THE
OLD ORDER AND
THE NEW

THE
OLD ORDER AND
THE NEW

A Novel of Africa

by

WILFRED FOWLER

THE MACMILLAN COMPANY • NEW YORK

Originally published in Great Britain by The
Cresset Press, under the title HARAMA.

First American edition,
The Macmillan Company, 1965

Library of Congress catalog card number: 65-11573
Printed in the United States of America

'The web of our life is of mingled yarn,

good and ill together;

our virtues would be proud if our faults

whipped them not; and our

crimes would despair if they were not

cherished by our own virtues.'

CHARACTERS

Harama the Mudela of Pela, *a Paramount Chief.*
Wood, the narrator, *an Assistant District Commissioner (afterwards a Provincial Commissioner).*
Daubney, *a Provincial Commissioner.*
Pomeroy, *a District Commissioner, later acting Provincial Commissioner.*
Elizabeth, *his wife.*
Metcalfe, *an Assistant District Commissioner (afterwards Deputy Civil Secretary).*
Burwash and Woolam, *Assistant District Commissioners.*
Ali, *Wood's servant.*
Hiro, *a groom.*
Arisi, *a member of Harama's household.*
Gela, *an orderly.*
Crane, *a District Engineer.*
Peggy, *his wife.*
Palthrop, *a District Medical Officer.*
Marchant, *a Forestry Officer.*
Margaret, *his wife (afterwards married to Metcalfe).*
Elliot and Firbank, *District Education Officers.*
Tansy, *Firbank's wife.*
Miller and Smellie, *District Police Officers.*
Brice, *a District Agricultural Officer.*
Keast and Stobart, *Foremen of Works.*
McFie, *a trader.*
Sedley, *a Medical Officer on special duty.*
Hilda Standfield, *a nurse (afterwards married to Wood).*
Ames, *a District Commissioner.*
Phyllis, *his wife.*

Gregg
Damer
Follet
Meakin } *Police Officers on special duty.*

Loftus, *an Army Officer.*

Fela Pereta, *Leader of the National United Democratic Alliance (NUDA).*

Pilama Mudi, *Leader of the National Independence Congress (NIC).*

Bowcott, *a Deputy Provincial Commissioner.*

Mathews, *Civil Secretary.*

Honourable Xanadu Cairngross, *Minister of Development.*

Crawley, *a Secretary.*

Calder, *a Crown Law Officer.*

Edith, *his wife.*

Zadeta, *a Minister.*

Dufu, *an opportunitist.*

Likema
Bauro } *associates of Dufu.*
Ritelo

Peake, *a Judge.*

Roebuck, *a District Commissioner.*

Ilse, *his wife.*

McIntyre
Bemena } *Assistant District Commissioners.*
Tai

Mena, *a District Police Officer.*

Demeta, *a District Medical Officer.*

Buramo, *a member of Harama's household.*

Holworthy and Pardy, *Police Officers on special duty.*

BOOK I

'What's past

is prologue'

CHATER I

[decorative rule]

The road from the rail-head at Huta became an impassable quagmire as soon as the rains set in but after six weeks of dry season, billows of powdery red dust had followed my truck as I jolted over the corrugated sun-baked laterite surface. It was in the half hour of tropical twilight of the second day and there was chill in the air when I reached the native town and drove up the road to the station.

Pela Station lay in a circle with buttressed mud houses lying back from short drives along the circumference. The road from the town passed the trading section, the polo field, the hospital, the clerks' quarters and offices and met the circular road at a tangent near the tennis courts. Daubney the Provincial Commissioner and Metcalfe an assistant D.C. were finishing a game with Pomeroy the D.C. and Burwash the other assistant D.C. Daubney, sallow after years in the tropics, was below average height but straight and compactly built and even at fifty active and quick on the court. A friendly smile enlivened his face when he came forward to meet me. Pomeroy, a handsome man with an assured manner, raised a hand, towelled himself, put on a sweater, blazer and scarf and ran a comb through his long fair hair. Burwash called out a greeting as he walked round the court collecting the balls. Metcalfe wiped his face in a towel and then slung it over his shoulder. 'Welcome back from the fleshpots,' he said.

Daubney said little at dinner and when we moved to chairs on the verandah he made no reply to my inquiries about people. I thought he was tired after tennis or maybe grudged putting me up for the night but then he spoke as though he had something to tell me.

'You are going to Mafi District.' He was about to continue when the *too too roo* of an owl came out of the darkness. 'That's a Scops owl,' he exclaimed, 'you don't often hear them so far north as this.'

3

'How soon am I wanted at Mafi?' I asked.

'You'll come with us to the Mudela's meeting tomorrow and leave the day after.'

I had hoped for the first few weeks of my tour in the station but I said nothing and Daubney continued. 'The Mudela's appointed a new district chief and wants someone to go there at once.'

A bat flew up and down the verandah. Daubney's head boy came for the coffee tray.

'His name's Kasta. He's got no traditional right to the position but he's very ambitious.' Daubney got up for a pipe. 'And he's a friend of the Mudela and as we have been urging him to choose literate headmen, I approved the appointment.'

We could no longer hear the owl and but for the *tchik tchik* of crickets and the wail of a distant hyena, there was silence outside.

'May I ask why I'm wanted at Mafi so soon?'

Daubney held a match to his pipe.

'Things aren't going too well. Tax collection's backward for one thing.' I waited for him to go on. 'The Mudela's asked for help as he doesn't want his protégé to fail or make himself unpopular by pressing his people too much. I'm posting you to touring duty in Mafi District and while you're there you must help Kasta with tax collection. You will report to Pomeroy.'

The fragrance of moon flowers wafted in from blooms on the creeper outside and an enormous white moth fluttered through the open shutters and stuck to the wall like a plaque. The whooping cry of a tree hyrax cascaded down the notes of the scale. Daubney went on talking but I was too sleepy to listen. I refused a night cap and climbed the dusty stairs to my bed.

Ali was in the room when I awoke. He had put a tea tray close to my bed and was hoisting the net. After a routine of greetings I asked him why he had not met me at Huta.

He stood back and glared at me.

'Meet you at Huta,' he said with a rising inflexion, 'how many times I go to the Provincial Office to ask what time you come?'

He seemed to want a reply. 'How do I know?' I said.

'I'll tell you. Eight times. D'you hear me? Eight times. Gela your orderly is my witness.'

'And couldn't you find out?'

4

He compressed fleshy lips and pushed his face forward.

'The Chief Clerk say every time he doesn't know.'

'All right,' I said, 'give me some tea.'

He held out the cup and saucer.

'What house do we have?'

'No house. We go to Mafi tomorrow.'

He stood stock still and his mouth fell open.

'Allah! so soon.'

'Tell the lorry driver to go ahead with my loads and Hiro to start now with the horses.'

He went out muttering complaints.

Sounds of movement rose from the compound. Daubney's servants exchanged greetings with people passing the house. The impatient cry of the bulbul, *quick doctor quick*, came out of the bush. The well windlass creaked and someone was splitting wood. A bugle call sounded as the police broke the Residency flag. Ali brought in a jug of hot water.

Palmyra palms towered on the right of the road to the town and beyond there were date palms. The great wall weathered by rain and wind was beginning to crumble but the arched gateways where roads converged on the town were still in good shape. We drove through at foot pace and moved cautiously along the main thoroughfare. There was a stench from the dye pits and the clack of looms in the weaving huts. We passed the throng in the corn market, turned at the mosque and entered the labyrinth of alleys which lead to the compound. A drummer announced our arrival and as we walked to the council hall Harama the Mudela of Pela came out to meet us. He was of middle height with a line of moustache over full sensual lips and a small goatee beard. He gave us a piercing glance from strong brown eyes and bowed slightly to Daubney and Pomeroy.

'Come this way,' he said, and we followed him into the hall. He pointed at chairs and then sat on a divan draped with leopard skins.

The district chiefs sat on mats on the floor and a scribe wrote while Harama consulted them. Time after time he pointed at Kasta giving him the name of his district according to custom.

'What's your opinion, Chief Mafi?' he repeatedly asked.

Kasta wore the embroidered gown of a person of rank. Each time his response was the same as he spoke with control in a deep voice and a suggestion of deference.

'My lord, these chiefs are older and wiser than I. How can a son speak in the presence of his elders?'

Harama commended him. 'What you say is good, Mafi.' He looked round the seated headmen and added, 'but we want your opinion.'

Harama listened to Kasta with careful attention and then told the scribe, 'let it be so'.

The meeting dispersed but Harama drew Kasta aside and stopped to talk to us in the horseshoe shaped entrance.

'This white-man is going to Mafi to help you,' he told him and then smiling at me added, 'isn't that so?'

'That is so, Harama,' I said.

Kasta inclined his head. I got a whiff of chypre and when he looked up I saw his eyes were outlined with antimony.

'He will be welcome,' he said.

Harama touched Kasta's arm. 'He will help you with tax collection.'

Kasta bowed again. 'His help will be invaluable.' He then spoke to Daubney and Pomeroy in accentless English.

'He can depend on my full co-operation and help.'

'I'm sure he can,' Daubney said.

Kasta looked full face at me.

'If you want anything you must ask for it,' he said.

Mafi was a sprawling town of mud and thatch houses set among granite outcrops ninety miles southward from Pela. The road enters at the foot of a massive rock eroded into the shape of a pear, passes through the town up rising land to the resthouse a half mile beyond. Arisi, Harama's representative—*Harama's eye* was the literal translation—stayed in the town with Gela my orderly; Ali and my cook slept in a hut in the compound. The resthouse was a circular mud hut with a thatch roof overhanging enough to cover a verandah where Ali put my bath and wash basin. The day we arrived fruit of a silk cotton tree opened and flossy kapok drifted lightly away with the lightest movement of air.

In the second month of the dry season the countryside was arid and brown and morning and evening skies were darkened by dust haze. At night the *harmattan* blew off cooling sands of the interior and the temperature fell. There were deaths from cerebro-spinal meningitis—*chigana*, they called it. It came each dry season when people passed it on by sleeping close to each other to keep warm.

On the second day I went to see Kasta. His house stood back from an expanse of hard trodden earth with a single tree in the centre where a water-seller sat every day with her pots. The mark of the Lion Paw denoting the rank of the owner, a Moslem prayer and a proverb were worked into the mud façade of the house. Vultures perched on the phallic symbols crowning the parapet in a row over the entrance. I walked through to the compound and Kasta came out and took me to his office in the private part of the house. A scribe started nervously, kicked off his slippers and crouched in salute.

'Show the white man our tax books,' Kasta told him.

The scribe fumbled in a cupboard, then placed a dog-eared ledger on the table, turned over pages and moved away.

'This is it,' Kasta said, 'you see the names of the villages in the first column; in the second column we have the assessments for the year and then twelve columns, one for each month with the amount still outstanding.'

'Who makes the assessments?' I asked.

'I do that based on the cultivated land and livestock in each village. The headman apportions a share to each man and collects it. He brings it here and I send it on to the treasury at Pela.'

I examined the ledger, checking each column in turn.

'Some villages have not paid very much. Look at this place Boji.'

Kasta peered at the book. 'Boji, oh yes, that's a big place, four or five hamlets.'

'Total assessment £1,562 but only £316 paid.' I looked at him. 'Why is that?'

Kasta grimaced and then laughed. 'It's personal. The village headman thinks he should have been made district chief.'

'But there are others,' I said as I looked down the list. 'Your total assessment's over £16,000 but you have collected less than £4,000.' I turned to him. 'It's not very good.'

7

Kasta looked back with hooded eyes and assumed an arrogant manner.

'Harama understands my difficulties,' he said.

I wondered if I had been too outspoken.

'I hope I can help you,' I said.

He smiled. 'That's good of you. I'm sure you'll be a great help.'

I looked at the book again.

'Most of the villages are in the south. I'll go to them first and then to Boji and the rest of them later.'

'The people will take your advice,' Kasta said. 'They will soon pay what is due.'

He escorted me to the square outside. The old water-seller crouched near her pots as we approached her.

'Allah preserve you,' she said in a quavering voice. 'May your life be long.'

Kasta flung up a hand in acknowledgment as we walked on.

'Let me show you what I am trying to do,' he said.

We saw the slaughter-house and public latrine and then inspected the market and a new type of stall he wanted to build. He asked my opinion of the building layout in the new part of the town.

'What I really want,' he said deliberately as we turned back, 'is a school. The Koranic schools are limited. Boys must be educated in the faith, of course, but under modern conditions they need broad based education.' He fell silent and then went on, 'and after a school, roads, piped-water and a hospital.'

'That's an ambitious programme,' I said.

He nodded. 'I suppose it is, I suppose it is, but that's what I dream of.' He looked dubious and with no sign of arrogance. 'There's no harm in that, is there?'

I was taken aback with a curious feeling of pathos.

'It's highly commendable,' I said.

We walked on in silence and then he remarked, 'people don't always understand one's efforts on their behalf.'

A small crowd in the square surrounded two men holding a horse. Hiro my horse boy moved forward and backward as the horse swung round and reared. It was a cleanly built chestnut of about sixteen hands, big in the quarters and short in the back with a deep barrel-shaped body.

'That's a fine horse,' I said.

Kasta turned with a quick change of mood.

'Are you interested in horses?'

'I've got a couple of weight carriers for trekking,' I said.

'I've got this horse for you.' He pointed at Hiro. 'Is he your horse boy?'

'Yes, but . . .'

He ignored me. 'Get on,' he said.

Hiro climbed on the horse's back. In a few seconds he had disappeared down the road. We stood a minute and then with a thunder of hooves he reappeared high on the horse's shoulders, coming back at express speed scattering fowls and goats and evoking shouts of approval. In a few seconds he had disappeared at the opposite end of the town, then returned trotting quietly. He slipped off the horse and bent low to Kasta.

'My lord,' he gabbled, 'this is the best horse in the world.'

'Take it for your master,' said Kasta.

Hiro got up and took the bridle of the sweating horse uncertain what to do next.

I protested, 'You cannot do that.'

'Why not?' Kasta demanded. He looked angry and I thought at first I had offended him but his lips turned down with amusement. 'It's nothing, I would like you to have him.'

Hiro rubbed down the horse while he waited.

'All right,' I said.

Kasta watched Hiro walk the horse away and then spoke again.

'Put that horse in for the races.'

'What races?' I asked.

'Huta Races. Put in two horses.'

I laughed awkwardly. 'You can't enter a horse until you have got a horse to enter.'

'Why not? all you want are two names. I'll find you a second horse.'

CHAPTER II

There was plenty of game. I had flushed ten or more birds within a few yards of my feet in the old cassava garden and they had gone rocketing away before I could take careful aim; there were even more in the long dry grass beyond. But after walking four or five miles and firing my cartridges I had brought down only three birds; two had run in the long grass and were lost, Gela carried the third, an old cock francolin with one foot missing— nipped off in a gin trap, I supposed. The gun had a long heavy barrel and my shoulder was sore where it had rubbed through my shirt. Grass seeds stuck in my stockings and a graze on my right hand smarted with gun oil and sweat. Gela would have politely agreed if I had explained that it was the gun and not I that had been at fault, but we walked on in silence.

It was dusk when we reached the outskirts of the town and I heard the muezzin clear his throat before he made his call to prayers. In the fading light we walked slowly up the hill to the resthouse.

Gela stopped suddenly. 'Kasta's there,' he said.

All I wanted was a bath and drink; I had no wish to see anyone. 'Where?' I asked.

Gela pointed with lifted chin at the resthouse. I saw the car when we drew nearer. The new Oldsmobile looked ostentatious against my old truck.

Ali had lighted an acetylene lamp and Kasta sat outside on a camp chair. He had been at Pela for a council meeting when I got back from my tour of the southern villages and I had not seen him since. I greeted him and Ali brought out my second chair. I wondered what could make Kasta miss his evening prayers.

'I've just got back from Pela,' he said. 'I had tea with the Provincial Commissioner yesterday. I told him you were doing very good work here. In fact,' Kasta laughed and placed his hands on his knees, 'in fact I said you were the best administrative officer I have known.' He gave me a quick glance. 'It's true, you know.'

I was displeased by his flattery.

'You've only known me, Kasta. No one else has been here since you became district chief.'

He made a cutting gesture with the flat of his hand.

'I've known many administrative officers, many. Harama knows what I think of you and I have told the Provincial Commissioner and Mr Pomeroy.'

'You embarrass me,' I said.

He moved in his chair.

'Why should you be embarrassed. I am a black man and you are a white man but I say with no disrespect of your position that I am old enough to be your father.'

Ali came out and adjusted the lamp and the hissing flame brightened.

'Why shouldn't I say what I think of you,' Kasta continued.

'It's very good of you.' It was a lame reply but all I could think of.

Kasta stayed another ten minutes and then called Ali and gave him a handful of coins.

'It's sad about Somba,' he said as we walked to his car.

'Somba?' I asked. 'Who's that?'

'Village Head, Boji. He went home and found his wife and baby dead with *chigana*.' The driver started the engine and the attendant opened the door but Kasta appeared reluctant to go. 'Yes, it turned his head and he wandered away and has not been seen since.'

I was not interested.

'You mean he's disappeared?'

'Yes, and I'm afraid he too must be dead.'

'I'm sorry,' I said.

Kasta was still slow to go.

'I'm seeing more horses tomorrow; if I see a good one I'll get it for you.'

The car headlights pierced the darkness like searchlights and a minute later I heard the three-tone horn sound somewhere down in the town.

The resthouse well became dry and I paid Lamu sixpence a day to fetch water from the town. He was old and he limped slowly up and down the hill following a donkey with two earthenware pots slung over its back. When it stopped he patiently rebuked it but if it failed to respond he lost his temper and cursed it with shrill incoherency.

The water Lamu brought was dirty and tasted earthy even after it had been boiled and filtered. Nothing could be done about it but Ali often complained, goading the old man through stages of explanation, explosion and incoherency to slow recovery and finally laughter.

I had just finished breakfast and looked up and saw Lamu through the hut entrance. The sun was still low and the old man looked pinched in the fresh morning air. I went out and found Gela and Arisi regarding him with sceptic interest.

'What's worrying Lamu?' I said.

Gela spoke. 'He's got some story about Posu.'

Ali spluttered with laughter. 'She's Lamu's concubine, the water-seller in front of Kasta's house.'

The old man was too angry to speak properly.

'You infidel pig,' he cried wagging a finger at Ali, 'how dare you defame me in front of the white man?'

'Leave him alone,' I said and turned to Gela. 'What's all this about?'

'Lamu takes water to the old woman. She says, "he hasn't come out".'

'Who hasn't come out?'

'Somba.'

'Village Head of Boji?'

'Yes, she says he went into Kasta's house three days ago but hasn't come out.'

Ali laughed as though the notion was ludicrous. He wagged his head. 'These old people!'

'Be quiet,' I told him. 'Gela,' I said, 'there's bad news about Somba. He's probably dead in the bush somewhere.'

'Exactly so, that's what I've heard.'

'Listen, Lamu,' I said, but his thoughts had wandered. He touched the donkey with his stick and limped down the hill.

I thought nothing of Lamu's mumblings until that evening.

Kasta had cleared five acres of land to the west of the resthouse where we exercised the two horses. They were walked fifteen miles every morning and in the evening I gave them three fast gallops of five or six furlongs.

Hiro got Mogu a boy from Kasta's compound to help him and at sundown they came back to the resthouse and hobbled the horses over pegs in the ground. I had taken to sitting in a camp chair watching them work. Community of interest drew us together and the boys laughed and talked freely.

Mogu dropped an armful of guinea corn heads in front of the chestnut.

'Hiro,' he said, 'ever escorted an invisible man?'

Hiro brushed the bay.

'What do you say, Mogu?' he asked.

'Ever escorted an invisible man?'

Hiro stood back, eyeing the bay.

'You are mad, you can't escort an invisible man.'

Mogu filled a bucket from a water pot and put it down for the chestnut.

'Oh yes you can, I've done it, I did it three days ago.'

Hiro passed a hand over the bay's quarters.

'Allah,' he laughed, 'why do you lie. Who can believe such foolishness?'

Mogu laughed. 'It's true. Kasta told me to escort Somba back to Boji. I said: Where is he? Kasta said: Can't you see him, you fool?' Mogu raised his hands in a gesture. 'Who am I to argue with Kasta? I said, long may you live my lord, and rode halfway to Boji and said: Farewell Somba, may Allah see you safely home, and then I came back.'

'And there was nobody there?'

'No one at all.'

The boys laughed as they led the horses to the stable huts at the back of the compound. I went into the resthouse and wrote three versions before I was satisfied. A horseman took the letter to Pela next day.

Pomeroy must have left as soon as my letter reached him and travelled all night. He refused my invitation to breakfast but accepted an offer of coffee.

'Have you mentioned this to anyone else?' he asked.

'No, only to you.'

Ali brought in the coffee and stayed to put clean linen away in a uniform case.

'Must he stay?' Pomeroy complained.

'He doesn't understand English.'

'Tell him to go.'

When Ali went Pomeroy looked grim.

'You're quite sure you've mentioned these suspicions to nobody else?'

'Quite sure,' I said.

Pomeroy sipped coffee and put down the cup. His expression was gentler.

'How long have you been here?'

'Nearly three months.'

'Three months,' he reflected. 'It's not long.' He shrugged his shoulders. 'Still, people do get things out of proportion when they've got no one to talk to.'

'There is that danger, I suppose.'

I may have sounded hesitant because he gave me a hard look and there was an edge to his voice.

'Better people than you have and plenty more will,' he said; then he smiled. 'If you are bothered again look the cause of your anxiety full in the face. It's fatal to thrust it away. Lift the thing up and examine it and if possible do something.'

I nodded. 'Yes,' I said, 'I see what you mean.'

'Now what about this affair?' he said in a business-like manner. 'An old water-seller told your water carrier that she saw Somba go into Kasta's house and not come out again.' Pomeroy held up his hands and wagged his head in mock reproof. 'That could be explained in a thousand ways. Maybe she fell asleep, maybe nature called her, maybe he came out after dark—it's not worth thinking about.' He put my letter on his knee and smoothed out the creases. 'And this horseman Mogu you mention. He was told to escort Somba but says he did not see him.' Pomeroy sounded exasperated. 'Really my dear fellow, anything could have happened. Somba might have gone ahead or taken another road. Surely the simple answer is the most likely one.' A hard look of appraisal came into his face. 'Aren't you possibly doing Kasta grave injustice?'

'Yes,' I said, 'possibly I am.'

He stood up. 'I'm sure you are and anyway if you must get wild notions, pick on someone else. Harama thinks highly of Kasta and if you are not careful you'll find yourself posted out of this province.'

I walked to his car with him.

'I'm sorry you've had this special trip here,' I said.

He put his hand on my shoulder and stood for a moment at the side of the car.

'That's all right. I'm ordering you to come to Pela once a month for some tennis and bridge.' He got into the car and raised his hand as he drove off. 'Don't forget, I want to see you once a month at Pela.'

As soon as he had gone I called to Ali, 'We are going to Boji tomorrow.'

CHAPTER III

Main road resthouses were falling into disuse as more people got motor cars but on bush tracks where we still travelled on horse or by foot they stood a day's trek apart at twelve to fifteen mile intervals. They were grass thatched mud huts with a table and chair and a door frame and window shutter often riddled by termites. Many of them were the resort of bats which left a throat-catching stink. Some were infested by scorpions which had to be stamped on or crushed with a stick before we could settle. But now after four or five hours of wearisome trekking they offered promise of comfort.

It was the third day since we left Mafi. The carriers had fought for light loads and gone ahead and after breakfast I followed with Ali and Gela.

There was high humidity as well as the great heat which comes before the first rains and my sweat sodden shirt clung to my body. The track wound like a red thread through the fired grasslands. Green shoots would appear when the rains started but now a fine white dust lay over the landscape. Thorn bushes and occasional baobob trees gave variety to the scene and sometimes granite outcrops loomed into sight through the haze where baboons glared down at us. Flocks of guinea fowl rose as we advanced on them and once a fine red kob with spiralling horns dashed across the track in front of us. The haze lifted as the day advanced and by noon circling vultures showed that the village was near.

A few minutes later the huts were in sight.

The carriers had put down their loads, littering the ground with their head pads, and sat waiting for payment in front of the resthouse.

'I want to see the man in charge,' I told Gela.

An elderly man stepped forward. A thin white moustache

curved over his mouth nearly touching the blob of white beard on the point of his chin. His eyes were bagged and his forehead was lined but he stood at attention, steady eyed and composed, waiting to hear what I had to say.

'You are an old soldier?' I said.

He stood straighter. 'Sergeant Sagala, number 3159, sir,' he reported in barrack English.

I gave him time to relax.

'Have you had *chigana* this year?'

'Ah!' he exclaimed as though I had surprised him. 'We must give thanks to Allah, there has been no *chigana* in Boji.'

The onlookers murmured, 'Amin, Amin, Amin.'

'None at all?'

The old man shook his head. 'None at all,' he declared and turned to the others, 'is that not so?'

'It's true,' they agreed.

'Have you all paid your taxes?' I asked.

'We must give thanks to Allah for good prices for our produce,' he said.

More people had gathered. 'Everyone paid?' I asked them.

'Yes, everyone, everyone's paid.' They spoke up like well taught children and awaited the next question.

'Where's Somba?'

That confused them but one man spoke.

'He's gone to Mafi,' he said and the others chattering among themselves then agreed.

I had one more question.

'Are Somba's wives in good health?'

They turned and pointed to two women with tightly wrapped cloths over their breasts. One pounded ground nuts in a wooden mortar and the other poured the broken shells and kernels from one calabash to another.

'They are there.'

I walked over the dusty ground to the two women. I knew my question would sound strange to them.

'Are your children well?'

They stopped working and looked up with nervous surprise.

'We must give thanks to Allah,' they said.

'Where's Somba?'

'He's not yet back from Mafi.'

Winnowed nuts piled up on a skin at their side.

'Those are good nuts,' I said.

'They are good nuts,' the elder agreed.

I left them and walked back to the resthouse.

'We return to Mafi,' I told Gela and Ali.

It was half past six by the time I had bathed and changed and the sun was sinking like a fiery red ball as I went down the hill to see Kasta.

The old water-seller sat with her pots but there was no one else in sight near the house. I walked through the entrance and found a youth in the compound feeding a young chimpanzee. I was unsure of my voice and sounded harsh when I spoke.

'Where's Kasta?'

The youth looked startled. 'In there,' he said nodding towards Kasta's rooms.

'Tell him I want him.'

The youth fed the chimpanzee the remaining boiled cas sava and pawpaw and went into the house. A minute later he came out and toed the chimpanzee before him towards the stables. Then Kasta appeared and stood leaning against the door jamb. His head was covered by a short tasselled hat and he wore a gown unadorned except for simple embroidery at the neck.

'I hope the boy did not disturb you,' I said.

He shook his head. 'I was doing nothing.'

His eyes remained watchful while I gave him a formal greeting.

'Yes?' he said waiting.

'I've just got back from Boji.' Kasta regarded me with sombre attention. 'Your information about Somba was wrong; there's been no *chigana* at Boji this year and Somba's wives want to know why he has taken so long to come home.'

Kasta looked away with haughty indifference.

'The people say everyone has paid tax,' I added.

After brief silence Kasta shrugged his shoulders and threw out his hands.

'It seems I was misinformed.'

'How could that happen?'

Kasta eased himself away from the door jamb.

'Somba must have started the story himself.'

I felt my efforts were feeble.

'What do you mean?'

Kasta looked back in silence and slowly smiled.

'What could I mean?'

'I don't know.'

'Somba absconded with Boji tax money of course.'

I recoiled from the falsity of his manner.

'You believe that?'

He heaved himself away from the jamb again and grimaced.

'What else can you suggest?'

'Very good,' I said, 'I'll notify the police at Pela.'

He raised his right hand.

'Do so with all speed.'

I left with no formal leave taking and forgot the fatigues of the day as I walked up the hill.

The women traders had moved at sundown to the ficus trees in the night market and wicks in shea butter produced a chiaroscuro effect and a murmur came from shadowy figures sitting and moving about in the gloom.

Ali came forward with a lamp when I turned in at the resthouse compound.

'There are people waiting to see you,' he said.

Anything unusual now seemed likely to plague me.

'What people?' I asked.

'The native court judge.'

'Tata?'

'Yes, and Gela and two strangers.'

I walked slowly towards them. Tata was nervous but had the manner of someone not to be deflected from what he had decided to do.

'You want to see me, Tata?' I said.

He moistened his lips.

'Yes, sir.' He pointed first at the taller and then to the other stranger. 'These two people, Pedelo and Raba, reported something to me this afternoon.'

My heart missed a beat.

'Something about Somba?'

He gasped and met my eyes with a darting glance.

'Who can say?' he said.

It was some moments before he again spoke.

'You know the old cassava garden on the road out to the west from the town?'

'Where I go shooting?'

Gela replied, 'That is the place.'

'Continue, Tata,' I said.

'There's a dry well there.'

'Yes,' I said, 'go on.'

Tata turned to the two men. They wore dirty garments of local weave and skins at their waists.

'These men went to look at traps. They set them for . . . '

'Never mind that, what happened?'

'There was an evil smell.'

'Coming from the well?'

'Yes, and this man Pedelo looked down and saw a white gown.'

'Is that true?' I said to them.

They were both very frightened.

'Yes, we saw it,' they said.

Tata, Gela and Ali now waited attentively.

'Arisi not here?' I said while I collected my thoughts.

'He's gone,' Gela said.

I shivered with an upsurge of fresh anxiety.

This new mystery must wait, I thought, if it were not part of the greater mystery which now filled my thoughts.

'We'll go to the cassava garden,' I said.

There were now hundreds of lights and the murmur of voices grew louder as we came abreast the market and then became fainter as we strode on and took the road out to the cassava garden. The stench of putrescence assailed my nostrils but nobody spoke as we walked in single file through the abandoned garden. Long-plumed nightjars flew to and fro hawking over the ground with the ends of their plumes floating behind like bats in the gloaming. Away in the bush a call came repeatedly *weet*, *weet*, *weet* with monotonous insistence.

Pedelo and Raba stopped and speaking in whispers urged me to look at the path. In the beam of my torch I saw the tracks of two pairs of feet in the sandy soil; they stopped at the well and retraced their way over the oncoming tracks.

Pedelo whispered and Gela reported, 'he'll go down the well if you will give him your torch.'

Ali demurred, 'Ah, no, take mine, you can't use the master's torch for that purpose.'

I held my light on the well diggers footholes as Pedelo lowered himself. When he came up he was bare to the waist and carried something wrapped in the garment he had been wearing. I held the light on it as he threw back three folds of cloth and uncovered a human head. There was a whimper from Ali; Gela gasped, 'Allah protect us.'

Tata spoke first. 'It's Somba,' he said.

I looked at the object again.

'How can you tell?' I said.

He pointed with shaking hand at the open mouth.

'I know those teeth.'

'And it's Somba's beard,' Gela added.

'Is the rest of it there?' I said to Pedelo.

'His neck was broken and the head came away.'

'Allah!' whispered Gela.

I left them and took the turning up the hill to the resthouse. The shea butter dips in the market were brighter or maybe they seemed so because it was darker.

It was nearly dawn and I heard cocks crow before I slept. I woke when the car came into the compound and for a moment I was untroubled, then I was possessed with fears of what the new day had in store for me. I pushed up the net and sat on my bed. It was a blue car and it was a relief to me that it was not Kasta's Oldsmobile. I thrust my feet into slippers and crossed the compound to the strange car. Harama sat next to the driver. I braced myself in readiness for anything he might have to say to me but as I drew nearer he called, 'we've got him, he's here.' Kasta in the hat and gown he wore when I saw him the night before sat at the back between two of Harama's policemen. His eyes met mine without a flicker of recognition and moved away.

Harama got out of the car. He must have been travelling all night but though his gown was dirty and creased he showed no sign of fatigue. I felt his authority as he regarded me with dust-rimmed eyes.

'Arisi brought me the news. I've seen Tata and Gela and the

two men. The scribe has told everything. Kasta was consuming the tax and paying him to say nothing. When Somba said he was going to see you Kasta strangled him with his own hands. They took the body to the old cassava garden after dark.'

A truck came up the hill and turned in behind the car. The scribe sat at the back with two policemen. He wept noisily like someone overwhelmed by hopeless despair. Harama looked at him with no change of expression. 'He's sorry now,' he said. I nodded at Kasta. 'He's not so sorry,' 'Ah, him!' Harama said, 'he's a proud hard man.'

There was nothing more to be said but Harama made no move to go. He regarded me again but with a frank open expression as though for a moment he had forgotten about Kasta and was thinking more about me. I returned his gaze and he smiled. Unuttered communication passed between us and in that brief instant I felt we were in absolute harmony and a bond had been formed. It was a rare and strangely disturbing experience.

Harama got back in the car, nodded and smiled. He spoke to the driver and then again turned to me.

'I'll see you in Pela,' he said as though it had all been arranged.

The driver pressed the starter and let in the clutch. The car went down the hill and the truck followed in the wake of dust it threw up. I thought about Harama long after they had gone.

CHAPTER IV

❧❧❧❧❧❧❧❧❧❧❧❧❧❧❧❧❧❧❧❧❧❧❧❧❧

When Pomeroy's letter came I wondered whether Harama had used his influence until I knew later what had happened. Burwash's dog went mad and bit him about his legs and arms before he could shoot it. Palthrop was worried about rabies and gave Burwash a course of injections. On the last day of the treatment a cobra in the rafters of Burwash's latrine spat in his face. He suffered intense pain and was blind for two weeks. A breakdown followed and Daubney sent him on leave. I was wanted in Pela to take over his work.

Pela was a small Provincial Station too remote and lacking in comfort to make it a popular posting. In the early days of British occupation it had been a military outpost and a rectangular area enclosing the offices was still called the Fort. Responsibility rested lightly on Daubney and he and his district commissioners, with the usual organization of specialist officers, administered an area half the size of Wales. The Governor and Civil Secretary at Belemba, eight hundred miles to the south across grasslands and rain forests, were too far away to have any impact on day to day happenings. Daubney did what he thought right and later reported. The administration of Pela Province was a benevolent and easy going thing.

Most people in the station worked from seven in the morning until two in the afternoon. In the late afternoon they played tennis or golf or walked round the station for exercise. Some people went hacking. Polo depended on sufficient enthusiasts to make it worthwhile. At night there were drinks and bridge. Two or three times a month someone gave a dinner party; finger bowls were put on the table and the host opened bottles of wine. Sometimes dirty food caused diarrhoea and vomiting and there were complaints of 'Pela tummy' next day.

I took Burwash's place with Daubney against Metcalfe and

Pomeroy at tennis. Once a week I played with Peggy Crane, the engineer's wife, against Pomeroy and his wife Elizabeth. The Pomeroys disapproved of Peggy but mixed fours were hard to make up and they accepted her until someone more to their liking appeared. Peggy was good hearted but she could be wearisome as her sense of humour was threadbare and offended some people. Long before the costume was commonplace she wore shorts for tennis, and at dinner at the Residency Daubney looked with a meditative eye at her long scarlet finger nails. Crane regarded his wife's extravagances with sardonic detachment. When Palthrop, the Medical Officer, came to the house he facetiously chided her with neglect of her lover.

Palthrop wore well-cut bush shirts and shorts and tan hand-made shoes; at night he invariably put on a dinner jacket. He was a handsome man with a brushed up moustache, long prematurely white hair and an eye glass. He looked more like an actor playing a part than a doctor, but Daubney thought well of him.

I enjoyed most the tennis Peter Metcalfe and I played with Robert Marchant, the Forestry Officer, and his wife Margaret. Margaret was a straight-backed blue-eyed girl about our own age. Fair hair neatly drawn back from a round bulging forehead, a pink complexion in spite of the tropics, and slightly prominent teeth gave her the look of a schoolgirl. She was a better player than Robert but always deferred to him.

Something had gone wrong with the career of Elliot, the Education Officer. He made up a weekly bridge four with Daubney and the Pomeroys but otherwise he sought no social diversions. Miller, the Police Officer, was an accomplished horseman and when he was not hacking or teaching beginners he beat a ball up and down the polo field by himself.

No one saw much of Brice, the Agricultural Officer, who was economizing for some reason and refused hospitality. The two foremen of works, Keast a Cornishman and Stobart a Cockney, shared a house and took advantage of their position in the Public Works Department to add to its comfort.

During the produce buying season a cosmopolitan community assembled in the trading section. McFie of the African Trading Company was the only trader who stayed on during the rains. He came from the same village in Ayrshire as Brice and though he was much older some sort of friendship existed between them.

I went every day to Harama's office in the town, sitting in dusty mud buildings correcting, advising and guiding native officials. Old men sat on the floor chewing kola nuts, gobbing behind cupboards when they wished to empty their mouths. Others moved slowly from room to room carrying a besom and sprinkling water to damp down the dust. I ran into difficulties when I attempted reforms. Harama told me if the old men were taken off the payroll they would have to beg for a living. 'These men served my father long before you people came to this country,' he said, 'and as long as they live there will be work for them.'

The weather changed. Midday temperatures rose to 112 degrees and sweat ran off me as I sat working. In my second month in Harama's office I drove home one day at two o'clock, leaving the crowded streets of the town, passing through the gateway up the road beyond the trading section and saw sticks, leaves and dust swirling round in a vortex rising into the sky. The whirlwind moved away from the road and went across country tearing up more and more dust and rubbish. That night the net was blown from my bed and lightning, followed by thunder, flashed over the sky. Next day blue black clouds piled up and there were gusts of cool wind. The wind dropped and immense drops fell out of the sky starring sandy dry earth. I went outside to smell the rain and by a freak of sound heard shouts in the town.

The rains came more often, sometimes with fierce squalls banging windows and doors, sometimes steadily for hours, leaving pools in the compound. Blades of green grass shot up, leaves appeared, millet and guinea corn were soon six feet high and the golf course looked like a hayfield. Overnight, scarlet lilies fringed the Residency drive, tulip trees and cassias burst into bloom and the *ponciana regia* near the sentry box was a gorgeous medley of red, yellow and green. The roads in the station became ankle deep in sticky red mud and the flat roofs of mud houses, softened by standing storm water, gave way leaving gaping holes. There were swarms of flies and at night, when lamps were lighted, flying ants sometimes infested my house. The biggest nuisance was mosquitoes which bit viciously and drove people under their nets early to bed.

Bridge started earlier. I went each Saturday night to the Residency to play with Daubney, Palthrop and Miller. On the first Saturday in September Miller and I had won our second rubber and we were finishing drinks before dinner when Daubney got up to answer the telephone.

'It's for you,' he told Palthrop, 'Margaret Marchant wants to speak to you.'

We could hear Palthrop's drawling expostulation. He replaced the handpiece, rang and asked for the hospital. He spoke quietly and came back to us.

'Margaret Marchant's a sweet girl,' he said with a sigh, 'but I wish she wouldn't choose Saturday night to worry me about her cook's wife.'

We went into the dining-room. 'Margaret's a sensible girl,' Daubney said as we sat down, 'she's not the sort to panic.'

'No,' Miller agreed, 'I wouldn't have said so either.'

'Perhaps you're right,' Palthrop concurred, 'I'll see the woman after dinner.'

Palthrop did not wait for coffee. He returned twenty minutes later.

'The woman's sick all right,' he said.

Daubney ruffled the cards over the table.

'What's wrong with her?'

Palthrop picked up a card.

'Could be anything. I can't say yet.'

The rubber ended at midnight and Daubney did not suggest playing on.

The rain had held off for three days and the laterite roads had dried but Palthrop insisted on driving me back to my house. He shook his head when I invited him in for a drink. 'I'll go round to the hospital before I turn in,' he said. Next day at Pomeroy's luncheon party Margaret Marchant told me the woman had died.

Rain fell every day for three weeks. The lush growth of corn and high grass gave cover to hyenas and night after night their cries started the station dogs howling. Miller lost his wire-haired terrier and next morning he saw the padmarks of a leopard in damp ground near his house. At the beginning of the fourth week the sun came out and dried up the courts. Metcalfe and I had our Saturday game with the Marchants, but Margaret asked us to stop at half past six. Brice who lived near them was ill and she was anxious about him.

'The poor man never sees anyone and he could lie there and die,' she said.

Marchant smiled but they got into their little bull-nosed car and drove round to their house across the station.

Nobody got good cards at bridge that night. Miller was still depressed about his dog and kept talking about it, and Daubney was in one of his taciturn moods. Palthrop was the liveliest of us.

'How's Brice?' I asked while Daubney was entering the scores in the book.

'His temperature's down and he's much better,' Palthrop said.

Daubney ordered drinks.

'What's wrong with Brice?' he asked.

'Margaret Marchant was worried about him at tennis,' I said.

Palthrop picked up his glass.

'I wish Margaret wouldn't fuss so much.'

Daubney looked at him.

'What's wrong with Brice?' he repeated.

Palthrop pursed his lips and wagged his head.

'Basically he doesn't eat enough, but added to that he's had a sharp go of fever.'

For an instant longer Daubney kept his eyes on him but said nothing. Soon after we got up to go.

I had taken over Metcalfe's work in the Provincial Office. I was glad of the change as I preferred dealing directly with Daubney to working for Pomeroy.

That Sunday morning my letter-writing was disturbed by a telephone call. I expected to be asked out for a drink, but it was Daubney speaking.

'Brice is on the d.i. list; you should wire the Civil Secretary.'

'The line is down, sir,' I said, 'no telegrams have gone for weeks.'

'Yes, yes,' he said, 'I know, but put the telegram in the post office and confirm by letter—we can't do more.'

I could hear Daubney breathing.

27

'Is there any hope for him?' I asked.

'I don't know,' he said and rang off.

At half past ten next morning Daubney pushed open the connecting door of our rooms.

'I've just heard from Palthrop that Brice died ten minutes ago,' he said.

Stobart drove a works van to Brice's house. Four cars were waiting in the drive. Pomeroy, Metcalfe and I followed just after in Daubney's car. Red clay caked our shoes as we walked to the grave. The wreath of frangipane blooms Margaret Marchant had made fell on the ground when labourers lifted the coffin. During the service a family of grey parrots squawked and whistled, following each other in rapid flight. I picked up the wreath and dropped it into the grave as we came away.

We went back to the Residency. It was still early but most people took whisky. I stood with Pomeroy and Palthrop on the verandah. McFie came out and joined us. It was Palthrop he wanted.

'Ian Brice and I both came from Fairlie in Ayrshire, I'll be writing to his parents tonight.' He hesitated, at a loss for words. 'Is there anything I can tell them?'

Palthrop shook his head. 'Not really,' he said.

Pomeroy broke the awkward silence.

'I suppose you issued a death certificate?'

'Of course,' Palthrop said, for some reason looking at me. 'He couldn't have been buried if I hadn't.'

'You put down cerebral malaria?'

Palthrop faltered slightly.

'Yes, certainly,' he said, 'it was a typical case.'

Pomeroy snorted and turned away. Palthrop took more whisky and opened his case for another cigarette. McFie remained with us staring doubtfully at Palthrop.

'He died from cerebral malaria, then?' he said.

Palthrop inclined his head and spoke with a formal smile.

'That is so,' he said, 'cerebral malaria.'

Hiro, my horse boy, turned up at the house two days after the execution of Kasta. He had been weeks on the road and looked tired. He brought a letter and a cheque for £112 from the secretary of Huta Race Club. I had got a first and second with the horses I had sent to the meeting and the secretary had sold them as I requested. After tea I got a strong manilla envelope from the office and went to see McFie. He could give me twenty-two five pound notes and two pound notes for the cheque. I had decided to send the money anonymously to the Toc H worker at Mount Abro Leper Settlement—a man named Luxton I had met on the mail boat.

McFie lived in a russet-coloured bungalow behind his firm's store in the trading section. The place was deserted but for the watchman who crossed the muddy ground and struck six on the length of railway metal which hung from a banyan. I took the steps up the verandah. Plants in wire baskets hung from the ceiling over the chairs and drinks stools were arranged underneath. There was a book and pipe on a stool near a deck chair.

'McFie,' I called, but there was no answer and I shouted again, 'anyone at home?'

A servant in a tunic jacket came out of a bedroom.

'Where's your master?' I said.

'On bed,' he said, 'he's sick.'

'How long has he been sick?'

The boy pursed his lips.

'Maybe two day or something.'

'Can I see him?'

The boy raised his chin towards the bedroom door.

'He's in there. I think he's sleeping.'

He took a step to the bedroom.

'Leave him,' I said, 'I'll come another time.'

I drove back to the station and put away my car. I endorsed the cheque and sent it to Luxton.

Brice's death cast gloom over the station. It was beginning to lift when McFie died. The rain held off for the funeral and after it was over I walked a mile down the road with Metcalfe. The rain came as we returned and we ran to Keast and Stobart's house for shelter.

Stobart lolled in a chair, his flaxen hair awry and his sensual loose-lipped features flushed and ugly. Keast sat across the room, swarthy, beady eyed and bad tempered. Empty bottles stood on the floor near the chairs. They each held a plate with a pasty.

'Well, well, look who's here!' Stobart exclaimed with fatuous jocularity, 'the administrators. What an honour!' We went in and sat down. 'Won't you condescend to come in gentlemen and rest for a moment?' he said.

'While you're here I'd better measure up you two,' he continued. 'Me and Keasty have put away two stiffs this week. The head carpenter's making two more boxes, just in case.'

'Cheerful bugger,' Keast said.

Stobart ignored him.

'There were twelve pairs of shoes in McFie's room, all with patent trees in them.'

Keast fetched two more bottles of beer from the cooler.

'If they had been big enough you'd have swiped a couple of pairs,' he said, but Stobart continued, 'and four nice suits and a dinner jacket in the wardrobe. Two palm beach, a blue with a pin stripe and a grey worsted. Very smart.'

He poured out beer and then started to laugh.

'Can you beat it, do you know where Keast comes from?'

'For God's sake lay off, can't you?' Keast said. 'It's not funny.'

Stobart laughed again. 'St Pissy!' he shouted, 'that's the name of Keast's hometown. Can you beat that—St Pissy.'

He laughed helplessly as though the thought was too much for him.

'It's St Bissey, you imbecile,' Keast told him, but Stobart went on.

'Keast, tell them about that horse your old man had. Captain you called it. Thirty years old, you said. It was the most bloody wonderful horse in the world. It could talk, couldn't it, Keast? Tell them about it.' He bit into the pasty. 'Hell, this is hot, why didn't you tell me?'

A grey-haired bitch with low hanging dugs walked slowly across the room and placed her jaw on Stobart's knee. She yelped when Stobart touched her nose with the pasty.

'That'll teach you to fart in church my girl,' he said.

Keast sounded angry. 'There was no need for that.'

Stobart took a swig of beer. 'Keep the bloody thing away from me then. I can't think what you see in it, anyway.'

Keast made no reply. He went into the kitchen and brought back two more pasties and opened two bottles of beer.

Stobart had fallen silent. He put his hand on my thigh and I found his shallow blue eyes fixed on me.

'Ever killed a man?' he said.

'Now he's started,' Keast sneered, 'next thing he'll be crying.'

Stobart scowled but kept his mad-looking eyes on me.

'Ever killed a man?'

I filled his glass from my bottle.

'No,' I said.

He ignored the beer.

'You don't know what it is to destroy a fellow creature then?'

'No, I'm afraid not,' I said.

Stobart pulled his chair round and faced me.

'I killed a man when I was seventeen years old,' he said, 'seventeen years old!'

'Did you?' I said.

He looked at me with incoherent anxiety.

'They gave me a rifle with a telescope in 1916 at a place called Bapaume in France.'

His eyes filled with tears.

'Drink some of your beer,' I said.

'They told me to take cover behind some stones when it was dark. In the morning the sun was shining and birds were singing. It was in April. A jerry climbed over the parados and went off behind the trench. I watched him take off his belt and push down his pants. I saw him squat—five hundred yards away, he was.' Stobart shook his head. 'I was only a kid, seventeen years old. He lay there for three days before they buried him. A place called Bapaume in France on April 18, 1916, it was.'

Tears ran down his face and his lips trembled. He dropped his chin on to his chest and wept noisily.

Keast got up and crossed the room.

'Why have I to put up with this bloody performance? You'd have thought we had enough trouble.'

He stopped walking about and stood glaring at Stobart.

'You bloody great booby you,' he shouted, then bending forward he added, 'you make me sick.' He pulled out darts from the board, 'come on you two,' he said to us.

CHAPTER V

A car pulled up outside the office and Harama came in. He gave me a formal greeting and added, 'I have to come to say I am sorry that the two white men have died.'

'Thank you,' I said, 'would you like to see the Provincial Commissioner?'

'No, give him my message and ask if there is any help I can give him.'

He sat on and although he had nothing to say I regarded his presence as further expression of sympathy. I was convinced that in some way he could help us and tried to think of some service we needed.

'Harama,' I said suddenly; he looked back with immediate attention, 'you know the telephone line's down and the road to Huta is closed. If we could let them know what's happened here maybe they could help in some way but it takes three weeks to get through by mail runners and three weeks to get a reply. I'm certain it wouldn't take you that time to get a message to Huta.'

'Allah!' he exclaimed, 'three weeks! If I give the order my horsemen will get through to Huta in five days.'

I told Daubney what Harama had said. Half an hour later he left for the town. When he returned he pushed past the messengers and petitioners.

'Tell everyone to come to the Residency at seven o'clock tonight,' he said.

'For a meeting?'

He spoke over his shoulder as he went through to his room.

'Yes, everyone should come.'

There was a feeling of suppressed hysteria but Daubney spoke easily and we listened in silence.

Two deaths coming so close together might be a coincidence he said, but he thought it his duty to prepare for worse. Peggy Crane stood up swaying slightly as she stared round at us. There was a dribble of lipstick at her mouth and her left cheek was smeared with mascara.

'Yes, do something before we're all dead. You're in charge, do something,' she cried. She started to sob. 'Why did I ever come to this country.'

Crane pulled her down before she could say more. The ugly scene made us uncomfortable. Elizabeth Pomeroy stared straight before her. Margaret Marchant made a move towards Peggy but Robert restrained her.

'Peggy's right,' Daubney said. 'I've asked you here to tell you my plans.'

Daubney said Palthrop ought to have help. Palthrop sipped his whisky with an air of unconcern.

'This is my idea.' Daubney spoke with great deliberation. 'Dr Palthrop disagrees, but he is completely co-operative.'

We all looked at Palthrop. He now had an anxious expression. Daubney went on.

'I arranged with Harama this morning for a relay of horsemen to take a letter to Huta. There are ways of getting through, he assures me, and we should have a reply in ten days.'

Daubney paused and glanced round the room.

'I've sent Dr Palthrop's case notes to the Senior Medical Officer at Huta and asked for a medical officer and sister to help us.'

Pomeroy spoke first. He sounded sceptical.

'Yes, but how are these people to get here?'

Daubney folded his arms.

'That is the problem. I've suggested a route of five hundred miles which should be possible if rain held off for a few days, but with the river Libia to cross. . . .' Daubney turned to Crane, 'could you lay on a raft?'

Keast and Stobart whispered to Crane.

'Yes, we could do that all right,' he said. 'Even in full flood the Libia's not more than seventy feet wide but it is deep, too deep for poling.' He looked at Keast. 'I think we could work a raft across with ropes.' Keast nodded. 'We could try.'

Three days of hot sun baked tyre tracks and foot prints on the station roads. There was tennis again but the day Metcalfe and I were to play the Marchants, Margaret sent me a note in her small round handwriting to say Robert preferred not to play and asking me to get Pomeroy to make up our four. After the game Margaret insisted we went to her house for drinks. 'Please come,' she said, 'you'll cheer up Robert.'

We followed her round the circular road. The Marchants' house, one of three built together on the far side of the station, was called the Schloss because of its turrets and massive abutments. It was gay with flowers which Margaret cultivated in pots along shelves on the verandah.

Elliot, grey-haired and old looking, raised his hand in salute when we passed him at the turn in to the drive. Margaret was at the door when we arrived. She looked troubled.

'Robert's gone to bed,' she said. 'He's got a headache and pains in the back.'

We made no move, then Pomeroy said, 'If Robert's mouldy we had better not come in.'

She stamped her foot. 'You must come in,' she said. 'We'll go up to the bedroom. Perhaps Robert would like a drink too.'

Robert Marchant lay in a large double bed. A Webley revolver and a torch lay on his bedside table. On Margaret's side there was a Bible and paper-backed book.

Robert murmured inaudibly when Pomeroy greeted him. Margaret urged servants to bring us chairs but we refused to sit. Margaret followed us downstairs when we left.

'You don't think Robert's sickening for anything?' she said. She looked at us anxiously. At first nobody spoke then Pomeroy said, 'I think you ought to get Geoffrey Palthrop to see him.'

I saw Harama's head messenger pass in front of the Office towards Daubney's room and two minutes later Daubney pushed open the connecting door and came in to me. He held up a letter. 'I've got a reply from the S.M.O., Dr Sedley and Miss Standfield should be here the day after tomorrow. You and Metcalfe must meet them at the Libia and bring them straight to the Residency.'

He whistled cheerfully as he turned back to his room. I called after him.

'Have you heard Marchant's ill, sir?'

He turned abruptly.

'Margaret's very concerned about him.' I said.

He blinked with a look of pain. 'Oh dear, I hope nothing happens to him.'

Five minutes later he held the door half open with his hand on the knob. He sounded relieved when he spoke.

'Robert's temperature's normal. I've just heard from Palthrop.'

Metcalfe and I went ahead in the first lorry. The recent sunshine had dried the road but Stobart and Keast brought labourers to dig us out if we got stuck.

The Libia is one of hundreds of minor tributaries to the vast river system draining the territory. During the dry season there is at most only a trickle and often no more than moist sand, but at the height of the rains yellow-brown water rises up the banks and the river becomes a torrent carrying silt and debris to the sea. It was in full flood when I got out of the lorry and walked to the bank. Metcalfe threw in a stick and it was carried away twisting and turning and sometimes submerged in the eddies and currents. As we inspected the raft the second lorry arrived with Keast and Stobart. They had bolted baulks of timber together round two empty oil drums. The raft lay on the sloping bank where high grass had been beaten down. The flow of water made a curve in the rope joining the raft to a tree on the far bank. More rope laying in a coil joined it to a tree on our side.

'It works all right,' Keast said, 'we've crossed four times.'

'Is that rope strong?' asked Metcalfe.

Stobart picked up the rope and offered it to us.

'Two inch manilla, we use in the yard for heavy lifting gear. That won't break.'

We stood in a group staring at the raft in silence.

'Let's try the crossing again,' I said.

The labourers levered the raft into the water. The headman shouted and the gang on the other side hauled on the rope while they let out slowly on our side. They brought the raft back and Stobart and I crossed together to wait for the doctor and nurse.

At four o'clock we were still waiting and my throat and mouth were dry from smoking. Stobart opened a bottle of beer; it frothed up warm and sticky. I walked for a mile up the road to kill time.

Five hours after we had reached the river the sound of a motor engine grew steadily louder and a fifteen hundredweight truck appeared round the bend in the road. A man of singular appearance jumped down. He was of middle size; his florid face was unshaven and his red hair was long and untidy. He wore a dirty white shirt with tightly fitting khaki shorts. His blue socks and black shoes were the part of some other rig. Mud plastered the gingery hair of his short thick legs.

'Well, here we are, better late than never,' he said. 'I'm Dr Sedley and here is Miss Standfield the nursing sister.' The girl stepped stiffly down from the truck and joined us. Her white overall was crumpled and her long fair hair hung down her back. Sedley laughed. 'We've not travelled *de luxe* exactly, but never mind, sister,' he said speaking to the girl, 'you'll soon have work to do.'

She was trying to coil up her hair and took pins out of her mouth.

'That will be a change for the better,' she said.

I caught a glimpse of Sedley's insensitive features as he turned to go to the truck.

'Let me show you the raft,' I said to the girl, 'it's quite safe, we've made two trial crossings.'

It started to rain and we went back to the truck.

Sedley and Stobart lifted out two black japaned boxes, a microscope, a large wooden chest and three suit cases.

'What have you got there?' I said.

'Books, instruments, drugs and a few odds and ends,' said Sedley airily, 'just a few things.'

'Palthrop would have all you want.'

'Well, you know what they say, better be sure than sorry.'

The labourers got the loads on to their heads and carried them down the bank to the raft. Sedley and Stobart crossed and the labourers hauled back the raft. In the rain and failing light the muddy fast-flowing river, sucking and roaring, looked menacing.

I helped Miss Standfield down the bank through the long

grass to the water edge. Without hesitation she stepped on the raft.

'Sit down,' I said, 'it's safer than standing.'

I sat down beside her. The rope stretched taut as the river tugged at the raft and water splashed up drenching us from violent eddies in mid-stream. I was jolted into the girl when they pulled the raft into the bank. Metcalfe stood waiting to help her but she stepped off unaided and followed him up the bank, bending low and touching the ground to steady herself. A yard from the top she slipped full length on her face. Metcalfe took her hand and drew her up to the road. She was plastered in ochreous mud.

Sedley laughed. 'You look a sight.'

Stobart opened a pocket knife and she scraped the thickest mud from her overall and then washed her hands in a calabash of river water.

The rain stopped when we had got half-way to Pela and we drove faster. Shea-butter wicks were burning in the night-market when we passed through the town and it was quite dark when we reached the station.

Miller was with Daubney when he came out to meet us. Neither had changed and I got a whiff of whisky when Daubney spoke. He said nothing about Miss Standfield's appearance.

'Robert Marchant's dead,' he said. 'It is a great shock. I was expecting better news when Palthrop came round here half an hour ago.'

A gasp came from Metcalfe.

'Where's Margaret?'

Daubney glanced at him.

'She's with the Pomeroys,' he said. 'Miss Standfield, Mrs Crane'll put you up now.'

'Oh no, I'll stay in the resthouse,' she said.

She would have said more but I interrupted.

'I'll join Metcalfe and you can have my house—everything's there.'

Keast and Stobart took away the lorries and the rest of us went into the Residency.

Sedley seemed restless and would not sit down.

'Where's Palthrop?' he said.

'Palthrop?' said Daubney vaguely, 'he left here to go to Elliot's place.'

Metcalfe sat up.

'Is Elliot sick now?'

'So I understand,' Daubney said.

Metcalfe clapped a hand to his mouth.

'No!' he gasped. 'Oh no. When will this end?'

Sedley stood in the middle of the room facing Daubney.

'I'd like to have a bath and see Palthrop,' he said.

Daubney got up to show him his room.

'We must have a p.m. on Marchant,' Sedley said as they moved off. 'It's essential, absolutely essential.'

His voice grew fainter as they went upstairs.

Daubney was not in the Provincial Office next morning, but at ten o'clock he telephoned.

'Come here,' he said. 'Margaret Marchant's sitting on the front verandah. Don't disturb her, she wants to be alone; come in by the side door to my office.'

We worked for an hour then Daubney looked up at the sound of a car in the drive.

'That's Palthrop,' he said, but as soon as he spoke Sedley's voice reached us. He sounded excited.

'Mr Daubney,' he shouted. 'It's yellow fever all right. I've got Marchant's liver here in a jar. You can see for yourself, it's typical.'

There was perceptible silence, perhaps for three or four seconds, then a single cry. I ran with Daubney to the verandah. Margaret Marchant lay on the stone flags near the chair where she had been writing.

Sedley followed us with the jar in his hands.

'Oh, I'm sorry,' he said. 'This is most unfortunate, most unfortunate. I didn't know Mrs Marchant was here.'

We listened in a drizzle of rain to Daubney reading the burial service again and then went back to the Residency. Elizabeth Pomeroy came in later with Peggy Crane and sat with her on a sofa.

Sedley stood up when Daubney asked him to speak to us.

38

'For yellow fever to go on,' he said, 'three factors must operate, the virus, the carrier and human beings. The only link we can break is the carrier, which is the mosquito, *aedes aegypti*. Here in this station you have seen how yellow fever clings to a place; the virus persists in the mosquitoes you find there. There's been a case in each of three neighbouring houses—four including the cook's wife—and I'm told McFie spent a lot of time in Brice's house. We shall find *aedes aegypti* breeding over there somewhere.'

Daubney told me to see that Sedley got any help he required. Next morning I found he had started work early and I cycled round the station and found him in Marchant's compound clutching a hammer. Keast was there too with a gang of labourers. Piles of soil and flowers and broken earthenware littered the drive in front of the house. Labourers tipped over the big pots and Sedley smashed them with his hammer.

I pushed my bicycle up the drive.

'What's going on?' I said.

Sedley looked up.

'Hello there,' he greeted me, 'we've found the breeding place.' He kicked the circular earthenware stands where flower pots had stood. 'It's in these things.' He kicked one of the stands again. 'This is where the trouble came from, water in all of them and thousands of larvae—absolute death trap.'

Sedley started to whistle.

'Isn't it dangerous to be around here now?' I said.

'Dangerous?'

'What if we got a mosquito bite?'

'Not at this time of day. *Aedes aegypti* feed in the evening.'

Sedley gave an encouraging shout as the labourers turned over two more big pots. He peered into the earthenware stands in which they had stood.

'Come here,' he said, 'look at that.'

Scores of tiny thread-like larvae wriggled through the water.

'*Aedes aegypti* breeding,' he said, 'every one a potential killer.'

He dipped out two larvae with a test tube and tied muslin over the top. Then he poured away the water on the stand and smashed the earthenware.

'You'll tidy up before you leave?' I said.

Sedley stopped breaking the pots with his hammer.

'Sure,' Keast said, 'we'll leave the place tidy.'

I was about to go. 'Don't tell Margaret the mosquitoes came from her flower pots,' I said.

Sedley straightened up.

'Why not?' he said, 'won't she be interested?'

'Oh for God's sake,' Keast burst out impatiently, 'have some sense, man.'

Sedley looked doubtfully from one to the other of us.

'It wouldn't be tactful, you think?'

Keast turned on him with a snarl.

'You bloody imbecile,' he said.

Sedley twisted round squarely and faced Keast.

'Why do you say that?' He spoke quietly in a reasonable tone. 'I don't follow you.'

I left them, cycled down the drive and turned in at the next compound.

Elliot's boy crouched on a mat, bowing in prayer to the East. A turkey cock with fluffed-out tail gobbled across the compound. Brightly coloured lizards a foot long basked in the warm morning sun on the front of the house. They scampered away when I propped up my bicycle. Books spilled out from shelves to camp chairs patched with goat skin and on to grass mats covering the floor. Elliot's pipes filled a rack on the wall and two lay in an ash tray with a tin of tobacco on a stool. Dust covered the papier-mâché horn of a gramophone at the end of the room. I climbed the spiralling staircase to the bedroom.

Hilda Standfield was staring out from the casement window. She turned smiling wearily when I entered, but held up a finger as I started to speak.

'He's asleep,' she whispered.

Without his false teeth Elliot's face had fallen in and his mouth had a pinched look. White stubble sprouted from his bony chin and cheeks. He looked frail in the big stretcher bed.

'He'll recover?' I said.

She gave him a quick glance and nodded.

'Oh yes,' she said, 'he'll recover but he will want a lot of care.'

An African woman sat motionless in the corner behind me. She was middle-aged but still comely and with a good figure.

'The white man will recover,' I said.

'If it is Allah's will,' she said.

Hilda followed me downstairs to the compound.

Elliot's boy had finished praying and now sat relaxed on his mat.

'You'll now be able to get away sometimes,' I said.

She compressed her lips and I wondered if I had said the wrong thing.

'I want more clothes from your house,' she said.

'I'll bring my car round for you this afternoon. Perhaps later on you would join us for a drink?'

'I'd like to,' she said.

'Metcalfe says Margaret Marchant may soon play tennis again. Would you care to make up a four sometimes?'

'That would be nice.'

We were plagued by earwigs. They were everywhere, in the binding of books, in clothes, and in food. It was harvest time. The rains had come to an end and the short hot period had followed before the dry *harmattan* season. The countryside was again turning brown. Seven-foot high corn had been cut and half forgotten views of the station came into sight again.

Margaret Marchant left when the roads were open and Metcalfe went on leave at the same time. Miller and Elliot followed soon after. Stobart had packed to go but Keast was staying on until the next dry season. There were a number of new people in the station. I handed over the Provincial Office to a first-tour cadet named Woolam and was attached to Pomeroy again.

CHAPTER VI

Harama was in the room with Pomeroy. Pomeroy waved at a chair and told me to sit.

'Harama has asked for a party to go into the Balaba Mountains,' he said. 'He sent envoys there last year but two of them were murdered.'

He turned to Harama, 'Two, you said?'

'Three,' Harama said, 'and a messenger early this year.'

Pomeroy looked thoughtful, but Harama smiled. He had strong white teeth.

'The pagans are really very timid,' he said.

Pomeroy laughed.

'Yes, it is true,' Harama said, 'they hide in the mountains when they are alarmed.' He shrugged his shoulders. 'During their festivals the young men get a little mad, it is dangerous to disturb them then.'

Pomeroy fingered a paper knife.

'You've asked for Mr Wood but what can he do?'

Harama cleared his throat.

'We want the pagans to make their homes on the plains. The land is more fertile there and they will grow better crops. In the old days they went up into the mountains to hide from slave raiders.'

'Yes, Harama, but what can Mr Wood do?'

'They will listen to him, I know. We want some of their Chiefs to come here for a visit. When they go back maybe they will tell their people we are friends and more will come.'

'What about the murderers?' I said.

Harama looked from me to Pomeroy.

'We should like them to give up the murderers.'

Pomeroy escorted Harama to his car. He was no longer interested when he came back.

42

'You've heard what it's about,' he said. 'Reckon to be away about three months.'

I dined with the Cranes that night. Palthrop drove me round to their house. He took a brush from under the dash board and touched up his moustache before he got out. Smellie, who had followed Miller, was there and Firbank the new Education Officer with his wife Tansy, a dark long-limbed girl who made me think of a spider.

We sat on rugs playing liar dice. Crane kept filling our glasses with Tiger's Milk. Tansy Firbank sat with her legs curled beneath her.

'Watch it, Tansy,' I said when Crane came round again, 'this is terribly strong stuff.'

She held out her glass.

'Yes, but it's nice, sweetie pie.' She smiled at Crane, 'right up, please,' she said.

We ate food with our fingers and then Smellie moved round to sit with Tansy. Firbank talked to Peggy. Crane and I got up and sat on pouffes. Palthrop remained alone on the floor, swaying from his waist and talking to nobody. I caught him looking at me with grave concern. Crane left me to fill glasses again. The five poker dice lay on the mat. No one wanted to play now. Palthrop got awkwardly to his feet and stood against the wall.

'It's outrageous,' he cried. His voice became a snarl. 'Outrageous,' he repeated, 'outrageous.'

Peggy Crane scrambled up and put her arm round him.

'What's the matter Geoffy darling, what's the matter sweetheart? What's worrying you, my sweet, what's worrying you?'

Palthrop shook her off and pointed at me.

'That young man may be going to a painful death,' he said.

'Oh no!' Peggy exclaimed with jocular horror, 'not that.'

Crane and Firbank looked blank.

'I'm taking a party up to the Balaba Mountains,' I said, 'but it's Harama's idea, Pomeroy didn't think of it.' 'Yes,' said Palthrop, 'and likely to get an arrow in your back and die in agony five thousand feet up in those rocks.' He put his hands against the wall on each side to steady himself. 'It ought to be stopped. Pomeroy won't go up those mountains—Oh no, he's reserved for better things. No pagan behind a rock will put a poisoned arrow in his back. No by God, Pomeroy will take care of that.'

Crane moved across the room to Palthrop.

'Take it easy, Geoff, sit down, I'll get you a whisky.'

Palthrop walked unsteadily to a chair and sat down. He was no longer excited. He looked old and tired. He beckoned to me.

'I'll give you an emergency kit in the morning.'

Palthrop's car was outside when I went home for late breakfast. He opened a box he had placed on the table.

'You've got to act quickly.' He took out an eight-ounce bottle. 'This is neat brandy,' he said. 'Get down as much as you can and then push the arrow through and cut off the shaft.' He unwrapped greased paper from a scalpel. 'Make an incision in the area of the wound and rub in this pot permang.' He opened a tin and showed me the crystals. Then he took out a five c.c. hypodermic syringe and an ampoule of yellow fluid. 'It's not easy but it can be done. Give yourself an intravenous injection and when you've done that,' he held up another eight-ounce bottle, 'drink a tablespoonful of this. Don't be afraid to let the wound bleed but finally cover it with a dry dressing. There's a packet of gauze, a roll of elastoplast and a bandage.'

He looked at me anxiously.

'You won't remember what I've told you—I have typed the instructions and numbered these things. Make quite sure you know what to do.'

I invited him to breakfast.

He shook his head. 'I've got to get down to the hospital.'

'Now listen,' he said, 'keep that kit within arm's reach every second you're in those hills.' He called Ali. 'Carry this and stay close to your master.'

Woolam rang when I was at breakfast.

'The big cheese wants to see you at eleven o'clock in his office.'

'Who, Daubney?'

'No, Pomeroy.'

'What's biting him?'

'Search me, pal.'

He rang off.

It was after eleven o'clock by the time I had arranged about carriers and got back to the D.C.'s office. Pomeroy looked at his watch but said nothing.

'You know the Balaba Mountains are in Mandated Territory?'

'Yes, of course,' I said.

He fingered the paper knife.

'It's important that there should be no casualties when you get up there,' he said.

I laughed. 'On whose side?'

He spoke quite seriously.

'I had the pagans in mind.'

His manner riled me.

'I'd have thought it important to avoid casualties at any time.'

'On no account must anyone in your party shoot,' he continued. 'I want to make that quite clear.'

I gaped with amazement.

'I haven't given a thought to such things,' I said, 'but it could be we might have to act in self defence or stop a murderer getting away.'

He looked displeased.

'As a last resort, if there had been an actual attack on you, it would be permissible for you to shoot, but you would never shoot first.'

My only feeling was of incredulity.

'What's this about?'

He ignored my question.

'If a pagan is killed in an affray you must conduct a most detailed inquest and prepare a full report.'

'I would anyway,' I said.

He now looked uncomfortable.

'Yes, but this would have to go to the League of Nations.'

'To the League of Nations!'

'Yes, actually to a Miss Rebecca Fancott.'

'Who's she?'

'I understand she's a New Zealand woman, an Assistant Secretary in Room 347 at Geneva.'

'Oh yes,' I said, 'and what would she do with it?'

'That's not our concern.'

I stood up. 'I'll try to avoid killing anyone,' I said as I made to go.

He tried to detain me.

'When are you leaving?'

'The day after tomorrow, I hope.'

He was fiddling with the desk knife again.

'We should be glad if you would dine with us the night before you go.'

Pomeroy was trying to be friendly and I should have responded but I spoke without thinking with the perverse intention of slighting him.

'Thank you,' I said, 'but I've arranged to go to Palthrop.'

He lifted his eyebrows.

'Pity,' he said. He looked down at his desk and opened a file. 'Some other time, perhaps.'

After the subdued light of Pomeroy's room the glare outside made me blink.

We trekked eastward fifteen miles a day over a dusty plain across dry river beds and past rocky outcrops to the mountains. I rode in front with Arisi and Gela; Ali followed with the carriers. We reached the foothills on the eleventh day and Arisi brought Berefa to me, son of a pagan woman and a plainsman. He wore a white close-fitting loin cloth and a check cap, and on the upper part of his body, hanging loose and unbuttoned, a black dress waistcoat.

We left the horses and half the loads and Berefa guided us, climbing easily and quickly with muscles shimmering under his polished brown skin.

For days we followed him up stony tracks, hand over hand up rocky hillsides and along precipitous ridges to clusters of deserted grass huts half hidden by boulders. At sundown when we camped he called out telling the people we came as friends and begging them to meet us. His voice echoed in the surrounding hills and must have carried miles in the still mountain air, but nobody came. The pagans deserted their huts, their corn stores and their goats and kept away from us.

Berefa's loin cloth turned grey and the police uniforms lost their smartness. I knew the carriers' names. A feeling of physical well-being came with hard climbing. A bond drew the party together and I felt relaxed and in good spirits. But I had seen no one outside our party since I had set foot in the mountains. I would start back after another three days, I decided. We were becoming careless and next morning, after we struck camp, the party got strung out. Ali, with a kettle slung over one shoulder and an aluminium teapot and water bottle crossed over the other and the emergency kit with sugar and tea in a haversack, followed Berefa. He was feeling for footholds and stretching up hand over hand up a rock face. I was twenty-five yards behind. A small man, about five feet high, came out of the high grass behind a rock to the left of the track. He had a goat skin about his waist and carried a bow. He dropped down on his right knee, drew back his bow string, and took aim. I noted with heightened perception that the skin touched the ground when he knelt, the bunching muscles behind his shoulder and that he was lighter-skinned than my people. Then I shouted and it was as though he had never been there, but an arrow stuck out from the calf of Ali's right leg.

The police ran and spread out in the high grass, searching among the rocks for the man.

Blood ran down Ali's leg when I drew out the arrow, a sliver of palm mid-rib, barbed shape, fire hardened and saffron-coloured at the tip. The bowman had released it too soon; it penetrated less than an inch. Ali coughed as he swallowed the brandy and exclaimed 'Allah', when I cut into his leg, but no other sound came from him as I followed Palthrop's instructions.

We camped there and at daylight Berefa reported he had drunk corn beer and talked to the pagans during the night. He told me their leaders wanted to see me.

I waited in my camp chair outside the tent. They came out in file from the long grass, ten of them, led by Berefa. Thirty yards away they paused and then in turn dropped their bows and arrows. I told the police to go. Four men came forward with Berefa and prostrated themselves and then sat on the ground in front of me. They came to surrender the murderers. I gave them cigarettes and we talked for an hour; two of them agreed to come back with us to Pela.

When we got down to the plain the carriers sang a marching song about a fabulous D.C. named Carter and every night until lights out laughter came from the police lines.

I left the main party three miles from Pela and rode straight to the station. Woolam was in the Provincial Office.

47

'Pomeroy about?' I said.

Woolam sat back in his chair.

'You could certainly do with a hair cut,' he said as he gave me my mail.

He lit a cigarette and continued to stare at me.

'Never mind my hair,' I said, 'where's Pomeroy. I've got a report he'll like.'

Woolam peered about his desk and then tapped the bell.

'Where's my ash tray?' he demanded when the messenger came in.

'Listen Woolam,' I said, 'where's Pomeroy?'

He held out a tin of fifty Goldflake.

'I imagine you'll find him at the Residency.'

'What are you talking about?'

'Pomeroy's acting P.C. and doesn't deign to come to this office.'

'You're joking.'

'Oh, no. He's been doing it for two months, you're out of touch my friend. Daubney got bilharzia. Geoff Palthrop took him to Huta Hospital. Pomeroy's been in the big house ever since.'

'I certainly am out of touch,' I said. 'Who's D.C. now?'

Woolam drew on his cigarette and inhaled.

'Guy Merrifield St John Ames,' he said.

'Never heard of him.'

'No?' said Woolam, 'maybe you haven't, but you will, my friend.'

Woolam puffed deliberately and inhaled again.

'I ought to see him, I suppose,' I said.

'You can't.'

'Why not?'

'Because at this moment he's in Faisi.'

'In the rain forest belt?'

Woolam tapped ash off his cigarette.

'Yes,' he said, 'that's where he is.'

'What's he doing down there?'

'Well may you ask. He's with Smellie, a C.I.D. Officer named Gregg and a red-headed doctor named Sedley.'

'Don't stall,' I said. 'What's this about?'

'It's about a Leopard Murder Society that Ames has uncovered at Faisi.'

'A leopard murder society!'

'That's what I said.'

'But he's only been here a couple of months.'

'Precisely.'

'Are you serious?'

'Completely.'

'Is there such a thing?'

Woolam pursed his lips.

'Pomeroy certainly thinks so.'

Pomeroy was walking from the Residency as I came out of the office. He wore a white sola topi, a heavy tussore suit and white buckskin brogues. There was a flower in the button-hole of his jacket.

'You've been away a long time,' he said with a hint of rebuke.

'Ten weeks,' I said. 'You thought I'd be away three months.'

His frown suggested it might be wise to show him greater respect.

'Did I?' he said. 'I can't remember what I said.'

He walked on.

'Should I report to you?' I said.

He paused and looked back.

'Good heavens, no, tell Ames about it sometime—I'm going to Faisi tomorrow.'

Pomeroy hummed a tune as he moved on.

I went to Keast after tea to get my hair cut. He was lying in a hammock on the verandah bare-legged and without a shirt. He dropped a newspaper and got down. He was morose and pointed without a word at a chair. He draped me in a towel and shook talcum powder on my neck and then moved the clippers up the back of my head.

'Are they pulling?' he said.

There was a leaping tiger tattooed on his forearm and on the other, from wrist to elbow, a highly coloured snake.

'They're O.K.,' I said.

He blew on the clippers, working them in his hand and then inspecting them closely.

'They're stiff,' he said.

He finished with the clippers and started with the scissors and comb.

His silence was uncomfortable.

'Pomeroy seems to fancy himself now he's in the big house,' I said.

He stopped with comb and scissors raised in his hands. 'Don't talk to me about that bastard,' he said. He untucked the towel, shook off the loose hair and draped me again.

'What's the matter with Pomeroy?'

He flicked my neck with a whisk and said nothing for a moment.

'Pomeroy!' he said with contempt. 'He gave a party when Daubney went. He invited everyone but me. I thought he'd forgot. Next day he stopped me on the road to explain that he couldn't invite me to a station party because I was a Grade II appointment.' Keast spoke venomously. 'Then he patted my back and said he knew I'd understand.'

There was not much I could say.

'What did you do?'

'Do?' he said. 'Nothing, I walked away.'

Keast combed out my hair and trimmed the long ends in front.

He fell silent and finished cutting my hair. He shook out the towel again and we sat down.

'I shouldn't let Pomeroy worry you,' I said.

He turned angry little eyes on me and stood up.

'Pomeroy worry me! That'll be the day,' he said walking quickly up and down the verandah, 'that bastard worry me!' He suddenly sat down again. 'Oh to hell with it, have a beer?'

'Thanks Keasty, I'd like one,' I said.

CHAPTER VII

Pomeroy did not go to Faisi. Ames, Smellie, Sedley and Gregg, the C.I.D. Officer, came overnight to Pela to meet Bullivant the Inspector-General of Police.

I was at a side table in Woolam's office writing my report when Ames came in with a payment voucher—a brown-eyed man with big ears, swarthy and fleshy about the face but good looking. He forced a smile in the manner of someone preoccupied with important matters when Woolam gave him his money and nodded at me as he went out. An hour later Pomeroy's orderly brought me a note ordering me to report at the Residency at noon.

I arrived a few minutes early and Pomeroy looked at his watch as though I was somehow at fault and then told me to arrange a table and chairs on the verandah for a conference of seven. I thought his orderly could have done it but when I had finished I asked him if there was anything else he required. He addressed me in a portentous manner.

'Hold yourself in readiness for special duty at any hour of the night or day during this emergency,' he said. He cleared his throat. 'I suppose for the time being you can regard yourself as my personal *aide*.'

Tyres crackled on the gravel and Ames came in. He put papers on the table. Pomeroy shook his head. 'Bullivant will be on my right,' he said, 'you'll be there.'

Ames moved his papers to the other side of the table.

Sedley came with the police officers. He beamed at me.

'You know what they say?' he said. 'Coming events cast their shadows before them. Miss Standfield was telling me how kind you'd been to her and five minutes later the S.M.O. came to my room. Before he opened his mouth I said "I'll leave for Pela tomorrow". You should have seen his face. "How did you know the P.C. had asked for you?" he said. . . .'

51

'Please sit down,' Pomeroy said, 'we've got a lot to talk about.'

I took the chair at the end of the table. Gregg, a strong-faced fresh complexioned man with unblinking blue eyes gave me a friendly smile and introduced himself as he sat on my left. Palthrop arrived breathless and sat on my right in the remaining chair.

Pomeroy cleared his throat. 'We want Colonel Bullivant to have as much factual information as we can give him,' he said as he looked round the table. 'Above all I want him to know our thoughts about the appalling developments at Faisi.' He turned to Bullivant with a smile. 'I have no doubt you will be seeing Sir William Perriam Pleydell.'

Ames shuffled the papers in front of him. Sedley listened, head on one side and arms folded. The police sat impassive. Palthrop's mouth drooped miserably and I caught a whiff of gin when he turned my way.

'I have made an interim report to the Civil Secretary,' Pomeroy continued, 'but I am anxious that Sir William should get the feel of the situation, know how our minds are working.' He raised his hands, 'it's the imponderabilia which are so important, the intangibles, the nuances, which it is not easy to put into writing.'

There was brief silence then Bullivant spoke.

'We can't be sure that the Governor will want to see me.'

Pomeroy smiled tolerantly.

'Let's face it,' he said, 'we are talking about murder on a scale unprecedented in the criminal annals of the territory. For years possibly wholesale murder has been concealed with fiendish ingenuity. Offenders have gone unpunished and for far too long the community has been at the mercy of a diabolical and inhuman organization.'

It sounded corny but everyone looked serious.

The green canvas punka creaked as it swung over our heads. Pomeroy smiled. 'Sir William will want a first-hand impression,' he said confidently. 'There is, of course, nothing new in the notion of a Leopard Murder Society, such activity has been known in Sierre Leone, Liberia, the Congo, and I believe in parts of Nigeria. But never before,' he said with a note of satisfaction, 'never before on a scale comparable with that manifested in this Province. Gentlemen, let us get this situation in true perspective. There's never been anything like it.'

Palthrop moved uneasily in his chair.

Gregg raised his eyebrows at me.

Pomeroy finished talking.

'Mr Ames, go over the ground bringing out the main facts.'

Ames shuffled his papers.

'Three hundred miles to the south, where the Province runs into the rain forest belt, there is an enclave of Yama people historically subject to the Mudela at Pela through conquest, but with no ethnological links with Pela people.'

This was old stuff to anyone who had served in the Province, but Ames spoke as though he were giving us the benefit of personal research.

'About a hundred thousand of them live in scattered villages, each family with its own house and compound sometimes two to three hundred yards from the next. They cultivate the land and do a bit of hunting. There are tracts of original forest, mahogany, ebony and iron wood, but much of the area has been cleared. The people grow yams, cassava, sweet potatoes, okra and groundnuts, but their agriculture is primitive. When the ground is exhausted they leave it fallow for four or five years, sometimes longer. Secondary growth shoots up immediately and in no time there is a dense impenetrable barrier of vegetation. Footpaths criss-cross the area to gardens, into the forest, to neighbours' houses, to . . .'

Pomeroy look at his watch.

'Yes, yes,' he said, 'that is enough background material.' He turned to Bullivant. 'I think that gives you a picture of the terrain and people.'

Bullivant spoke across the table to Ames.

'Are there missions down there?'

Ames responded as though to cue.

'No, the missions haven't got in yet.'

'Can you tell us something about the social habits of the people?'

'They are gregarious,' Ames said in the manner of someone sure of his subject. 'They meet in secret societies with elaborate rituals and binding oaths. They stubbornly hold on to old beliefs, looking for supernatural causes for mishaps, consulting oracles for guidance and making sacrifices.'

Bullivant listened with close attention. There was more of it.

Ames had read it all in a report on the area by a D.C. named Faggot, and Pomeroy knew it.

'Thank you, Mr Ames,' he said. 'That will do by way of introduction.'

Their eyes met.

'Continue Mr Ames,' Pomeroy said with a bland smile, 'tell us about the killings.'

Ames inclined his head.

'Very good, sir,' he said, 'as you wish.'

'I first went to Faisi five weeks ago. The resthouse caretaker told me when I arrived that a woman had been missing after going out to pick yoka and had just been found mauled by a leopard.'

'Yoka?' said Bullivant.

Ames turned towards him with immediate attention.

'A wild spinach, sir,' he said. 'It has a mild aperient effect, I believe.'

'Yes, all right,' Pomeroy said.

'I asked to see the body,' Ames continued. 'The left arm had gone. The neck was missing. The head was detached and the soft tissue removed.' Ames looked at his papers. 'The breast bone and some ribs had also gone. There was no sign of the heart and lungs. On the back there were cuts and some puncture wounds.'

Ames picked up his silver pencil, holding it horizontally between his hands and leaned over the table.

'I stayed on eight nights at Faisi. In that period seven deaths were reported.' He wagged the pencil for emphasis. 'Seven deaths in eight days, I have the details here.' He looked at his papers. 'A triple death of a woman and two young daughters, a double killing of two wives and two separate cases of women, one of them in advanced pregnancy. Mutilations followed a pattern. Decapitation with neck missing, tissue stripped from face and skull, one or both arms severed, hearts and lungs removed, and so on. The point which I wish to press is that on all these bodies there were clean incised wounds and punctures on the backs.'

'Well?' said Pomeroy.

Ames carefully placed the pencil on his papers and paused.

'I must confess,' he said after reflection, 'it was some time before the possibility of a Leopard Murder Society occurred to me. I am not a doctor. I was not qualified to draw an inference from the similarity of the mutilations. But of two things I am sure—very many people, women and children mainly, hundreds probably, have been done to death at sundown on bush paths at Faisi. And now,' he went on slowly, shaking his head, 'people are afraid, very very afraid.' Ames looked at Pomeroy. 'I reported to the acting Provincial Commissioner when I got back here.'

Pomeroy looked down the table.

'We needed post-mortem examinations and reports on these bodies,' he said. 'At my request Dr Palthrop, the Medical Officer, went down to Faisi with the District Commissioner.'

Bullivant and Gregg turned slowly towards Palthrop. A look passed between Ames and Smellie and then Ames turned over his papers and Smellie took a cigarette.

'Dr Palthrop.' There was a hint of impatience in Pomeroy's voice. 'You examined a number of bodies I believe?'

Palthrop had been moodily smoking, showing no interest in what had gone on. He looked embarrassed and his eyes flickered. 'Yes, I examined six bodies,' he said. 'Four females and two males, small boys with their mothers.'

'Well?' said Pomeroy.

Bullivant and Gregg waited expectantly, but it was some moments before Palthrop spoke.

'I was told the mutilations I saw were typical of many bodies.'

'You formed an opinion as to the cause of death?'

'I did.'

'And what was it?'

'I formed the opinion that the six people had been savaged by a wild animal, probably a leopard.'

Pomeroy looked at Sedley and then turned again to Palthrop.

'You saw puncture wounds and incised cuts on the backs of the bodies?'

Palthrop made a perceptible effort to assert himself.

'I did,' he said.

A clock chimed one and a houseboy came in with a decanter of gin, a bitters shaker and a jug of water. Sedley asked for sherry.

Pomeroy became impatient as the boy went round with the gin.

'Get the sherry and leave it with Dr Sedley,' he said.

'Now, Palthrop,' Pomeroy continued. 'These cuts and puncture wounds you saw were caused by an animal?'

'I can accept no other hypothesis.'

'You do not believe these people were murdered?'

'I do not.'

'Thank you,' Pomeroy said, in the manner of someone resolved to be fair, 'we are grateful for your opinion,' then with a significant pause he looked down the table. 'Reason might well reject the idea of an elaborate murder organization.' He would have said more but Bullivant interrupted.

'Can we hear what Sedley thinks? You have seen some of these killings?' Bullivant said.

Sedley was pouring out sherry.

'Oh yes, I've examined five bodies.'

'What did you find?'

A stream of sherry ran across the table as Sedley continued to pour.

'Oh, I am sorry,' he said to Pomeroy. 'That was clumsy.' He looked helplessly round the room. 'Can I wipe it up?'

Pomeroy cut off his apology.

'Never mind that, tell us about the injuries you saw.'

Sedley lifted a brief case on to his knees.

'I have full reports here.'

'We'd like to see those later,' Pomeroy said, 'tell us in general terms what you saw.'

'The bodies were as Mr Ames has described—with minor variations.'

'You saw puncture wounds and cuts?'

'Oh yes, they were present in all five cases.'

'How do you suppose they were caused?'

Sedley spoke slowly with precise diction. There was a trace of north country accent in his voice.

'In my opinion they were caused by a knife not less than six inches long and on the non-cutting side about a quarter inch thick.'

'Then the wounds must have been inflicted by a man?'

'Or a woman.'

'Yes, yes,' Pomeroy agreed, 'and it follows that the mutilations and removal of organs and tissue was the work of a human being?'

'That is my opinion,' he said. He sucked noisily at his sherry and put down the glass. 'Of course there's a lot we don't know, a very great deal, but we are justified in proceeding on the hypothesis that murder has been done,' he stuttered slightly, 'and on a remarkable scale at that.'

Pomeroy appeared to watch rather than listen while Sedley spoke. He gazed up from bushy eyebrows with compelling intensity; then his face softened.

'On quite remarkable scale,' he concurred. 'Thank you Dr Sedley.' He looked down the table again.

'Well, gentlemen, where do we go from here?'

Bullivant stretched back in his chair.

'We've got a direct conflict of expert opinion,' he said. He spoke to Palthrop. 'Would you like to enlarge on what you've said?'

Palthrop pressed in his eye glass. The sad little gesture made me uncomfortable.

'If the possibility of murder is admitted,' he said, 'we are faced with a problem of forensic medicine.'

'Precisely,' Pomeroy exclaimed, and there was a laugh from Smellie.

Palthrop winced and appeared unwilling to continue.

'Go on,' Bullivant said.

Palthrop fingered his moustache and took a deep breath. 'What I'm trying to say is that medical opinion here should be just one piece in a jig-saw puzzle with many other parts to fit in. What grounds have we for asserting these people were murdered—similarity in the mutilations of the bodies and cuts and puncture wounds in the back? Leopards would tend to savage their victims in much the same way.'

Pomeroy shifted in his chair.

'What about the wounds in the back?' he asked.

Palthrop pursed his lips.

'Clawing when the animal struck.'

'Cuts and punctures four inches deep?' Sedley asked with a sceptical smile.

Palthrop shrugged his shoulders. 'Why not, if the animal struck hard?'

Sedley shook his head and smiled.

'Oh come, doctor, it's not possible.'

'Let's leave that now,' Bullivant said. 'I'd like to hear more from you from the medical angle.'

'We know so little,' Palthrop said wearily. 'In matters of this kind medical opinion cannot be decisive. But one thing I can say. With all the instruments I've got in my theatre I couldn't strip a fresh skull as cleanly as those that I saw down at Faisi, and I don't think Dr Sedley could either. Are we to believe that there are Faisi people who can and in the dark and in the middle of the bush?' He rubbed out his cigarette end. 'Can I have another drink, please?'

'Palthrop's got a point there,' Bullivant said.

Ames spoke to Pomeroy in an undertone and Pomeroy nodded. 'Gentlemen,' he said and tapped the table for attention, 'it is important that we get these killings into proper perspective. We may well be entering a field of strange and horrible practices. We may just be raising a veil concealing devilish and incredible skills, at the thought of which the mind boggles and reason protests. I beg you don't let us dismiss as impossible something we don't understand.'

Palthrop muttered and took a sip of his gin.

Pomeroy was now speaking strongly.

'Faggot, in his report on the Faisi people, speaks of their belief in a form of lyncanthropy. Where it is believed man can transform himself into an animal and an animal into a man you have conditions where a leopard society could flourish.'

Palthrop pushed his empty glass to one side.

'I don't get it,' he said.

Pomeroy compressed his lips.

'No?' he said. 'I should have thought it obvious.'

Gregg spoke for the first time.

'What are the possible motives for the murder of so many women and children?'

Ames lightly tapped the table with his silver pencil.

'May I?' he said to Pomeroy. Pomeroy nodded. 'I think it would be unwise,' he said, 'to look for the sort of motives which provoke murder in European society. Primitive man is often acutely sensitive to slights, and where human life is lightly regarded, murder is an obvious reaction.'

Pomeroy nodded agreement.

'Motives may be insignificant in our eyes but for the Faisi people,' he lifted his hands in a gesture, 'they might be enough to unleash a devilish sadism.'

'Yes, but why women and children?' Gregg said.

Pomeroy looked serious.

'We don't know all the answers at present, but we shall get them.' He raised his right hand to give emphasis. 'There may be a ritual significance in these killings. There is plenty of evidence of human parts being used in charms and being placed before fetish objects. As I see it there may well be a combination of personal and ritualistic motives in these murders.'

Palthrop stood up and bowed.

'Will you excuse me, please,' he said, 'I've got sick people to see.'

CHAPTER VIII

I was at the house writing notes on the conference when Harama
came in.

'I must thank you for bringing the hill pagans to Pela,' he said.

I put down my pen.

'I enjoyed it,' I said.

He sat relaxed and at ease regarding me with a benevolent
smile.

'I'm sorry your boy was wounded.'

I laughed. 'He's all right; he never stops talking about it.'

'Arisi says you saved his life.'

'The arrow did not go in very far.'

'Tell him to come in, I should like to speak to him.'

'Ali,' I called.

Harama took out a five pound note and gave it to him.

Ali prostrated himself. He brushed dust from his clothes when
he got up from the floor.

Harama waved him away.

'I want to talk about this trouble at Faisi,' he said.

I felt on dangerous ground. Pomeroy and Ames would not
approve of my joining in a speculative discussion with Harama
about the affair.

'Maybe you ought to see Mr Pomeroy or the D.C.,' I said.

He shook his head. 'No, it's you I must talk to.'

'I'm a very junior officer, Harama,' I said. 'I do just what I'm
told.'

He made a gesture as though brushing aside my objections.

'Why haven't I been told about the leopard murders?' he asked.

'I don't know, Harama,' I told him.

'I have people down there who report every month to me.'

'They've not mentioned these murders?'

'Never.' He fixed puzzled eyes on me and for a moment was

silent. 'I reckon to know what's going on in this province long before white men.'

I spoke without thinking.

'Perhaps your people are hiding the truth from you.'

He glared in angry surprise.

'If they are there will be trouble.' His expression hardened and then relaxed as he nodded slowly in thought. 'No, that's impossible. You and I will go down to Faisi and get to the bottom of this.'

The course of the conversation disturbed me.

'I can't do that, Harama. I'm posted here to help the acting Provincial Commissioner. I work to his orders.'

He looked disappointed but sat a few seconds longer and then got up and went out to his car. When he got in he let down the window. 'I'll think about this,' he said and then spoke to his driver.

Ali joined me as I watched the car turn out of the compound.

'Ah,' he declared, 'he's a man, that Harama.'

Pomeroy sent for me and kept me standing in front of his desk.

'I hope you're not seeing too much of Palthrop and Crane,' he said. 'You're not confirmed in your appointment you know.'

I said nothing and his manner changed.

'You've got quite a good record and it would be a pity to spoil it.'

There was an open telegram on his blotter. He gave me the code book and pushed the message towards me.

'What's this about?' he said.

It was in double Playfair Code and took a long time to decipher.

'*Reference your discussion with Bullivant stop Barr senior pathologist arriving Pela the fourteenth stop inform Palthrop and provide all facilities required for possible autopsies at Faisi.*'

It was from the Civil Secretary.

I wrote it out *en clair* and gave it to Pomeroy. He read it carefully and for some reason turned the paper over and looked at the back.

'This is it,' he said, 'now we're getting somewhere.'

Barr was in his late forties, a slimly built man with close-cropped grey hair. I found him forbidding at first but an engaging

61

smile and an attentive manner redeemed his severe appearance. I dined at the Residency the night he arrived; he must have been tired but he listened politely to Phyllis Ames chattering about her school days and he got Elizabeth Pomeroy talking about her children. He was first up to open the door when the women went out. Pomeroy struggled to retain the dignity of his position. He told me in a curt voice to take Barr to the hospital next day to meet Palthrop. The party broke up when Barr went to bed.

Barr had been gone with Palthrop for nearly two weeks. Pomeroy's nerves were on edge and he was talking about leaving for Faisi when Ames arrived with Barr's reports. I had been called to the Residency a few minutes before.

'Well?' Pomeroy said.

'It's murder,' Ames stated.

Pomeroy glared at him but said nothing.

Ames yawned as he sat down and stretched out his legs. His eyes were bloodshot and he was unshaven.

'Where's Palthrop and Barr?' Pomeroy said suddenly.

Ames puffed at a cigarette.

'They're a day behind. I left them at Malu.'

I started to move off as Pomeroy broke open the envelope. 'Wait,' he said, 'I didn't tell you to go.'

He muttered as he fingered the sheets of typescript, 'multiple injuries, stab wounds, sharply pointed knife, sharp instrument....'

He tossed the reports on to his desk and went to his safe for the code book.

'Check it,' he said when I had ciphered his report to the Civil Secretary, 'and then mark it "Clear All Lines" and send it to the post office at once.'

It was just before sundown. Chairs were out in the garden and George and Peggy Crane were sitting with Palthrop. I heard Crane talking as I walked up the drive.

'He's an expert, Geoff,' he said, 'the man's got a hell of a reputation.'

Palthrop looked tired and ill. His hand shook as he lifted his glass.

'He's wrong, I tell you,' he said. 'He's a gentleman and he's got a good brain, but he's quite wrong about this.'

Peggy suddenly got up and laid her hand on Palthrop's shoulder.

'Geoff, why should you worry. Forget about it. Stick to your hospital work. Everyone knows you're doing a good job. Mr Daubney asked specially for you to be sent here. He'll be back in a few months.'

'Thank God,' Palthrop muttered. 'Daubney's a sahib.'

'Well, there you are Geoff,' Peggy urged. 'You've got plenty of friends, John here, Tansy and Derek Firbank, and us.'

Palthrop's forehead twitched. 'Pomeroy's trying to run me out. He wants to label me as incompetent—he's been gunning for me since the yellow fever business.'

Crane flicked away a cigarette end.

'You make me tired Geoff. He can't run anyone out. He hates my guts but what do I care.'

We sat on and the sun went down like a monstrous red orange. Fruit bats squeaked in the mango trees and crickets were setting up their nightly racket in the dry grass. There were celebrations of some sort in the town and we could hear drumming. When sand flies began to bite, Palthrop's boy came out and pushed mosquito boots on his feet. He went back into the house and brought a pillow case to cover Peggy's legs.

A patch of torchlight moved jerkily up the drive. We fell silent waiting to see who it was and then Keast appeared out of the gloom. He wore khaki shorts and a dirty open necked shirt.

'Sit down Keasty,' Palthrop said. 'Help yourself.' Keast remained standing.

'I don't want a drink.'

'Well anyway sit down.'

Keast stood over Palthrop. He seemed very angry. 'I've been out looking at the bridge at mile eighty and I've just heard,' he said. 'Don't let that bugger from Belemba worry you Geoff.'

He apologized awkwardly to Peggy.

'The expression is not new to me, Keasty,' she said. 'We've been saying the same thing in not quite the same words for the best part of two hours.'

Palthrop stirred.

'He's a nice man, but he's wrong,' he passed a hand over his face, 'I'm sure he's wrong.'

Keast pushed out his chin.

'Of course he's bloody well wrong.'

Peggy raised her hands in despair.

'What a help you are Keasty.'

Keast leaned forward with outstretched arms as though addressing a crowd.

'These buggers are not going to take the micky out of Geoff. I'll see to that.'

Crane said nothing. Peggy sighed and reached for the decanter.

Pomeroy no longer came to the Provincial Office and kept me full time at the Residency. A hundred police were drafted to Faisi and two officers were attached to Gregg. Smellie was brought back to Pela but Ames remained with the police.

The dramatic developments turned stale and I felt no expectant interest as I worked on the messages. Pomeroy too was less agitated. I had begun to sit with him and Elizabeth on the verandah at about eleven o'clock every morning for coffee. It came as a shock to me that he lacked self-assurance; I found that it was after fits of irresolution that he was apt to be most arrogant. He had taken to consulting me in a light-hearted manner and though he treated my opinion with scorn he nearly always did what I said. Elizabeth, with tacit admission of a secret between us, began to confide in me as she sat at her needlework. Pomeroy had a special nerve tonic sent out by the Army and Navy Stores. He was fussy about his health and at night drank hot milk mixtures. His servants were not allowed to keep fowls lest early morning crowing should disturb him. The cooing of pigeons affected his nerves and we had twice shot round the house but they always returned. I preferred to think of him as domineering and ruthless, and it disturbed me to have his weakness exposed, but it helped Elizabeth to talk about him, so I listened with an occasional comment.

Pomeroy too was often genial and it was no burden to play the subordinate part which he gave me.

In the fourth week at the Residency a telegram came in at three minutes to eleven. Pomeroy put down his pipe.

'Come on, coffee,' he said.

I looked again at the telegram.

'This is marked Priority, I ought to finish it first.'

64

He slapped my back. He was in one of his boisterous moods. 'Leave it, boy,' he said, 'let it wait.'

We sat on the verandah-chairs. He clapped his hands and sang 'I can smell coffee, beautiful, beautiful coffee.' He kissed Elizabeth when she came out with the tray. 'Dead on time as usual. You're a marvel Liz, an absolute marvel. She looks nice today, doesn't she John—that's the sort of wife you want.'

Elizabeth smiled as she poured out our coffee. We had a second cup but Pomeroy talked on with fatuous loquacity. It was half past eleven before we got back to work.

My interest was roused as I deciphered the first groups of the message. I worked on and wrote it out in full.

'*Governor travelling self-contained with A.D.C. and Inspector General of Police. Wishes arrangements to be made for early visit to Faisi stop His Excellency wishes to address as large a representative body of Faisi people as possible.*'

It was from the Governor's private secretary.

'H.E. wants to visit Faisi,' I said.

Pomeroy snatched the message. He flushed and his face seemed to swell.

'Why the hell didn't you tell me sooner?' he shouted.

'I gave it to you as soon as I had finished it.'

He put the message on his blotter and although there was no wind, placed a paper weight on it.

'Listen,' he said, 'if I entrust you with responsible work, I want quick action and no sloppiness, and furthermore, no excuses. If the work's too much for you, say so and I'll make other arrangements.'

I looked at him calmly and caught a fleeting glimpse of uncertainty.

'Very good,' I said.

'Now let me see what's this about,' he said in the manner of someone who had settled a point. He re-read the message, slowly replaced it and glared at me.

'Well?' he asked as though putting my judgment to the test, 'what do we do now?'

Before I could reply his orderly brought in papers from Woolam.

Pomeroy put the flat of his hand on the message.

'Get out,' he shouted, 'and don't come in here again.'

The old man looked startled, then hurried away.

Pomeroy turned the key in the door.

'Well?' he said again.

'The P.S. will want a programme,' I said.

Pomeroy blew down the stem of his pipe, refitted it and opened his pouch.

'It's what goes into the programme that matters.'

He filled his pipe and held a match to it.

'Well?' he said when his pipe was alight.

'You and Ames will escort H.E. from the provincial boundary. You'll offer him this house for his night stop and ask him if he would like a small dinner party.'

Pomeroy put down his pipe.

'Small dinner party, indeed,' he said scornfully, 'what the hell do you think he's coming here for. He'll want to discuss the Faisi affair.'

He waited for my reply.

'I should put it to him,' I said.

Pomeroy was writing.

'Yes, and what else?'

'We'll have to mount a quarter guard and get a big flag. We'll have to arrange for one night each way at Malu and two or three nights at Faisi.'

He pointed his pipe at me.

'Where's his entourage going to sleep?'

I picked up the message and read it.

'They're travelling self-contained and that means they're bringing tents and equipment.'

He relaxed slightly.

'You think so, do you? Maybe you're right.'

He went out to tell Elizabeth and then came back and drafted a reply.

'What do you think of that?' he said.

I rewrote the reply. 'Yes, all right,' he said when he read it, 'send it off,' and then pointing to me he added, 'and tell that postmaster there must be no delay on the line.'

It was lunch time when I had ciphered the reply. I stood for a moment before going.

'Shall I take your instructions to Ames?' I asked, 'and maybe Gregg should come back with him too?'

Pomeroy spoke decisively. He pocketed his tobacco and keys.

'Leave tomorrow,' he said.

'Keast should come too with whitewash and furniture to do up the resthouses,' I suggested.

'Of course,' he said, 'and see to it that there are new seats and plenty of sand in the resthouse latrines.'

He remained standing at his desk.

'Have a gin before you go,' he said.

I demurred—'I don't think I ought to.'

'Come on, boy, it'll do you good. I'll have one too.'

I followed him along the verandah to the chairs near the flower tubs.

'Liz,' he shouted, 'John's staying for a drink.'

CHAPTER IX

We had driven southward three hundred miles, descending four thousand feet to the northernmost tip of the rain forest belt. After the night stop at Malu the increasing humidity began to affect us. If Keast had not grumbled I would have suspected the onset of malaria. We turned off the road at the resthouse signpost and followed the track for three miles through old fallow land where luxuriant new growth brushed the sides of the truck. Then we came to high trees and entered the forest. The close-knit canopy overhead kept out the sun and in the gloom of the track the stagnant air was heavy with the sweet sickly stench of corruption. We drove on until we came to a clearing. There were mangoes with yellowing over-ripe fruit, some paw paws and three massively buttressed silk cotton trees. As we pulled up at the resthouse purple black clouds like gigantic puffs loomed up against the afternoon sky.

Untrimmed timber supported thatch over low mud walls. Forestry officers on an enumeration survey had built the place. The entrance opened into a living-room with a bedroom on each side. The living-room jalousies and a shutter frame in one of the bedrooms had been destroyed by white ants. Whitewash on the walls inside was falling off in dirty white flakes.

Keast walked stiffly after our long journey. 'You'd be summonsed if you kept Grade A cattle in a dump like this in England,' he said.

While we were looking for a place for our kit, Ames's boy came in through the back entrance.

'There's no room here,' he said.

Keast glared at him and then told Casper, his own boy, to put up his bed in the room on the left.

Ames's boy watched with disapproval as Ali and Casper brought in our boxes.

68

'Where are the white men?' I said.

'Gone out,' he said.

'When will they come back?'

He shrugged his shoulders.

'They don't tell me what they do.'

We had bathed and changed and taken chairs outside for a drink when Ames and Gregg appeared. Ames read Pomeroy's letter in silence, passed it to Gregg and went into the resthouse.

Gregg sat with us and called for a drink.

He drew on a cigarette and then shook his head when I asked about progress.

'Things are going badly,' he said. 'We've just seen the remains of a woman half a mile up the track. There have been four murders in ten days.'

The other two officers arrived while we talked. Damer, the senior, a dapper man with well-formed features, a clipped moustache and greying hair plastered down on his skull, spoke in a precise manner and appeared to give thought to the most commonplace utterance. Two fingers of his right hand were missing which I supposed was the result of a war wound. Follet, the other C.I.D. officer, was younger, a tall man with long legs and big hands and clumsy in movement, but his light blue eyes and untidy fair hair gave him charm likely to appeal to women. He was shy at first, giving me quick side looks while we talked, but later, when he was more at ease, he rearranged his kit and moved his bed to give me space.

Ames took the head of the table, constantly mopping his face with a small hand towel. His sulky eyes and drooping mouth made him look ugly. Damer and Gregg kept up forced conversation but no one else said anything. The storm broke while we were eating and soon there was a patter of drops from leaks in the thatch. The boys made a commotion when they came in to move beds to dry places.

Ames shouted, 'Stop that bloody noise and get out.'

Throughout the meal Keast had been eyeing Ames with sullen dislike.

'Casper,' he shouted, 'move my bed to a dry place at once.'

Ames slowly looked up and glared at Keast.

'You can move your bed and get to hell out of here,' he said.

Keast put down his knife and fork and leaned forward with his hands on the table and made a move to get up.

'I'd like to give you a poke,' he said with vicious pugnacity, 'by God, I would.'

The rain on the thatch and the patter of drips on the floor suddenly seemed louder. Follet continued to eat, absorbed in the acts of cutting his food and forking it into his mouth.

Damer took a sip of beer and touched his mouth with his napkin.

'The rainfall in these forests is well over two hundred inches a year,' he said. Gregg laughed but Damer continued, 'but there's a place in the British Cameroons and also somewhere in India where the annual fall exceeds four hundred inches.'

Ames pushed away his plate; he stood up without a word and went to his bedroom. We could hear him cleaning his teeth and spitting while we went on with the meal.

Gregg and Ames left at daylight and after breakfast Damer and Follet went on a round of the police posts. Keast's carpenter started work on the shutters and jalousies and two other men mixed whitewash. The air was still but it was not yet hot as I walked through the forest. Half a mile from the resthouse I turned off at a path which fell away with gradual descent to a swamp where a wine tapper was at work in a clump of raffia palms. He encircled a palm with a sling of twisted fibre, joined it at his waist, and by skilful manipulation, leaning back, rapidly climbed with foot movements like walking. With a rope he lowered a full calabash and then descended and emptied it into a pot. He worked quickly, lowering overnight oozings from the tops of palms and drawing up and fitting empty calabashes to new tappings. When he had finished he hooked his sling and rope over his left shoulder and balanced a full calabash at each end of a pole over his right shoulder and carried the pot on his head. I looked up at the narrow-necked calabashes he fixed in the palms.

'When do you come for those?' I said.

He laughed as though I had said something funny.

'This afternoon I come,' he said.

He set off at a quick lope up the path to the main track.

By the time I got back the carpenter had cut out the rotten

joinery and was shaping new timber to replace it. The other men were whitewashing the walls.

Keast was in a bad mood. 'This is a waste of time,' he said. 'White ant will be in this timber in a month.' He nodded at the labourers cleaning the walls, 'and all this is eye wash. Why can't the Governor see how people live. He'll go back to Belemba and say we've got good resthouses.'

Damer and Follet returned at four o'clock. Follet had a dazed look and made no reply to my greeting.

'What's wrong with him?' I asked Damer.

Damer looked tired but without the strained appearance of Follet.

'I hadn't noticed anything,' he said. 'We've been busy today. Man murdered at a place called Wapa. Head severed, stripped of flesh, left arm missing and intestines removed and dumped about ten yards from the body. And there was a girl about six at a place called Mangula, seven miles away.

'Any suspects?' I said.

'Not really.' He seemed unconcerned. 'We've pulled in a lot of people for questioning.' He shook his head. 'These odd cases have no special significance. We've got to tear the whole organization apart.' He gestured with his mutilated hand. 'Then the killings will stop. A pattern is forming—we'll get the answers.'

He whistled as he left us to inquire about tea.

'I'm leaving tomorrow,' Keast said. 'I can finish work by mid-day and get to Malu before dark. I'm not staying here.'

After dinner we moved to long chairs outside. Insects surrounded the lamp like a vapour. Flying beetles with humming flight crashed against the glass and fell down. Night birds and chattering monkeys, and sometimes the roar of bigger animals, broke into the pandemonium of crickets and frogs.

Damer buttoned the cuffs of his shirt and smeared citronella oil on the backs of his hands.

'I've never known worse mosquitoes,' he said, 'not even on the coast of Nigeria.'

I was too overcome by the heat to make a reply. He lit a cigar, holding the match with little finger and thumb.

'I see it this way,' he said, inspecting the end of his cigar. 'There are three kinds of persons concerned, paid murderers, private murderers and those who hire murderers.'

Follet slapped at a mosquito and wiped away blood.

'And the people who buy parts of human remains,' he said.

'Quite so,' Damer concurred, 'four kinds, and the fourth we must expect to find among the leaders of the fetish cults.' He fell silent as he puffed at his cigar, and then added, 'it is surprising that the penis is never removed.'

Keast slapped angrily at a praying mantis and got up.

'Anyone like a beer?' he said.

He spoke with such vehemence that Damer looked surprised.

'Not for me, thank you,' he said politely, 'I seldom drink after dinner.'

Keast turned to me. 'You?'

I shook my head. 'No thank you Keasty,' I said.

Follet yawned.

'I'll split a bottle,' he said, 'to put back some sweat.'

Keast went into the resthouse and returned with two glasses and two bottles of Carlsberg.

Damer calmly went on when Keast had opened the beer.

'If my assumption is correct, the killings have five possible explanations, revenge, bravado, ceremonial rites, the greed motive of paid killers, and lastly, sadistic vice. The mutilations suggest that all five could sometimes be combined.'

Follet said 'Yes' as if good manners required it but neither Keast nor I said anything. Damer, puffing thoughtfully at his cigar, continued.

'Our problem is twofold. We must discover who traffics in human remains and we must learn the secrets of the Leopard Society.'

I was inattentive and he stopped talking. 'Go on, you were saying?' I said.

'I was saying our problem is twofold.'

'Well, how far have you got towards a solution?'

He spoke with an air of candour. 'We've made no progress at all. We've seen no paraphernalia, no leopard skin cloaks, no masks, no counterfeit pads—nothing. Our best hope is to pick up a member of the society and get him to talk. There are people who could tell us about meetings, about the hierarchy of the organization, about their ceremonies, office holders and so on.'

'It won't be easy to get one of the members to talk.'

'No, but there must be outsiders who have suspicions.'

I felt sleepy and it was an effort to listen.

'They're too scared to say anything,' I said.

'That is precisely our difficulty. They fear the society more than the police.'

'Can you blame them?'

Damer turned to me with a smile and touched my knee.

'Not I,' he said, 'but we shall see that they do fear the police. I feel the vital information we want is within reach. We'll get it.'

Keast picked up the empty bottles and glasses.

'I'm going to bed,' he said.

There was no wind in the clearing but I could see shadowy movements in the tree-tops. Sweat cooled on me and I felt chilly.

'I think I'll turn in,' I said.

Large drops of rain fell as we folded the chairs and took them inside.

Keast was already asleep and I could hear Follet's deep breathing but Damer sat at the table in the middle room making notes. His lamp was still burning when drowsiness overcame me.

The caretaker brought two men to cut the grass round the house and whiten stones along the edge of the path with lime Keast had left me. There was nothing much more I could do.

I missed Keast. The police officers were away most days. In the evening Damer worked on a drawing board producing a series of curves and some nights he developed film and made prints. Follet was poor company. He was moody and drinking a lot and I disliked the abusive manner in which he spoke to the servants.

The fourth day after Keast left Damer and Follet got back early. At half past five we were in pyjama trousers drinking tea and discussing the Governor's visit when the caretaker rushed into the room and stood gibbering, too breathless to speak properly. Follet put down his cup.

'Get out,' he shouted, 'don't you come in here like that again.'

Ali had just returned with hot water. He glared at Follet.

'Can't you see there's trouble?'

I cut off Follet's rejoinder.

'Hold on,' I said to the caretaker, 'talk slowly. What's wrong?'

He pointed with a trembling hand.

'I've seen a bad thing up there. It is better you come.'

We put on slippers and followed him along the track. Ten yards on from the point where the path turned down to the swamp we came upon a pole, two broken calabashes and an earthenware pot on its side. The air was heavy with the sickly smell of palm wine. Flies buzzed round a pool of blood on the path.

'Allah,' said Ali, 'it's the palm wine tapper.' He went on a few paces. 'Look,' he shouted. The ground was disturbed and a low tunnel had been forced through dense secondary growth. 'He's been taken in there.'

He got down on his knees and began to crawl into the bush.

'Come back,' Damer said, 'we mustn't disturb the ground.'

Follet's servant was carrying a machete. Ali took it and started hacking through vegetation. Damer followed, oblivious to scratches. We found the body twenty yards in from the track. The head was detached and soft tissue removed. Part of the neck, one arm, and some internal organs were missing.

'Look at his back,' Damer said. 'That's typical. See those stab wounds, half an inch long and deep? I'd like to get hold of the implement they use.' He opened his camera. 'The light's not good. I'll try an open aperture at a twenty-fifth.'

Follet remained on the track and looked blank when I pushed my way out. There was no expression in his voice.

'They got a woman and a girl here about a month ago,' he said.

Then Damer came out. He rolled on the film and asked me to hold the camera while he tightened his pyjama cord.

'I'll develop that tonight,' he said as he took the camera. 'It'll be something more to show H.E.'

We sat round the resthouse table. The Governor told Harama to sit next to me so that I could interpret. Damer had marked crosses on a map of the area, big black crosses for men and smaller for boys and red crosses for women and girls. He had inked in a square and using it as centre had lightly drawn a number of concentric circles.

'That is the centre of the contaminated area,' he said, pointing at the square. 'All murders have occurred within eight miles of this point and most within a radius of five.'

The Governor put on reading glasses and studied the map.

'Mostly women and girls,' he said.

Damer put three sheets of squared paper on the table.

'Quite so, sir,' he said. 'These curves show the trend. Three times as many females as males.'

Damer handed him photographs. He frowned as he looked at them one by one and then put them down and took off his glasses.

'What are we doing about all this?' he said to Bullivant.

Bullivant made a gesture towards Gregg.

'Mr Gregg is in charge of the investigation. Will you explain to the Governor,' he said.

'We've set up ten police posts in the eight miles circle.' Gregg pointed at the map. 'They are marked "P" here.'

The Governor replaced his glasses and looked again at the map.

'Yes,' he said.

'We've declared a curfew from six o'clock until dawn and patrols go out from each post.' He turned to Damer. 'Have you got the time diagram?'

Damer spread out another sheet of squared paper.

'The times of the day are shown vertically and the dates on the horizontal. We fix the times as close as we know.' Gregg pointed at the diagram. 'You'll see that they all fall within the hours of five and seven, mostly in the late afternoon.'

The Governor looked in turn from the map to the diagrams and took off his glasses again.

'This analysis seems thorough but are you getting anywhere with your inquiries?'

For some reason Gregg stood at attention.

'No, sir,' he said.

Damer shuffled forward.

'If I may say so, I think the facts will become known to us at one single stage, perhaps when we least expect it. I do not think we shall progress by a gradual accumulation of information.'

The Governor pursed his lips. There was criticism in his question.

'Has any person been charged with murder yet?'

There was awkward silence.

'No, sir,' Gregg said.

'No!' the Governor said. 'Are the local people helping?'

'They've given us no help at all, sir,' said Gregg.

Pomeroy was slightly in the background and appeared impatient at not being brought into the discussion.

'We are dealing with people of diabolical skill who have thoroughly cowed the population.'

The Governor turned and faced him. Pomeroy moved awkwardly under his speculative gaze.

'Your people have arranged meetings for me?' he asked.

'Four separate meetings have been fixed,' said Pomeroy.

The Governor took out a cigarette case and Pomeroy at once struck a match.

'Let's hope they'll do some good,' he said to him.

The Governor spoke at the meetings we arranged for him. Bullivant, the Inspector General of Police, and Harama came with him. He said Government was determined to stop the murders and bring to justice those who were responsible. If village heads and others in authority did not help, circumstances would be made uncomfortable for them and their people. Government would stop at nothing to put an end to the terror. If Government had the support of the people the end would come quickly and easily. If not, it would take longer and be more painful for all concerned but the end would come just the same and the murderers would be hanged and those who helped them would be punished. The people listened in silence and then dispersed.

I was conscious of anti-climax at the conference the night before the Governor's departure. No one felt that our biggest gun had made impact on the barrier of secrecy which faced us. The Governor looked tired. He had refused to be carried in a hammock and like the rest of us had cycled or walked to the meeting places.

'We must bring these murderers to justice,' he said, 'but we are, of course, concerned with far more than a police operation. It's a social problem. We need schools, roads, hospitals and markets. The people are turned in on themselves with their cults and secret societies. Why are there no missions here?' he asked Pomeroy. 'Have they been asked to come?'

'Not as far as I know, sir,' Pomeroy said.

'Well, bear it in mind. In the meantime there is an obvious need to make closer contact here. There is virtually no administration.'

'Virtually none,' Pomeroy said in a tone which suggested he shared the Governor's concern.

'Post someone here to work independently of the police. Someone young who can get about and gain the people's confidence—Harama suggests Wood might be suitable.'

'Very good, sir,' Pomeroy looked at me. 'Wood can remain here for the time being and I'll let Mr Daubney know your wishes when he returns.'

'Do so,' the Governor said.

Gregg moved his kit into my room. After breakfast he left with Damer and Follet on a round of the police posts. I sat on drinking coffee after they had gone.

Harama came in just after nine o'clock.

'I thought you had gone back with the Governor's party,' I said.

'I've got a man I want you to see,' he said, 'his name is Boningo, he will help you.'

'I need plenty of help,' I said.

He laughed and went out.

'Boningo,' he called.

A man of middle height, thin, with cracked smooth skin, came into the room. He wore a shirt of strong white material and a cloth hanging a few inches below his knees. He took off a greasy velour hat.

'This is Boningo,' Harama said. 'He is my man.'

Boningo bowed low showing a scab on a bald patch and looked up and regarded me with jaundiced bloodshot eyes. 'Harama is my master,' he declared, 'I will do what he says.'

CHAPTER X

'Certainly you may witness the ceremony,' Boningo said. He hitched up his cloth and turned to the others. 'Do we not welcome the white man?'

They were elderly men, bare to the waist and draped below in cloths. Two slung raffia bags over their shoulders.

'That's magic material,' Boningo said. 'We must outdo the power of the Leopard Society.'

Six of them carried elephant tusks. Ralaka, a grizzled man with stretched scaly skin, put down a bundle of palm leaves.

'He's welcome,' he said in a quavering voice.

'He's welcome,' said Sena, a young man with a calabash, 'he's welcome if he does not interfere.' The rest of them murmured agreement.

Boningo again raised his hat. Grey bristles sprouted on his bony chin and a whispy moustache hung arc-shaped over his mouth. He showed blackened teeth when he smiled.

'You heard what they said?'

'I will not interfere.'

I was last in the file as Boningo led the party through the forest. The high trees and the tangle of vegetation hemmed us in like a tunnel. Sweat trickled down the back of the man just ahead of me with a tusk over his shoulder. Beyond the green black verdure bordering the path the forest was alive with animals, reptiles and birds. Though I saw no one I had a feeling we were watched. I started nervously at the crash of a falling branch. Occasionally the gloom of the path was relieved by a shaft of warm sunlight piercing the overhead canopy and throwing a patch of bright light on mouldering leaves. I saw a reddish-brown butterfly with deep violet spots and a wing span of a swallow, and once, through a break overhead, I caught a glimpse of an eagle hovering with outspread wings. We walked in silence, stepping across roots and climbing over fallen tree trunks. Blood pounded in my head and I began to wonder if I could keep up with the party. Then Boningo turned with raised hand. He spoke to Ralaka and they and the six men carrying the tusks went ahead. A few minutes later we came up to them in a clearing where about three thousand men were assembled. Twenty-five elders straggled across the clearing to meet us. Boningo waited, solemnly greeting each one in turn and asking if all their men were present. Then he took off his hat and said he wanted to start. He cleared his throat and began in a loud voice.

'You all know about the terrible crimes, crimes which are disturbing the peace of your village, the Faisi district and the whole of our tribe—dastardly crimes, horrible crimes, evil crimes,' Boningo became impassioned raising his clenched right hand. 'You all know that since the days of our forefathers our elders and family heads must know all about our secret societies.' Boningo paused dramatically and levelled his forefinger at the crowd. 'There are people now present who know about this Leopard Society.' He paused again, looking slowly round the silent assembly. 'There are murderers here present,' he shouted, 'murderers of innocent women and children, evil men bringing shame and sorrow into our midst.' He put his face in his hands and then went on with renewed passion. 'You are murdering each other under cover of leopard killings and selling parts of your wretched victims for money,' he past in a paroxysm of disgust, 'selling parts of your fellow men for money. Can man fall lower than this?' He took a few paces to and fro with downcast head and continued, 'and when the District Commissioner uncovered your devilish practices and brought police to our forests what help did you give him? You who know, what did you tell him? and remember,' he said with a lift of an arm pointing quickly round the crowd, 'you, you, or you may be the next victim and your mutilated remains befoul the paths of our forests.' His expression changed and he spoke imploringly. 'My countrymen, my friends, we are all Faisi people, I beg you to stamp on this devilish thing. Even if you are afraid to talk to the police,' his voice rose to a shriek, 'stop killing your women and girls.' He spoke to Ralaka and turned again to the crowd. 'You all see these emblems,' he pointed first at the palm leaves and then at the tusks, 'the *karato* and the *litimi*, our people have always revered these emblems of peace. Look at them carefully.'

The tusks were placed in a circle and Ralaka lay palm fronds across them. Tago, a big man and darker skinned than the others, went to a house on the edge of the clearing and brought back a goat. He tied its feet together and placed it between the tusks. Sema got water for the calabash bowl and held out a hand for the raffia bags; from one he took out brown lumpy material and dropped it into the water and then from the other he sprinkled yellowish powder and slowly stirred the mixture. He paused and was about to add more powder but decided against it and continued stirring with a slow left to right motion.

Boningo held up his hand. 'Everyone stand,' he shouted, 'all village headmen and heads of families come forward to take the *gamola* oath.'

The crowd moved and the murmur of talk rippled through the clearing.

'Silence!' Boningo shouted. 'How dare you talk!'

About three hundred men came out and joined the elders. Two of Boningo's party arranged them in a line, and in tense silence Boningo drew his hands over his face and trembled as if moved by violent emotion. He spoke in a harsh voice and gesticulated as he walked along the line.

'You bind yourself to conduct all your affairs according to our emblems,' he pointed at the palm leaves and tusks, 'you will instantly report what you know of any secret society concerned with the taking of life.' Boningo paused and raised his hands over his head. 'You will have no part, neither you nor your people, in a leopard murder society.'

Sema stirred up the fluid in the calabash bowl and walked behind Boningo down the line, touching the tongue of each man with a stick he dipped in the fluid. In turn each man reached down and touched the ground with his fingers and then passed his hands over his face.

Ralaka cut the goat's throat and splashed blood on to the palm leaves. Boningo raised his hands again and proclaimed 'Let our troubles end this day, let leopard murders cease. We spill the blood of this goat to save the blood of innocent people. Let the power of *Gamola* strike dead all who break this oath.'

Tago blew five times on the smallest of the tusks and Boningo raised his hands again and commanded the assembly to shout 'there will be no more leopard murders'. The shout echoed in the confined space of the clearing and a flight of hornbills went over with staccato cackling cries and monkeys chattered somewhere close to in the forest. Ralaka dipped the palm leaves in the goat's blood and went round the edge of the clearing laying one across each of the paths into the forest. 'All must step over a palm leaf,' he said in a quavering voice. 'Let nobody look back until he gets home.'

When the crowd had gone Boningo raised his felt hat and showed his blackened teeth in a smile. His voice was hoarse from shouting.

'Good-bye, sir,' he said. 'That was the most binding ceremony known to our people. None can defy it.'

His party moved to a house where the froth of palm wine oozed out of narrow-necked calabashes.

Before supper we sat outside. The arms of our chairs became wet in the cooling air, but we preferred the risk of rheumatism to sitting inside.

We were having our first drink as a patch of torch light moved towards us over the ground.

'Here's Follet,' Gregg said.

'He's late again,' Damer said.

The light moved nearer.

'He's taking too much out of himself,' Gregg added.

Follet came up quickly and blinked at the lamp. He was in shorts and an open-necked shirt and wore plimsolls. He looked angry, and, ignoring Gregg's greeting, turned to me.

'You were out with Boningo today,' he said.

His eyes were hard and he glared with dislike.

'Yes,' I said, 'why?'

'The performance today was at Iluma?'

'Yes, a clearing about three miles to the north.'

Gregg sat forward looking first at Follet and then at me.

'What's this about?' he said.

But Follet kept glaring at me. He spoke in a broken voice and timed his utterance, it seemed, for effect.

81

'Constable Mika was murdered this evening at Iluma.'

Gregg gasped. 'Mika, your orderly?'

Follet's outburst embarrassed me. I felt an irrational urge to defend myself.

'You can't connect that with the meeting,' I said.

The lamp light caught scorn in his face.

'No?' he said, 'you don't think so. I've been checking up. Boningo's had six meetings and there's been an immediate murder at each place.'

Damer spoke for the first time.

'Figures have gone up since the meetings started.'

Follet was working himself into a frenzy, muttering to himself and walking up and down in the lamp light. He was sweating and his long hair was lank and untidy. He suddenly faced us.

'They're laughing,' he cried, 'they're behind the whole thing.' He came close to me, 'and they're using you as their tool.'

'Rubbish,' I protested, but he ignored me and turned to Gregg.

'Please, sir,' he said impulsively, 'let's pull in Boningo and his gang. We're getting nowhere the way we are going on.'

Damer caught something of Follet's excitement.

'Brian may have something there,' he said. 'They're an organized body and the people are scared of them. They could be leading us up the garden path.'

Gregg resisted the pressure of his two officers.

'This is pure surmise, we haven't a shred of proof.'

Follet scowled and spoke with suppressed fury.

'We'll get it,' he said, 'just let's pull the bastards in.'

Gregg looked serious.

'Sit down, Brian, he said, 'let's have a drink and talk the thing over.'

I was left out of their discussion and nobody said anything when I excused myself and went into the resthouse.

'Bring food,' I told Ali.

'Aren't you going to wait for the others?'

'Bring food,' I said.

Later on when he brought me a pudding, he said, 'The white men have gone somewhere.'

I was in bed when they got back. I heard the low hum of talk as they ate supper. Then Gregg came in quietly with a dimmed hurricane lamp and sat in the camp chair between our two beds.

'Are you awake?' he said.

I eased up on my elbow.

'Yes,' I said, 'where have you been?'

He disregarded my question.

'It is quite true. Mika was murdered just this side of Iluma. They found his baton and cap on the path; his body was thirty yards inside the forest.'

I was now fully awake.

'What are you going to do?' I said.

'God knows, I don't know what to do.'

He lit a cigarette and in the light of the flame I caught a glimpse of sombre bewilderment. I pushed out the net and sat on the bed.

'Give me one of those cigarettes,' I said, 'if you don't mind drinking out of your tooth mug I've got a bottle of whisky here somewhere.'

I padded across the room in bare feet and took a bottle from a box. I pulled my chair round and we sat talking in whispers.

Gregg broke off what he was saying. 'Listen,' he said, 'do you hear that?'

Someone was weeping.

'That's Follet, that boy's got me worried.'

The weeping went on; it was like that of an ill-treated child, hurt and abandoned to grief. Damer's deep snores seemed unfeeling as the weeping continued.

'He's cracking,' Gregg whispered. 'He's got some crazy idea that you're mixed up in these murders.'

The chair creaked as I stood up.

'Me?' I said, 'for God's sake what does he mean?'

I felt Gregg's hand on my arm.

'Sit down,' he said, 'don't be stupid, I only mentioned it to show how unbalanced he is.'

I steadied my nerves and overcame an impulse to see Follet.

'He's mad,' I said, 'he'll have to be moved.'

I slept late and when I awoke I could heard Gregg talking to Damer in the next room. My mind turned at once to Follet's monstrous suggestion and while I shaved I had further doubts and wondered whether Damer shared his belief and was persuading Gregg of my complicity. With a fit of panic I wondered how I would be placed if Gregg did not trust me. I shirked meeting them and delayed a few minutes, putting away clothes. Follet had finished breakfast and had a cup of coffee before him, but the other two were still eating. Follet gulped his coffee and stood up when he saw me. As I sat in my place Damer gave me a curt 'Good morning', and looked down again at his food.

Gregg smiled. 'Hello, slept well?' he said.

I was annoyed by the relief I felt at his greeting.

'Why didn't you wake me?' I said.

A mail runner reported after Damer and Follet had left on their rounds. He had been longer than usual on the journey from Pela.

'Why are you late?' I said.

He was bedraggled and tired-looking but he made an attempt to stand at attention.

'I only travel by daylight,' he said, 'I'm afraid of the forest.'

'We'd get our mail in half the time if they sent horsemen,' Gregg said.

'There's too much tsetse South of Malu,' I said.

There were three home letters in girls' handwriting for Follet with one each for the rest of us and a certain amount of official material. I read a letter from Pomeroy.

'Dear me,' I said, 'Pomeroy wants me back at Pela for ten days to a fortnight.'

Gregg put down the letter he was reading and looked at me.

'Go back to Pela—what the hell for?' he protested. 'We need you here. It was agreed with the Governor that you should stay. I've a good mind to write Bullivant.'

'Pomeroy dislikes Ames, and Woolam's got plenty to do,' I said. I read the letter again, 'and I suppose he wants a first-hand account of what's happening. And anyway,' I added weakly, 'a break might be a good thing for me.'

Gregg flicked a cigarette end through the open shutter and looked thoughtful. He lit a new cigarette and looked at me again.

'Maybe you're right,' he said, 'but not for too long.'

CHAPTER XI

Peggy peered into the darkness. It was the fourth time in half an hour she had gone to the window.

'Are you sure he knows where to come, Geoffrey?' she said.

Palthrop drew on his cigarette.

'I told him we'd be here if he arrived after eight o'clock.'

Peggy came away and stared anxiously at Palthrop.

'But does he know our house?'

Crane spoke over his shoulder as he went round the room with cigarettes 'For God's sake woman relax, he can ask, can't he? He's probably picked up a bit of stuff somewhere and we won't see him till morning.'

Peggy furiously pumped at the pressure lamp.

'There's no need to be coarse,' she said, 'for all you know he may have killed himself.'

Crane breathed heavily. 'Can you beat it,' he said. 'You'd think we were expecting Royalty.'

Peggy's nerves were on edge. 'This place is like a morgue,' she said turning the gramophone. The gramophone began to play 'A room with a view and you. . . .'

'Must you?' said Crane.

She stopped the music.

'Why don't you do something to entertain our guests?'

He shook bitters into his glass and added gin.

'If they don't like it here they know what to do.'

Palthrop yawned. 'What a rude fellow you are, George,' he said and added, 'Got any ice, Peggy?'

Peggy walked with quick short steps to the kitchen, but was back in an instant. 'Now the ice machine has packed up,' she said, and was about to say more, but raised her hand and went to the window. 'Be quiet everyone, I think I can hear a car.' We stood in a group round the window.

A green Lagonda towing a trailer came round the circular sweep and pulled up in the light at the door.

'Manny,' Peggy screamed, 'where have you been, sweetheart?'

As Loftus stepped stiffly out she clutched him in a wild embrace. Crane smartly slapped her bare shoulder. Loftus turned with a smile to Tansy. 'I don't think we've met,' he said.

'Never mind all that,' Palthrop said, 'where the hell have you been?'

Loftus walked round to the front of his car.

'Come here,' he said. The big off-side lamp was a mess of feathers and blood.

'I hit a guinea fowl. I had to go carefully when it got dark.'

Peggy had recovered her spirits.

'You musn't drive so fast, Manny, you'd break so many hearts if you got killed.'

A corporal of the Frontier Force sat in the passenger seat.

'Get my bags out,' Loftus said.

'Eat dirty, Manny,' Peggy said, 'don't bother to change.'

Loftus unclipped the tonneau cover and the soldier took out two rifles.

'The Manlicher,' Loftus said, 'the Mauser, now my gun and the ammunition.' The soldier helped him to lift out the heavy box. 'That's all, thank you Dudu.'

Loftus's animal vitality brought new life to the party. There were more drinks and talk became shrill. The flickering light grew dim, Loftus sat next to Tansy, furthest away from the lamp.

'Derek', she suddenly called.

Firbank was talking to Peggy.

Tansy raised her voice.

'Derek,' she cried, 'Can we go to Faisi?'

'No, of course not,' he said turning again to Peggy.

Tansy got up and crossed the room.

'Why not?' she said. 'You never do anything I ask.'

Firbank brushed cigarette ash from his shirt.

'There are no schools there.'

Palthrop came to life.

'All the more reason for going, old boy,' he said. 'Start some. Break new ground, be a pioneer.'

Firbank turned his head slowly.

'I wish you'd mind your own business, Geoff,' he said, but Palthrop went on, 'go down and reconnoitre, boy, put some pegs in the ground and mark out the site of a new school.'

'Please can we go, Derek?' Tansy said.

Crane got up to order dinner.

'Give in early, Derek, and save yourself trouble,' he said.

It was midnight when we went in to the dining-room. Loftus moved across the room to me.

'I didn't expect to find you here,' he said. He gave me no chance to reply. 'I can only stay three weeks, I've got to get back for the Boka Polo Tournament by the fifteenth of next month.'

He darted off to sit next to Tansy.

Palthrop sang: 'Caviare comes from a virgin sturgeon. . . .'

The boys took away the soup plates and Crane carved a duck.

'Remember to sign Pomeroy's Visitors' Book,' he said from the side table.

'He'll write to the General if you don't,' Firbank said.

'And Elizabeth Pomeroy won't invite you to the Residency for a drink,' Peggy added.

Palthrop drooled on: 'A virgin sturgeon's a very nice dish. . . .'

'I'll do it first thing in the morning,' said Loftus.

The rains had not started at Pela and after the forest I found the countryside dusty and dry.

The sun was not up and it was still cool as I walked from Woolam's house to the Residency. The air was full of swallows sweeping low to catch the cicadae rising before the fire as a prison gang burned off dry grass. Brown kites with mean little eyes and feathery white legs, almost squat in appearance, waited on the ground in advance of the flames and then rose laboriously flying off with a mouse or small snake. A big cane rat with stiff back hair like porcupine quills leapt through the fire. Prisoners chased it and one man threw himself full length and caught it.

I stopped to speak to the tennis boy. Pomeroy wanted a game after tea and the courts needed marking. There was the sound of a motor-car engine and ahead of me one of Keast's road gangs gave way for Manny Loftus's Lagonda coming round the curve from the Residency. I walked towards him when he pulled up a few yards in front of me. A tarpaulin sheet was tied over the loads in the trailer and bags were piled up in the back of the car. Corporal Dudu sat in the front passenger's seat. Loftus, still gripping the wheel, kept his elbow at rest on the door and leaned over to speak. He was bare-headed and his dark hair was brilliantined and well brushed. His khaki bush shirt with badge holes in the epaulets was creased from fresh laundering.

'I didn't expect to see you last night,' he said.

'I've been here for a couple of weeks to help Pomeroy.'

'You are going back?'

'Yes, in four or five days.'

He pressed the starter.

'I'll see you then,' he said.

I raised my hand and he drove off towards the road to the south.

Elizabeth passed my coffee.

'Where's Captain Manbyn Loftus staying?' she asked.

Pomeroy glared at me.

'M.L. here?' he said, 'what the devil does he want?'

I shrugged my shoulders.

'I don't know, local leave, I suppose.'

'Local leave indeed, local leave,' he repeated with scorn. 'These soldiers are always on local leave. God knows when they work.'

'Where's he staying, John?' Elizabeth said.

Pomeroy gaped, perplexed by the interest she showed.

'What's it matter anyway?'

'He signed the book this morning,' she said. 'We must invite him to dinner.'

Pomeroy replaced his cup on the tray.

'Oh, he did, did he? Well write him a note.'

'Where's he staying, John?' Elizabeth asked again.

'With Geoffrey Palthrop, I believe,' I said.

'I'll ask Dr Palthrop to come too,' Elizabeth said.

Pomeroy demurred automatically, but he still seemed pleased that Loftus had called.

'Must you,' he said with distaste. 'I swore I'd never have that clown in my house.'

Elizabeth bridled and spoke with unusual asperity.

'We can't invite his guest without asking him too.'

Pomeroy yawned.

'*Noblesse oblige*, I suppose, *Noblesse oblige*. I must say I think more of M.L. for calling.'

Elizabeth stood up.

'Can your orderly take the letter?'

Pomeroy took a cigarette.

'Of course.'

I had begun to feel uncomfortable.

'Loftus left Pela this morning,' I said.

Elizabeth blinked as though I had struck her.

'What a pity,' she said as she sat down again, 'We'd have had him to lunch if I had known.'

'Well you didn't,' Pomeroy said. 'It's time we two got back to work.'

Elizabeth fixed her eyes on me.

'When will he be back, John?'

'I don't know, Elizabeth, I'll let you know if I hear.'

'Please do, in plenty of time if you can.'

I followed Pomeroy back to his office. Five minutes later he put down his pen.

'Where's Loftus gone?' he asked.

'I don't know,' I said.

He looked down again and took up his pen.

'I'd like to know what he's come for.'

Loftus's tent was dwarfed by the trees and looked like a boy's plaything on the edge of the compound.

I drove up to the resthouse.

Gregg had taken off his clothes and was resting. He wrapped a towel round his waist and came out to meet me.

'You'll have to move in with us,' he said. He nodded at the other room. 'Firbank and his wife are in there.'

'Tansy Firbank here!'

'Yes, but thank God they're leaving tomorrow.'

While we were talking Tansy came along the path with Damer and with Meakin, the new man, followed by Loftus and Firbank. She wore drill jodhpurs and a white shirt. She laughed at something Damer said and then Damer and Meakin laughed at something she said in reply.

'Who the hell does she think she is?' Gregg grumbled, 'and look at that old fool Damer. Can you beat that?'

'Get out of sight,' I said as they drew nearer.

'Hello, John,' Tansy shouted, 'where have you sprung from?'

Damer was smiling and eyeing her as we stood talking but Meakin, a small man with receding fair hair and prominent blue eyes, was not at ease and laughed unnecessarily. He moved to one side when we were joined by Loftus and Firbank.

Loftus was carrying a shot gun. His ivory complexion was dark at the chin and over his mouth. He smiled, and for some reason I thought of a lizard.

'Dine with us tonight?' he said. 'I've got a couple of guinea fowl, they'll go well with red currant jelly.' He apologized to Damer and Meakin. 'Four's a tight fit in my tent.'

'You are the limit, Manny,' Tansy said, 'fancy bringing red-currant jelly to bush.'

'When are you going back, Derek?' I asked Firbank.

'Tomorrow,' he said.

'Oh, no,' Damer said. 'You can't take Tansy away. We're only just getting to know her.'

'We're going back tomorrow,' Firbank said without any expression, 'or at least I am.'

Damer took Tansy's arm with ponderous gallantry.

'That's an idea, you leave Tansy with us,' he said and then turned to Tansy, 'you don't want to go back, do you my dear?'

Meakin laughed to show he was concerned in the play.

Tansy looked from Damer to Firbank. She was being very silly.

'How ever could I get back to Pela?' she said.

'I'll run you back,' Loftus said.

Firbank started to say something but Damer shouted, 'Hooray, it's settled, Tansy, you're staying.'

Tansy looked from Loftus to Firbank with a weak smile.

'What do you think, Derek?' she said. 'Manny will bring me back.'

She drew away when he put his hand on her arm. There was an uncomfortable silence and he turned and walked to the rest-house.

90

Damer spoke first.

'Tansy, my dear, your lord and master takes a dim view of our plan.'

Tansy looked dubious and stared at the resthouse and then looked questioningly from Damer to Loftus.

'He didn't look pleased, I'd better tell him we were joking.'

Loftus touched her arm.

'You do no such thing. Stay on a couple of days. I'll run you back.'

Tansy opened her soft mouth and looked meltingly at Loftus.

'Would that be all right, Manny?'

He patted her arm.

'Sure, that'll be all right.'

I left them and went into the resthouse. Gregg was standing in his tin bath soaping himself.

'Tansy Firbank's not leaving tomorrow,' I said.

'You mean she's staying here?'

'That's the idea.'

Gregg sponged himself and reached for his towel.

'She's bloody well not and I'll tell her myself.'

I unlaced my shoes and pulled off my stockings.

'You'll have to work that out with Loftus. He's the snake in the grass.'

He stopped drying himself and glared at me.

'Don't look at me like that, it's not my fault.' I protested.

'What the hell's it got to do with Loftus? We require this resthouse. We've got work to do.'

I stripped off my clothes and shouted for bath water.

'Loftus might be able to help us.'

Gregg snorted.

'Not when there's any skirt in sight. I wish he'd go back to his polo and gin parties. I've got no time for play-boys.'

The camp bed was strapped in a roll and three tin boxes stacked in a corner. There was a wash basin on a tripod. He had turned over a camp bath to serve as a side table. Tansy was wearing a crimson dress which enhanced the effect of her warm colouring. She had done her hair differently and since I had seen her earlier she had enamelled her finger nails. She had left off mosquito boots as I suppose she thought her legs looked better without them, and wore high-heeled sandals on her bare feet. Loftus wore a black tie, white shirt, dress trousers and a blue cummerbund. Firbank and I had put on open-necked shirts and grey flannels.

Dudu had cooked the food earlier and gave us soup, casseroled guinea fowl and a savoury. Loftus opened a bottle of Chambertin and afterwards, in candle light, we drank coffee and cointreau at the camp table.

Firbank was half drunk when he came. He had three cocktails before dinner and had drunk most of the burgundy. He sat swaying in his chair unable to light his cigarette while Tansy talked gaily to Loftus.

There had been a murmur of thunder while we were at dinner. Through the tent opening I saw yellow lamp light from the resthouse but all round it was quite dark. Then in a blinding blue flash I saw the trees quite clearly. There was more lightning and explosive thunder. Above the clamour of the forest I could hear wind in the tree tops.

'Tansy, you ought to get back,' I said.

She looked at Loftus.

'Do you think it's going to rain, Manny?' she said.

He pursed his lips.

'No, I think it's a false alarm.'

Tansy smiled at me.

'We'll stay a bit longer.'

A minute later she complained of the heat in the tent.

Loftus filled Firbank's glass but I shook my head.

'No?' he said, and then spoke quietly to Tansy. 'Like a breath of fresh air?'

She stood up at once.

'I'd love it,' she said and then added to me, 'take care of Derek. Perhaps he ought to turn in.'

'Don't go out,' I said. 'It's madness to go walking about in the dark.'

Tansy hesitated.

'Are you sure it's all right, Manny?'

He took her elbow.

'Yes, it's all right.'

He patted my shoulder as they went out.

'Not to worry, my boy, I'll take care of her.'

As they disappeared into the darkness I slapped Firbank's knee.

'Wake up you fool, Tansy's outside with Loftus.'

'To hell with them,' he said, 'give me some more cointreau.' He bent down and picked up his cigarette, 'and a light, there's a good fellow.'

I could no longer hear the wind in the trees and the forest was quiet. Then the rain started to fall. It came in a deluge, droning as it beat on the canvas. Dudu came to close up the tent.

'Leave it,' I said, 'the rain's not coming in.'

We sat on a few minutes and I was wondering what I ought to do about Tansy. There was a folded ground sheet on the camp bed and I thought I might go out and look for her.

Firbank took more cointreau.

'They'll get wet,' he said, 'and serve them bloody well right.'

I shivered in spite of the heat in the tent and knocked over the chair as I sprang up. Above the noise of the rain I heard screams.

'Get up you sot,' I shouted at Firbank, 'something's wrong.'

I met Gregg outside carrying a rifle. Damer had a revolver and Meakin was flashing a torch.

The screams became louder.

Gregg sounded angry.

'She's over there by the cotton trees. Hold your light steady, you fool,' he told Meakin.

Firbank pushed forward between us.

'Tansy, Tansy, where are you,' he shouted.

'She went out with Loftus,' I said to Gregg.

'Well, she's alive.'

We found them under a cotton tree. Loftus was trying to say something but Tansy kept screaming and clinging to Firbank.

'It's snakebite,' Loftus said, 'we ought to get her inside.'

Firbank put his hand on Loftus's chest and pushed him, and turned to Gregg. 'Give me a hand.'

Loftus moved back when Gregg took Tansy's legs and helped Firbank carry her.

I flashed my torch over the sodden leaves. Then I examined the tree. On the inside of a buttress, a few inches from the foot of the trunk close to Tansy's heel marks, I saw the pincer jaws and lobster-like body of a scorpion. It moved sluggishly and the venom sac in the spiked tail was empty. I stooped cautiously and picked up a stick. I crushed the scorpion and pushed the mushy pulp on to a leaf.

The rain had stopped, fireflies sparkled, and the pandemonium of frogs and crickets became louder; an animal barked some-where out in the forest. A group of house boys silently made way when I turned in at the resthouse.

Tansy lay on her camp bed and Firbank was holding her hand trying to comfort her. A pan of water was heating on a primus stove.

'What are you doing?' I asked Gregg.

He spoke shortly.

'Sterilizing a razor blade. We'll have to make an incision and rub in potassium permanganate.'

'It's a scorpion bite,' I said.

He turned back on me.

'Scorpion bite! How do you know?'

I showed him the scorpion.

'Thank God,' he said. He paused for a moment. 'If she had worn mosquito boots it would not have happened. Meakin, you've got some ammonia.'

Gregg tapped Firbank's shoulder.

'Dab the spot with ammonia and give her a good shot of brandy. She must keep her weight off her foot and she'll be better in a couple of days.'

Tansy's face was twisted with pain but she had stopped moan-ing and was grumbling at Firbank.

'Why did you make me come to this horrible place? You know I didn't want to come.'

Firbank tried to placate her.

'I'm sorry sweetheart,' he said. 'We'll go back to Pela tomorrow. Have some more brandy.'

Tansy was still in pain when Firbank helped her out of the rest-house. There was a clamour of birdsong at the back of the house. Later it would be hot but at eight o'clock in the morning it was pleasant outside.

Loftus strolled slowly across the compound and joined us as Firbank helped Tansy into the car. He smiled at her cold reply to

94

his greeting. He suggested putting the seat back to give more room for her leg.

There had been a murder the previous evening and Gregg and the two officers left as soon as the Firbanks had gone. Loftus made no move and I accepted a cigarette from him. The boys were airing beds in the sunshine and throwing sheets and pyjamas over a clothes line.

'I'm going back to Pela tomorrow,' Loftus calmly informed me.

Even so early in the day his ivory complexion was darker at his chin and over his mouth. I suddenly felt he was a stranger.

'You're not,' I said.

There was an ugly little smile on his face.

'No?' he said with laconic arrogance.

I was tempted to hit him, and spoke without thinking.

'Why can't you leave people alone?'

He feigned bewilderment.

'Leave people alone? I don't understand.'

I left him and went back to the resthouse.

I had an acute headache and I asked Ali to make tea and bring aspirin. I decided to unburden myself to Gregg and was wondering uneasily how he would receive my proposals when I had a rigor and felt my heart fluttering. I had been chilled by the rain. I recognized the symptoms. I had an attack of malaria.

CHAPTER XII

Ali sponged me twice a day and changed my bedding, and from where I lay I sometimes saw him through the open shutter hanging out my sodden pyjamas and sheets. He clucked his tongue when I left food he brought or shook my head at hot drinks between meals. For eight days I sweated on the camp bed with aching limbs and a throbbing headache. My morning temperature was just above normal but it rose as the day advanced and by sundown reached one hundred and four. The thermometer stood in a meat-paste pot of Dettol solution on a box at the side of my bed. I became obsessed with the thing and got an irrational feeling it was to blame for my slow recovery. When I dozed off into half sleep I was confused by a persistent dream that I was in my bed at home in England and I was overwhelmed with self pity when I awoke with slow realization of the bare dusty room, the leaking thatch and the shabby camp kit stacked in the corner. Gregg moved his bed into the room with Damer and Meakin but he came in each morning and evening with Ali to see me. He urged me to be patient and let the fever run its course.

I woke late on the ninth day with acutely perceptive senses as though a muffling veil had been raised. When Ali brought in the basin I washed myself and shaved for the first time since my illness, and then got up and moved shakily to my boxes for a book. At eleven o'clock I had a visitor. Manny Loftus came on tip-toe into the room. He looked at me and then smiled.

'How are you?' he said gently. 'You've had a bad time they tell me.'

I put down the book.

'I thought you'd gone to Pela,' I said.

He showed no embarrassment as he drew up a camp chair.

'I didn't stay. I saw Harama and he collected all the gin traps in the town—twenty-three—I brought them back. The A.T.C. have wired Belemba for another three dozen.'

He spoke quietly. Heavy doses of quinine had dulled my hearing and I strained to hear him.

'Gin traps?' I said.

He drew the chair closer.

'I've got news for you. In five days we've trapped six leopards in the area where the killings have been worst. And that's not all.' His dark eyes gleamed and I caught a whiff of his hair lotion as he leaned forward. 'And that's not all. Two nights ago I was with Boningo and Dudu at a place called Soka—three huts and a fetish shrine at the turning two miles down the main track. There'd been a killing half an hour before we got there.' He lit a cigarette. 'A seven-year-old girl had been playing with two little boys outside one of the huts. They said she went into the compound to pee and they heard a scream and saw a spotted animal with a long tail carrying the girl across the compound and then jump through the fence and disappear into the forest. We found a clear trail of pug marks into the compound; where the child was seized they were close together and showed the imprint of claws. On the far side of the fence there were again four pug marks close together where the animal landed after its leap.' Loftus paused—'It's a pity to bother you with all this when you're ill. Do you want me to go on?'

'Yes, of course,' I said.

'We followed the pug marks and found the remains. The head was stripped of scalp and facial tissue. Bush was pressed down and we saw more pug marks and a pile of shit. A bit further on there was a long scratch mark on the ground where the beast cleaned its claws.'

Loftus took a wallet from his bush shirt pocket.

'Look at these,' he said. He showed me four gingery hairs.

'You found those?' I said.

He put away the wallet. 'I did,' he said, 'a yard from the body.'

He looked at me in thoughtful silence.

'Have you spoken to Gregg?' I said.

'Yes.'

'What did he say?'

Loftus shrugged his shoulders.

'Gregg? Nothing. Damer says the pug marks were faked and the hairs planted.'

'Does he explain the shit?'

Loftus snorted.

'What are you going to do?' I said.

He looked surprised.

'Me? I'm waiting for Harama to send the traps. That'll take another week, but I've plenty to do. We ought to get some results with sixty traps.'

'Aren't you due at a polo tournament soon?' I said.

He frowned. 'They'll have to get someone else.'

Ali came in with a mug of Ovaltine.

'When you're up we'll get really going on this,' Loftus said.

He smiled and raised his hand as he went out.

I was sitting in my long chair when Gregg came back at five o'clock. He was tired and dispirited.

'You are looking better,' he said.

'I'll be up tomorrow,' I said.

He spoke automatically.

'Don't rush it, you must get your strength back.'

He did not go, but stripped off his shirt and stood staring through the open shutter.

'Manny Loftus looked in this morning,' I said.

Gregg slowly turned and regarded me with watchful eyes.

'Oh yes?' he said.

'He was telling me about the trappings and the killing at Soka.'

'Well?'

'There must be a lot of leopards in the forest.'

Gregg made a weary grimace.

'Of course there are, you wouldn't expect a leopard society to operate here if there weren't.'

'I suppose not,' I said.

Damer and Meakin arrived while we were talking. I could hear them moving about in the other room and one of them shouted for bath water.

Gregg spoke with a faint expression of mockery.

'Who asked Loftus to come here?'

I had a qualm of uneasiness as he waited for my reply.

'I did,' I said.

He looked at me with a crooked smile and then folded his arms and stared through the shutter again.

'I thought so, and I should like to know why?'

I felt my disadvantage and I was too weak to assert myself.

'I was influenced by Geoffrey Palthrop's opinion, but what do you think Pomeroy and Ames would have done if I had said so?'

Gregg turned quickly.

'You could have told me.'

'I should have told you,' I said.

Gregg was immersed in reflections and made no reply when his boy announced his bath. He looked at me again.

'You're a more complex character than I took you for. I don't know how your mind's working and I don't know what you think Loftus can do.' *106465*

'He's a shrewd and competent person,' I said.

'Maybe,' he said, 'but I don't like him.' He waved his hand. 'That's beside the point—what is important is that Sedley and Barr, the top pathologist, both say the bodies they saw were stabbed.' He wagged a finger at me. 'The same injuries have appeared repeatedly on the bodies we've seen.' Gregg's voice became hard. 'And don't under-rate Damer. He's no fool.'

I protested at being forced into a position I was unprepared to defend.

'Don't pick on me, I've said nothing. I know what people think of Geoffrey Palthrop, but I reserve the right to my own opinion.'

Gregg suddenly laughed. 'Skip it. Can I bring my bed back now?'

There was something clandestine about Loftus's morning calls. He waited until Gregg and the other two had gone and then walked from his tent and tip-toed into my room. The third time he came he brought a jar of Brand's essence and a bottle of Tio Pepe and showed Ali how to mix them with an egg for me.

'This will put you right.' He looked at me with a benign smile. 'One for elevenses and another at sundown.'

'How are things going?' I said.

He gave a faint shrug. 'According to plan. We've now killed twelve. I've sent to Pela for gunpowder for Boningo's people. When we've got more traps from Harama and go further afield it'll be too much for Dudu and me; they'll have to go round with their muzzle loaders.'

That night Damer was in an expansive mood. He whistled as he cleared his papers when the servants came to lay the table.

'There've been significant developments,' he said at dinner. 'We've had no killings in the worst area this week. The two we've had have been on the edge of the eight-mile circle.'

'I'd noticed that,' Gregg said.

'I've always believed our methods were sound,' Damer continued. 'If we prevent new crimes we're achieving something. It's costly in manpower but close policing is the long term solution to our problem.'

There was a rumble of thunder in the distance. It came nearer until it seemed over the resthouse and then the rain fell, keeping us indoors after dinner.

Damer lit a cigar and then spread out his map.

'I should like to move Police Posts six, seven and eight away from the centre.' He pointed with a pencil, 'and place them here in the form of an equilateral triangle.'

He looked at Gregg. 'What do you think, sir?'

Gregg seemed tired, but he tried to be attentive.

'It's certainly worth considering,' he said, 'but let's watch developments over the next couple of weeks. I should prefer a more definite lead.'

Damer put his elbows on the table and rubbed his chin. He then took out a pair of calipers and measured points on the map.

He nodded. 'On reflection, I think you're right, sir. We'll be running into difficulties over communications. We want to be sure about what we are doing. It could be that we'll have to set up a new headquarters.'

Gregg got up and stared out through the open door.

'The rain's stopped.' As he spoke renewed uproar came from the forest and flying ants began to swarm round the lamp. 'I'm going to bed,' he said.

For three days I did not go beyond the compound. On the fourth day after breakfast I walked a quarter of a mile through the forest. The sun was not up but the effort brought sweat out of me. At half past eleven Ali came in with the sherry and beef essence.

'There's a lorry from Pela outside,' he said.

I went to the middle room and peered through the jalousies. Harama's half ton truck stood near Loftus's tent. Dudu was directing local people unload kegs of gunpowder and steel traps. Loftus stood a few paces away watching them. He had not called for three days. I supposed he had been too busy, and I was relieved as I did not want to associate too closely with him.

The people filed off into the forest carrying the kegs on their heads; the remainder followed with the traps. There was a puff of exhaust smoke and the truck circled inside the compound and turned off down the main track to the open road. Loftus spoke to Dudu and went into his tent. Then I saw Ali stroll across the compound and get into conversation with Dudu. Five minutes later Loftus came out of the tent wearing puttees and carrying a rifle.

With the return of my strength I went further each day. The third day after the truck appeared I walked four miles through forest to Boningo's place. He told me his people had destroyed five leopards. Boningo raised his hat. 'The Captain is our saviour,' he said.

A mile from the resthouse on the way back I met Ali running towards me. His white clothes were saturated with blood.

'What's wrong?' I said.

He was too agitated to speak properly.

'A leopard's hurt Dudu.'

'Good God,' I said. 'Is he dead?'

I increased my walking pace towards the resthouse and Ali found it hard to keep up with me.

'No, but I think he will die.'

We walked faster as though it was important for us to get back quickly.

'How did this thing happen?' I said.

'I go with the Captain and Dudu to see the traps this morning. First trap, nothing, second trap, nothing, third trap a big male leopard caught by the back foot.' Ali touched his right leg. 'He was snarling and trying to pull out of the trap. Dudu turned to give the Captain his big rifle then the leopard pulled out of the trap and leapt at Dudu.' Ali clawed the air with his hands. 'Dudu fell down and then got up and the leopard leapt on his back.' Ali clawed the air again. 'The Captain went mad. He beat the leopard's head with his rifle and then he shot him five, six, plenty time. After that he kicked him f'ss, f'ss, f'ss. I helped him carry Dudu. When we got back he took one drum of petrol, a bottle of brandy and two blankets for Dudu. He did not speak. He just drove away very fast like a mad man and leave everything.'

I said nothing and we kept up our fast pace. Loftus's tent was there with Dudu's tent and the latrine screen behind. The trailer rested at a tilt with it's shaft pointing upward but there was no sign of the car. I told myself that even if I had not known that Loftus had gone I would have been aware of the emptiness of the little encampment.

'Won't the Captain come back?'

'No,' I said.

Gregg and the two police officers were away each day. I wondered what they did but I was unwilling to ask. Gregg was still friendly but his manner changed. He confided in me less and talked more to Damer and Meakin. Damer's jubilation at the lengthening period without killings disturbed me. He talked about the cycles of activity of the leopard murder society and the probability of a period of quiescence. He believed there was an esoteric link between the society and the number of leopards in the forest. I began to wonder how long I could stand it and I sometimes found Gregg's eyes on me when we sat over drinks.

Loftus had been gone ten days when Gregg spoke to me one night as we turned in. There was sudden decision in his voice.

'I must get on the end of a telegraph line,' he said. 'Will you drive me to Pela?'

'Yes, of course,' I said.

'Tomorrow?'

'Very good,' I said, 'we'll leave in the morning.'

The forest grew thinner the further we travelled from Faisi and by the time we reached Malu we were in orchard scrub country.

We spent the night at Malu and left at dawn raising billows of dust as we jolted over the red earth road. A large flock of crown birds rose, beating their wings, thrusting out their long necks and carrying their legs at an angle. They uttered a trumpeting call, turning their heads from side to side as they flew. Gregg said nothing in reply when I said it was a remarkable sight.

Harmattan haze cleared as the sun rose higher filling the cloudless sky with glaring white light.

Gregg was impatient. We stopped only to pour in petrol and let out air from hot tyres.

It was five o'clock when we drove through Pela up the road to the station. Pomeroy and Elizabeth were on the tennis courts. He was cursing a ball-boy while Elizabeth waited to serve.

'Shall I stop?' I said.

Gregg took off his sun glasses. His fingers were stained from cigarette smoking.

'No,' he said.

'What shall I tell him tomorrow?'

'I asked you to drive me here. It's time I wired a progress report.'

Smellie was hacking on the road ahead as we followed the big circle round to the resthouse.

'Here's Smellie,' I said, as I slowed down.

Gregg sat back and stretched himself.

'Keep going. I don't want to see anyone.'

The caretaker unloaded the truck. I opened our chairs. Gregg took out whisky and glasses and poured two nips. A shout came through the doorway.

'I'd recognize that truck anywhere.'

Keast, in native sandals, shuffled in with his bitch. His bow legs were bare and his open shirt exposed a hairy chest.

'I spotted you from the other side and I said to myself, that's Wood's truck, and so I came over.'

'It's nice to see you Keasty,' I said. 'Have a drink?'

He shook his head. 'I've just finished tea.'

Gregg was on edge and I was tired from driving, but Keast stood there with his right hand on the knob of his stick. His face puckered as he stared at us.

'What's eating you, Keasty?' I said.

'I want you to see something.'

I had no intention of moving.

'Have a heart. We've just got in from Malu. I'm going to bath and when I've eaten I'm going to bed.'

Gregg gulped his drink.

'I'll bath first,' he said.

Keast turned on him quickly.

'No, you don't, you must come too.'

Gregg made no attempt to be civil.

'I've got work to do. I'm not moving from here.'

Keast stood his ground.

'I've been waiting weeks to tell you about this.'

Gregg paused thoughtfully and lit a cigarette. After a moment of silence, he said, 'All right, what d'you want us to see?'

'I want you to come round to Stacey's house. It won't take you long.'

'What on earth for, Keasty?' I said.

An air of mystery came into his manner.

'Come over and you'll see for yourself. You won't be wasting your time.'

Keast lifted his bitch into the back of the truck. The three of us pressed together on the seat. We passed Derek and Tansy Firbank. Tansy held up her hand but I waved through the window and drove on.

It was my first visit to the Forestry house since Margaret Marchant had left. Burned-up tufty grass covered the bed where I had often seen her at work. Footprints and the impress of tyres remained in the rock-hard clay of the drive. There were no flower pots in front of the house and the candy-striped curtains had gone. Keast shouted through the open door 'Can we come in, Stacey?'

Stacey, in blue striped pyjamas came down the spiralling staircase. His drawn thin face was unshaven. He looked searchingly at us, making an effort to overcome langour.

'You're ill,' I said.

He shrugged his shoulders.

'It's nothing, a little dengue; that's all.'

Keast was impatient. 'Can they see what you showed me?'

'Come in,' Stacey said.

Bird skins and feathers littered the dining-room table and a paper bag lay on its side spilling out white powder.

We followed Stacey through a pantry out to the compound behind the house to a thatched structure about ten yards to the right of the servants' houses. Birds fluttered or quietly perched in home-made cages stacked in rows under the shelter. Stacey peered in each cage to see if the birds had water.

Keast touched his shoulder. 'We haven't come to look at birds,' he said.

Stacey turned and called to a boy and then spoke to Keast. 'Someone must hold your bitch.'

We walked on to a second shelter and an ammoniacal stench of animal urine assailed our nostrils. A heavy wooden cage fronted with strong metal mesh was raised on stones under the thatch. With effortless grace a half-grown leopard strode restlessly to and fro, turning without pause at each end of the cage. Long back legs made its head seem low as with each stride it placed big front paws with deliberate precision. A roll of light furry flesh hung down from its belly. Its testicles stuck out in a tight little pouch under a long tail curling up at the tip.

'They are much bigger in the shoulders than Indian leopards,' Stacey told us, 'and heavier and longer in the body. The fur is darker. . . .'

'Show them those things,' Keast said.

Stacey gave a start of surprise.

'They're in a box at the back of the hut.'

Four clean white skulls lay in an old beer case. My heart stopped beating. At first Gregg made no movement and uttered no sound. His jaw fell open and he stared at Stacey aghast. Then he said hoarsely, 'what's the meaning of this?'

Stacey laughed awkwardly.

'They're Sooty Mangabeys,' he said.

'He means monkeys,' Keast said impatiently and then added, 'show them what you showed me.'

At a word from Stacey the boy went off and came back clutching a monkey's head by its fur. He stood on a box and dropped the head through a trap door at the top of the cage. The leopard pawed the head once and resumed its restless striding and then settled down placing a front paw on the head. With slow deliberate movement it stripped away fur and flesh from the bone with long rasping licks of its tongue.

Stacey's sick face flickered with interest.

'It's curious how this one goes for Sooty Mangabeys. I had one before which would touch nothing but Diana Monkeys, you know the ones with the white chest.'

Gregg's thoughts were not in his eyes.

'What are you going to do with it,' he said.

'I'm shipping it to Bristol Zoo. What I really want is a young gorilla.'

Gregg was no longer listening. He turned and walked round the house to the truck.

CHAPTER XIII

Pomeroy gave a party when Daubney came back.

Shea butter dips along the drive flickered like fairy lights. A police orderly in dress uniform of red and gold Zouave jacket opened car doors and Pomeroy stood in the hall with Elizabeth greeting guests with extravagant warmth. He had a flower in his button-hole and his fair hair was newly trimmed and well brushed. Even if his benevolence was feigned he was an impressive man as he came forward with outstretched hand.

'Everyone must have a cocktail,' he said waving his hand at a servant holding a tray. 'It's obligatory, they're Peggy's specials.'

There was a bar and cold buffet in the dining-room and arm-chairs were placed among the hydrangea tubs on the verandah.

Maybe Peggy's cocktails touched off explosive relief, or maybe we were glad to see Daubney back, or maybe, as Peggy said, it was just time for a party. As the evening advanced people shed inhibitions and got noisy. The men took off their jackets and loosened their ties. Pomeroy moved about the house pawing his guests and urging them to drink.

At eleven o'clock he came out to the verandah where we were dancing. He had put on a cook's hat and apron and was carrying a napkin.

'Grub's in,' he called. 'Come and fetch it.'

Palthrop had stayed a long time with Daubney but I saw him alone after supper.

'Hello,' he said, 'I've had a nice letter from Barr.' He touched his moustache and cleared his throat. 'A very nice letter indeed. I sent him photographs of Dudu. . . .'

Pomeroy joined us. He was sweating profusely and had become very boisterous.

'Geoffrey, my boy,' he said, 'I must apologize.'

Palthrop stood with one hand in a pocket and his eye glass

hanging over his cummerbund. There was a speck of dried shaving soap on the lobe of his right ear.

'Apologize!' he said with a start. 'What on earth for?'

Elizabeth joined us before Pomeroy could reply.

'Geoffrey,' she cried, 'why haven't you a drink?'

Palthrop made a slight bow.

'I won't have another, thank you Elizabeth.'

'What nonsense, Geoffrey, you must.'

Palthrop bowed again.

'Well, if you say so, dear lady.'

Elizabeth hurried away in search of a servant.

Pomeroy gripped Palthrop's arm in the manner of someone conferring a favour.

'Geoff,' he said, 'I want to apologize for my past attitude towards you.'

Palthrop frowned and looked at me and then faced Pomeroy again.

'What are you talking about? You've got nothing to apologize for.'

Slowly Pomeroy smiled with his eyes fixed intently on Palthrop.

'We part friends, boy?'

'Of course,' Palthrop said.

Pomeroy, still smiling, raised his hand in half salute and moved on. Palthrop brushed up his moustache and looked down the verandah.

'I must say that was extraordinarily civil of Pomeroy,' he said.

Elizabeth brought him a drink.

'You must look after Geoffrey,' she told me, then as she was going she half turned and added, 'I have something to tell you.'

I left Palthrop and followed her into the sitting-room.

'You'll be the first one to know. Douglas is going into the Secretariat next tour.'

'Really, Elizabeth,' I said, 'to do what?'

'The Civil Secretary wants him to be deputy in charge of the Political Division.'

'That's marvellous,' I said.

She was no longer animated. 'The poor dear would be a lot happier if he wasn't so terribly ambitious.'

There was bedlam around us. Elizabeth frowned as though the noise was too much for her.

'Still, I think he's better with ideas than dealing with people,' she said.

'I am not so sure,' I said.

Pomeroy was lying blindfold on the floor with a roll of newspaper in his hand. Keast also blindfold lay at his side. They were playing a game.

Elizabeth sighed. 'He hates every minute of it, it's his act for improving staff relations and of course Mr Daubney is here.' I said nothing and Elizabeth went on. 'This has been a horrible tour. Such ghastly things have happened and nobody likes Douglas.'

'I wouldn't say that,' I said, but she ignored me.

'It's ridiculous with you so young that we should owe you such a lot. How old are you, by the way?'

'Twenty-three,' I said.

'Yes, it is ridiculous,' she said.

She blinked as though she might cry, but made an effort to regain her composure.

'Mr Daubney told us Peter Metcalfe's also posted to the Secretariat.'

I laughed, glad of relief from embarrassment.

'Poor fish!' I said. 'What's he going to do?'

Elizabeth shrugged her shoulders. 'An assistant secretary of some sort, I suppose.'

'Well, well, well,' I said, 'the future of the territory is assured.'

Elizabeth did not smile.

'Mr Daubney saw him with Margaret Marchant at Lord's,' she said.

George Crane joined us, his face shining with sweaat nd his shirt stuck in wet patches on his muscular shoulders.

'Dance with me, Elizabeth?' he said.

Elizabeth smiled. 'I'd love to George.'

Daubney slipped off to bed, and the party got noisier.

At three o'clock Pomeroy looked tired. The boys had started to empty ash trays and take away glasses. I was the first to go and Elizabeth came out and walked with me down the drive.

I would not have chosen the day after the party to go to Buala but for weeks petitioners had worried Harama about a boundary dispute and I had arranged to go with him to settle it. When Hiro reported at breakfast that my grey had a saddle sore and the big chestnut was limping, I had a good excuse for postponing the trip.

Arisi and Gela were waiting with their horses at the back of the house. They were shocked when I suggested we put off the inquiry.

'Harama is expecting you,' Arisi said.

I stood wondering what I should do.

'You might cycle,' Gela said, 'it is only twelve miles.'

I looked at Arisi.

'The path is hard,' he said, 'you'll get there quite easily.'

They waited for my decision.

'You two go on with Harama, I'll overtake you by bicycle.'

Buala lay to the north of Pela. For the first five miles the route was along a well-trodden market track. Men with donkeys laden with ground nuts gravely saluted me and prayed Allah I arrive safely. Files of bare-footed women moving easily with head loads and swinging their arms gave me nervous looks as they kept on their way. Six miles from Pela I stopped at a cluster of huts, a locust bean tree and a well. Two men and three children gathered to watch me straighten the front wheel.

'How far is it to Buala?' I asked.

The men looked at each other.

'Buala?' the older one said. 'It's a long way.'

'Yes, but how far?' I said.

'Not too far,' said the other.

'Can I get there by bicycle?'

They thought again.

'If it is Allah's will,' the old man said.

The younger man called after me, 'Harama and two men are a long way ahead.'

I turned off at a shade tree and took a narrower track and almost at once came to sand. From then on I was compelled to push the bicycle for two or three hundred yards at a time. Sweat poured out of my body saturating my clothes and dripping off me as I walked.

I had pushed the bicycle through sand for more than a mile when I saw vultures in the haze ahead circling over acacias and shea-butter trees. Ten minutes later huts came into sight.

Harama had finished the inquiry. I followed him through the village and a mile on to see four cairns marking the new boundary. There was nothing to keep us. Harama rode back to Pela with Arisi and Gela.

By midday the haze cleared and the sun was mercilessly hot.

My sodden shirt seemed to be hampering me. I tore it off and dropped it. The bicycle too had become a burden and after the fifth fall I left it and began to walk. But I became tired of walking and I sat down to rest. The periods of rest lengthened and I thought it better to lie down. When I got up I was giddy and began retching. I needed to rest again after walking a few yards; I kept getting up and trying to walk. I slipped off my trousers as I thought I could move better without them. Then I was seized with cramp in my stomach; I doubled up and fell in a thorn bush. Cramps came to both my legs and then to my back and arms. Every movement I made set up cramp in some part of my body. I started retching again and spewed up blood. With some dim process of reasoning I decided it was better to remain where I was than attempt to move on. I began to feel indifferent and it seemed of no consequence what I did. I watched blood dripping from thorn scratches form globules in the sand.

The sun turned red and glaring as it began to go down. A lizard came in quick tentative darts towards my feet. A bustard flew slowly overhead. Someone spoke. I opened my eyes and found Harama gripping the bridle of his horse with his right hand and pulling me with his left.

'Wouldn't it be better if you got up?' he said.

'No,' I said, 'I don't want to get up.'

I was relieved when he left me. Then almost in no time it was dusk and a crowd was around. They had lashed poles together with bark strips and made a litter. Four of them lifted me on to it and the crowd raised it over their heads and moved forward. The next thing I knew was Geoffrey Palthrop looking down at me.

'Hullo, Geoffrey,' I said, 'what are you doing here?'

Keast and Harama were with him.

I greeted Harama in the vernacular. I could not recall what I was supposed to be doing with him. It seemed close but just beyond my reach and then I remembered.

'We've got to settle a boundary dispute at Buala,' I said.

I felt tired and turned away from them.

'No you bloody well don't.' Palthrop's voice seemed a long way off. 'Drink some of this.'

I sipped the fluid.

'It's brandy,' I said and then retched and vomited blood.

They wrapped me in blankets and put me on a mattress at the back of their truck. Palthrop pushed a needle into my arm and I remembered nothing after the engine started.

I struggled with blankets and found I was wearing blue silk pyjamas. I was at the back of a car and through the window I saw the yellowish glow of sunrise in the morning haze. I recognized the back of Geoffrey Palthrop's head.

'Geoffrey, where are we going?' I said.

He stopped and came round to me. He felt my pulse and then gave me a spoonful of salt mixture.

'I'm terrible thirsty,' I said.

He spooned a lump of ice out of a vacuum flask.

'Try this,' he said. 'I'm afraid to give you anything to drink.'

He bared my arm and gave me an injection.

'Try to relax,' he said.

It was bright daylight when I awoke and we were outside the produce stores near the railway siding at Huta. The car was on the roadside in the shade of a mango tree and Palthrop was pouring water from a bottle into a mug. A crowd formed while he shaved and rubbed powder over his face. He brushed his hair and then, staring critically into the driving mirror, brushed up his moustache. He put in his eyeglass and started the car.

We left the produce stores, driving through the crowds in the trading section and then turned up the hill past the banks and insurance offices and beyond to the reservation. He turned in at a drive and pulled up under a *porte-cochère* at the hospital.

I heard someone say: 'Patients are not admitted here, please go to the main entrance in the next block.'

I thought it a pleasant voice and then Hilda Standfield looked through the window. She was wearing the veil and overall of the nursing service.

'Well,' she exclaimed, 'goodness me.'

She turned to Palthrop.

'Acute heat exhaustion, dehydration and haemorrhage,' he said. 'He only wants nursing.'

BOOK II

'There is occasions

and causes

why and wherefore

in all things'

CHAPTER XIV

~~~~~~

For twenty-five years I had been given to up-country postings and I was surprised when Peter Metcalfe, who had been promoted Deputy Civil Secretary, wrote asking if I were interested in the post of Provincial Commissioner, Belemba. It was providential, he said, that Bracey Smith, who had been doing the job, had been invalided out with heart trouble as a vigorous man with a fresh outlook was needed.

I was not sure that I was a good choice and moreover my inclination was to finish my service with people not so politically advanced as the Belembanians. But I distrusted my own judgment and wrote back to say that I was willing to be considered. It was a key post and I was flattered when Mathews the Civil Secretary wrote personally to say that I had been selected to fill it. The unexpected appointment meant cancelling a posting to Pela Province, where I had spent most of my service, and my doubts were renewed when a letter came from Harama written by one of his scribes but endorsed with his personal seal. 'You will be among strangers,' he wrote, 'among people you will not understand. We want you in Pela where everyone knows you. It is Allah's will that you come back to us and there can only be trouble if you do not.' There was a lot of it and much of it was extravagant and fulsome. Harama was becoming senile or the scribe had taken liberties in composing the letter.

Morning traffic from Muda, fed from avenues and crescents named after Governors and Secretaries, flows slowly along the main road for three miles to Belemba. It cuts through the golf course, passes the military barracks, then further on, Police Headquarters and later the high walls of the Prison. There is an unpainted Methodist Chapel, a school and a miscellany of African shops and ramshackle houses, a new petrol station and beyond on a ridge overlooking the town, the main government offices. The road turns away on entering the town and becomes Wilberforce Street where Syrians and Indians competing for business in piece goods and cloth stand in shop doorways waiting for customers and African traders display Japanese enamel ware, oil lamps, bags of salt, imported second-hand clothing and all kinds of ironmongery. A white-sleeved constable on a dais where Wilberforce Street meets the Front, waves on or halts the traffic making for departmental stores, the banks, the oil companies' offices and other new buildings facing the harbour. The Front follows the harbour outline easterly for two miles to the customs sheds, warehouses and docks and then another two miles to the airport; on the west it passes Government House, a spacious three-storeyed building clean and white like a spa hotel at the end of a drive, then a row of old colonial houses, classical in proportions but now shabby and costly to keep up. There is the tennis club, the yacht club and finally the beach where fishermen pull up their canoes and dry their nets on the sand.

High Street turning off Wilberforce Street to the right and running parallel with the busiest part of the Front is a thoroughfare of taverns, rackety printing presses, patent medicine stores, and premises of uncertain purpose. Here motor cars, hooting incessantly, move slowly among cyclists, handcarts, and hawkers into a jostling throng of women in tribal dress, northerners in robes and loose baggy trousers, traders in tailored suits and shirts, and beggars exposing deformities. Concrete buildings of overseas firms unable to find sites on the Front tower next to old houses built by Africans who learned their trade as slaves in Brazil. Alleys lead into a warren of old mud block buildings and shanties of packing case timbers, flattened oil drums, or old corrugated iron where squatters pay rents to the descendants of the original landowners. Clerks, artisans, and book-keepers live in a new part of the town and come daily to work in buses or on bicycles while their children, girls in blue, green or red tunics, boys in short trousers and jackets with badges make their way to the secondary schools. You get used to the exuberant vitality, the colourful squalor and noise of Belemba but at first impact they shake you.

A year ago a conference in London agreed on a legislative assembly of elected members and government by ministries, and the Governor's executive council became the Council of Ministers with an African majority. It was decided that a date for full independence would be fixed at a second conference to be held within three years. The aircraft with the returning delegates taxied up the runway and came to a halt in front of the airport terminal buildings. Fela Pereta, leader of the National United Democratic Alliance, and Pilama Mudi, leader of the National Independence Congress, appeared arm in arm at the top of the gangway and then embraced each other in full view of the wildly emotional crowd which had been there since morning to meet them. Before leaving the airport they issued a statement. '*We have thrown off the yoke of imperialism and return as comrades victorious in the first stage of our fight for freedom. With God's help we shall continue the struggle together, fighting shoulder to shoulder, until we have won the precious prize of full independence.*'

A lively nationalism brought a multitude of fissiparous associations, tribal societies, splinter groups, trades unions, ex-servicemen's leagues with secretaries, chairmen and presidents all trying to make themselves heard. Hardly a day passed without some declared ultimatum, some demand, some indignant protest or some new party manifesto. The political scene was highly coloured, animated and constantly changing but the trend of affairs led inevitably with gathering momentum towards independence. The stress of events was too much for the alliance of NUDA and NIC, and at the first election to the new legislature the parties were attacking each other with all their old ferocity. NUDA were returned and Pereta became the first Chief Minister.

Bracey Smith had gone before I arrived at Belemba and Bowcott, the deputy, was acting P.C. He was known to be eccentric, outspoken and indifferent to his effect on people. There were times, I was told, when for weeks he adopted the slow speech and accents of a countryman. His language was often obscene. For long periods he was apt to be vegetarian. He had recently brought a year of abstinence to an end with a bout of drunkenness. His clothes were unpressed and he wore nickel-rimmed glasses to correct short sight. He was a strange man but by the third day I found myself drawn to him.

Our offices were arranged on the ground floor. Miss Malling occupied the room adjoining mine, a smiling girl whose biggish limbs and ruddy complexion belied her lively intelligence. Baga, the African administrative officer who dealt with the routine of the office, had a room on the other side. Bowcott's room was next to Miss Malling's and beyond was Mr Munga, the Chief Clerk, the main office and the typing pool.

I sat under a ceiling fan at a desk facing french windows opening on to a low balcony from which I could see the town sprawling down to the harbour. One of the telephones rang during my third morning in the office. Mathews the Civil Secretary said he wanted to see me.

The heat of morning had drawn beads of sweat and I mopped my brow as I followed Mathews's secretary into his room. He looked up and regarded me with unwavering tawny eyes.

'Be seated,' he said, pushing cigarettes towards me. He then looked down again at the desk. A maze of small veins made patches of red on his face. His high brow caught the light from the window when he looked up in thought. Wide flaring nostrils, a pointed nose and thin lips left him with no pretence to good looks.

He replaced his pen and blotted the paper. He read what he had written, made an amendment and blotted the paper again. He touched the bell and the girl came in. He held out a file.

'Government House,' he said, 'at once, please.'

He turned, fixing his strong eyes on me again. His diction was clear and precise.

'We have given you the most difficult posting in the country.' He paused to see the effect of his statement. 'The Governor himself suggested you and I may say that with the greatest respect I fully shared his opinion.' I knew this was nonsense because Peter Metcalfe had contrived the posting. He stared with sombre intensity. 'It is our intention that you spend two tours here.' He grimaced and made a slight gesture. 'Traditionally your work here is to advise the Governor through me on affairs in the town. Belemba is the focus of the Colony's political activity so your advice may be of the greatest importance.'

The strange luminousity in Mathews's eyes held my attention. As he talked flecks of froth appeared on his lips.

'For this particular post more than any you must bring a certain philosophy to your acts and decisions. The old benevolence is offensive. Today the need is for bold, imaginative and generous ideas.'

Mathews paused again.

'Do I make myself clear?'

'Yes, I think so.'

'We must move apace; there must be no foot dragging. Progress must follow converging lines towards a balanced unity of political, economic and social development. Unless we can clearly see this as the object of all we do, say, and think, we have no right to be here, no right at all.'

He frowned as he leaned over the desk.

'Do you agree?'

'Certainly,' I said.

'Normally the process would take time.' Mathews rocked his head and added judicially, 'maybe ten years, but we must move faster. We must leave this country as a going concern long before that. For historical reasons Belemba and the district is backward and that's what makes your job important—perhaps I should say more important,' he bared his teeth in a momentary smile and then went on a little complaisantly, 'at my suggestion the Legislature voted expenditure of half a million for a local development programme. It will be up to you to see that that money is well spent. Bracey Smith made very little headway,' Mathews pursed his mouth in disapproval, 'of course his health was bad but I don't think he had the right feeling towards change. He was unreceptive to new ideas.' Mathews spoke as if thinking aloud and then suddenly checking himself he resumed his sombre appearance. 'The Governor and I hope for better things from you. Above all we expect you to consult African opinion about all you do. The people must participate in your decisions. It is not enough to give them what we think they ought to have.' He bared his teeth again in a smile. 'Your means could possibly be more important than your ends. More important than anything you must work through the Ministry of Development.' He looked at his watch. 'I must ask you to go now, come and see me when you've had a chance to work out your plans.'

He looked down with no further interest in me and I went out.

119

I talked to Bowcott for hours about the development plan; my respect for him grew the better I knew him. Beneath his strange exterior, and in spite of human frailties, he was a dedicated man possessing more than the ability expected of an intelligent well-read man; he was gifted with insight into the motives of people and with my doubts and uncertainties I knew I was an open book to him.

We interviewed people to find who would work together on our committees. We asked both political parties and trades unions to send representatives. The town council nominated three members; the Women Traders' Guild sent their president with three women supporting her. Bowcott persuaded the old famililies to choose some of their people and got six leading men in the town of independent opinion to join us. With the help of the committee we drew up the plan. We proposed improving living conditions in the old part of the town, we worked out a loan scheme to help tradesmen and craftsmen, we decided to make grants to community centres and encourage boys' and girls' clubs; adult education classes were to be started, we planned to level and drain an area of waste land and mark out football pitches and a running track. I had long sessions at the Ministry talking to Gerald Crawley the Permanent Secretary—Bowcott, who had known him at Oxford, called him Creepy Crawley and for some reason disliked him. The Honourable Xanadu Cairngross, the Minister, sometimes sat with us asking questions with bold unblinking gaze. He agreed to take our plan to the Council of Ministers.

CHAPTER XV

It was not easy to find time to visit the outlying districts but after repeated requests by Tollemache the D.C. I left my work in Belemba to meet the Tosho people and hear appeals from their court.

A messenger shouted 'Order' when I entered the council hall and everyone stood up until I sat down with the Chiefs. I listened to their eloquence for two hours repeatedly telling them that what they asked me to do they could now do for themselves.

And then I heard the appeals. Three cases related to land tenure and two were matrimonial disputes. The land cases were identical in principle. The traditional law was certain and the facts had been well established. I upheld the native court judgment.

The first of the matrimonial cases was on the refund of bride-price. The man had paid money to a girl's father and given presents to the mother and to the girl in consideration of marriage but the girl had married another man. I again upheld the native court and ordered the brideprice and the value of the presents to be refunded. The respondent in the last case was a man of forty who, though dressed in native costume, looked out of place in the rustic court. A young man in coat and trousers sat in the body of the court with a note-book. I supposed them to have come out from Belemba in the cream-coloured Zephyr standing outside. The respondent gave his name as Moses Tarova, plaintiff in the original action claiming a declaration of title of the five month pregnancy of a woman named Melody Hama. He spoke good English and readily admitted he had not seen the woman for two years.

'And you claim title to this pregnancy?'

'Certainly.'

'Even though it is not your flesh and blood?'

His eyes narrowed and he spoke in a harsh voice.

'That's nothing to do with it. The court of original jurisdiction in its wisdom found in my favour. My claim to the unborn child is based on sound customary law. If an infant is conceived in this woman while she is my wife, when the child is born it is mine, and mine only.'

I found myself disliking him—that was perhaps why I asked the question.

'This woman left you for another man?'

He reacted immediately; he pushed his face forward and spoke with a sneer.

'Yes, she did, but she is still my wife.'

I looked away from him and faced the appellant. She was a young woman about twenty-two wearing a wrapped skirt, a loose white blouse and a twist of cloth round her head. She was obviously pregnant but there was nothing else remarkable in her appearance.

'What have you to say?' I asked after the clerk had explained what had been said.

'Because this man has plenty of money he thinks he can do what he likes. I never wanted to marry him, my father made me. I'm not his wife; over a year ago I asked for divorce and paid the brideprice into court.'

She held out a court receipt.

'Is that true?' I asked the clerk as I examined it.

He was embarrassed and looked for help from the court members behind me.

'Yes, it's true,' he said.

I examined the paper.

'This receipt is for seventeen pounds.'

Tarova raised a finger at me.

'I paid over fifty pounds for this woman and until its paid back to me in full, she's my wife.'

I ignored him and spoke to the clerk.

'When the woman asked for divorce, was a summons served on the respondent?'

The clerk turned over enclosures in the case file.

'Give me the file,' I said.

I found a copy of the summons to Tarova with a sworn statement of service.

'Appeal allowed,' I told Tarova. 'This woman is not your wife.

If you do not withdraw the sum deposited in court within a week the appellant may recover it.'

I endorsed the court record with my findings. The woman knelt on one knee and thanked me and then went off with a man of about twenty-five who had been standing behind her throughout the proceedings.

It was some moments before Tarova spoke, then he came forward to the table.

'I refuse to accept your judgment, I shall see the Minister. How can people like you alter the finding of a native court. They know, you don't. . . .' He was furious; he would have gone on but I stopped him.

'Anything more from you and you'll be charged with contempt of court.'

The young man with the note-book took his arm and led him away but he looked over his shoulder as he went out.

'This is not the end of this case let me tell you.'

I lit a cigarette and a moment or two later I heard a car started and through the open doorway saw the Zephyr move off.

When the court rose they asked me to look at their school. I stood at attention while the school band played a verse of God Save the Queen on home-made instruments. The children sang a song of welcome and then the headmaster showed me his class rooms and I signed his visitors' book.

The chief and three of his elders in the embroidered gowns they had worn for the meeting, and the court clerk still carrying his record books, walked with me through the village. Tosho was at the end of five miles of earth road turning off seven miles up the trunk road. It was difficult to believe I was only twelve miles from the noisy traffic and stress of life in Belemba. I was refreshed and encouraged because the people appeared to think I could help them. I had left unfinished work but I was easily persuaded to delay my return.

The bright midday sun shone vertically downwards beating back from the red hard-packed earth with eye-straining glare. The ochreous red of mud huts gave no relief but beyond there was the green of bananas, cocoa trees, towering kola nut trees and mangoes. They were taking me to the Infant Welfare Centre they had built from their own rates. It was a whitewashed mud block building, corrugated iron roofed with green painted doors and window frames. Entrance was through a covered space in front where patients sat waiting on benches and beyond a door led to three small rooms.

The midwife came forward a few yards to meet us.

'Welcome, Sir,' she greeted me.

She was a little over five feet but quite self-possessed and much less nervous than some of the men I had met that day.

'Good morning, midwife,' I said. 'What is your name, please?'

'Miss Comfort Makolo, Midwife Grade III.'

Her white cap and apron had lost their first freshness and an inch and a half of braided petticoat appeared below her blue uniform. Her complexion was not black, more a rich chocolate colour and shining with health. There was a speck of clinker in the corner of her right eye. She looked like a healthy young person who slept well.

'How old are you, Comfort?' I said.

'Eighteen and seven months, sir.'

A crowd of villagers formed an arc behind me as we talked. Seven women on the benches sat unmoved by the activity around them. Some held very young babies, others were large with advanced pregnancy.

'May I come in?' I said.

She showed me the labour room with its high table and red rubber sheet, the douche room with its drain, the drug store, two beds with adjoining cots, the tiny office where she kept her scales and records and a table for writing.

'How many deliveries did you have last month?' I asked.

She replied like a schoolgirl sure of her work.

'Eleven admitted and nine domiciliary deliveries.'

I nodded, but she stood eagerly waiting for more questions.

'Have you many ante-natal patients at present?'

'Twenty-seven.' She offered me an exercise book. 'Here is my register.'

I glanced at the ruled pages and the well-formed schoolgirl writing.

'I have also nineteen mothers and babies attending,' she said.

I complimented her on the cleanliness of the centre and on her neat records. 'You are doing good work here,' I said.

For the first time her formal manner deserted her and she looked shy.

'Is there anything you want?' I said. 'Something you need for your work?'

'I should like a gate at the entrance of the verandah,' she said. She meant the open waiting room. 'It would keep out the sheep and the goats at night, they come in to sleep and we find their faeces and urine on the floor in the morning.'

I inspected the entrance and told the Chief to have a gate made. Before leaving I glanced at the seated women; curiosity had roused some from their lethargy. One of them held my attention; she alone of the seven did not look up. In her arms was a baby whose staring glassy eyes stood out from a skull-like head and whose tiny limbs stuck out like sticks from a frail blown-up body.

'This baby is very ill, midwife,' I said.

'He is very ill, sir,' she calmly replied. 'He has miasmus, he cannot digest milk and will inevitably die.' Before I could protest she added, 'and the woman is very ill too, she is anaemic.'

'Can't something be done for them?'

The midwife pursed her lips.

'I am giving the woman an iron tonic but there is nothing we can do for the baby. I told the mother to bring it when doctor came last week but she didn't come.'

'Why not, why didn't she come, doesn't she want the baby to get well?'

The midwife clicked the knuckle joints of her right hand.

'You know our people,' she said. 'The man's been buying native medicine for them.'

'Yes, yes, I understand,' I said. 'Could anything be done for them in hospital?'

Her mouth fell open as though I had lifted the discussion to a level of unreality.

'Oh yes, but how can they get to Belemba?'

'I'll take them,' I said, 'I'm going there now, they can come in my car.'

A murmur of applause rose from the crowd and for some reason I felt ashamed.

'Ask the woman if she will come,' I said.

The woman looked surprised and answered in a low voice when the midwife spoke.

'She will come if her husband agrees,' the midwife said.

'Is the man here?' I asked the Chief.

'Yes, he is a blacksmith; we passed him on our way here.'

'Tell him to come,' I said, 'and tell him to come quickly. I have already been here too long.'

I walked away a few paces in a mood of growing impatience. I lit a cigarette and waited. Something was wrong that such distress and misery should exist unrelieved.

The blacksmith wore short trousers and a garment of hard-wearing locally-woven cloth. He was slightly above average height and sparely built, and although he was clearly surprised by my interest in him, he looked back fearlessly with intelligent eyes. I steeled myself for opposition.

'Your baby son and your wife are very ill,' I said. 'I want to take them to hospital in Belemba—if they stay here the baby will die and maybe your wife will die too, maybe they will die if I take them to Belemba but there they will have a chance.'

He made a gesture of hopelessness.

'Do whatever you think best, master,' he said, 'take them to Belemba and if it is the will of God they will recover.'

I touched him on the shoulder and felt hard muscle.

'With God's help they will recover,' I said.

The circle of spectators murmured 'Amin, Amin', and stood waiting for the next act in the drama. The woman nodded wearily when the blacksmith spoke to her.

'Get her into the car,' I told the midwife.

The baby whimpered when the woman got in. The woman then took the baby and the midwife turned and darted into the building. She returned with a mackintosh sheet and spread it over the back seat of the car and a brown red-edged blanket which she wrapped round the woman. I pressed the starter and reversed and then straightened to make way down the earth track. Once again the midwife darted away; she returned with a yellow card and handed it through the window to me.

'Here's the baby's case-history,' she said.

I took the card and put it under the dash-board.

'Thank you,' I said. 'Good-bye.'

I walked ahead of the woman through the swing doors into the odiferous interior of the women and children's hospital in central Belemba. I supposed people who worked there became accustomed to the blend of strong disinfectant and unwashed bodies, but it caught me in the throat as I awaited the Sister. She raised her eyebrows as she looked from me to the woman. She read the midwife's card, and then looked at the infant with professional interest.

'You are a miserable shrimp,' she said good-humouredly, 'we must see what we can do with you.'

CHAPTER XVI

The hum of the ceiling fan drowned most of the sound from Miss Malling's room. But I had become aware of voices, mainly the angry voice of a woman and I got up and pushed open the door. Miss Malling was standing four feet away with her back to me. She turned at the sound of my movement. Her self-possession had deserted her and she was flushed and spoke with a shrill voice.

'I've told them you've got an appointment with the Director of Public Works.' She looked at the people facing her and added with exasperation, 'they won't let me fix an appointment, they say they must see you now.'

The room seemed full but there were only six people, two white women and two Africans and two half-caste boys about six and eight years old. A hard-featured woman about forty with muscular arms and rough red hands, wearing a dirty white blouse and navy blue slacks, stepped towards me.

'That's right, mister,' she said, 'we want to see you.'

'Call the Director of Public Works and say I can't keep my appointment,' I said to Miss Malling.

She was about to speak but changed her mind and raised her eyebrows in silent disapproval.

'You can come in,' I told the woman.

They took some time to get seated.

'Why have you come here?' I said when they were settled.

A man of about twenty-seven, with close-set features and restless eyes, spoke first. A wisp of smoke rose from a hand hanging loose at his side. Seated next to him was a tired looking white girl about six months pregnant.

'We were told in the Civil Secretary's office you would see us.'

'You've been to the Secretariat?'

'We've just come from there.'

I spoke to the big woman in trousers.

'What do you want?'

She nudged an African about her own age sitting next to her. 'Show him your hands,' she said.

He raised misshapen claw-like hands and held them out at the level of his face.

'All right,' I said.

He placed his hands on his thighs and stared at the wall behind me.

'Do you know what that is?' the woman said.

'It's some rheumatic condition, isn't it?'

'Some rheumatic condition,' she said contemptuously. 'That's rheumatoid arthritis. Do you know how he got it?'

'No,' I said.

'Seventy-two hours in an open boat in the North Atlantic in winter.'

'You were in the Merchant Navy?' I asked him.

He fumbled in a jacket pocket and brought out a discharge book.

'Yes, he was, and gets no pension,' said the woman.

'I'm sorry,' I said as I returned the book to him.

The woman kept her eyes on me.

'Well?' she said.

'I don't think there is anything I can do,' I told her.

'Yes there is,' she said. 'You can find work for us.'

'Work?' I said doubtfully. 'He can't do much with hands like that.'

'It's me who wants work, he's done nothing for five years.'

I looked at her with renewed interest.

'What work can you do?'

'Office cleaning.'

'No, you can't, not in Belemba.'

'Why not?' She raised her voice. 'I did it in Cardiff and I can do it here.'

The two boys moved closer, pressing against her. Though the pathos of the situation dismayed me I felt obliged to speak firmly.

'No you can't, there is no work you can do here.'

The children waited expectantly for her to speak, but the woman remained silent for some moments looking at me in bewilderment, then in a puzzled tone she asked: 'Well, how are we to live?'

I had no answer for her.

'I can't say, if you will give me your name and address I'll see what can be done.'

'Mr and Mrs Suma and Gerald and Peter,' she said.

I wrote what she told me.

'Where are you living?'

'We are staying with my husband's brother in Spinga.'

I knew the place—a mushroom village three miles away on the main road, much too far away for a white woman to walk in the tropics.

I turned to the tired white girl. She yawned nervously but her husband glared at me.

'You want work too?'

The girl edged close to her husband.

'Yes,' he said. 'My wife is a qualified teacher—she's worked four years for L.C.C. schools.'

'What about you?' I said to him.

'I'd accept work in the administrative service or in the secretariat.'

'Oh yes,' I said, 'what makes you think you'd be offered a job like that?'

He started to speak but his wife interrupted.

'He's studied law and public administration.'

'Where?' I said.

'At the London School of Economics.'

'Are you qualified?'

He scowled.

'No, not yet.'

He would have added something but his wife interrupted again.

'There's a good explanation for that.'

He flushed but remained silent and the girl chattered on. 'He gets headaches and finds it hard to concentrate. He's well up in his work but never does himself justice in examinations.' She met my eyes uneasily and added, 'there are people like that.'

I looked from one to the other.

'How long have you been married?'

The girl answered, 'four years.'

'You were teaching all the time?'

'Oh yes.'

I picked up my pen. 'Let me have your name and address,' I said.

'Mr and Mrs Sangu, 27 Jubilee Street,' the man told me.

I made a note and replaced the pen.

'I take it we'll be hearing from you soon?' he said.

His manner offended me.

'Your wife won't want to think about work at present.'

'She'll be all right for two more months.'

He fascinated me and I stared at him with interest. My reflection was disturbed by Mrs Suma.

'Give a girl a chance, can't you?'

He turned on her furiously.

'Mind your own business,' he said.

His wife put a hand on his arm.

'Please, please, Toga,' she begged, and then looking at the older woman she said, 'I promise you I'll be all right.'

'You take it easy, dear. You don't look strong to me.' She glared at Sangu. 'Don't mind him.'

Sangu raised his voice. He seemed beyond himself with fury.

'Will you keep out of my affairs,' he shouted.

Mrs Suma turned away with a shrug.

'That will do now,' I said, 'if you want to argue among yourselves do it outside.' Then looking at Sangu I added, 'you are at liberty to write about work.'

When they had gone I sat blankly staring through the french windows. I was sure I was right in being non-committal because it would have been wrong to encourage hopes of an easy solution to their problems. But now a reaction set in and I was suddenly oppressed by a feeling of sadness. These people needed help and I was afraid I would fail them. On impulse I telephoned Edith Calder. 'Edie,' I said, 'I'd be glad if you and John would come round for a drink one night soon.'

The earliest day we could arrange was ten days ahead. I put down the telephone and almost at once there was a call on the direct line from Government House.

'H.E. would like to see you,' the Private Secretary said.

'Now?'

'Yep.'

'What's it about?'

'I don't know; he's just out of a meeting of the Council of Ministers.'

The guard at Government House gate were eating their midday meal partly concealed by a high croton hedge. The sentry slapped the butt of his rifle as I turned up the drive. A greyhaired major domo with three rows of medal ribbons came out and opened the door of my car. As I stood waiting I became depressed by a melancholy thought of the growing inconsequence of things which had once meant so much to me. Gleeson the A.D.C. hurried across the polished parquet of the hall.

'H.E.'s expecting you,' he said with a formal smile, 'come this way.' He pushed open a door. 'Wood's here, sir,' he announced and then turned back to me, 'you'll have a gin?'

The Governor was in the book-room where he did most of his work. He was a tall man, even taller than Mathews, with a good-humoured though slightly saturnine countenance, short cropped dark hair turning grey and a fine strong face. He gave an impression of excellent physical condition and of an alert and lively intelligence. It was hard to imagine a man more trusted by African leaders and who could command greater loyalty from his subordinate officers.

'Come in, Wood,' he said, 'come in and sit down.' He had taken off his jacket and had been reading *The Times*. 'Sit here and you'll get a bit of breeze from the fan.' He held out a cigarette box. 'Cigarette? light?' I puffed at the cigarette. I recognized his restless and talkative mood.

'I've just come from the Council of Ministers,' he said. He tossed the newspaper on the desk. 'Things go wrong when you least expect it. Do you know Zadeta?'

'Minister without portfolio?'

'Yes, but he wanted something to do and has now taken on the entertainment of official visitors.'

The Governor finished his gin and touched the bell. The servant came in and refilled the glass and then stood waiting to give me a second drink.

'Zadeta was very angry today,' the Governor said. 'He was not told about the M.P.s we've just had.' He paused for a moment looking straight at me. 'I suppose you made the arrangements?'

'My office did. The deputy Civil Secretary asked us to take care of them.'

The Governor nodded. 'A failure in communications, I suppose. Metcalfe had not been told about Zadeta, nor, for that matter, had you.'

I shook my head. 'No,' I said.

The Governor resumed after a moment's reflection.

'Apart from being upset over the principle, Zadeta and his friends don't feel the M.P.s were shown the right things. They think they must have gone away with a poor impression of Belemba.'

I felt embarrassed as if I were at fault.

'I'm sorry, sir,' I said, 'I didn't arrange their programme and I must say that I've been too busy to inquire what was done for them.'

'Bowcott looked after them?'

'Yes, but it's my responsibility.'

The Governor was unimpressed.

'Yes, all right,' he said, 'but there's another thing. Bowcott upset one of the party. I think it was Sturt. He's a bit of a thruster but I am sure he means well.'

'Oh dear,' I said, 'I am very sorry, sir.'

'Yes, I know you are. But remember you must get on with the ministers.' His face hardened and for a moment he seemed no longer friendly. 'So just watch it in future.'

He touched the bell again.

'Another gin?' he said and then pushed the heavy cigarette box across the table between us, 'and a cigarette?'

Bowcott was still in his room when I got back.

'I was hoping to find you,' I said.

The ash tray on his desk overflowed with cigarette ends and there was ink on his fingers. He had loosened his tie and his hair was awry.

'Actually I was just about to go,' he said.

He got up and took his jacket from the peg behind him.

'I've been talking to H.E. at Government House,' I said.

He polished his glasses with the end of his tie, regarding me with weak pale blue eyes.

'Oh yes,' he said tonelessly. He held his glasses up to the light of the window then breathed on them and rubbed them again with his tie. 'What's biting him?'

'What happened about the M.P.s on Saturday?'

'Sebastian Paling kept me up till two o'clock drinking my whisky and sneering at his colleagues.'

'Never mind him, what happened during the day?'

Bowcott replaced his glasses and looked at me with a meditative eye.

'I showed them round the place.'

'What did you show them?'

'What did I show them?' he said as though reflecting, 'oh, I showed them the slum buildings and the shanty houses, then I took them to the old market and we looked at the ju-ju stalls and the charm dealers. They watched mammies dancing for a time then I met them at the Boys' Remand Home.'

The presentiment I had begun to feel did not fail me.

'You suggested they walked from the old market to the Remand Home?'

I felt his eyes fixed on me.

'Yes, I thought they would see things better that way.'

'Over a mile in the heat of the day?'

There was a suggestion of mockery in his question.

'As much as that d'you think?'

I raised my voice slightly.

'You know it's at least a mile.'

He said nothing.

'Did you take them to the College of Technology?'

He shook his head. 'No,' he said.

'The Trade Centre?'

'No.'

'The Teaching Hospital?'

'No.'

'The Women's Training College?'

'No.'

'The House of Assembly?'

'No.'

'But you did show them shanty town and the mammies dancing in the market?'

'Yes, I did do that.'

Bowcott broke the strained silence.

'As a matter of fact they said they didn't want to see anything else when I met them at the Remand Home.'

'You saw to that; you made them so hot and thirsty they'd had enough.'

Bowcott passed a hand over his face.

'Just about, just about, I suppose you might say that.'

His stratagem seemed childish.

'O.K.,' I said tartly, 'I get it. But I don't think you've been very clever.'

He met my eyes coolly. 'No?' he said politely with raised eyebrows. 'No?'

The gin I had drunk at Government House had gone amiss and I was tired and hungry. I spoke with a quick spurt of temper.

'Because you were too lazy, or too astute, or something, they saw nothing of what's been done in the place. You in your bloody wisdom contrived it.'

He flushed and pushed his face forward.

'You're like the others—eye wash, eye wash, eye wash all the bloody time. You encourage these people. They're like a girl who conceals a gin-stinking uncle forgetting that one day he's bound to walk in and fall flat on his face in front of her boy friend.' Bowcott paused. 'Your concrete edifices are nothing—they see them everywhere. Let them see the things the people are not so proud of and in any case,' he added, 'I'm not a Cook's guide.'

I spoke firmly. 'Listen, Bowcott,' I said, 'you and I do just what we are told these days, not what we think we ought to do, and what's this I hear about you and Sturt?'

He looked back at me with a faint smile.

'What about Sturt?' he said.

'You seem to have given him offence.'

'How?'

His manner was guarded. I felt myself losing patience again.

'Did you talk to him at all?'

He shrugged his shoulders. 'He's a fatuous little man; he boasted that in three years he travelled more than ten thousand miles in Africa.'

'Well?'

'I asked him if he had learned anything in that time.'

'What did he say?'

'Nothing, he didn't speak to me again.'

'You were a bit dim, weren't you?'

Bowcott yawned. 'I don't know, maybe. What's it matter anyway?'

'I don't know,' I said, 'but remember we don't touch this sort of thing again. The Council of Ministers from now on.'

Bowcott picked up keys, cigarettes and lighter and slipped some files into a brief case.

'They're welcome,' he said with a sour grin, 'they're welcome.' He looked at me questioningly. 'Was there anything else you wanted to talk about now?'

'No, that's all,' I said.

CHAPTER XVII

The big American car pulled up under the *porte-cochère*, the driver opened the door and Edie stepped out.

'Go back to the office and wait for Master,' she told him.

'Where's John?' I said.

'Where do you think?' she laughed, 'where he always is—in that office of his.'

Edie was a true blonde with cobalt blue eyes, a creamy sun-burned skin, a generous full-lipped mouth and a well formed chin. She had a trick of smoothing back her hair when she talked to you. I supposed her to be thirty as I looked at her plump shoulders and the suggestion of a roll of flesh above the strapless bodice of her dress. She had stuck a hibiscus bloom in her hair—a mistake, I thought—and for some reason she wore sun glasses.

'It's nice of you to come, Edie,' I said.

She sat on the wicker chair to the right of a low table on the verandah and put her sandalled feet on a pouffe. 'Am I the only guest?' she cried in mock alarm.

'I'm the one who should be nervous,' I said. 'What'll you drink, Edie?'

'Nervous of me, darling, nonsense.' She took a cigarette from the box on the table, 'God knows I'm harmless. Can I have a gin and lime, please?'

'Gin and lime,' I told Ali.

I lit Edie's cigarette and poured out whisky and water for myself.

'I always admire your tiles when I come here,' she said.

I looked at the black and white marble.

'There used to be a lot of them about. They say they were brought out as ballast by the Portuguese slavers.'

Edie got her cigarette drawing and then sipped her drink.

'When's Hilda coming out?' she asked.

'Not this tour. There's nowhere she can leave the children.'

She tapped ash off her cigarette.

'I don't understand people like you,' she said. 'You give up too much. You might as well be in gaol or a convent or something. I don't get it. Life's too short.'

'Maybe you're right. It's too late to change our arrangements. Someone's got to make a home for the children.'

'You're wrong, you know,' Edie said earnestly, 'you are dead wrong. Anyone can look after children but only a wife should look after a husband, and if she doesn't the chances are someone else will.'

'That's what they say,' I said.

'Well, why don't you do something about it? Two people like you oughtn't to be separated so much. It's not right.'

I was almost apologetic.

'Maybe next tour we'll make other arrangements.'

'You won't,' she jeered. 'I know you two. Why don't you dump your children in a boarding school like we do and think of your-selves a bit?'

I was beginning to wonder how I could change the subject when she fell silent.

'Edie, I want to ask your advice about something,' I said. 'It's a delicate subject but you can help me better than anyone.'

'Well, shoot, what are friends for?'

I touched the bell for more drinks.

'Two married couples, black husbands and white wives, came by the mail-boat and have asked me for help. It's the first time I've come up against this sort of thing.'

Edie gulped her drink and took a cigarette.

I snapped my lighter and offered a light.

'Go on,' she said.

'I've seen young doctors and lawyers with white wives at the cinemas and in the shops who are making a very good go of it, but I can see no future for the people who've been to see me. One was an invalid seaman, and the other a failed student with a school-teacher wife.'

'Can I have another drink, please?' Edie said.

'Yes, of course—I'm so sorry.'

She took the decanter and poured out a lot of gin and added a dash of lime juice. She shuddered when she sipped the drink, then put down the glass and leaned across the table and touched my arm.

'You don't mind if I call you Jack, do you?' she said.

'No, Edie, of course not,' I said. 'Nobody does but I wish you would.'

'Listen, Jack, why do you worry about these people, let them get on with it.' Her voice became suddenly harsh. 'They are just people and nobody forced them to marry and come out here. They can stop in England and get children's allowances, national assistance, out of work pay and all the rest of it. They're free agents. Forget about them.'

'Edie, I daresay you're right, but what you say doesn't help me. I've got these people sitting on my office doorstep and I've got to do something about them.'

She was silent and then spoke wearily. 'Yes, I see what you mean. You can take it from me there's no future for those women out here.'

'What do you mean?'

Edie ignored my question.

'Jack, you don't think there is anything wrong in a white woman marrying a black man, do you?'

The turn in the conversation disturbed me and I reflected that I didn't know Edie as well as I thought I did.

'No, Edie,' I said. 'A marriage like that need be no more chancy than a marriage between people of the same race; if a couple like each other and know what they are about, why shouldn't it work?—in fact, we know it can. It's got nothing to do with being right or wrong and it's certainly no one else's business.'

Edie was silent; she had become withdrawn. Four or five cars passed the house. It was nearly eight o'clock. I supposed there was a party on somewhere.

Ali came out to empty the ash trays and to decant more gin.

A trader in a dirty white gown and a fez kicked off his slippers and edged along the verandah towards us. His boy stood a little apart with a large bundle on his head.

The trader repeated a greeting and bowed slightly. 'I have some very nice things here,' he said. 'I sell very cheap to you master. Maybe you like to buy something for madam?'

Edie laughed.

'On your way, my friend,' she said. 'We've seen all you've got plenty times.'

'Do not be impatient,' he said, 'I have many new things to show you. I came here first so you could see. Bring the things,' he told the boy.

The trader sat cross-legged on the tiles slowly untying the bundle. With dramatic deliberation he spread out the sheet.

'Ivory from the Congo, very cheap.' He gave the crude carvings a front place on the sheet. 'Ah, now here we have Benin brass work and leather from Nigeria, very good handbags and wallets and these pouffe covers. And camel hair blankets from French country, good for the bed when it's cold. All very cheap. Look at this thorn carving.' He held up the figure of a woman carrying a child. 'Isn't that beautiful, and this ebony work from Dahomey. You like one of thess ebony heads?'

He went on without stopping, picking up and putting down what he offered for sale. Then he looked from Edie to me and spoke as though he were doing us a favour.

'What would you like?' he asked.

'There's nothing new there,' Edie said easily. 'Master's been in this country a long time. Why do you come here with such rubbish?'

He started to plead.

'On your way,' I told him.

He suddenly laughed. 'Master is a great man, I must not annoy him.'

He repacked his bundle crossing the sheet over and knotting it carefully. The boy lifted it up to his head and went down the steps.

The trader ceremoniously took his leave.

'I will return when I have something worthy of master.' He pushed his feet into his slippers and followed the boy.

Edie broke a brief silence.

'You're not broad-minded or decent, are you, Jack?' she said.

'No, far from it.'

'You've nothing to do with the London School of Economics or the Fabian Society or the British Council or anything like that?'

'Do I look it?'

'No, I can't say you do.'

We smoked in silence. I found it difficult to bring the conversation back to my problem and I began to hope that John would soon come to take Edie home.

'I'll tell you something, Jack,' she said, as though she had been thinking. 'Marriage to an African out here can only work if he's a good provider. If the woman's going to survive at all she's got to have a house, furniture and one or two servants; she's got to have a car of some sort and enough house-keeping money to get the kind of food she's used to; and another thing, she's got to have enough money to go back home when she needs a change. This country's not like England, but girls with a training can get jobs here if they are not having babies, and if their husbands get good pay they're O.K., and let's face it—many of them are better off than they ever thought they'd be. I am, for one—John's Senior Crown Counsel and everyone says he'll be the first African Attorney-General and what's more important, he's a good husband. We've been through a lot together. . . .'

Edie's voice broke and she started to cry. I shifted uneasily wondering what I should do.

'I hope I have said nothing to upset you?' I said.

She took a handkerchief out of her bag and dried her eyes. She put away the handkerchief and clicked the bag.

For twenty minutes Edie did most of the talking. She lit a fourth cigarette. 'I've never talked like this to anyone before,' she said.

'It's most interesting,' I said and then added what normally I would not have dared to say. 'You've adjusted yourself wonderfully well and made a great success of your marriage.'

'Oh, it's not at all bad—I've been very happy with John. Sometimes on leave we run into trouble. We book rooms by letter or telephone and when we arrive they sometimes suddenly discover the room is wanted.'

'When they see John is black?' I said.

'Yes, of course, what else?'

'Has it happened often?'

'Often enough, and in a different way it was just as bad when we took the children to a nursery school near Hayward's Heath and the woman said "I wasn't expecting a coloured gentleman" as though John was a tame baboon; she asked him if he spoke English as if it was a trick of some sort. She ignored me and didn't give John a chance to say anything. "Everyone's welcome here irrespective of race, creed or colour," she said. I could have kicked her in the teeth.'

Headlights swept over the garden as a car turned up the drive. Edie stopped talking, and then added, 'this looks like John.'

It was late and anyway I was unwilling to go over the subject again.

'Tell me what I ought to do,' I said as I stood up.

'About those people?'

'Yes.'

'Send them back to England.'

'I can't make them go even if I had the money for their passages.'

'Well, give them the chance, if you can; it's up to them after that.'

I switched on the *porte-cochère* light. Calder must have sent his driver home because he was alone. He looked tired.

'I am so sorry I'm late, Mr Wood,' he said.

I put a hand on his shoulder and laughed; he was notorious for his prodigious capacity for work and lack of punctuality.

Edie called out from the verandah 'don't call him Mr Wood, he's Jack to us now.'

Calder followed me to the chairs. He had a small bald patch on the crown of his head and the shortly cut fuzzy hair at the sides was prematurely white. There was probably an Hamitic strain somewhere in his ancestry as his features were finer than those of most coast negroes.

'Hello, John,' Edie said, 'just remembered you've got a wife?'

'Hello,' he said amiably giving her a quick look. And then added with a smile 'You're plastered, dear.'

'Plastered?' she said with an indignant inflection. 'Plastered!— did you hear what he said, Jack?'

He remained standing.

'Sit down, John,' I said, 'and have a drink.'

He looked at his wrist watch.

'It's half past nine, we ought to go,' he said.

'Just one for the road.'

For some reason he looked at his watch again.

'Could I have some Coca Cola, please?'

Edie disappeared into the house while John sipped his drink. She removed the hibiscus bloom and repaired her make up while she was away. She refused another drink but took a cigarette.

'I've been wanting for a long time to ask you something,' Calder said. He pointed towards the garden. 'How do you manage always to have such beautiful cannas?'

'The secret is horse manure,' I said.

'Horse manure—dear me,' he said, 'as easy as that.'

'Yes, but it is no good if it's fresh. It must be composted and plenty of it.'

'Horse manure!' said Edie incredulously. 'Listen to them, for God's sake.'

Calder ignored her. 'Where can you get it,' he said.

'Send a lorry and some labourers to the Polo Club Stables.'

'Would you kindly ask if I can have some?' he said.

'No, I will not, John,' I said. 'The secretary is George Bolitho and he works for Shell. You must ring him tomorrow and tell him you will be sending for a load.'

'Of course, you must ask him yourself,' Edie said. 'Don't be ridiculous.'

'Ah, well,' Calder said.

He stood up. 'Come on, Edie, it's time we went home.'

'I'm ready, Mr Future Attorney-General,' she said taking his arm and turning to me she added, 'Jack, we must love you and leave you.'

I opened the car door for Edie.

'Come and see us soon,' she said.

CHAPTER XVIII

I got out of bed, bathed and dressed. Sleep had relieved me of doubts and as I ate breakfast I became more sure that what I intended to do was right.

Instead of turning in at my office I drove on to the Secretariat. Impatience had made me too early; the official bus bringing private secretaries from Muda followed me into the compound and clerks were just dismounting and pushing their bicycles through the main gates. When I climbed the staircase the Financial Secretary's messenger told me Barlow was not in his office; he gave me the *Courier* and suggested I wait. I stared at the shipping in the harbour. A tanker, low in the water, came smartly in with the morning tide making for the oil wharf. The harbour ferry tied up and passengers crowded down the wide gangway on their way to work. The *Amelia Buckland* moved steadily away from her moorings to start another day in her endless task of dredging the fairway. It seemed as if I had seen it all a thousand times before. I glanced at the paper. 'Monster Mass Meeting of Protest,' I read in banner headlines and below in smaller print "'Hungry men are angry men", says Alefa Bula, Railway Union Boss.' I felt no wish to read about the railway. The local press had long debased superlatives. I looked at my watch and found five minutes had passed. Sitting about waiting for Barlow was no way to start a day. Five minutes later I lit a cigarette and opened the paper. I saw my name in a two inch column box of heavy type headed 'Reader you may well ask'. It was not a leader; it was a presentation of tabloid journalism.

'*Our legislators in their wisdom,*' I read, '*have appropriated a substantial part of our revenue to encourage the indigenous inhabitants of Belemba and the surrounding districts to help themselves in commercial, industrial and agricultural enterprise and they have placed the responsibility for disbursing these funds in the able hands of our Minister of Development. We make no apology for reminding our readers that we advocated this measure no less than seven years ago but an imperialistic government of alien officials abetted by African stooges—men who had sold their birthright for a mess of white man's pottage—saw no good in our proposals. Those days have passed and we have won the first fruits of our struggle for freedom; today we have a legislative assembly composed of a majority of our own elected representatives, but alas the putrefying dead hand of white officialdom still lies across our affairs. We hold no brief for Mr Gabriel Dufu—it is enough for us that he is a law abiding patriotic citizen. Like other thoughtful people, he recognizes that malnutrition and dirty food are twin evils in the lives of many of our people. He sees it as his duty to serve the under-privileged, the less fortunate of our fellow men, by producing cheap wholesome food of high nutritional value under scrupulously hygienic conditions. Surely, it was for such a scheme as this that our legislators decided that the taxpayers—our money—should be lent, surely the Honourable Mr Xanadu Cairngross, M.L.A., our able Minister of Development, would bless this enterprise. What then is holding it up? Mr Dufu is not a rich man but he has faith in his project and is willing to invest his savings in it but he needs more money—that is why he asked the Belemba Development Board for a loan. The advisory committee supported Mr Dufu's application but for some reason the final decision rests with the civil servant, a paid official. This official chose to flout the advice of his committee and has refused Mr Dufu's application. Who is this official?—he is one John Gledhill Wood who at present occupies the office of Provincial Commissioner, Belemba. By what right does this official oppose the wishes of the people? by what right does he obstruct a worthy enterprise? READER YOU MAY WELL ASK!'*

I dropped the paper. It was an adroitly shaped piece with a malicious twist, and its falsity outraged me. Dufu entered government service from school but after a few years had resigned under pressure. Later he had worked for the African Trading Company and lastly for Curtis Millicrap the contractors. There was now no one in the town who would give him work and he was making a living out of politics, organizing petitions and becoming active on the hooligan fringe of NUDA. Dufu came to me for an unsecured loan of £2,000 to install power-driven corn mills. He had no detailed scheme and no proposals for loan repayment. The application was impertinent and Dufu laughed when I rejected it. Munga, the Chief Clerk, came into my room after he had gone. 'That man's a rascal,' he said, 'I hope the Board are not lending him anything; if they are they'll never see it again.'

I picked up the paper again and was re-reading the piece when Barlow appeared.

'Seen this?' I said.

He laid a briefcase on his desk and then took off his jacket and hung it on a peg.

'I never read those papers,' he said, 'you'd soon be round the bend if you took any notice of what they print.'

He sat behind his desk and filled a pipe from an oiled silk pouch. Barlow had got a saddle nose by boxing at Cambridge; this and a prognathous jaw and beetling eyebrows gave him a rugged appearance.

'I hope you haven't been waiting long,' he said.

I told him about the white women and their black husbands.

'As I see it there's only one thing to do,' I said. 'We must offer these people the chance of going back to the U.K. on the understanding that they'll get no special consideration if they remain here.'

Barlow drew on his pipe. 'I see what you mean,' he said, 'but where are you going to find money for passages; that's your problem.'

I was nettled by his obtuseness.

'I want an allocation of funds from you for that,' I said distinctly, 'enough for four single third-class passages and two halves.'

Barlow looked startled; he put down his pipe in an ash tray.

'It's not possible, old boy, a year ago, yes, but not today. My Finance Committee consists entirely of African-elected members.' He picked up his pipe and pointed the stem at me. 'Do you know, we've had to stop grants to Boy Scouts, Y.M.C.A., and to the Mission to Seamen. Anything to do with Europeans is out these days.'

His face fell into grim lines. I returned his gaze. It was always like this, I thought. I was perplexed and angry. There was always difficulty of some sort.

'Can't you try?' I said. 'What does the committee suppose will happen to these white women?'

His pipe had gone out. Barlow looked at me and replied as he held a match and puffed.

'They couldn't care less, old boy; you can take it from me, they couldn't care less.' He made a gesture. 'After all, why should they?'

I fell silent for a moment and Barlow continued in a conciliatory tone. 'You wouldn't believe how difficult things are today.'

'No?' I said frigidly.

I returned his gaze and detected fleeting uncertainty. 'Can't you try?' I pressed and saw him beginning to weaken.

'Frankly, I don't like it,' he said, 'but if I put up a few things for them to shoot down and agree to something they want, I might get it through.'

I stood up to go. 'You'll do your best, I am sure,' I said.

'I'll give you a ring on Thursday. Mind you, I can't promise anything.'

He unstrapped his briefcase and drew out red striped secret files. His gesture was ostentatious.

'Thank you very much,' I said.

He began writing and made no reply.

I left him and passed on my way down the stone staircase to the court yard where I had left my car. I wondered if I should do anything about Dufu as I drove back to my office.

The telephone in Miss Malling's room rang repeatedly. She had complained of toothache and had gone to the dentist. I pushed open the door and picked up the handpiece. Barlow's Secretary asked me to hold the line. I had heard nothing from him on Thursday and it was now Friday and I was afraid that he had failed.

'It's O.K. old boy,' he said. 'It's in the bag. I've just signed authority for you to spend up to £300.'

He brushed aside thanks and rang off. I put down the telephone and then dialled Aston Beauchamp Lines and reserved third class accommodation for four adults and two children on the next homeward-bound mail-boat. I returned to my room and sent for Mr Munga. I told him to have the people in the office by ten o'clock in the morning.

I had not seen them for a month.

'I've got something to tell you,' I said when they were seated. 'It's not an offer of work and I doubt whether I shall ever have one for you—at least not for the sort of work you would like.'

I caught Sangu watching me with narrowed eyes.

'Why have you brought us here then?' he asked. He shook off his wife's hand. 'What's the idea of wasting our time?'

'Be quiet,' Mrs Suma said angrily, 'we want to hear what he's got to say.'

Sangu shot a supercilious glance at her. 'God give me strength,' he muttered.

'This is not an offer of work,' I told them again. They listened with close attention while I spoke as gently as I could. 'What I have to offer are passages back to England for anyone who wants to take them. Nobody is bound to go but those who don't mustn't expect special consideration because they happen to be a European.'

Mrs Suma replied immediately. 'We'd like to go back as soon as possible.'

'What about you, Mr Sangu?'

He said nothing at first, but when he did speak his voice was quiet.

'Are you suggesting my wife and I return to the United Kingdom?' he said.

He waited watchfully for my reply.

I shook my head.

'I am not suggesting anything,' I said patiently, 'I am only telling you that there is a passage available for you both.'

He pulled his chair closer to my desk.

'I don't understand,' he said with reflective emphasis, 'this is my own country. Why should I want to leave it after being away so long?'

Mrs Suma interrupted to ask if they could leave. I nodded and they got up; the two children looked back as they went out.

'You haven't answered my question,' Sangu reminded me.

'Mr Sangu,' I said wearily, 'I don't want to argue. I've told you, and the other two, that I'm not able to offer you work—at least not with the sort of pay you would accept—I wish I could.

148

Instead, I'm saying that I can offer you a passage back to the U.K. where you and your wife might be more comfortably off than you would be here. That's all.'

Sangu put his arms on my desk and leaned forward.

'Your suggestion is monstrous, monstrous.'

I caught the fanatical look I had seen before.

'Very good,' I replied. 'If you don't want to accept the offer, there is no more to say.'

Sangu stood up. 'Come on,' he said to his wife, but she remained seated.

'What's the matter with you?' he said.

'I want to go back to England,' she said.

Her face was thinner than it had been a month before. There were dark lines under her eyes. She had a strange feverish animation, and patches of red showed on her cheek bones.

He shouted, 'What do you mean?'

'You heard what I said. I'm going home. You've made no arrangements for me. We've got no money and there is nowhere for me to have my baby.'

She started to cry. Sangu looked angry.

'If you go, you needn't come back,' he said.

She shrugged her thin shoulders; her indifference exasperated him.

'And by that I mean you needn't come back now—today.'

She sat silently looking down with her hands in her lap

'You needn't worry,' I told her. 'One of our welfare workers will take care of you until you sail.'

Sangu's mouth fell open.

'How dare you separate husband and wife?'

'Mr Sangu,' I said very slowly. 'I'm not separating husband and wife, you and your wife must choose as you like. I wish I had more acceptable suggestions to make to you.'

'Oh, no,' he said. 'Oh, no, you are the agency coming between my wife and me. You are directly responsible for separating us. Just because I am an African and she is a European you are making this trouble.'

I passed my hand over my face.

'Please be quiet,' I told him, 'I'm only trying to help you.'

'Quiet!' he shouted, 'when you are breaking up my marriage.'

Sangu's raised voice brought Miss Malling and Bosa to the door.

Sangu looked wildly from me to Bosa.

'Be very careful, policeman,' he cried, 'if you lay a hand on me I'll sue you.'

Bosa was unmoved by the warning. He touched Sangu's arm.

'Come on, my friend,' he murmured gently, 'don't make trouble here, please,'

Sangu shook off Bosa's hand and made a gesture of brushing his coat sleeve. He looked back from the door. 'You won't get away with this, when we get independence you'll be the first.'

Miss Malling came in after he had gone.

'Are you all right, Mr Wood?' she said. 'Would you like some coffee?'

I smiled at her concern for me. 'Tell Miss Orchard to arrange something for Mrs Sangu until the mail-boat goes.'

I lit a cigarette and wondered whether I had done right. I smoked half the cigarette and rubbed it out; worry would change nothing. I took a file from the heap on my desk.

CHAPTER XIX

The morning had been hot and I had worked late; it was half past three when I pushed back my chair after lunch.

'I'm going to my bed,' I told Ali, 'put out tennis clothes and bring tea at four.'

I turned on the ceiling fan, undressed and lay on my bed. I woke out of deep sleep when Ali came in. A teapot, milk jug, cup and saucer stood on a tray at the bedside. For a few moments I did not feel like talking.

'Pour out tea,' I said.

He filled the cup.

'What's the time?' I asked when I had taken a sip.

'Half past four,' said Ali and then went on crossly as if it were my fault he was late, 'there's a man waiting to see you.'

'Run a cold bath,' I said.

I took another sip, drank again and put down the cup.

'More tea,' I said.

Ali poured a second cup, turned off the bath tap and went to a cupboard for tennis clothes.

'Why didn't you tell him to go to the office in the morning?'

'I did tell him, but he refused to go.'

I slipped off the bed and went to the bathroom.

'Well, I've no time to see him now,' I said.

I was fresher for the cold bath and towelling. I pulled on white clothes, checked my bar-tickets, stuffed a pound note in my pocket to get more, took my racket and a sweater from Ali and went downstairs. The car was under the *porte-cochère*. I opened the off-side front door to dump the gear on the seat then I saw a man in an embroidered gown and round cap coming towards me. It was the blacksmith from Tosho. He might have come in by lorry to Belemba but he must have walked three miles up to Muda. I wondered how he had found the house.

151

'You've come a long way,' I said. 'How's the baby?'

He smiled. 'He is fine,' he said, 'very fine.'

He looked over his shoulder and I followed his gaze to the woman. She was bright-eyed and her skin was shining with health.

'Is it a man baby?' I said as I peered at the sleeping infant.

'Yes, he's a man,' she said with a proud smile.

'Let me see him.'

She loosened the cloth and eased the child into her arms and held him out to me.

'He's strong now,' I said.

'Yes, he's strong.'

The child opened his eyes and caught sight of me. The man and woman laughed when he yelled and with playful remonstrance rebuked him.

'He doesn't like me,' I said.

'Ah! yes, he likes you,' the woman said. She tightened the cloth wrapping the infant securely on her back and stood with glowing face not sure what to do next.

A relationship had become established which I could not deny —a relationship which made demands on me. I took out the pound note and gave it to the man. 'Buy palm wine for the naming ceremony,' I said.

The woman knelt gracefully and thanked me; the man pulled off his hat and kicked off his sandals, dropped on to his hands and knees, lowered himself and lay flat on his face before me; then he pushed himself on to his hands and knees again and rose to his feet. I was overdue for tennis but I touched his shoulder and told him to get in my car.

I drove them down Wilberforce Street as far as the Front. The woman thanked me and walked slowly towards the lorry park. The man hesitated and then came round to the driver's door and spoke through the window.

His manner was furtive. 'Master,' he said awkwardly, 'you are number one boss for Belemba?'

'Yes, I suppose I am,' I said.

He looked behind him and up and down the Front and spoke quickly. 'If Nida Binta does not stop preaching somebody will kill him.'

He uttered the warning reluctantly and before I could reply he turned and walked after his wife.

Next morning Herbert Gregg the Commissioner of Police made his Friday call. We might meet two or three times in a week, but we always kept free time to talk on Friday mornings. I had known Gregg so long that a bond existed between us— a bond which made concealment between us impossible.

'Take off your cap, Herbert, and sit down,' I said.

He put his cap on my desk and pulled up a chair. He took out a case from his tunic pocket, offered me a cigarette and took one himself. We had not much to say to each other and when we rubbed out our cigarette ends he stood up.

'Do you know a man named Nida Binta?' I said.

He shook his head as he buckled his belt.

'Should I? he asked as he put on his cap.

'I don't know. I was warned yesterday that if he doesn't stop preaching he may get in trouble.'

Gregg was unmoved.

'Mission splinter groups, I suppose, setting up a rival concern. He'll get slapped if he's not careful. What did you say his name was?'

I repeated it and he wrote it in a note-book; he saluted and went out.

I ate breakfast slowly after Sunday morning service and then finished my weekly letter to Hilda. It was after eleven o'clock when I reached the beach and walked over the Bahama grass above the sand looking for somewhere to sit. White-gowned followers of the Lord's Annointed, a corrupted Christian cult, crouched on the ground in a casuarina grove while their leader, a long-haired man in yellow, faced the sea with outstretched arms. I walked through the casuarinas scuffing dry sea wrack as I went down the beach to the sea. Great green-grey waves rolled in from the ocean breaking with a roar on hard white sand and finishing with a ripple of froth high up on the beach. I stripped, waded into the warm sea and dived under the waves, swimming a stroke or two between rolling breakers before diving again to avoid being tumbled. I had enough and came out. I lay back with my head on the towel and let the sun shine on my body. I would turn red and burn and later in the week my skin would peel but I felt too relaxed and lazy to care. I shut my eyes and dozed, and stress and fatigue seemed to drain out of me into the yielding sand underneath.

Somebody touched my feet and a voice spoke.

'You'll pay for this; won't you ever learn sense?'

I sat up and blinked. Herbert Gregg in bathing trunks, a beach shirt and a straw hat from the market, stared down. I looked up at him, admiring his lean muscular figure.

'Hello Herbert,' I said. 'Where did you spring from?'

'I'm with people called Payne further along.'

'Payne?' I said, 'who are they?'

'You don't know them. I saw you cavorting in the sea and I thought I'd join you.'

I wondered what he had come for.

He sat at my side and drew up his knees. The hair on his chest was turning grey at the same rate as his moustache and the remaining hair on his head.

'I've found out something about that man,' he said.

'What man?'

'Nida Binta, the man you told me about.'

'The renegade mission teacher?'

'He's no mission teacher. He's boss of the League of Enlightenment.'

'Really,' I said, 'what's that?'

Gregg reached behind me and took a cigarette from my tin. I gave him matches. For a few moments he puffed in silence.

'I don't think it's any kind of a racket,' he said. 'He's got some followers who say their object is to free people from fear of old superstitions.'

'Does he know what he's talking about?'

'He's actually a weaver by trade, a big husky man with a couple of convictions for fighting.'

I took a cigarette from my tin. Gregg gave back my matches.

'I don't get it. What's he doing, how's he annoying people?'

'He preaches at night in the streets. One of his henchmen opens a folding table, another lights a lamp and a boy carries a stack of books and lays them on the table in front of him. It's an act, of course, but it impresses the customers. He has worked up a line of talk and preaches about a supreme being he calls the Great

Enlightener. All this is harmless and can't possibly cause trouble but he finishes up by jeering at the pagan cults—provocative talk. He's been initiated into most of them and has got hold of some of the paraphernalia they use in secret rites.' Gregg shook his head. 'There'll be trouble, bound to be sooner or later, it's emotional, they won't stand for anyone treating their societies with contempt.'

I tied the towel round my head. The sun was overhead and getting hotter and I was afraid my scalp would burn.

'What sort of crowds does he attract?'

'About two thousand was reported for last night's meeting.'

'Can't you move on a crowd of that size?'

'They hold their meetings in a *cul de sac* or alley away from main traffic. The crowds go to them and you can't say they cause an obstruction.'

We sat watching surf rolling up the beach with the incoming tide. Three Greek youths ran past with a beach ball.

'You ought to do something, Herbert,' I said. 'That man's sticking out his neck.'

'Do something!' Gregg said, 'just tell me what.'

'He can be told to lay off.'

Gregg snorted.

'He's no saint and maybe he's lacking in sense, but he's got guts. He won't be scared off.' Gregg added in a more conciliatory tone, 'a couple of men will go to the meetings. If there are developments maybe we'll have to do something, but I can't think what.'

A boy with a wet loin cloth came with a basket. I took a florin from a trouser pocket and chose three flat fish. The boy took the coin and moved on without speaking.

'Where did you get your information?' Gregg asked.

'What information?' I said.

'About Binta.'

'I can't tell you, Herbert.'

He regarded me with amused surprise.

'What do you mean, you can't tell me. Are you trying to sell me short?'

'Honest to God, I can't tell you, Herbert. The whole thing's too long and complicated. I'll tell you someday if you must know.'

We stopped talking about Binta and said nothing for five minutes. Then Gregg took another cigarette and got up. He brushed loose sand off the back of his thighs and then took off his shirt and shook it. 'I must go,' he said and then left me.

CHAPTER XX

The humidity was oppressive after the air-conditioning of the house. Nobody was in sight but I drove slowly with deliberate care. There had been nothing but champagne and brandy to drink; the food had been flown out from France. The massive crystal chandeliers, wall mirrors and gilt brocade furniture were like something out of a film set. I was still marvelling at the vulgarity of Hyne's hospitality as I turned up my drive.

Without raising a hand Hyne made £20,000 a year from his agencies and he had put money into cinemas, timber buying and copper mines; he owned the best hotel in the town. He had never married and now at sixty he made his home in Muda with Nina, a beauty of uncertain ancestry he called his housekeeper. He appeared to like me, maybe because I knew the village in Staffordshire where he was born. But it was the first time I had been to one of his parties. Germanacos the Cypriot was there with his wife. An American director of one of the oil companies on a hurried visit to the country came late; his exquisitely-groomed wife laughed a lot and tapped my arm and for some reason called me Mr Brady. A swarthy man with an accent, though he said he was British, asked me to arrange an interview with the Governor; he told me he had come out to buy scrap metal. Fagio, head of the Italian contractors who were building bridges and roads, talked about big game shooting in Ethiopia. There were two other people, a man and a woman whose names I did not hear properly. They all belonged to a world which was strange to me, all except Alabami, the African business man who turned up at most parties. He wore a badge and had a pen clipped in his breast pocket. His tie was held in place by a gold chain. We found common ground in a farce we always played with great solemnity. He would have me believe he attached great importance to the advice I gave him on how to make money. The latest idea was a dance hall with a first-class band and a restaurant.

'The chef?' he said after I had greeted him.

'French or Swiss,' I advised, 'and you'll have to pay him £2,000.'

He looked doubtful. 'Can you get a really first-class man for that? Food is so important.'

'To be safe, make it £2,500,' I said.

He took out his diary, unclipped his pen and wrote, 'Chef, French or Swiss, £2,500.'

Hyne called across the room. He wanted him to talk to the scrap metal dealer. Alabami made a sad grimace, replaced his pen and blew on the wet ink. 'There's not much chance to talk here,' he said, 'may I come round and see you?'

'Of course, Mr Alabami,' I said, 'any time.'

With the exception of Alabami I disliked them all. I felt softened by being in their presence.

I put the car away and walked wearily to the house; my shirt and jacket stuck to my body and more than anything I wanted sleep. I banged the glazed door. The small boy usually waited up for me when I was late, but it was Ali, a blanket hitched over his shoulder, who fumbled sleepily with the lock.

'Is Dula sick?' I said as I pushed passed him.

Ali was now wide awake and glaring at me with out-thrust chin and angry eyes.

'Where have you been?' he said.

He had served me twenty-five years and was growing old, but there were times when I found his impertinence intolerable.

'How dare you speak to me like that,' I said looking down at his pinched face.

He ignored my rebuke.

'That man's here,' he spat out.

I threw my jacket over a chair.

'Don't talk in riddles,' I snapped back. 'What man?'

'This man who come here with woman and baby.'

'The blacksmith from Tosho?'

'Yes, him.'

'Why didn't you tell him to come in the morning?'

'Tell him?' Ali's voice rose to a squeak. 'Tell him? I tell him twenty times but he say no, he must see you now. Now he must see you, he says. The man's crazy. I ask him what he want, he says it's important but can't tell me. He can't tell me.'

'You could have telephoned.'

Ali lowered the lamp and put his hands on his hips. 'Telephone?' he said in a whisper, and then much louder, 'I telephone eight place I can't find you. How can I telephone you if you no tell me where you go?'

'That will do,' I said. 'How long has he been here?'

'He come just after you leave, about eight o'clock.'

'What's the time now?'

Ali switched on the hall light to look at the clock.

'Quarter to two,' he said.

'And he's still here?'

'That's what I say.'

'Tell him to come in.'

'In here?'

'Where else? and bring me some whisky.'

Ali stopped in his tracks. He affected amazement. 'You want whisky now after all the drink you've had?'

I felt my temper rising.

'Just do what you are told with less talk.'

The decanter, the jug and the glass were on a tin tray. I supposed it to be a gesture but I said nothing. He poured out whisky and added water.

'Leave the tray,' I said, 'and tell the man to come in.'

I unknotted my tie and tossed it on to my jacket. The blacksmith kicked off his slippers in the hall and came into the room blinking sleepily in the light. He was wearing a creased jumper and loose cotton trousers. A whiff of stale sweat and palm wine caught me in the throat when he drew near.

'I'm sorry you've had to wait so long,' I said.

He lowered himself and lay flat on his face on the carpet.

I touched his back. 'Get up,' I said.

He made no reply. I had thought of him as a calm person, but now as I looked at him he was moved by some strong emotion. I touched him again and then he stood up.

I pointed to a chair.

'Sit down.'

He clutched his arms across his chest and remained standing.
'They are going to kill Binta tonight,' he said.
I looked at him with incredulity and horror.
'Tonight?' I said. 'If what you say is true, he must be dead now.'
'It's true,' he said.
I told him again to sit down and I went to the desk for paper and pencil.
'Who are they?'
His face worked and he shivered violently. He seemed unable to speak. I took a glass from the cabinet and half filled it with whisky. He held it with both hands and lifted it to his mouth.
'Who are they?' I asked again.
I waited with paper and pencil.
He spoke in a choked voice.
'Abbas of Tosho, Alogawa Saba of Luala and Stamala of Langa.'
'You know certainly?' I said as I wrote.
He looked stricken.
'Yes, I know certainly.'
I stared at him for a moment and then went out to the telephone in the hall.
Gregg replied almost as soon as I had dialled his number. He sounded tired.
'I've got some news about Binta,' I said.
I heard him draw in his breath.
'O.K., O.K., I know,' he said. 'I've just come from the office.'
'He's been murdered?'
'Yes, what else are you ringing about?'
'I can give you the names of the murderers.'
I heard him draw in breath again.
'Hold the line,' he said, 'I'll get some paper.'
He came back. 'O.K., go ahead,' he said.
I read out the names and addresses.
'Are you sure about this?' he said when I had finished.
'Yes, certain.'
'I'll see you in the morning,' he said, and the line went dead.
I returned to the sitting-room. The man sat upright on the edge of the chair opposite clutching a thin cloth hat with his right hand and staring at me as though in a trance. After a few moments of silence he spoke.

'We bring three kola nuts, three peppers, a fowl, a bottle of palm oil, a large calabash of palm wine and a giant snail.' He spoke in an expressionless monotone. 'We take off our clothes and every man, one after the other, bows down before the *pupedo*.'

I leaned forward straining to hear. His voice had dropped and he spoke huskily in the Bugi dialect.

'*Pupedo?*' I said, 'what's that?'

His mouth fell open and he looked surprised. My interruption displeased him. He tilted his head and glowered at me with hooded eyes.

'It's a crocodile skull with shells fixed on it,' he said. 'When we meet he daub blood on it.'

My heart-beat suddenly raced and blood pounded in my head. In that brief instant of smouldering resentment he communicated something to me which made Binta's murder unimportant. Fatigue and sleepiness left me; I knew I was being told about *Ulo*, a fabulous organization about which neither anthropologists nor police knew anything except that it existed. The poignancy of the experience was unbearable. He was struggling with powerful inhibitions, entrusting me with his life, and maybe that of his wife and child too. I overcame an impulse to silence him.

'Continue,' I said, but it was some moments before he spoke.

'We cut off the tip of the snail shell and dip the middle finger in the moisture and rub it over our heads. We pour palm oil on the ground in front of the *pupedo*. We sing and clap our hands and dance to drumming.'

He told me about elaborate ritual, the titled officers of the cult and about a complex language of signs and pass words. Much of what he said was incomprehensible and sometimes he dropped his voice and was inaudible. Fifteen minutes passed and he fell silent, shifting uneasily in the chair and staring about the room with an air of surprise. I poured out half a glass of whisky for him and took the same for myself. He shook when he gulped the neat spirit and put down the glass.

I asked the question with studied unconcern. 'Did Binta belong to the cult?'

He looked perplexed. I poured out another half glass of whisky for him and sat waiting for him to speak. He put his hand round the glass but did not drink. He seemed to have forgotten his annoyance.

'We meet every nineteen days just after midnight. About twenty days ago our master said Binta must be punished for revealing our secrets. He said he must come to the next meeting.'

'Did he come?'

'He insulted our cult and said he would never come again to the lodge.'

'Continue,' I said.

'At our meeting twenty-one days ago the master sent three men to fetch him. They went off in the dark sounding a bull roarer and crying "Trouble O, Trouble O".' He lifted up the glass and looked into it and put it down again without drinking. 'Binta beat them with a stick and drove them away. We had a meeting two days ago. We were told to wait in the outside place while six of the big men went to the small place inside. The master told me to bring in five fowls. I carried them by their tied legs, three in one hand and two in the other.'

He took up the whisky and shivered again as he gulped it. He put down the glass and drew his right hand across his mouth.

'Yes?' I said.

'They gave me a knife. "Cut their windpipes" they said, "and if they die face up on their backs Binta can go free, if they die any other way he must be killed." One by one I cut the windpipes of the fowls. They fluttered about and then died on their sides. The master sprinkled blood on the *Pupedo* and told me to go.'

'Yes?'

'I waited with the others outside. Then a voice spoke—"Nida Binta has betrayed this secret and powerful cult and has defied an order to be judged by this lodge. Abbas, Saba and Stamala are ordered to kill him", then we all shouted "kill him! kill him!"'

I poured out a drink and lit a cigarette. He looked drowsy.

'Go on,' I said.

'We cooked the fowls with the peppers and snails and ate the food and drank palm wine. After that we danced. When it started to get light everyone went home to his house.'

'That was two days ago?'

He yawned and nodded. 'Yes, two days ago.'

He slumped in the chair breathing noisily in deep sleep. I shook him but he showed no sign of rousing. I took another drink, lit a cigarette and went outside. Stars shone brightly out of a clear sky; it was much cooler and I shivered. I finished the cigarette and flung the stub on the lawn and went indoors. The man was sleeping where I had left him. I put a stopper against the open door and with lights blazing on the ground floor I dragged myself upstairs to my bedroom. I threw off my clothes and got under the net.

Sleepiness and fatigue pressed on me like a weighted blanket; to wake and move was a struggle but the telephone rang insistently. My limbs would not respond when I tried to get up, my head throbbed with a sickening pain behind my eyes and when I did sit up, I felt giddy. It was half past three when I left the man asleep in the chair. After champagne and brandy it had been unwise to drink half a bottle of whisky and smoke so much.

Ali was taking the call downstairs when I picked up the telephone. I told him to get off the line and then Gregg's voice came through.

'I hope it's not too early for you?' he said.

It was still not quite light and I had to peer at the watch on the table.

'It's quarter past six,' I said.

Instead of the amused tolerance with which he usually spoke, his voice was excited.

'I've just got in. I've got something to tell you. I'll be round in about fifteen minutes.'

'Like hell you will,' I said. 'Make it an hour.'

I replaced the telephone. Ali came in and tossed up the net.

'Make strong tea and bring aspirin,' I said.

'You left the door open last night,' he accused me, 'and all the lights on.'

'Never mind about the door, get tea,' I said.

'You want tea in bed?' he asked querulously as he picked up my dress trousers.

'That's what I said.'

He was about to say more but our eyes met and he remained silent. He took the studs and cuff links out of my shirt, picked up my underwear and tossed it and the shirt into the basket. Then he moved leisurely downstairs for the tea.

I dribbled sauce on the avocado pear and gouged out a spoonful.

Through the open window in the hibiscus bush at the side of the drive I saw a sunbird, not more than two inches long, with blue-green crown, gold-green upper parts, blue metallic throat and deep crimson breast—it was an exquisite little creature. It moved rapidly from flower to flower, sometimes hanging upside down as it inserted its beak and sometimes hovering with rapid wing beats as it inspected a bloom. There were steps on the gravel and with an angry *tweet* it flew off.

'Hello, Herbert,' I said when Gregg came in, 'have some breakfast?'

He sat down facing me across the table, unshaven and tired looking. He shook his head. 'I'll have a cup of coffee.'

'Get another cup,' I told Ali.

I filled the cup and passed it to Gregg. He stirred the coffee and then took out a cigarette case.

'Do you mind if I smoke?' he asked.

I shook my head. 'Go ahead.'

I finished the avocado and Ali took away the plate. I looked across at Gregg.

'Well?' I said.

He tapped cigarette ash into his saucer.

'That was a wonderful tip you gave me,' he said with a faint smile.

Ali brought me toast and a boiled egg.

I broke the top of the egg. 'Tell me about it,' I said.

Gregg sipped the hot coffee.

'The duty officer telephoned at ten o'clock. I was playing bridge at the Fergusons. He told me a man had been murdered at Bari. It was a routine report but I was fed up with bridge and had a sudden impulse to go down to the station.'

I took a mouthful of egg.

'It was Binta?'

Gregg nodded. 'Yes.'

I looked at him saying nothing at first, and then remembered what he had said on the beach.

'I thought you had men standing by at his meetings.'

Gregg's face hardened.

'They ran when the trouble started; they're for the high jump all right.'

'Tell me about it.'

'You know the Bari district?'

'The slummy area between High Street and the Front?'

'Yes, where there are all those narrow streets and old houses.'

'I know.'

'They're a strange lot there, they'd told Binta to keep away.'

I finished the egg, took some toast and marmalade and poured out more coffee for Gregg.

'He had been saying too much?'

Gregg paused to light a new cigarette from the stub.

'I suppose so,' he said.

'But he had his meeting?'

'Yes, he had his meeting. There must have been a big crowd, nearly two thousand, and most of them hostile.'

I poured out another cup of coffee and asked Gregg for a cigarette.

'He had guts,' I said.

Gregg grunted. 'He was asking for trouble.'

'Go on,' I said.

'A man standing at the front of the crowd asked him whether sterility in women could be cured by the god *Poro*. It was a put up question. Binta sneered at him and asked what good was a handful of stones. Another man shouted and soon there was pandemonium. A bull roarer sounded above the din and someone screamed "Ala Kako O". The crowd stampeded and made off. A few of Binta's people remained but ran when three men attacked him. One struck him down with a stick and a second grazed the side of his head with an axe. One of Binta's people, a man named Ubas, stayed on and tried to pull him away by his arms and shoulders, but they beat him about the head. When he made a second attempt they stabbed him. Before he collapsed he saw Binta's head split open and blood spurting out. Ubas's friends found him bleeding in the road and brought him to the station. We got a statement from him before we took him to hospital and from four other people who saw the start of the thing. We weren't getting anywhere until I got your tip. We found the three of them at Stamala's place, a house with a beer licence just outside the town. There was blood on their clothes; there was a fourth man with them drinking gin. The body was trussed up at the back of a fifteen hundredweight truck in the compound. We pulled in the fourth man as an accessory; I reckon he'll come clean, but anyway the case is open and shut.'

Gregg yawned. My head ached with waves of pain. We stood up and went to easier chairs in the sitting-room. Cars passed outside on their way to Belemba. I told Ali to bring fresh coffee. Gregg seemed tired but unwilling to go. I looked at my watch.

'There was another report this morning.' He spoke slowly. 'It might interest you.'

I waited for him to speak.

'Yes?' I said. 'You were saying?'

'The constable on beat duty at the end of the road pulled in a man about four o'clock this morning for suspicious behaviour. He said he had just come from your house and was on his way back to Tosho. He gave his name as Maleto.'

Gregg roused up and looked straight at me.

'Oh,' I said, meeting his gaze uneasily, 'he said his name was Maleto. What happened?'

'I said he could go.'

'Where is he now?'

'In Tosho I suppose.'

'You won't want him as a witness?'

Gregg grinned sourly. 'Witness for what?'

'The Binta case.'

Gregg shrugged his shoulders.

'How can he help us there?' he said.

I made no reply and Gregg stood up.

'I want a few hours shut-eye before I try to do any work today.'

I walked out through the *porte-cochère* to the drive and went with him as far as the road. We stood there for a moment.

'I hope you know what you are about,' he said as he turned to go, 'I don't.'

I gave his arm a friendly squeeze.

'I am not sure that I do either,' I said.

'Watch your step,' he said as he walked off.

CHAPTER XXI

Mathews sent for me. He had no complaint but said he had heard that I tended to be aloof and wanted to advise me. It was important that I should be accessible, forthcoming and ready to go half way to meet people in public affairs.

I asked him to be more precise.

'I always consult the advisory committees,' I said. 'Attendance has fallen off, but that's not my fault. I'm always accessible.'

He stood up and put his hand on my shoulder. He was only a year or two older than I was, and I found the gesture offensive.

'Adopt a flexible attitude. These urban communities are unlike the people you've been used to. You must adjust yourself.'

I was unsettled by my session with Mathews and wondered who had been talking to him.

I pushed open the door to the adjoining room. Miss Malling was cleaning her machine; she had turned it on its side and was dusting it with a soft brush. 'Have you got anything for me?'

She shook her head. 'No, nothing.'

She had on a blue overall.

'I haven't seen you wearing that before,' I said. She peered at the machine and took up the brush. 'Why should you?' she said as she started to work.

For a minute I watched her.

'Do you turn away many callers?' I asked.

She was at once on the defensive.

'I either make appointments or tell you who comes.' She put down her brush. 'Why do you ask?'

'The Civil Secretary says I am too aloof.'

'Rubbish,' she said, and took up her brush again. 'If I may say so you see far too many people.'

Bosa followed me down the passage to the main office.

Mr Munga the Chief Clerk immediately stood up and greeted

me. Only at the height of the hot season he left off a waistcoat. Strong character and intelligence compensated for his lack of education, but he occasionally showed resentment of the young graduates who had passed over him to posts which he thought himself better able to hold. He was inclined to be pompous but I admired him for the gratitude with which he spoke of British officers who had helped him. I returned his polite greeting.

'Are you busy?' I said.

'I am always busy,' he said. 'I have not been home before seven o'clock for weeks.'

'Well, don't overdo it.'

He made a slight bow. 'Thank you, sir.'

'Mr Munga,' I said, 'would you say the public have difficulty in seeing me?'

Munga frowned. 'On the contrary, sir, I think you permit too many liberties with your time. Things were different when Mr Bracey Smith was here.' He shook his head, 'far different, nobody wasted his time.'

He escorted me to the door and I went on to Bowcott's room.

'What about tennis?' I said.

He removed his pipe. 'All right,' he said.

'We'll go straight from here this afternoon.'

I returned to my room and worked until one o'clock and then went back to Muda for lunch.

I returned to the office looking forward to tennis. About three o'clock the sky became overcast. Half an hour later gusts of cool wind came through the windows disturbing my papers; the gusts grew stronger turning the papers into a swirling mass. I locked the windows and rang for Bosa to pick up the papers, then stared at the darkening sky. Flashes of lightning were followed by thunder claps. The wind dropped and rain almost obscured the street below where wayfarers pressed against the walls of the Secretariat for shelter. A low and almost unending rumble of thunder now blended with the rushing splashing sound of the rain. The fierceness of the storm spent itself and the heavy rain gave way to a steady fall. Bowcott came in and joined me at the window.

'Pity about tennis,' he said.

The sky had cleared when I left and there was promise of a fine evening. A few people were on the golf course and I could hear the shouts of the crowd half a mile away on the Football Association ground. The rain had little effect on the sandy soil and we might have been able to play, I thought, as I drove up the road.

It had been an unsettling day leaving me vaguely uneasy but I regained tranquillity as I walked round the garden weeding the lawn and repairing damage done by the rain. Ali came out about half past six to say there was a telephone call. It was Margaret Metcalfe. After we had exchanged greetings she said: 'I really rang up to ask you to supper next Thursday.'

'Isn't there something on that day?'

'H.E.'s having a drinks party for Proclamation Day—come straight on here from Government House.'

I returned to the garden, but almost at once Ali called me again.

I retraced my steps and picked up the instrument a second time. I did not recognize the African voice. I thought there had been a mistake and was about to replace the telephone when I caught the name Dufu.

'You want to see me in High Street tonight?' I said in surprise.

'Yes, Mr Wood, at number 29. It is an important matter about the Development Programme.'

I thought of Mathews's talk about meeting people half-way. My instinct was against it, but I agreed.

'I'll send a car for you at nine o'clock,' Dufu said.

I disliked the suggestion.

'I have my own car.'

Dufu insisted. 'It's not wise for your car to be seen in High Street at night.

Argument would be wearisome and slightly ridiculous.

'All right,' I said.

My forebodings returned to me. My office was the place to see people.

I bathed and had an early supper. At half past eight a small car came up the drive. I could smell the exhaust in the sitting room where I sat waiting.

The driver sprawled in his seat with his face turned away smoking a cigarette.

'Put out that cigarette,' I said.

His rejoinder was inaudible but he kept the cigarette between his lips. He drove very fast along the crown of the road, slower past the police barracks but faster again as soon as he was out of sight of the man at the gate. My office watchman sat on the entrance steps talking to an old woman. The lights of people working late formed an irregular pattern on the dark façade of the Secretariat. He drove slower down Wilberforce Street and as he turned into High Street he pressed on his horn and swore at someone crossing the road. He braked and spoke over his shoulder; 'Dufu told me you get out here.' I pushed down the door handle and before I could ask directions he drove off. A man wearing thong sandals and a cotton gown was urinating into the drain. I waited until he had finished and then enquired 'My friend, where is number 29?'

'You P.C.?' he said.

'Yes.'

'Dufu told me to wait for you—this way.'

I walked behind him. He stopped and watched two men on upturned boxes playing draughts beneath a street light. They played at high speed banging down pieces with noisy clatter and raising shouts of laughter from idlers lounging round the lamp standard.

My guide stopped at a shop with weathered joinery and a sign board fixed over the door 'The International Trading Company and Commercial Agency'. The only sign of business enterprise was an advertisement for an aphrodisiac.

'In there,' he said waving his hand towards the open door, 'go in there and then up the stairs. Dufu's waiting for you.'

A naked bulb hanging from the ceiling spread a poor light through the room and just reached a roughly fitted counter where a boy sat facing the door. He ate with his fingers from a basin of meal, spitting gritty fragments on the floor, then dragging his hands across a dirty vest he slowly turned over pages of a copy of *Life* magazine.

'Mr Dufu here?' I said.

He lifted his chin towards a gap in the counter.

'Through there and up the stairs.'

I passed beyond into the light of a second lamp in a passage and then climbed a staircase. Loud talk punctuated by a burst of laughter reached me from a room above. The noise ceased when I knocked and Dufu opened the door.

Over-enlarged photographs of an African man and woman flanked a pendulum clock on the wall. Green patterned linoleum covered the floor. The chairs, padded with kapok, the table and a glazed cupboard were copies of furniture in government quarters. Net curtains threaded along string draped the windows. The shade of a standard lamp cut off the light into dim and bright on the green washed walls. I felt an irrational sadness. Someone striving for respectability had done their best for the room. I looked beyond Dufu and saw Likema, a middle-aged man who called himself a produce dealer but it was by money lending that he had grown rich. He never attempted to dissemble his dislike for the British. It was his money which had paid for the uniforms and equipment of the Freedom Fighters, an organized group of young hooligans which worked to his orders until it was declared a proscribed organization. Next to him sat the lawyer Bauro, a slightly built man with close set fine features, who had made a good start at the bar but had become unreliable through excessive drinking. He now made an uncertain living fishing in troubled waters, petition writing and accepting work no other lawyers would take. The fourth, Ritelo, a labour boss of some sort, flirted light-heartedly with the World Federation of Trades Unions but did nothing in return for remittances from Warsaw and Prague. He was a hearty man, big and going to fat. There was nothing complex in his character. With an engaging sense of fun he had once frankly admitted to me that he was a rascal and since then I had liked him. I was surprised to see him seated at the table with the three other men.

I looked quickly at each man in turn but said nothing. Dufu then drew out a chair and invited me to sit. He reached for a bottle of White Horse Whisky and stood over me.

'Have a whisky, Mr Wood,' he said and then added, 'or if you would prefer it we've got some cold Heinekens.' He picked up a bottle of beer from the floor. Bauro who had been regarding me with a puzzled expression leaned over the table clutching half a glass of neat whisky in his right hand. Under dark brown pigmentation he looked grey and there were purple rings under his eyes.

'Give him whisky,' he told Dufu. 'You like whisky, don't you white man?' he added, eyeing me in a puzzled manner.

Dufu became busy with the bottle and glass.

'I won't have a drink,' I said. 'I have come here at your request and I would like to hear what you have to say.'

'Oh, pity, pity, pity,' Bauro declared with grotesque dismay; he brightened, 'have a cigarette—that's it, have a smoke,' he suggested. 'Give him a cigarette, Ritelo.'

Ritelo turned the lid on a fifty tin of Capstan, threw the circle of foil on the floor, shook up a few cigarettes and held out the tin.

'No, thank you,' I said. 'If somebody won't tell me why I am here, I shall go.'

There was hostility in Likema's face. Ritelo was embarrassed. Bauro still looked puzzled, staring at me open mouthed and slightly amused. Dufu was the only one who appeared self-possessed.

'I'm sorry, Mr Wood,' he said in a frank open manner. 'I'm sorry our hospitality is unwelcome to you.'

'Skip it,' I said. 'Why did you ask me here?'

He sighed. 'Well, it's really in your own interest. We want to help you.' He looked at the others. 'Isn't that so?'

'Yes, sure, that's right,' Bauro said. 'We want to help you, white man.' He poured himself more whisky. 'Eh, Ritelo, boy, isn't that right, we want to help him, don't we?'

'Yes, that's right,' Ritelo said awkwardly.

Likema scowled when our eyes met and looked away.

'There's a movement growing against you in the town,' Dufu continued. 'There will be a demand for your removal.'

I interrupted him before he could say more.

'What are you talking about?' I said, 'what movement?'

Dufu gave the other three a quick side look and then faced me again with unwavering eyes. 'They are saying you are out of sympathy with the aspirations of the people,' he spoke slowly as though choosing his words, 'they say that the tide of events has overtaken you and that you are out of harmony with the times. They are beginning to say you should go.'

I had got over the first stab of apprehension and was angry.

'Never mind about that, just tell me what it is you have to say.'

Dufu raised his hands in a gesture of good-humoured exasperation.

'Mr Wood,' he begged, 'please don't lose your temper, you

must be realistic.' I said nothing and he went on, 'We are in a position to help you. We can make your Development Programme a great success.'

'My Development Programme, what's that got to do with it?'

Dufu shrugged his shoulders and made a weary grimace. Ritelo moved heavily and leaned forward to take a cigarette from the tin. Bauro laughed as he splashed more whisky into his glass; he slapped Likema's thigh. 'The Development Programme, that's it,' he said. Likema moved his leg but continued to gaze at me.

Dufu smiled wryly. 'Yes, it's the Development Programme we want to talk about.'

A rhinocerous beetle flew through the window straight at the lamp and fell on its back buzzing helplessly on the table. Ritelo reached for it and carefully picked it up. All eyes were on him as with a rending sound he slowly crushed it between his forefinger and thumb. He stood up and tossed the dead beetle through the window. There was a tinny sound of impact as it struck a sheet of galvanized iron in the street below.

'Yes,' I said, 'go on.'

'If the Development Plan is a success, you will get the credit.'

'What about this movement in the town?'

Dufu laughed. 'Oh, that,' he said as if it were nothing, 'we can stop that.'

'Sure we can; it's a cinch,' Bauro said.

Ritelo drew on his cigarette. 'It's up to you, Mr Wood.'

I thought he was trying to be helpful.

'In what way?' I said.

'Well . . .' he began.

Dufu raised his hand. 'We agreed that I should do the talking.'

Likema suddenly came to life.

'Well, get on with it,' he said.

For the first time since I came into the room Dufu appeared unsure of himself.

'Very good, Mr Likema,' he said. 'I'm just coming to it.'

He assumed a business-like manner. 'You have under your control a large sum of money for loans to local enterprises?' He paused waiting for my assent, but I said nothing. 'In the coming week you will receive three different applications for loans of £3,000. If you approve these loans your Development

Programme will be a success and you will enjoy great personal popularity.'

The suggestion was so fantastic I could hardly believe he was serious. A moment passed before I could speak.

'What if I refuse?'

Dufu was no longer suave; his face was expressionless.

'You won't refuse.'

'No?' I said.

'If you do it will be the end of you as far as your future in this country is concerned.'

I stood up.

'Wait a minute, white man,' Bauro struck in huskily, 'don't go.'

'Well?' I said.

'Take it easy, don't be hasty. Do you know why Jimmy Hyne is always praised in the papers?'

Likema spoke furiously.

'You talk too much,' he said. 'I'm a fool to have anything to do with you.'

Bauro yawned. 'What's it matter, he'll never make anything stick.'

'You open your mouth too wide,' Likema rebuked him. 'One of these days you'll get us into trouble.'

'O.K., O.K.,' Bauro said easily, 'anything you say, Papa, anything you say.' He grinned drunkenly at me. 'I never said a thing to you, did I?'

I pushed the chair back and put my hand on the door knob. No one spoke, but as I opened the door and went down the stairs sounds of laughter came from the room. The boy was sitting where I had seen him half an hour before, still fingering the magazine.

The draught players had gone but lights came from a beer shop and somewhere up the road a radio set blared dance music.

I walked to the junction of Wilberforce Street then, after standing there for five minutes, decided to go on to the top of the street to the taxi rank on the far side of the hospital. There was no wind and after the rain the night was humid and still.

I walked up the street to the hospital. There was still a few palm oil dips flickering where women sat at the roadside. Insects swarmed round a lighted display case outside the United

174

States Information Services Reading Room. There was a photograph of a smiling negro in baseball kit, a group of black and white children queueing for polio injections, more black and white children in a class room, an American General clasping the hand of a negro soldier. There were more photographs of the same kind and in large neat lettering across the top the words 'No Colour Bar Here!' A watchman in khaki drill sat on an empty beer case against the wall. He was smoking local leaf in a short-stemmed pipe.

'That's a good pipe?' I said.

He took it out of his mouth, regarded it critically and grinned amiably, 'Yeh,' he said, 'it's a good pipe.'

I gave him a shilling and walked the rest of the way to the cab rank.

I told the taxi driver to take me to Gregg's house. There were four cars in the drive, so I gave Bowcott's address, but found the house in darkness. I told the driver to take me home.

CHAPTER XXII

Cars were parked along the Front for half a mile. Women dressed with special elegance—it was before half past six so they wore hats and gloves—and men in their best suits streamed through Government House gates joining the lengthening queue moving up the drive towards the Governor and his wife.

Gleeson announced guests and then after a handshake and greeting they moved forward on to the main lawn like cattle released into pasture. There were nine hundred present, every-one who had signed the Governor's Visitors' Book in the past year, forming a gay assembly against the bright green grass and the shrubbery.

Ali threaded his way through the crowd and came straight to me. There were about a dozen glasses of a brown fluid on his tray.

'What have you got?' I asked.

He was slightly on ceremony. It was a distinction to be among the outside servants asked to help at a Government House party.

'Rum cocktails,' he said, 'very good.'

I took a glass. It was potent but extremely palatable, a mixture of lime juice and overproof rum and additional ingredients, the secret of Government House steward.

'Yes, all right,' I said, 'I know.'

The drink had quick effect, guests stood relaxed in animated groups or moved about, bright-eyed, looking for friends. More than half were Africans—they increased with every Government House party—well dressed and smiling, a little reserved but ready to talk to anyone who spoke to them. Others bustled about in the crowd with the elaborate assurance of people showing themselves at ease in familiar surroundings.

Mathews, with a glass of lemonade in his hand, stood listening attentively to Pereta while Cairngross, Zadeta, two other

176

Ministers and some NUDA party leaders formed a small group around him.

Edith Calder wore a hat modelled like a dahlia, a close-fitting cream dress and black elbow-length gloves.

'Hi, Jack!' she greeted me.

'You ought to be proud of John,' I said to her.

She flushed with pleasure. 'I am.'

She sipped her drink and turned down her mouth in comic distaste.

'Where is he?' I said.

'He's around somewhere, the poor dear's tired and didn't want to come.'

A woman elbowed her way towards us and stood just behind Edie, a self-possessed important-looking person.

'Someone wants to speak to you, Edie,' I said.

'Mrs Calder,' the woman began, 'I really don't know how to apologize for what happened on Tuesday. Not seeing Mr Calder with you I didn't know who he was. . . .'

Edie cut her off. 'That's all right,' she said, 'quite a natural mistake. You probably thought he was my chauffeur.'

Edie turned to me again but the woman remained standing. 'I wouldn't have had such a thing happen for worlds. You will apologize to Mr Calder for me.'

Edie's face hardened and she said nothing. The woman waited a little longer before she moved off.

'What's biting her?' I said.

Edie snorted. 'She fancies herself. Her husband's in the Development Corporation or International Credit Bank or something like that. They had a drinks party on Tuesday. John dropped me at the door and went off to park the car. That woman asked him what he wanted when he came back—he wasn't allowed to come in for about ten minutes. I went out and found him arguing with a house-boy. I refused to stay.' Edie sipped her drink. 'Silly woman.'

I grinned at her. 'That's not very polite, Edie.'

She grimaced. 'Somebody ought to tell her the time.' Edie took a cigarette from a servant and I snapped my lighter for her.

'Thanks, Jack,' she said. 'I must move round now. Come and see us sometimes.'

Dr Edube Perigo was standing apart with his hand outstretched on the curved handle of a walking-stick near the baobob tree in the corner of the garden. He wore a well-cut dark suit, a grey homburg hat and shining black boots; a gold watch chain stretched over his waistcoat. He was seventy or more and as he stood there, unaware of my interest in him, I caught a glimpse of resignation and calm, almost of detachment, in his lined slightly emaciated face. He had been one of the Governor's nominated members in the old legislature and the first African member of the Executive Council. He had thought it his duty, many people thought wrongly, to stand for election to the new house. The press had pilloried him and in a cartoon in the *Courier* he had been shown with bowed head and outstretched arms mumbling, 'thank you, massa', to a grotesque caricature of a top-hatted white man.

'Good evening, Dr Perigo,' I said.

He turned strong guileless eyes on me and courteously raised his hat.

'Good evening, Mr Wood,' he replied in a deep melodious voice.

Dr Perigo shook his head at the servant but I took another drink and a cigarette. He turned his head to the right and then, as though thinking out loud, he said, 'Times have indeed changed; there are people here tonight I wouldn't have in my house. When I was invited first to Government House thirty years ago it was an honour, but not today. Anyone who calls himself a politician is welcome.'

I followed his gaze. I saw first the tall figure of Mathews and then the Governor now at the centre of the circle. Pereta was introducing Dufu to him and Likema was waiting. A shout of forced laughter followed a remark by the Governor and another came after Dufu spoke.

Dr Perigo broke the silence as we stood idly watching.

'They are very merry,' he said.

'Yes,' I said, and as I spoke there was more laughter and even Mathews smiled. The Governor was gesticulating and looking from one to another in the circle and finally wagged a forefinger at Pereta. Pereta raised his hand in protest and pointed an accusing finger at the Governor and said something which brought renewed laughter. Guests turned and looked at the widening circle. Suddenly the Governor left and moved into the crowd, greeting people and sometimes stopping to talk.

'He's good at putting people at their ease,' I said.

'Yes,' Dr Perigo agreed, 'he does his best.' He spoke with slight irony, though not unkindly, 'but he puts the wrong people at ease.'

We stood in silence and I was wondering how soon I might go when he came out of his thoughts.

'I despair of my people. They have fine clothes, motor-cars, and plenty of money and they regard all these things as important. They lie and bribe and no one thinks the worse of them for it— in fact, silly people are sorry for them if they get into trouble.'

'That's not true, Dr Perigo,' I said, 'you are too severe.'

He looked straight before him and at first made no reply.

'Possibly,' he said slowly, 'but that's how it seems to me. Maybe we are moving too quickly and trying to do overnight what took centuries in your country.'

'Dr Perigo,' I said, 'public morals were very low in England a hundred and fifty years ago.'

'So they tell me,' he said, but not as though he believed it, and I began to feel impatient.

'There is a creative minority in this country which cannot be denied. Progress and change are inexorable. Some people may make capital out of this and some may get hurt, but does that really matter. Wisdom and decency must eventually prevail.'

Dr Perigo transferred his walking-stick to his left hand and laid his right hand on my arm. He smiled. 'I know what you mean, Mr Wood. Don't misunderstand me. Fela Pereta is a young man of the highest principles. His father was my closest friend. Fela still comes to my house to pay his respects. He has many difficulties; it's not easy to hold together a large mixed party. Pilama Mudi's also an upright man. Maybe it's my age. Perhaps I resent the opportunities of youth today, or maybe . . .'

A shriek made us turn. I recognized a secretary from the Labour Department. She was one of three young women looking with shining eyes at a fair-headed young man named Lever who owned a red sports car.

'I stopped when I heard his whistle,' Lever was saying. 'When he came to me I said, "Yes, constable, anything wrong?" '

'Go on Mike,' one of the girls said.

'Old flatfoot saluted and said "Yes suh, this is a one way street suh." "That's all right, sergeant," I said, "I only want to go one way".'

The young women laughed. 'That shook him, Mike,' one of them said.

'You're telling me it did,' Lever shouted. 'By the time he had sorted out that lot I was on my way to the Airport.'

'You're a scream, Mike, you really are,' the first girl yelled and then playfully flicked out his tie.

'Hey, shut up, lay off, can't you,' Lever said. He pushed the girl away and replaced his tie. Almost immediately a pretty dark girl flicked it out again.

I looked at Dr Perigo and without a word we walked along the edge of the lawn and found space near a bed of cannas at the other end of the garden. Late afternoon sunlight had given way to early dusk and suddenly coloured lights appeared in the trees. The buzz of talk grew louder and the band played with renewed animation.

I stayed with Dr Perigo although conversation had lapsed again. Just as I was about to move off he broke the silence.

'Did you follow the trial?' he said.

The trial of Abbas, Saba and Stamala had ended that morning. Two English lawyers and five Africans had appeared for the accused men and at one stage it appeared as though the prosecution might fail.

'Yes, I did,' I said. 'It was a very fair and painstaking trial.'

Dr Perigo grunted and then pointedly, as though he thought I ought to know, he asked 'Who instructed those lawyers?'

It was no doubt idle conjecture by Dr Perigo. Indeed many other people had asked where the money to pay lawyers had come from, but I fancied something sinister about the manner in which he put the question.

'What do you mean Dr Perigo?' I said. 'I suppose their families raised the money, mortgaging their land and borrowing from moneylenders, but why should I know?'

He looked at me and shrugged his shoulders.

'I thought you might know.'

Before I could think of anything to say we were joined by the Bishop. He drew Dr Perigo aside and I left them.

A stab of foreboding made me uneasy. I fancied a suggestion in Dr Perigo's question that I had special knowledge. Though I told myself it was absurd I could not divest myself of uneasiness; the thought persisted that I was entangled in something evil from which I could not escape unscathed.

Conversation rippled over the crowd and there was more laughter. I had stayed so long with Dr Perigo that I felt cut off from the gay little groups around me.

The band broke into the National Anthem and when the music ended guests moved away from the lawn and surged down the drive in an orderly mass. Edie Calder's yellow hat was unmistakable in the light from the lamps on the gates. Leisurely-moving guests looked at me with astonishment as I pushed forward to overtake her.

'John,' I said, 'who instructed the people against you in the trial?' Before he could reply I said, 'it was a man named Likema, wasn't it?'

He returned my gaze with curious eyes.

'It was supposed to be secret,' he said, 'who told you?'

'What did it cost?'

'About eleven thousand pounds, they say.'

'Thank you, John, bye-bye, Edie,' I said.

I turned back to look for my car.

CHAPTER XXIII

Shaded lights inside broke the darkness and threw patches of light on the verandah. The murmur of conversation and a high-pitched voice followed by laughter came through the french windows. Crawley raised his hand and smiled at me. He was talking to a fair rather faded woman. Mrs Bennet, wife of the Director of Public Works, looked puzzled by something Bowcott was telling her. Palmer, the Auditor, in earnest conversation with Metcalfe, frowned slightly as though resenting interruption. Mrs Crawley, looking chic and well groomed, shook her head at a servant offering a decanter. The men got up clutching their glasses when Margaret rose to meet me. A bald fleshy man with a mottled complexion stood at her elbow. There was a red rose in his button hole and a single eye glass hung from a black silk cord down the white waistcoat he wore with his dinner jacket.

'You've not met Mr Peake?' Margaret glanced at him as she spoke. 'I should really say Mr Justice Peake,' she said. 'He's just been transferred from British Guavaland and has come to us as first puisne judge.'

'How do you do?' I said.

'Wood, did you say?' He appeared to be making an effort of memory. 'No, I think not,' he said after eyeing me carefully. 'I don't recall you.'

Margaret turned to the fair woman. 'And Mrs Peake,' she said.

The woman tapped ash from her cigarette and forced a smile at me.

A single piece of polished mahogany to which twelve people could sit with comfort formed the top of Metcalfe's dinner table. It shone in the light of three-branch candelabra showing a trace here and there of the tools of craftsmen who had shaped it. There was artistry in the sprays of correleta looped like a chain down the table and in the frangipane and bougainvillea blooms

182

tucked in cunningly-folded napkins. Margaret had brought out her Waterford glass and best silver.

Margaret faced Peter across the table; she put Peake on her right and I sat on her left facing Mrs Peake on Peter's right. Mrs Peake was still smoking when we sat down and asked for an ash tray. Margaret tilted her head towards Peake, listening attentively. Mrs Crawley on my left told me about their new house at East Grinstead and gave me an account of the holiday they had spent in Norway. She asked about my family and then got into conversation with Palmer on her left. Mrs Peake talked to Peter in a clipped and affected accent. Above the hum of conversation she spoke across the table to her husband.

'Mr Metcalfe knows the Baileys, dear.'

Peake broke off his conversation with Margaret.

'Really,' he said in a fruity voice. 'Neville and Andrea were very close friends of ours in Trinidad.' He then resumed what he was saying to Margaret. There was a break in Mrs Peake's loquacity and when I looked up I was surprised to find her staring at me. I felt slight constraint.

'Were you glad to leave British Guavaland?' I said.

'Oh, dear me, no,' she said. 'We were extremely happy in B.G. Sir Rollo and Lady Skipton were very friendly—very friendly. I suppose we were at Government House on an average twice a week. Sir Rollo insisted on keeping our Friday night bridge four whatever happened—he was a sweetie.'

I waited while a servant poured out wine.

'Why did you leave?' I said when he moved on.

'Why did we leave?' repeated Mrs Peake with a shrug. 'It was just time to move if Francis is to get a C.J. ship. There will be four vacancies in the next five years.' She broke off, smiled and took up her glass.

I looked at her in silence.

'You get a K even if you are C.J. of a place like Zanzibar or Mauritius,' I said.

Mrs Peake smiled. 'Yes, that is so,' she said.

Margaret touched my arm.

'I knew I had something important to tell you. You'll never believe it—we've seen a pair of Hankinson's short-billed honey eaters in the compound!'

'No?' I said, infected by her pleasure. 'Are you quite sure?'

'Yes, quite, quite sure,' she said with a touch of impatience. 'There's no doubt at all. They're nesting in a Jacaranda tree near the boundary. Both Peter and I have seen them several times.'

'This is tremendous news,' I said. 'They've never been reported as far south as this before.'

'No, never, I knew you'd be interested. It knocks old Bauer's theory into a cocked hat. Peter says . . .'

Peake leaned towards her, lowering his head and saying something to claim her attention. She gave me a regretful smile as she turned to him.

'I insisted on two separate and distinct conditions before I accepted this transfer; first of all I said . . .'

I listened without interest as he droned on about himself until Mrs Crawley diverted my attention.

'I haven't seen you playing tennis lately,' she said.

'Tennis!' I said. 'I've got no time for such frivolity.'

'Nonsense, Gerry plays twice a week, sometimes three times when Mr Mathews wants a game.'

'That's why he's so sunburned and handsome.'

She laughed. 'I wouldn't know about that.'

Bowcott's voice rose above the conversation. Mrs Crawley darted a quick glance at him. 'It's that rum,' she said. 'It's got a delayed action they tell me.'

Bowcott, with elaborate gallantry, stood up and held the door when the women went out. The men moved closer to fill up the chairs. Peake leaned forward. Tufts of gingery hair stuck out on the backs of his thick fingers as he went through the process of lighting a cigar. He inspected the burning end, puffed twice, and looked again at it.

'I was talking to the C.J. last night,' he said. 'I told him that I had got a reputation for severity. Always scrupulously just, I hope, but severe.' Peake chuckled. 'I have always found that the best deterrent to crime is a wholesome fear of the law with all its severity but with all its humanity too. I remember when I was in Northern Rhod. I was sitting at Ndola and I had a man before me—I think he was charged with stealing by finding; he got away with a box which had fallen off the back of a car—anyway

184

that doesn't matter. After the two witnesses had given evidence for the prosecution he tried to speak. . . .'

I listened apathetically, watching him fouling a finger bowl with cigar ash.

'I said to him, "Wait, my friend, if you wish to speak you'll get a chance later on". . . .'

Bowcott suddenly interjected.

'A vigilant police force and judges who are prepared to sit and finish cases—not work when they feel like it, and worry about their dignity and whether they are getting proper respect; that's what is needed more than anything. Your talk about severity and fear of the law is so much nonsense.'

Peake's mottled complexion turned deep red, but he controlled himself.

'Really,' he said with bland dignity. 'I find your views interesting. Would you tell me precisely on what authority you speak on this subject?'

Bowcott grinned mockingly. I felt misgivings as I waited for him to speak.

'Yes,' he said, 'on precisely the same authority as you do—that of an unsuccessful barrister who couldn't make a living at home.'

Peake tapped more ash in the finger bowl and then laughed awkwardly and looked round the table.

'He's got a droll sense of humour, I must say.'

Metcalfe pushed on the decanters but there was an awkward silence before conversation became general again.

Palmer spoke across the table to Metcalfe in the angry tone he often used.

'What bloody impertinence, it's got nothing to do with him. Why can't he mind his own business?'

'What's the matter?' I said.

Crawley puffed on his cigar. 'H.E. told Peter that Africans should be admitted to all clubs.'

'He's right, of course,' I said.

Palmer put down his glass and slewed round in his chair.

'You mean you agree with him?'

'Certainly,' I said, 'he's absolutely right.'

Palmer compressed his lips and peered at me.

'You shock me,' he declared with incredulity. 'I would never have believed it. Are we to have no place where we can meet with our kind and relax. After a hard day's work must I be forced into the company of people with whom I have nothing in common?'

He kept his eyes on me, waiting for me to speak.

'I don't know,' I said, 'but I'll tell you this, if I were on a club committee I'd insist on African membership on the same conditions as Europeans.'

'Why?' Palmer demanded, 'give me a few reasons why.'

'Listen,' I said, 'whether you like it or not there's an African political party government running this country.'

'Well?'

'You could find the golf course turned into a housing estate, barges tied up at the yacht club wharf and goats tethered on the grass courts.'

Palmer seemed perplexed and faltered when he spoke.

'I don't follow you.'

'There's more to it than that, but never mind, skip it. . . .'

Palmer stared at me scowling but saying nothing. Peake looked from one to the other of us smoking gloomily and adding to the mess in the finger bowl. Bowcott hummed a tune as he splashed brandy into his glass, and Peter Metcalfe leaned over and with his table napkin wiped up the drops on the polished mahogany.

'Keep going, John,' he said.

'Well, as I see it, it's no good putting in your time in an office and even doing a lot of overtime and then thinking you have done your duty. We are here in this country to help the people develop their political institutions—we can't live apart if we are really sincere.'

I knew I was talking too much.

'Keep going,' said Peter, 'you're doing fine.'

'Oh well, it seems to me there must be goodwill all round— we've got to make a greater effort as part of our jobs. We mustn't think of black and white. We are all people, equal partners, working together for the future of the country. Anyone who can't see himself this way I honestly believe should get out now.'

Nobody spoke and I went on.

'I sometimes wonder what good was done in the good old days

of the twenties and thirties. We kept the peace, certainly, but what progress did we make, I don't know.'

I put out my hand for the decanter.

Bowcott leaned over the table wagging a forefinger.

'If we four were young Africans,' he said very distinctly, 'we should all be agitators for Independence, and you,' he said pointing a finger at Palmer, 'would be a fanatic and a bloody nuisance to the police, and maybe, some day, Prime Minister.'

Peake frowned majestically.

'I'm not sure that those remarks are in the best of taste,' he said.

Nobody else spoke until Crawley broke in with the manner of a tolerant and fair-minded man. 'I certainly can't go all the way with John, but I think there is a great deal in what he says. We, of course, have Africans to our house. . . .'

Bowcott belched noisily.

'You mean, Creepy,' he said calmly, 'you mean you have your Minister to the house sometimes.'

He belched again and took a cigarette.

Crawley flushed. 'If you don't want to address me by my sur-name,' he said pettishly, 'please call me Gerry like other people.'

'Yes, I will, by God, it's a splendid name for you.'

Crawley gave him a supercilious glance.

'I must say you have a most engaging sense of humour.' He turned away. 'I think we have to recognize the emerging creative minorities and go more than half way to meet them,' he said.

Bowcott splashed more brandy into his glass.

'Does that mean something, Creepy?'

Peake and Palmer listened to Crawley with close attention. Bowcott was humming again and occasionally laughed. Metcalfe raised his eyebrows at me as he pushed the brandy and cigarettes across the table.

Crawley went on. 'In some ways I think we must concede that there are Africans—not many as yet perhaps—' he paused slightly —'but definitely some who in certain respects are our equals. We ought to recognize this and arrange our thinking accordingly. Changes are taking place in Africa—there's no denying it—big changes.' He drew on his cigar and looked at me with approval. 'I can go quite a way with you, John,' he said.

Palmer had been waiting for a chance to speak but Bowcott forestalled him. He spoke in a thick voice.

'Creepy, you are a bloody hypocrite, you always were one for getting in on the ground floor. Racial equality, that's the thing now, eh?'

He had both his elbows on the table. In his right hand he held the upper plate of his false teeth. He licked the high white metal pallet and then carefully inspected it; he licked it again and then replaced the plate in his mouth.

'You're an imbecile, Creepy,' he said, then raised his voice. 'Some Africans equal in some ways to white people, indeed! I know any number who are in every way infinitely your superior—morally, intellectually, physically. Who the hell do you think you are, anyway?'

Palmer leaned forward and pinched the wick of a spluttering candle and a wisp of smoke floated away. Peake cleared his throat and shifted in his chair.

'Well, really,' he declared.

Nobody took any notice of him; all eyes were on Crawley. His boyish features became ugly as he looked from Bowcott to me.

'Don't you think it's about time you did something about this man?' he said.

Bowcott laughed. 'What can he do, Sonny Boy?'

For some reason I felt angry. 'Be precise,' I said.

Crawley made a gesture of contempt.

'Do you agree with him?'

'Not always.'

He glanced at Bowcott with distaste.

'Do you agree with what he has just said?'

If I had not been nettled by his manner I might have avoided trouble, but in some confused way I knew I had to choose between right and wrong. I found myself saying, and knew it must sound silly, 'If you mean, do I know Africans who are in every way your superior, the answer must, of course, be in the affirmative.'

Peter Metcalfe replaced stoppers in the decanters and shut the boxes of cigarettes and cigars.

'Let's take a look at the garden,' he said, 'the girls will be wondering what's happened to us.'

I spoke to Bowcott outside.

'Your performance tonight has been masterly, you must be proud of yourself.'

He took my arm in a grip.

'You musn't worry about Creepy,' he said, 'and that old phony's not worth a thought.'

'You don't understand,' I said. 'It's Peter Metcalfe I'm worried about. You placed him in an impossible position.'

The others had returned to the house. Bowcott held me back and we stood together on the lawn. The moon was in its first quarter and in the dim light I got a glimpse of his face. He had sobered and looked anxious.

'I must apologize to Peter,' he said.

'I suggest you push off home.'

'You think I'm drunk?'

'Yes, I do.'

'You are, of course, dead right.'

Without another word he turned and walked across the lawn towards the drive to the road.

'Where's Dikon?' Margaret asked when we joined the women.

'He's asked to be excused,' I said, 'he's not feeling well.'

She looked at Peter and then turned to me again. 'Shouldn't someone have gone with him?'

Peter put his hand on her arm.

Mrs Crawley took a cigarette from a gilt and enamel case and snapped on a flame from a matching lighter.

'I shouldn't worry, Margaret,' she said, 'he'll be all right in the morning.'

Peake grunted and was about to say something when the telephone rang. Peter came back to say Gregg wanted to speak to me.

Gregg's voice sounded a long way off when he replied to me.

'Ali told me where to find you,' he said, 'call in if you are on your way home in the next half hour.'

'What's the matter?'

'I'll tell you when I see you.'

I put down the handset and found people standing up ready to go when I returned to the sitting-room.

There was a light in a room upstairs and I threw gravel at the window. Gregg looked out and called to me to come up.

I opened the door and climbed the stairs. There was a bundle of polo sticks and a saddle in the corner of the room. Gregg was sitting at an untidy desk in dressing gown and pyjamas. He had been typing but now the machine had been pushed aside and sheets of typescript lay on the blotter in front of him.

'Have a cup of tea?' he said, 'I brew my own up here with the electric kettle.'

I shook my head but took a cigarette.

'I'm glad you looked in,' he said. 'There's something I must tell you.'

'Yes?' I said.

He pushed back his chair and stood up; he locked the typescript in a wall safe. He remained standing, looking at me with an air of concern.

'Well,' I said, 'what is it?'

He sighed and passed his hand through his thinning hair.

'I am afraid they're gunning for you, old boy,' he said keeping his eyes on me.

His manner seemed ominous.

'Gunning for me,' I said, 'who's gunning for me?'

'Likema seems to be the prime mover.'

'Likema?'

'That's what I said.'

'I don't get it, what's all this about?'

Gregg raised his hands in a gesture.

'You must have got up against him somehow.'

'What's he aiming to do?'

Gregg looked troubled.

'Discredit you, run you out of your job—I don't know.'

I was disturbed by what he said.

'Can he really do this?'

Gregg grunted. 'You'd be surprised,' and then added, 'just a minute.'

He went out and returned with a boy in khaki shorts and a vest.

I looked at the boy carefully; he gazed back embarrassed by my stare, but unafraid.

'You were in a shop in High Street a couple of weeks ago?' I said.

The boy nodded. 'Yes, 29 High Street. You came in at 9.10 p.m. on Thursday, June 17, and you left at 10.17 p.m.'

'He's working for you?' I asked Gregg.

'Tali, tell the Provincial Commissioner what you have told me,' Gregg said to him.

The shade of Gregg's goose-neck lamp shed a pool of light on his desk. Tali stood in semi-darkness at the end of the room.

Gregg leaned forward and spoke again to the boy.

'Now, Tali,' he said, 'tell the Provincial Commissioner everything.'

There was a white glint from his eyes as Tali looked up and nervously yawned. He opened an exercise book with a picture of a crocodile on the cover.

'Can you see?' Gregg said.

'I know what I have written,' he said.

'All right, go on.'

'On May 4, Primo Likema called Sali Dufu, Gasu Bauro and Dina Ritelo to 29 High Street to meet him at 8.15 p.m.'

The effect of drink at Metcalfe's party had worn off. I felt cold sober and anxious.

'That's before I saw them,' I said.

Tali frowned at my interruption.

'Four weeks and three days before,' he said.

Tali looked to Gregg for guidance.

'Continue,' Gregg said.

'Likema said he had called them to discuss a matter of importance. He said the Provincial Commissioner was the enemy of our people and there would be no progress until he was moved. Ritelo did not agree. He said the Provincial Commissioner was a good man and he would not stop to hear him slandered. Likema became angry and said he would make trouble for Ritelo if he refused to co-operate.'

Tali looked up.

'When I have more information I will report what Likema knows about Ritelo.'

He looked down again.

'Ritelo got excited and attempted to assault Likema. Dufu and Bauro held him until he grew calm. Likema told them that opposition to the Provincial Commissioner must be arranged.'

Tali's manner was impersonal and I found it hard to believe he was talking about me.

'Likema ordered Bauro to organize protests by the traders against the market stall allocations. He told Ritelo he must get the railway and dock workers to strike against the Provincial Commissioner. Ritelo started to shout again. He said he must have some reason for a strike. Likema told him he would have to think of one. Ritelo said he refused to have anything to do with Likema's plan. He said Likema wanted to make use of the unions to work off a personal grudge against the Provincial Commissioner. Likema warned him again and Ritelo stopped talking. Likema said Dufu must talk to disgruntled people and find out as much as he could against the Provincial Commissioner.'

'Stop,' I said, 'why are they doing this?'

Tali looked from Gregg to me.

'I do not know yet,' he said. 'Likema is concerned in so many things. The Provincial Commissioner must have crossed him somehow.'

'I barely know the man,' I said.

'Go on, Tali,' Gregg said.

'Likema gave them each fifty pounds. At first Ritelo refused to take anything but Bauro told him not to be foolish.'

Tali turned over a page.

'On May 9 and 11, Dufu reported to Likema.' Tali spoke regretfully. 'I do not know what was said.'

'Never mind,' Gregg said, 'tell the Provincial Commissioner the rest of it.'

'On May 15, Bauro arranged a protest meeting of traders at the market for five o'clock. He drove past at half past five but only seven people had come. He came back at six o'clock; there were only three people there then and he left for the Occidental Club in Gladstone Road.'

'There was no meeting?' I said.

Tali shook his head. 'There was no meeting; in fact, the traders are pleased with the changes.'

There was a scurry and squeaking of rats on the ceiling boards. Tali gave an upward glance and then looked down again at his notes.

'Has Ritelo done anything yet?' I said.

'I have no information but I do not think so.'

He went on from his notes.

'On June 17, Likema called Dufu, Bauro and Ritelo to 29 High Street at seven o'clock. He told them he would get development grants for them. He said the Provincial Commissioner had been warned against refusing so many applications. They agreed to ask for three thousand pounds each. Likema told Dufu to telephone the Provincial Commissioner to come to 29 High Street. Bauro and Ritelo said he would not come. The Provincial Commissioner came at ten past nine and left at seventeen minutes after ten. He refused to listen to them.'

'Did they expect me to?'

'Likema knew the Provincial Commissioner would refuse as he had already refused Dufu. He wished only to stir up feeling. He told them if the Provincial Commissioner were moved they were certain to get grants.'

'Yes,' I said.

'They left at twenty minutes past ten. Bauro was drunk. Dufu and Ritelo helped him downstairs and telephoned for a taxi. Dufu afterwards went to the Hot Cha Cha Club in Wilberforce Street.'

'Go on, Tali,' Gregg said.

'On June 27, Yalu Bensato came to 29 High Street.'

'Who?' I asked.

'Bensato, the editor of the *Graphic*,' Gregg said.

'The paper owes Likema three hundred pounds for news print. Bensato has had the money to pay but has spent it. Likema knows this and has been pressing him.'

'Thank you, Tali,' Gregg said. 'That will do.'

'I can go?'

Tali's sandals went slap slap on the stairs.

'That boy's a treasure,' Gregg said. 'Have a cup of tea? It won't take a minute.'

'What's all this about? What does Likema want?'

Gregg plugged in the kettle and busied himself with a teapot and cups.

'Honestly, old boy, I don't know. People are scared of him but he's losing his influence. He's got nothing on the political leaders—he goes for the small fry.'

'Like me.'

'I shouldn't worry, it may come to nothing.'

Gregg's assurance was too facile.

'You don't believe that?' I said.

He poured out the tea and handed me a cup.

'Maybe not, still it won't help to worry.'

'It's not very nice to know people are plotting against you,' I said lamely.

I refused a second cup of tea and he came down the stairs with me to my car.

'I'll keep you informed of developments,' he said. 'At least we know what's happening.'

Ali was waiting up for me when I got back to the house. I told him to put whisky and cigarettes in the bedroom.

CHAPTER XXIV

I awoke in half light, for an instant untroubled, then as I stirred and my mind became active I gave way to thoughts that something was wrong. I stripped off sweaty pyjamas and looked with distaste at the dirty glass and the cigarette ends on the desk where I had sat six hours before. Traffic sounds came through the bathroom window while I shaved.

After days of cooling rain the heat was stifling. Lush green verges along the roadside seemed to have sprung up overnight. Scarlet and green of flame of the forest, the funereal bloom of frangipane, purple bougainvillea, leafy mango trees and hibiscus bushes flowering in red, white and yellow, distracted from the ill-kept lawns and straggling hedges of officials' houses.

A spasm of homesickness came to me while I waited at the end of the road to join the morning traffic. It persisted until I reached the town and then my spirits revived. The heat after the rains gave a strange quality to the light and ships visible in a silver and azure haze appeared to be high out of the water. The clang of sailors chipping plates came across the harbour above the sounds of the town.

I turned in at the yard and put my car away. The head messenger regarded me speculatively when he greeted me. I looked to see if Bowcott was in; he was there with a litter of maps and papers on his desk. Community development had become his interest and earlier in the week he had been away touring the outlying districts.

We said nothing about the party the night before. He talked about the roads and bridges the people were building and suggested schemes we could help with grants from development funds.

'I called at Tosho on my way back,' he said. 'They think a lot of you there.'

I laughed. My self-esteem was partly restored.

'It's a good thing someone does,' I said. 'How's my friend the midwife?'

'She's O.K. She asked me to tell you Maleto was dead.'

I remembered the blacksmith as not much over thirty.

'Dead?' I said. 'How?'

Bowcott gave me a searching glance.

'He was sick for a couple of days, came out in boils and died. Why do you ask?'

'When was this?'

I was conscious of Bowcott's curious eyes.

'About six weeks ago,' he said, 'or it may have been more.'

I stared back at him and shook my head.

'The body will be putrescent and in any case I'd never get an exhumation order.'

Bowcott took a cigarette from the tin on his desk, snapped his lighter and puffed.

'Do you mind telling me what the hell you're talking about?' he said.

'He was murdered.'

Bowcott looked at me sombrely.

'Why do you say that?'

'I have my reasons.'

'I should be very interested to hear them.'

'Do you know anything about the *Ulo* cult?'

'It's a criminal secret society, isn't it?'

'You might call it that.'

'Well?'

'Maleto was a member. He gave me the information which led to the conviction of Abbas, Saba and Stamala.'

Bowcott tapped ash off his cigarettte.

'It's really only a hunch?' he said.

I shook my head. 'No,' I said, 'it's a certainty.'

'How do you know?'

'I just know.'

A flicker of admiration in his face passed and he became serious. 'You're navigating dangerous waters, aren't you?'

I looked at my watch.

'It's a quarter to nine,' I said.

Bowcott pushed a newspaper across the desk.

'Seen today's *Graphic*?'

I picked up the paper.

'It's the first leader,' he said.

It was headed 'A Damning Indictment' and it began:

A contemporary with typical disregard for truth has averred that we of this journal support John G. Wood, Provincial Commissioner of Belemba. We wish to go on record as holding no brief for him—holding no brief, nay, this is not enough, we believe it our duty to arraign him before the bar of public opinion on five separate counts.

The duty laid upon the fourth estate is sacred and not to be treated lightly. Truth sometimes is to be found at the bottom of a well, but wherever it may be we shall find it. For months we have watched the ineptitude of this man with growing concern. But because we believe in justice we suspended final judgment. We should have been happy if he had proved our assessment of him to be wrong and this leader need never have been written. Events have shown us to be right. Some may say in the present mood of our people he is irrelevant. There is nothing new in the bungling incompetence of expatriate officials; we know too that many of them are making a puny last stand to preserve the status quo. They will soon be swept aside by the tidal wave of events sweeping over our country. But this John Wood is different. Holding the key executive position of Provincial Commissioner of Belemba he acquires significance out of proportion to his normal potential as an obstructive interloper. Time and again we have detected his meddling hands in matters which do not concern him. His ignorance, incompetence and ill will can no longer be ignored— a stage has been reached when we must make known without equivocation our detestation of him and all he represents. Unlike our contemporary we do not expect our readers to be content with platitudinous generalities. We shall be particular in our denunciation; we shall specify the grounds on which we base our charge. Wood must answer five counts in the indictment we have drawn up against him. First—that he has failed to discharge the duty laid upon him by the Belemba Development Ordinance. He has scorned schemes which our people have prepared with painstaking care to bring benefits to their fellow men. He has denied them loans which he has no right to withhold. Evidence is not wanting to show that he has used the formal authority which the law gives to him to thwart the intentions of our legislators.

Second—he has intervened in the administration of courts of customary law and prevented the dispensation of justice. Statutory law still gives the Provincial Commissioners power to hear appeals from our customary courts. This anachronism is overdue for amendment but as long as it remains on the statute book we expect expatriate officials to confine their activities to the correction of technical mistakes and errors in form. John Wood is not content to do this; he assumes the right to pronounce on customary law and to upset the considered judgment of the revered elders who sit on the bench of Tosho court.

Third—he has broken up the marriages between Africans and Europeans. One of our young men came home with an English bride. The girl was welcomed by her husband's family. All was set fair for the future happiness of the young couple until they fell foul of John Wood. Perhaps he thought one of our young men was not good enough for his countrywoman. We are not psychologists, we cannot penetrate the labyrinthine workings of this man's mind. It is enough to say that as a result of his interference the young couple are parted at a time when more than ever the young woman needs the help and support of her husband.

Fourth—he has frequented resorts in Belemba where no senior official should be seen. We do not set ourselves up as arbiters of moral behaviour. We believe in the adage of 'live and let live'. But we must face it—there are resorts in Belemba of which we are not proud. Those who frequent them belong to a strata of society about which we know little and care less—but not all. When the Provincial Commissioner of Belemba is seen in one of these places and moreover when it is remembered he is responsible for issuing the licence on which it depends for existence, the onus rests upon him to show that he seeks only innocent amusement and that his conduct is blameless.

Fifth—he deliberately misled a British parliamentary delegation on a visit to Belemba, concealing from them our progress and achievements. We are by nature a hospitable people. We welcome visitors. We particularly welcome visitors who come to this country with sympathetic interest in our aspirations. It is our pleasure to show them our modest achievements—and not all of them are modest. There is nothing wrong in drawing the attention of our visitors to the progress we are making. Indeed, it is our duty to do so to promote better understanding. John Wood must answer the charge that he deliberately concealed from a British parliamentary delegation public institutions which to some extent are a measure of our progress and instead limited their sight-seeing to survivals which in no way represent the present stage of our development. We shall not readily acquit him of this crime.

Reader, we shall be content with these five counts. We could add more but these are enough. This man is a menace; he is an enemy of our people. He must go and go soon.

I threw the paper down. 'Must I read this nauseating muck.'

Bowcott spoke with unaccustomed gentleness.

'Don't let it get you down,' he said, 'no one takes that stuff seriously.'

Bosa had the *Graphic* open at the leader. He looked puzzled when he greeted me. Miss Malling was standing at a filing cabinet.

'Mr Mathews asked for you just after eight o'clock,' she said, 'and Mr Pereta, Mr Mudi, Dr Perigo and several other people have telephoned that you should ignore the newspaper.'

'It's kind of them, very kind of them.'

She smiled. 'May I give you the same advice?'

'Thank you,' I said.

I telephoned to Mathews. He asked me to be at his office at eleven o'clock. He sounded amiable but his request increased my uneasiness.

Two hours passed normally. Noise of traffic and the cries of hawkers came from the street; the siren of a French-line ship whooped spasmodically. I could hear children shouting tables in the Seventh-Day Adventist Mission School about a hundred yards behind the office. More people telephoned about the *Graphic's* leader. John Calder said he thought an action for libel would succeed.

It became much hotter as the day had advanced and I entered the Secretariat just before eleven o'clock with sweat pouring down my face. Three small arm chairs were set out in front of Mathews's desk. The Hon Xanadu Cairngross, holding a tin of Churchman cigarettes, sat to his right, Gerry Crawley sitting in the chair to the left half rose greeting me with a flashing smile. Cairngross said nothing. Mathews pointed at the middle chair.

'Sit there, please,' he said.

I was aware of calm in the room. It gave me the feeling that I had been discussed and something concerning me had been decided.

'Mr Cairngross and the Permanent Secretary have been good enough to come here at my request,' Mathews said. 'His Ministry is interested in much of the work you've been doing.' He looked at Cairngross. 'That's so, isn't it?'

Cairngross said, 'That is so.'

'And I am concerned with the remainder of it.' He looked thoughtful. 'It seemed a good thing to me if we met here.'

His manner suddenly changed. He broke off and became solicitous.

'Are you bothered by the glare?' Without waiting for my reply he lowered the venetian blind over the window behind him. 'I should have thought of that before.'

I watched him closely when he sat down.

'Has this got something to do with attacks on me in the papers?' I asked.

Mathews smiled. 'What's that?' he said in a puzzled tone.

'This meeting, this discussion.'

'Yes, something, I suppose you might say.' He laughed. 'They've been having a go at you haven't they?'

Crawley laughed too but there was no change in Cairngross's expression.

'No,' Mathews continued in a frank manner, 'I hope we don't take too much notice of the papers. There is more to it than that.'

'More to what?' I said.

Mathews raised his eyebrows.

'You've been here just over a year now?'

'Yes,' I said.

'Yes,' he concurred, 'actually thirteen months.'

He looked at a file on his desk.

'You came after Bracey Smith. The Governor and I thought you suitable for the posting.' He turned over the papers in the file. 'Have you liked being here?'

'Oh, yes,' I said.

'It's not easy?' he suggested with a smile.

'It certainly isn't, sir,' Crawley said, 'particularly for an officer with no previous experience of Belemba.'

Mathews looked from Crawley to me.

'No, I suppose not,' he said with a glance at Cairngross. 'In the circumstances Wood has done well.'

The partiality of his manner worried me; it was unlike him.

'With the greatest respect, sir, I think he's done very well indeed.' There was a suggestion of defiance in Crawley's vibrant voice. He spoke as if his opinion might not be popular but no one would shake him.

Mathews said nothing; he looked at Cairngross.

'Minister?' he said.

Cairngross rubbed out the cigarette.

'My colleagues in the Council of Ministers and I are not unappreciative of Mr Wood's good qualities.' He bunched his lips. 'It could be that there is something in what the Permanent Secretary says. Perhaps it's difficult to change after working for years in the Provinces. Anyway, we feel Mr Wood could be used to the greater advantage of our people up-country somewhere.'

He waved his arm indicating the wide area open to me. He was about to add something but seemed to lose interest.

Mathews bared his teeth. 'Wood,' he said blandly, 'what do you think?'

It was impossible to pierce the tough covering of his personality.

'You and the Minister have decided that I have been a failure here and must be moved?'

'Oh, no,' said Crawley, but Mathews made no comment.

'You are, of course, both quite right. There are forces here with which I feel quite unable to contend.'

Cairngross, with a lighted match in his hand, glanced at me before drawing on his cigarette.

Mathews closed the file and looked at his watch.

'We asked you here so that the Minister and I might have a personal word with you. I don't think it would help to say more than we believe that you would serve the territory to better advantage somewhere in the provinces.'

His voice had hardened.

'You may make arrangements for your leave now.'

'Is that all?' Cairngross said.

'Yes, Minister, thank you for coming.'

Cairngross got up and walked towards the door. Crawley picked up the Churchman cigarettes and followed him.

They left the door ajar for me. Mathews stood looking down at a note on his blotter. A feeling of injustice engulfed me. Everything had not been said. I stood rooted to the patch of Wilton carpet in front of his desk.

'I'm being badly treated,' I said.

Mathews looked up, instantly alert again.

'Oh,' he said, 'in what way?'

'The opposition to me has been artificially contrived.'

Mathews's mouth opened slightly and I caught the luminous glow in his tawny eyes.

'You are probably right,' he said judicially. There was renewed interest in his voice. 'I had not thought of that, I must say.'

I returned his stare.

'Is it right, therefore, that I should be ignominiously removed from my work here?' I said.

Mathews face relaxed as he looked at me, then it slowly took on a puzzled expression.

'Ignominiously removed from your work here?' he said, 'I don't understand you.'

I felt my temper rising.

'I wouldn't have thought it difficult,' I said.

His manner changed again and he spoke with acidulous precision.

'What you think and what you feel are of no consequence.' He scowled at me. 'You are *non persona grata* with the Ministers.' He shrugged his shoulders. 'It is not worth inquiring why. You've got to go.' He reminded me of a big cat. 'I'd have thought the whole thing was obvious,' he said as if appealing to reason.

He looked again at his blotter and sat down, took up his pen and started to write. I left him, carefully closing the door behind me.

I went to Metcalfe's room. He was dictating to his secretary. He told the girl to go and listened while I told him what had happened.

'I'm sorry, old boy,' he said, 'very sorry. It's unwise to stick your chin out.'

'What do you mean?' I said.

He shrugged his shoulders and grimaced.

'I suppose you ought to have made adjustments and played it more their way.'

I was stupified with surprise.

'Do you mind telling me precisely what you mean?'

'Don't look at me like that,' he said, 'you've got to be practical.'

I was filled with revulsion, not on account of the words he used, but because of some suggestion of surrender.

'Does Margaret know about these practical adjustments?'

He flushed deep red.

'Leave her out of it,' he said.

'I'm sorry, Peter.'

There was an uncomfortable silence.

'I mustn't keep you from your work,' I said at last.

He made no reply and I left him. Bowcott was the person I should have seen first.

CHAPTER XXV

My successor had not been named but I made a list of files I thought he ought to see and I was emptying the drawers, throwing away a collection of personal papers, when the Civil Secretary's telephone rang. Metcalfe spoke; there was constraint in his voice.

'Have you arranged your passage?' he said.

I tried to sound friendly.

'I'm flying by B.O.A.C. the day after tomorrow.'

If I had not heard his breathing I would have thought we had been cut off.

'You'll have to cancel it,' he said.

'What's the idea?'

'I can't tell you any more.'

I was tired and I had begun to look forward to my leave.

'What's the matter with you, this is a direct line, nobody can listen in?'

He ignored my outburst.

'You are to come to a meeting at Government House at one o'clock.'

'When can I go on leave?'

'I don't know,' he said.

He rang off before I could say any more.

It was hot and there were crowds in the street when I came out and the traffic was slower and more congested than usual. A Volkswagen 'bus went by with a loud hailer repeating 'Independence now, Independence now, Independence now'. An Opel followed and someone in a big Buick blew a bugle through an open window. There were more cars behind and I waited until I could get into the slow moving stream. A boy ran alongside shouting 'Go home, white man'.

I laughed. 'You bet that's what I want to do.'

He kept up with me still running with the car.

'Give me a cigarette,' he said.

I tossed a cigarette through the window.

The Inspector General of Police and Gregg were already at Government House. Barlow the Financial Secretary and Pascal the Attorney-General came after me and then Metcalfe and John Calder. Gleeson offered us cigarettes. 'H.E. should be here soon,' he said. At the same instant a voice reached us.

'Tell me then, what is the right thing to do for the country?'

There was an inaudible murmur and the voice rose again.

'It's no use talking like that, we are not controlling events, we are not deciding anything.'

The Governor came into the room with Mathews long striding and very alert. Mathews sat in the chair on his right.

The Governor looked round the table at each of us as if to satisfy himself that everyone was present. He showed no signs of stress or dejection but more of determination to come to terms with a problem.

'I won't keep you long,' he said, 'but I must tell you there is a constitutional crisis and there may be demonstrations and possibly disorder.'

Gregg interjected. 'There is a meeting in Wilberforce Square this afternoon.'

The Governor raised his eyebrows and looked at Gregg and me in turn. 'You two can handle that.'

'As you know,' he continued, 'there are two years to run with the present constitution, which as you know is virtually internal self-government, but today, on the motion of an opposition back-bencher, a man named Sigo, a NIC member from Basali, the House resolved unanimously that full independence should be granted forthwith.' The Governor breathed hard. 'I don't think anyone was ready for it but the Council of Ministers obviously, I suppose, allowed a free vote.' He compressed his lips. 'When the House rose this morning I called an emergency meeting of the Council. Though they didn't seem happy about it the Ministers told me that they were in full agreement with the House and asked me to take immediate steps to give effect to their wishes.' The Governor paused and made a slight gesture. 'They were not prepared to talk about anything else. Without exception, though

I fancy with some reluctance, they handed me their portfolios and resigned. I asked them to reconsider their decisions and reminded them that it had been agreed that the present constitution was to provide a three year period of consolidation. We talked for an hour and for a time I thought I had persuaded them but no one was willing to be the first to give way.' He shook his head. 'A few minutes later we were back where we started and they were absolutely adamant. They would talk of nothing but immediate independence.'

No one spoke and the Governor passed his hands over his face and then suddenly smiled at us. 'That's the position.'

I do not know why I spoke first, or indeed why I spoke at all. 'They must realize that independence cannot be granted immediately. It would take time to complete the formalities even if agreement was reached.'

His voice cracked—I supposed he had been talking a lot.

'Yes, in the meantime, they say, ex-officio members would not be expected to sit in the House nor in the Council of Ministers. Pereta would preside over meetings of the Council. I would assent to all bills as a matter of course. They say there is no point in waiting; they've had all the experience they require.'

I again broke the silence. 'Do you not think there is an inevitability about these things? Once a movement of this sort begins it gathers momentum and it is impossible to retard it even though it may be in the best interests of the people themselves to do so.' Mathews looked at me with surprise but no one said anything and I went on. 'If we accept this I think our task becomes less complex and therefore, to some extent, easier.'

The Governor leaned over the table and took a cigarette. Pascal snapped his lighter. The Governor drew heavily and blew out smoke.

'You're right,' he said. 'Wisdom, experience, patience, become of no avail. We have to come to terms with a state of affairs we can't change very much.' He shrugged his shoulders. 'It is a matter of timing. We could do a lot to help them in two or three years.'

Mathews spoke for the first time.

'The important thing is to do our best for the territory in the short time left to us.'

The Governor jerked his head round.

'Of course it is,' he said, 'of course it is, we all know that.'

Situation reports came through from patrol cars while Gregg and I sat chain smoking and gazing at the blown up street map on the wall. There was nothing for us to do. The meeting in Wilberforce Square had lasted three hours and more than ten thousand people were still there cheering the speakers and chanting 'Independence now, Independence now'. At half past four Mudi and Pereta spoke in turn telling the crowd to disperse and go home without making trouble.

The receiver crackled as the reports followed.

'*Acker White calling Control. Wilberforce Square meeting break-ing up, but crowd of about three thousand forming in Gladstone Road. Over to you, Control.*'

'*Control calling Acker White, Control calling Acker White. Report developments. Out.*'

It was fifteen minutes later before we got the next report.

'*Acker White calling Control, Acker White calling Control. The crowd includes big hooligan element. Now moving down Gladstone Road to Front. Over to you.*'

'*Control calling Acker White, Control calling Acker White. Thank you, Acker White.*'

Gregg grimaced, but almost immediately the receiver crackled again and a signal came from the Front.

'*Plum Purple calling Control, Plum Purple calling Control. A hostile mob of about two thousand now moving along the Front. I have deployed fifty men across the road and hold fifty in reserve. Request reinforcements to contain situation. Over to you, Control.*'

'*Control calling Plum Purple, Control calling Plum Purple. You are doing fine. Disperse mob and restore order. Prior Palmer reporting to you with one hundred men. Out.*'

I followed Gregg into the yard. Two police officers, one African and one European, came forward and saluted.

'There's a schemozzle on the Front,' Gregg said turning to the white man. 'Report to George Crawshay immediately, and you, Josh, stand by with your lot,' he told the African officer.

Gregg turned to go back to the Control Room.

'I'll see if I can help,' I said.

I drove from Police Headquarters passing the Prison and the Methodist Chapel. I left the Government Offices on the Ridge and turned down Wilberforce Street to the Front. The policeman on point duty halted me and came round to the window.

'You can't get through,' he said, 'there's a riot.'

There was a roar like breaking surf.

'Hear them?' he said.

He listened, oblivious of my presence.

'Bloody fools,' he murmured. 'They're mad.'

There was no traffic but he returned to the dais to signal me on.

Fifty helmeted men with whicker shields and staves rested in reserve on the grass verge. I left my car outside Pargetter Haymes Motor Showroom and walked to where Prior Palmer and Crawshay stood in the road. Police were deployed from the water side across the road to Cheetham's Hardware Store. In front there was a vacant area about twenty feet deep and beyond a frenzied mob advancing and jostling forward but being pushed back by the police. The noise was deafening as the crowd came forward, pushing, shouting and shrieking time and time again. One man was raising his arms and shouting as he led the rushes. I stepped a few paces ahead to meet him. Sweat poured down his face as he gesticulated, advancing and retreating before me in a mad dance. He suddenly came close and tilted his chin in my face pressing against me. His black cotton shirt hung open showing the chest and stomach of an immensely strong man. He pushed his face at me baring black pointed teeth and glaring with bloodshot eyes and then tore his shirt down the front allowing it to hang in rags from his waist.

'White man,' he declared dramatically raising his arms, 'I want to die for Africa.'

I looked him in the face.

'O.K.' I said, 'go ahead.'

I turned aside, but he barred my way.

'What's the matter with you?' I said.

He leaned back, pushing out his chest and holding his arms in an attitude of surrender.

'Shoot me,' he said, 'go on, white man, shoot me down like a dog. I want to die for Africa.'

I looked at him in silence for a moment.

'You are a foolish man,' I said, 'why can't you go away.'

The policeman behind me stepped forward and pushed him.

'Shame,' he shouted. 'Shame on you for striking a brother.'

The policeman pushed again.

'Get moving,' he said.

The man squared up, his head poised on a powerful neck, and raised his muscular arms. 'Imperialistic stooge,' he jeered, 'you are an imperialistic stooge.'

The policeman gripped his baton.

'Stooge of the imperialists,' the man said.

The policeman moved towards him.

'Leave him,' I said.

The crowd opened around us.

'This man offered violence,' the policeman said, 'he should be taken into custody.'

'Leave him,' I said.

A ring formed about us as I looked the man up and down. The whites of his bloodshot eyes were yellow tinged and he frothed at the mouth.

'My friend,' I said to him.

He made a wild sweeping motion with his left arm.

'I'm not listening to you,' he said.

'I want to tell you something.'

He paused suspiciously.

'What is it?'

'Do up your fly buttons.'

He looked down and clumsily did up his fly. Someone in the crowd shouted 'your fly's undone, Bimo'.

'Why do you insult me?' he shouted.

'I did not insult you,' I said. 'I told you your fly buttons were undone.'

He suddenly laughed and slapped my shoulder.

'You humbug me, white man, I am serious, I am very serious.'

I laughed. 'On your way, Bimo,' I said.

There was a shout of laughter as the crowd surged forward again and I found myself looking at a short man with heavily rimmed glasses. He wore a panama hat on the back of his head and a short fawn-coloured shirt. He spoke with the bustling manner of someone who had no time to waste.

'Are you in charge here?' he said.

I took a deep breath. My feet were aching and my throat was sore.

'I could be,' I said, 'why?'

'Because I demand to see the Governor.'

'You demand to see the Governor?'

'Yes, certainly, my group has certain proposals to make.'

Prickly heat on my arms and shoulders had set up maddening irritation.

'Tell me about them,' I said. 'Let me hear them, friend.'

He looked at me severely.

'We take grave exception to certain provisions of the existing constitution regarding the transfer of power.'

'Go on,' I said.

He raised his forefinger.

'Dealing first on grounds of principle,' he said, 'the agreement reached at the last London Conference had two way application. There were two parties to it—you follow me? So either party can propose variations of the original agreement. It is on this basis that my group has prepared a six-point memorandum for submission to. . . .'

'Why don't you write to the Governor about it?' I said.

He was disconcerted then looked thoughtful. 'You think that would be better than presenting it in person?'

'Much better,' I said.

'Thank you,' he politely said with a bow. 'I am grateful for your advice.'

He went off pushing his way through the crowd.

I turned at a touch on my arm. I recognized him at once.

'Good afternoon, Mr Alabami,' I said.

He wore an elaborate native costume and traditional hat with a badge inscribed 'Freedom'.

'How nice to see you here,' I said.

He pushed his fingers into his ears and made a comic grimace.

'You can't hear yourself think,' he said.

'I haven't seen you for months,' I said.

'No, but I've been thinking a lot of something you said at Jimmy Hyne's party.'

'Yes?'

'You remember we were talking about a dance hall?'

'Yes,' I said, 'non-stop dancing; there's money to be made in that, but Mr Alabami,' I added gravely, 'it must be well run. It must be respectable.'

'You advised me about the chef. Can I come round and see you sometime?'

'Of course,' I said, 'any time.'

He looked at his watch and then gazed over the milling crowd.

'Do you think I can go now?' he said.

He gazed at the crowd again and then raised his hand to greet someone.

'You've been prominent in the demonstration,' I said, 'everyone has seen you by now.'

He turned uncertain eyes on me.

'You think so?'

'Yes, sure.'

'Well, cheerio,' he said, 'I'll be round some day to see you.'

'Cheerio,' I said.

He kept to the edge of the crowd shouting greetings to people he recognized.

Dufu pushed himself in front of me. There was a youth with him wearing a tee shirt with the word 'Superman' across the chest.

'Good afternoon, Mr Dufu,' I said. 'Call off the hooligans and let's go home.'

'I don't understand you,' he said. 'This is a spontaneous demonstration of popular disapproval.'

I turned my back on him and walked across the road in front of the police. A small man danced about barring my way and then suddenly flung off his jacket. A row of medals was pinned to his shirt.

'I fought for freedom,' he shouted.

The dramatic gesture miscarried. People behind jostled him and he got into argument with someone who trod on his jacket.

The European staff of Cheetham Bros., Pargetter-Haymes, Anglo-African and the African Trading Company were in the windows of their showrooms like spectators in a grand stand watching events in the road. There was now less noise and the crowd had stopped pressing the police. Gregg joined me.

'Hello, Herbert,' I said.

'It's in the bag,' he said, 'it's finished, they're clearing away at the back.'

He lit a cigarette and we stood together in the middle of the road.

'Another half hour at most,' he said.

Prior Palmer came up and saluted.

'Yes, Tim?' Gregg said.

'Message from Civil Secretary, sir. No opposition to be placed in the way of demonstrators. They should be allowed free movement along the Front.'

Gregg's face creased in bewilderment.

'What?' he said. 'Are you sure he said that?'

'Quite sure, sir.'

Gregg shook his head.

'I don't get it, Tim, but not to worry, the show's finished.' He looked at me. 'What's Mathews talking about?'

'Search me,' I said.

A Land Rover pulled up behind us. It was Prior Palmer again.

'The Civil Secretary wishes to speak personally to you and to the Provincial Commissioner,' he said.

I sat with Gregg in the Land Rover.

'Commissioner of Police and Provincial Commissioner calling Civil Secretary,' Gregg said.

The radio distorted Mathews's nasal voice.

'I have responsibility for peace and good order, and I order the police now to withdraw and allow free movement to the assembly of people now on the Front.'

Gregg spoke angrily. 'But, sir,' he said, 'the rioters are dispersing.'

'Do as I say,' Mathews said.

'You realize that these people may re-form and march on Government House, sir,' Gregg replied.

Mathews spoke slowly.

'Please obey my orders forthwith, that is to say, immediately. I have told you repeatedly I will not tolerate unnecessary force in dealing with the public.'

Gregg's eyes blazed as Mathews's voice continued. 'Confirm when you have . . .'

Gregg slapped the switch down.

'The fool,' he said, 'the fool. Why can't he keep out of this?'

Gregg got down and shouted to his officers. 'Tell your men to fall in by the trucks ready to return to Headquarters.'

Two of them saluted and moved off, but Crawshay stood his ground.

'It's too soon, sir,' he said, 'there'll be trouble.'

Gregg lay a hand on his arm.

'George, I couldn't agree with you more,' he said with great emphasis, 'but it's the Civil Secretary's orders.'

Crawshay's jaw dropped. 'We've got to pull out?'

Gregg raised his hands in a gesture of helplessness.

'I'm afraid so, George, I'm afraid so.'

Crawshay swore. 'Very good, sir,' he said, 'if that's the way it's wanted.'

'That's the way it's wanted, George, but don't blame me. I'm just a bloody flatfoot, not a politician.'

Nothing happened at first, then movement developed like water through a breach in a dam and in less than a minute men streamed along the road with arms raised shouting and urging others to follow. Someone started a shrill ululation and more in the crowd took it up until a growing volume of barbaric sound filled the air. There was a crash and a tinkle of glass. Pargetter-Haymes showroom window was broken. The youth I had seen with Dufu threw a bottle through Cheetham's window. Stewart, the manager, came out waving clenched fists above his head. Then the Anglo-African window crashed, the African Trading Company and the insurance office next door.

It was too late to turn and I drove my car forward. A stone skimmed the bonnet and ricocheted away. The next struck the windscreen and an opaque web slowly spread through the glass. More stones came and someone ran after me belabouring the back of the car with a pole.

I drove up Gladstone Road round Wilberforce Square, now deserted, and joined Muda Road. One thought persisted, I had not cancelled my air passage, and I had nearly finished packing. I was leaving for home next day. Whatever happened, nothing would keep me back, nothing at all.

It was barely seven o'clock when the telephone rang. My head ached and I felt ill. I had smoked and drunk too much the night before with Bowcott. I thought it was something to do with my air passage. I picked up the telephone.

'Good morning, Mr Wood,' came the slightly accented voice. 'This is Fela Pereta.'

I was too taken aback to speak easily.

'Good morning, Mr Pereta,' I said.

He kept unusual hours, I knew. He might have worked for two or three hours already.

'You're going home today?' he said.

I shifted over in the bed to hold the telephone more easily.

'Yes, at noon.'

'You are not coming back to Belemba?'

'No,' I said, 'I don't know where I'm being sent when I return.'

'I am sorry you're not coming back here.'

'It's nice of you to say so.'

'Things haven't been easy for you, have they?'

'Well . . .'

'I know all about it.'

He hesitated and I waited for him to go on.

'Our politics are difficult sometimes, very difficult. People can get hurt who don't deserve it.' He sighed. 'It's a pity but it can't be helped.'

'Maybe,' I said, 'that could be so. Sometimes ends justify the means.'

'Thank you,' he said, 'thank you for all you've done.'

'It's kind of you to telephone,' I said.

'I don't agree with what they wrote in the *Graphic*, I'd have stopped it if I had known.'

'I know you would have done.'

'I'll see you sometimes when you come back?'

'I hope so.'

'Mr Wood,' he said, 'you know those people who made trouble yesterday were just common hooligans?'

'Yes, Mr Pereta, I know that, you find them everywhere.'

'Ah, well, I must ring off. Good luck, Mr Wood.'

'Thank you, Mr Pereta. Good-bye.'

Forty-eight hours later I was in England.

CHAPTER XXVI

I had left it rather late, but there was always a lot to be done at the end of leave. The porter at the lodge pointed to the out-building just visible three hundred yards away in the hospital grounds.

'They're doing them over there,' he said. 'Just follow the road as far as the main block and then turn to the left and you'll see the place on your right.'

I turned up the side road to the building—there was something impermanent about it as though it had been put up in a hurry for a wartime purpose—stacking chairs were set out in rows in the over-heated room. More people came after me. Some looked like aircrews or soldiers, and there were boys in R.A.F. uniform. Two women waited ahead of me, one with a girl of five at her side and a boy of three wandering about the room, and the other, an older woman, with a ten-year-old son sitting next to her reading a comic. The younger woman was anxious.

'They can't make you have the injection,' she asserted. The older woman spoke as from greater experience.

'They won't allow you on the aeroplane if you don't.'

'You really have to have it then—they say it can't harm you, but how do they know?'

The girl threw off the hand of her brother and stood closer while her mother droned on.

'They ought to let people choose whether they want to be injected—after all, it's their business.'

The conversation lapsed. The boy put down his paper and demanded how much longer there was to wait. A nurse opened a door and at a signal the waiting people got up in turn and disappeared into an inner room. The two women, animated by this activity, resumed their chatter, talking mainly about their husbands.

In my turn I went through the open door following the woman with the children. She was talking to a nurse but in the impersonal routine of the place no one gave her attention and she moved on unwillingly. I gave my full name and age to the nurse, took off my jacket and bared my left arm.

A white-coated pathologist with glasses fitted a needle to a syringe and drew up a milky solution.

'Do you have a reaction to eggs?' he asked.

'Reaction to eggs?' I said.

'Yes, do you get a rash after eating eggs?'

I shook my head.

'No, nothing like that.'

'Have you been vaccinated lately?'

'Not lately.'

'Any other inoculations?'

I again shook my head. 'Nothing recently.'

'Have you been inoculated against yellow fever before?'

The inquisition was irksome. The pathologist was probably at his kindergarten in the far-off days when I had four deep injections in the stomach. The nurse was probably not born.

'Yes,' I said wearily, 'several times.'

The nurse daubed spirit on my arm and the pathologist pushed in the needle.

'This is one of the least troublesome of the inoculations,' he said informatively as he pressed down the plunger.

'Good,' I said and then rolled down my shirt sleeve and put on my jacket. The nurse gave me a certificate and I returned to the waiting room. I took my raincoat and hat and went out into the dim light of late January afternoon. It had turned colder and the rain had become sleet. The green bus swallowed up the hospital visitors with whom I had waited. The wet road reflected orange street lights and added to the medley of fluorescent shop lighting and the lights at crossings and traffic stops. I sat chilled and damp during the slow journey through sprawling suburbs to the old part of the town. I alighted and with sleet beating against my trouser bottoms I walked a quarter of a mile past stone Victorian architecture to the house.

'You're late,' Hilda said.

'I had to wait,' I said.

216

I sat down facing the fire.

'Sir Douglas Pomeroy has made a speech in the Trustee Council,' she said as she dropped a newspaper.

'Where are the children?' I said.

'I told you at lunch they were going out to tea.'

'It's a filthy night,' I said.

'You'll soon be in the sunshine and away from it all.'

'I'd rather stay here.'

'Well, you'll be retiring soon.'

'I'll put in a couple more years if they want me.'

Hilda went out and returned with a tea trolley.

'It is strange that you should be going back to Pela as P.C.,' she said.

'I am quite pleased to finish up where I started, but it's different now—radio station at Pela and a landing ground at Niko. All-season road to Huta and double carriageway bridges over the rivers.'

I poked the fire, added a log and stood up and pressed it in with my foot.

'I can't help thinking of two silly women at the hospital this afternoon.' I said. 'They were objecting to injections.'

'Did you know them?'

I shook my head.

'One woman said her husband was an agronomist.'

'What on earth is that?'

'A fancy name for someone concerned with the economics of agriculture. The other woman's husband is a dye chemist.'

'A dye chemist?'

'Yes, I suppose he's employed by one of the research groups.'

'What strange people they have nowadays.'

'They're more important than we are.'

She smiled at me.

'Nonsense! You're depressed, you always are at the end of your leave.'

I stood up with my back to the fire.

'You're an Imperialist. Your day has passed.'

'Has it? I never knew that before. The trouble with you and your friends is that you have worked yourselves out of a job.'

217

My spirits rose at the pleasure I saw in the face of the customs officer; it was the same with the man at the immigration desk. They both waved me through with a smile at Belemba Airport and outside an inspector of police saluted and greeted me by name. I felt a surge of affection for these African officers and wished I could somehow show what their friendliness meant to me.

Peter Metcalfe was at the airport to meet me and later that night at the club both he and Herbert Gregg urged me to rail my car to Huta and follow by air a week later, but I preferred the long road journey to waiting a day longer than necessary in Belemba.

The tarmac road ran through the rain forest like a knife cut; ahead lay the earth roads of the orchard scrub country. As I poured out tea from my flask the whooping cries of an animal came out of the forest and a procession of hornbills flew out with rustling wings and harsh cackles. It was the second day of my journey; I had come three hundred miles since I left Lobo that morning after a night stop with Bairstow the P.C. I felt lethargic in the stagnant tepid air of the forest country. Concrete block houses with corrugated iron roofs on the road up from the coast had proclaimed the prosperity that had come to the people. The engineers who built the road could not have foreseen the traffic which would pass over it—six wheeler lorries, petrol tankers, convoys of new vehicles going northward; and south-ward, lorries laden with gigantic logs, coffee, ground nuts, palm kernels, sisal and cotton.

At three o'clock I crossed the northern provinces boundary and reached the junction I looked for. There were rusting skeletons of two derelict lorries and a giant ant hill pointing up like a monolinth. Women in drab indigo cloths jostled in the roadside market of palm thatch stalls. I waited for the roadside dealer to hand-pump petrol out of a drum and looked at the sign post— Alagba 41 miles, Ukige 164 miles and Huta 383 miles.

Hot sun had dried the ground after the first rains and a cloud of dust followed the car as the earth road wound through the forest, past massive clumps of bamboos, along the edge of banana groves and through cultivated land where half-naked men stooped at work with short-handled hoes. I was off the main highway and compelled to go slower. Goats wandered across the road and then charged head down to safety, fowls fluttered squawking out of my way and naked brown children shouted 'white man, white man.' On the outskirts of Alagba I played with a whimsical notion when I overtook a file of women, the oldest of them misshapen by years of hard work and child bearing, carrying logs of dead wood on their heads; younger ones followed with infants tied on their backs with young girls in the rear with a few sticks or a branch.

'Ladies, what are your views on constitutional development?' I thought I might ask them.

I reached Alagba just before nightfall and drove through the government station.

Tennis courts at the club were deserted but a shout of laughter came from the building as I turned at the Rest House sign post. A large black car stood in the *porte-cochère*, an enormous Cadillac with massive chrome fittings and high flaring tail fins, and above the rear number plate a large letter M in cast aluminium. I pulled up behind it and got out cramped and with a headache from eyestrain. At the new resthouses you could get a bed and a bath and food and drink if you booked in advance. Long distance calls were uncertain and even if Metcalfe's secretary had got through there might not be a room for me. I braced myself for argument and pressed the bell at the desk. Dogs were forbidden in the resthouse, I read on a baize-covered notice board. Visitors were invited to write their complaints in the book provided for the purpose. There was something about meal times and the payment of accounts. A dog-eared letter addressed to W. O. Rook, Esq., M.B.E., looked long unclaimed. I kept my finger on the bell push. A steward in an unbottoned tunic jacket came from the kitchen. His cheeks were symmetrically scarred with tribal marks and there was a razor-scraped parting in his crinkly hair. He shook his head when I asked if a room was reserved for me.

'You get a message from Belemba yesterday?'

He shook his head again and pursed his thick lips.

'No,' he said with a blank expression, 'I get no message about you.'

'I'm Provincial Commissioner of Pela,' I said, 'can't you arrange something for me for one night?'

He showed no interest and sucked a tooth regarding me with unchanged expression.

'All the rooms are booked.'

We had reached an impasse.

'Can I use your telephone?' I said.

He glanced at the instrument and again pursed his lips.

'What's the D.C.'s number?'

He cracked the finger joints of his left hand and looked away as though my presence wearied him.

'Number one.'

The bell at the other end rang for a long time before a voice announced 'D.C. go on tour'.

'Who's speaking?'

'Operator.'

'When D.C. come back?'

'Next week, I think.'

I replaced the telephone. The steward stood waiting for me to go.

'Can I see your bookings?' I said.

He raised his chin towards a paint-lined board behind him. There were chalked entries against each of the ten rooms. I looked again.

'Four rooms for the Minister?' I exclaimed incredulously. 'What Minister?'

'Mister Mutsawaga—Minister of Social Services.'

I did not know the name. There had been a reshuffle of ministries and a newcomer must have come in.

'What's he want four rooms for?'

'Secretary say he want four rooms, so we book them.'

I thought there was a chance that the Minister might not require them all.

'Where's Minister now?' I said.

He was regarding me with distaste and seemed anxious to close our discussion.

'He come back for dinner.'

'Bring me whisky,' I said. 'I'll wait for him.'

It was still early, barely a quarter past seven. Not many people would come across from their rooms before eight o'clock. I was the only person in the lounge when the steward brought my drink. I added water to the whisky and lit a cigarette. I picked up a picture paper and hoped the Minister would come soon. I was tired and depressed, and prickly heat was bothering me. The expedition was madness. Two hundred and eighty miles from Belemba to Lobo and three hundred and sixty-two from Lobo to Alagba—I had travelled more than six hundred miles in two days of the hot season, and was still only about half-way.

There was something wrong with the electricity supply. The naked lights flickered and then became dim and the ceiling fan circulating slowly sent tobacco smoke away in eddies but brought no relief from the heat. There were now twelve people in the lounge—four couples and four men sitting alone, tired looking and sitting quietly while waiting for food. The steward put the third tot of whisky on the cigarette-scarred table. Then the Minister swaggered in with a rustle of native costume. He wore a round cap decorated with gilt filigree work. The listless white people looked as he and his four companions found chairs. It was Cairngross and it was his big black Cadillac outside. With the nationalist movement some leading people with English names had looked back into their ancestry for an African name and had discarded European clothes for traditional costume. The flowing gown seemed to add to his exuberant vitality—he was certainly the dominant figure in the room. He clicked thumb and finger and called to the steward. The steward stood talking after he had brought them drinks. 'Who?' I heard the Minister demand, 'who did you say?' When the steward again spoke Cairngross replied as though with an effort he recollected of whom he spoke. 'Wood?' he said, and then he and his companions turned and stared at me. I crossed the room and greeted him.

'I didn't know you had left the Development Ministry,' I said.

The five of them looked at me with curiosity—three older men I supposed to be NUDA party members from the town, a young man was a secretary or an official of some sort.

Cairngross took a cigarette from a round tin of fifty.

'I haven't seen you for a long time—how are you? where are you going?' He spoke with a momentary flicker of interest.

'I've come up from Belemba, Minister,' I said, 'I'm on my way to Pela.'

'Pela!,' he echoed, 'that's a long way.' He yawned. 'The steward says you've not got a room.'

'No, Minister, there was no time to book.'

He pointed at the secretary.

'Take his room,' he said and told the young man, 'you can sleep in the town.'

He nodded at me and turned again to his companions. Their laughter and raised voices reached me after I had gone in to the dining-room. They were still sitting at the table when I came out.

CHAPTER XXVII

At talks in London after the failure of the interim constitution, the date for Independence was fixed. The House was dissolved and in the following election campaign NUDA promised universal primary education, and expansion of free medical services, a programme of water supplies and local government reform. They were returned with a working majority over NIC and at once got to work. The Local Government Bill went through just before I got back from leave and James Roebuck the D.C. and his assistants—McIntyre a New Zealander and two Africans Bemana and Tai, had already travelled thousands of miles in the heat and dust of the dry season, holding meetings in markets, under trees, in schools and in native court houses consulting the people on a new local government structure for Pela Province.

Over the years the old dynastic rule had been modified but with gradual changes it was doubtful whether Harama had noticed it. In the new arrangement a figure-head position was reserved for him but powers of decision were vested in councils. When I explained this, as I did repeatedly, he nodded and assured me that he supported the changes. I always left him feeling that although he said he was anxious for progress he took the view of a well-disposed onlooker not personally concerned who hoped all would go well.

The Minister approved our proposals for ten district councils to act as electoral colleges for the Central Council at Pela. Then followed registration of voters, the revision of lists and the gazetting of polling stations. We all felt the strain of the work. Roebuck had rings under his eyes and got short-tempered with McIntyre. I often saw the light in his office when I went to bed.

Everything became a matter of politics. NUDA sent loud speaker vans from Huta and these were followed from village to village by NIC vans. When crowds gathered to listen to dance music speakers harangued them asking for votes. Not much was said about local government; the speeches were about freedom and democracy and the rights of the common man. The voting symbols of the parties— the Bull of NUDA and the Ram of NIC— were plastered on walls and tacked on to trees.

A week before the election Harama asked me to see him but as I was leaving the Residency, Hophni Mena, the Superintendent of Police, came into my office. There had been scuffles and stone throwing in Pela and in three other places. Four men were in hospital and a NUDA van had been wrecked. Twenty men were in the police lock-up and party lawyers had come out from Huta trying to arrange bail and accusing Mena of discrimination.

'When we pull in hooligans we don't ask what party they support,' he said, 'and my men know it.'

Mena's curly black hair was grey-streaked. He was in his late forties but he was a tough little man and at one time had been well known as a middleweight boxer. He had been a constable in Gregg's Faisi party and this formed a bond between us.

I put my hand on his shoulder. 'You carry on as you are. Life's not easy for you, I know.' He gave me an attractive smile and I grinned back at him. 'I'm with you, Hophni,' I said.

'That's all I want to know, sir.'

He saluted and went out.

I was late for my appointment with Harama.

A drummer at the compound entrance announced my arrival and a servant took me to the inner chamber where Harama saw me when we were alone.

A photograph of his father in Chief's regalia—too blurred by over-enlargement to be recognized—hung on a wall facing a lithograph of Queen Victoria. A reproduced photograph of George V talking into a microphone hung next to a print of Edward VIII looking boyish in an Admiral's uniform. Matching portraits of George VI and Queen Elizabeth hung on each side of the door and over the door a new photograph of the Queen and Prince Philip with the royal children. A war-time print of Sir Winston Churchill was beginning to fade. Behind Harama's chair a glazed door closed over a baize-covered board where the badges of the C.M.G., the C.B.E., and the Queen's Medal for Chiefs hung from fading ribbons tacked on to the baize.

The servant moved Harama's chair nearer the table, bowed, and withdrew.

I heard muttered voices and the rustling of gowns and caught a whiff of sweet scent. I stood up when Harama shuffled into the room, and put down his horsetail switch on the table. He was too breathless to speak but held my hand in a two-handed clasp. He lowered himself into the chair, rested his arms on the table and greeted me with a benevolent smile.

'Welcome, old friend,' he said, 'it makes me happy to see you.'

He wore a soft white fez and a lemon-coloured gown of strips of local silk. His eyelids were blue rimmed with antimony and his fingers and nails stained russet-coloured by henna. A cataract was forming over his right eye and his hearing was failing.

'I'm glad to see you, my friend,' I said.

Harama eased his gown at the back. He smiled again. It was an honest old face rather than clever—serene, simple and strong.

He cleared his throat and leaned over the table.

'I don't want this local government,' he said.

He hitched up his gown again and yawned as he awaited my reply, but I had no quick answer.

After a few moments silence Harama continued, 'The way we have always done it here is good. I sit with my counsellors and everyone talks. I listen to all they say.' He made a slight gesture. 'Soon we know the right thing to do and everyone agrees.'

He picked up his switch. The hair fell back as he held it up. 'You know,' he said smiling again, 'I always do what my people tell me.'

A lizard slipped on the grass mat and scuffled over the floor. Harama started to cough. He wiped his watering eyes and spat into a cloth. He put the cloth on the table and leaned back in his chair.

'Well?' he said.

I felt in despair, not because the work would be halted but because I had a presentiment of trouble to come.

He kept his eyes on me and he looked disappointed when I said nothing.

'You always give good advice,' he said.

I spoke gently with slow deliberation.

'I don't understand, Harama. I thought we'd settled all this.'

'Yes but these people have been bothering me.'

I took out a cigarette and asked permission to smoke.

'What people, Harama?'

He struck the table bell.

'Tell Buramo I want him,' he said to a servant.

Buramo, the son of a concubine, was a child round the house when I first came to Pela. He had been educated at Huta and trained as a teacher but Harama had taken him back in the house.

He greeted me, and then turned to Harama.

'Buramo,' Harama threw out his hands, 'tell the white man about these people who have been here.'

'Mr Tasak and the other two people?'

'Yes, yes, those people.'

'Tasak, NUDA secretary from Belemba,' I said, 'has he been here?'

Buramo bowed. 'Yes, he came here and asked to see Harama.'

'What for?'

'He wanted Harama to announce his support for NUDA.'

Harama looked at me expectantly, but it would have been unwise for me to say anything.

I waited. 'Well?' I said.

Harama leaned over the table towards me shaking the horse-tail. At first he seemed too angry to speak, then he raised his voice, 'I drove him away. I told him the Pela people are my children—we don't have parties here.'

I looked at Buramo.

'What did Tasak say?'

'He threatened Harama. He said they wanted to help Harama, but if he did not co-operate the party would oppose him.'

'I see,' I said.

Buramo's eyes met mine and we looked at each other in silence. Then he said, 'That's not all. Three days later a NUDA loud speaker van came through Pela saying Harama was oppressing the people. He was paid a big salary and it was wrong of him to take presents.'

Harama shifted in his chair and started to tremble.

'Do you hear what they said about me?' he shouted. 'My people are happy. That's why I don't want this new local government.'

Buramo was waiting to speak.

'Mr Arep, NIC secretary, was here yesterday but Harama refused to see him. Before he left he said they were disgusted with NUDA and were determined to support Harama.'

Harama banged the table. 'Support me! Who are these insolent dogs. I don't want people going about making speeches about me.'

He now had a wild, worried expression. He wiped his face with the cloth and fell silent. The effort of talking had been too much for him.

Buramo was intelligent and balanced but with his deferential courtesy I could not tell what he was thinking.

I spoke quietly in English.

'The local government reform must go on. It's the law, it's approved by the House of Assembly. There's no turning back.'

He smiled ruefully. It was the first sign of feeling he had shown.

'Most assuredly. That's what I keep telling Harama.'

'He should get on terms with the political parties.'

'He won't do that.'

Harama looked suspiciously at Buramo and then turned to me. 'You agree we stop all this local government business?'

Buramo excused himself and went out.

I slowly shook my head.

'That's not possible, my friend. We can't stand still. We must go on. All our plans are approved by the Minister.'

'A black man minister?'

'Yes—Mr Kanato.'

'You obey him?'

'Of course.'

Harama looked incredulous. He did not believe me. I tried to speak patiently but we had been over the ground so many times before.

'Times are changing, Harama,' I said wearily, 'Africans are taking over the Government and I have told you many times before long the white man will go.'

'That's it,' he exclaimed. 'I don't want the white man to go. They brought my people many good things like . . .' he paused and looked anxious and then his face lightened, '. . . like corrugated iron and lamp oil.'

227

I said nothing and he repeated.

'Yes, corrugated iron and lamp oil,' as if challenging me to deny it.

I was wasting my time. When I got up to go Harama accompanied me along the passage. Outside the sun beat fiercely down on the hard-baked clay of the compound. A drummer at the doorway stirred when he saw Harama and began a routine of traditional praise.

'Hail king of the Universe, benefactor of the poor, Allah give thee great riches and grant you long life.'

Harama blinked in the glare as the drummer kept up the meaningless rigmarole. Scores of red and blue lizards clung quite still on the wall in the sun. There was a constant thud of women pounding yams. Other women stirred pots while keeping watch on pinkish tomatoes grouped in half-penny piles, chillies, red peppers, kola nuts, matches tied in bundles of ten, and packets of salts. Naked children playing in the sun with leather amulets at their waists wetted the ground. In the shade of a mango heavy with yellowing fruit a class of small boys recited the Koran while their elderly teacher moved among them with a thong. An old woman with dangling breasts squatted in an open doorway spinning cotton at the end of a stick and nearby an old man sat with his back to a tree talking to himself and plaiting a horse hobble; another old man lay fast asleep on the ground. A girl giggled while she sat between the legs of a companion dressing her hair.

Harama stood framed in the horseshoe shaped doorway. He had forgotten his annoyance and seemed to breathe an air of benevolence over the horde of dependants. He touched my arm, 'I want your photograph,' he said. I felt impatient. I wanted to tell him, 'those days are finished for ever,' but as I shook his hand I said 'Yes, of course, I'll be honoured.'

I had left the windows closed and the car was like an oven when I drove out into the road. The driver of a Volkswagen bus marked with the Bull of NUDA was cursing people in front as he forced his way through with continuous hooting.

The election was not decided on village pump politics. For weeks NUDA loud speaker vans had proclaimed a vote for the Bull would bring new roads, water supplies and free primary schools and hospitals, and there was talk about the oppression of chiefs. NIC promised to keep taxes down, better prices for produce, secondary schools, support for Harama and respect for native law and custom. When we counted the votes we found some villages had voted *en bloc* for the Ram and others, a few miles away, had given all their support to the Bull. Some villages boycotted the election and this may have tipped voting in favour of NUDA, as when Roebuck announced the results next morning they had got majorities in seven of the ten districts and would therefore control the Central Council.

Mr Kanato, the Minister for Local Government, flew up from Belemba to Niko. He was a graduate of Durham and before entering politics had been principal of a teaching training college. He stepped down from the aircraft—a small man with bushy hair and rimless glasses, wearing a well-cut suit—and came forward with outstretched hand.

At ceremonies we arranged for Kanato he made a speech and presented each council with a warrant of their duties and powers. He spent the last night at the Residency and we talked about local government until two in the morning. I had persuaded Harama to receive him, but when I drove down after breakfast Buramo came out with a message that Harama was sick and unable to see anyone. Kanato's face hardened, but he was soon smiling again and sent back a message that he hoped Harama would soon recover. The incident was not mentioned on our way back to Niko.

The task of making the councils work fell on Roebuck and the intrusion of politics into every discussion made his task harder. A proposal by a NUDA member would be rejected by NIC and the same thing happened the other way. Only politics counted. The Central Council with a leavening of teachers and traders in the NUDA majority did better. But Harama was an obstruction. He did not recognize the limitations of his position and tried to dictate to the council, ignoring the agenda and often returning to subjects which had been previously discussed and resolved. Meetings were held up on points of order with many people talking at once.

One Sunday morning I stopped to talk to the Reverend O. B. Alomo outside the mud block church the Anglicans had built beyond the polo ground about a mile from the station. We had raised money to pay for a roof and he wanted to thank me. He showed me a lectern someone in England had given him. He talked fluently and well about the Church's problems. A note of anxiety came into his voice.

'The old days of schools and medical missions are gone. We led the way, but now we must acknowledge that government can do these things better. It's a matter of money.'

'I suppose you're right,' I said, 'but you get Government grants.'

We sat on the verandah facing a patch of brown grass. A bare-foot boy in white shorts and a book in his hand stood waiting to speak to Alomo.

'Come back in half an hour,' he said gently.

He collected his thoughts.

'Grants did you say? Yes, on conditions. That makes us dependants of the Government, doing work for them which they could do better. It's no good running mission stations on a shoe-string with no real impact on public affairs.' He looked sad. 'What good am I doing here, what contacts have I made?'

I reassured him. A fowl fluttered up to the verandah. His dog barked and he gave it a tap to silence it.

'No,' he said, 'we ought to concentrate our efforts at the centre; we should meet new problems which have come with education and political progress, not wait until they are forced on us. May-be Christian churches should unite and build a college for the ministry—a centre for the best brains we've got. . . .' His voice tailed off and he grimaced, 'anyway, we've got to do something.'

There was nothing helpful I could say. I had letters to write and I wanted to get back to the station. He walked with me be-tween the crotons bordering the path to the road.

'I suppose we've all got our problems,' I remarked senten-tiously.

He spoke with immediate contrition.

'Yes, indeed, of course, you must be worried about Harama.'

He awakened the anxiety I had pushed to the back of my mind. I must have been abrupt because he looked startled when I replied.

'Why?' I said, 'why should I be worried about Harama?'

Alomo looked at me with questioning eyes.

'I thought you might be,' he said. 'At the Council meeting on Thursday some of the NUDA young men abused him. Even a year ago such a thing would not have been possible.' He opened the gate for me. 'Maybe it's as well he doesn't hear much, but you can't help wondering how it'll all end.'

'I suppose you can't,' I said. 'Good-bye Mr Alomo.'

'Good-bye Mr Wood.'

CHAPTER XXVIII

There was no longer enough work to keep me fully employed. In the old administration we had been concerned in everything that went on, our opinions were consulted and carried great weight and there was always plenty to do. With the coming of ministerial government the administration had become bureaucratic and more in the hands of specialists in Belemba who wrote direct to departmental officers and I often heard only in gossip what was being done in the Province. Roebuck and his assistant D.C.s had their hands full guiding the new councils and carrying out the local government reform, but there appeared nothing of any consequence for me to do. I decided to visit the pagan settlements in the plains to the south of the Balaba Mountains. There were five of them and only a few groups of elderly people remained with the ancestral shrines in the mountains. It had been a great achievement by Harama to persuade the pagans to come down to the plain.

The flat earth shimmered in the heat haze and powdery dust, not red laterite as in other parts of the Province, but yellowish brown, penetrated the car and got into my nose and throat. I did the journey in just over five hours. Berefat was fingering Moslem beads when he met me and wearing a gown and red fez. He showed me their schools, the infant welfare centre and the market. I sat outside my hut just before sunset. I became chilly and put on a jacket. Smoke rose from evening fires, then I watched the glowering sun go down. Ali brought me a drink and I sat on in the darkness fascinated by the crackle and glow of a mountain bush fire.

I returned to Pela the following day.

I spent an idle week in the station and then accepted an invitation from the American Evangelical Mission to the opening of an extension to their hospital at Faisi. I stayed on two days and their education supervisor, a tireless woman wearing octagonal glasses and jeans—she came from Pasadena, she told me—took me round their rural training centre where Faisi men ran a co-operative farm and their women in monogrammed overalls learned cooking, dressmaking and weaving.

'We aim to train the whole family,' she said, 'and so raise the standard of living. Next year we are going to start a model village where they can put our methods into practice for everyone to see.'

Next day she drove me through the forest in a Jeep to see their primary schools. A nurse came with us to show me their clinics.

The mission superintendent saw me off.

'Come again, Mr Wood,' he said, 'it's been good to have you with us for a few days.'

'I've been very impressed by your work,' I said.

He beamed. 'Yes, I think our efforts have been blessed.'

'How long have you been here?' I asked him.

'We came down here first twelve years in December with Harama. He'd been begging us to come for four years before that.' He gave a little nod. 'Great man, Harama, but for him we wouldn't be here. Pity he's a Moslem—still, maybe. . . . How is he now?'

'He's pretty old.'

'Yes, I guess he must be. Give him our greetings. Say we hope he'll come and see us one day.'

'I'll do that with pleasure,' I said.

An air letter was waiting for me at Pela. Hilda had written to say she could join me for four months.

The fifty-seven miles from Pela to Niko is a two and a half hour's run except after heavy rain when patches of mud make the short road impassable and you have to keep to the tarmac over the longer road. I left the Residency at six o'clock and it was half past eight when I signed the P.C.'s Visitors' book at Niko and drove on to the airport. My car looked shabby parked next to a new Chevrolet.

Niko is not a place for mails or refuelling. It does not appear in the internal air services timetable. It is an old R.A.F. staging post

233

now only used as a 'flagstop' where one aircraft a week linking the overseas service puts down if two or more passengers request in advance. The waiting-room was forlorn as though onward progress had overstretched itself and retreated. Fly-spotted pictures of English castles hung on the walls and advertisements of airlines, fouled by lizard droppings, made ineffectual appeal from a side table. A weighing machine marked in kilograms was labelled 'Out of Order'. I walked across the room and out through the door on the other side. A messenger in the shade of the roof overhang stared out at the runway. At a quarter to nine a clerk in peaked uniform cap rode up on a bicycle. I followed him into the office attached to the waiting-room.

'Who's disembarking?' I said.

He looked at a signal form.

'Two passengers—Mr Ramachandrai and Mrs Wool.'

'The name is Wood,' I told him.

He looked again at the paper and shook his head.

'No,' he said, 'Wool.'

I let it go. I was impatient and restless and my tongue and throat were sore from smoking.

'Is the aircraft on time?'

He examined his wrist watch and then stared through the window at the runway.

'I think so,' he said, looking again at his wrist watch.

The Dove touched down at five to nine. The clerk and the messenger wheeled the steps into place and the door opened. An Indian came first carrying a zippered document case. I saw a pink vest through his nylon shirt and got a whiff of his scent. Hilda followed with her night-stop bag and some parcels. As we walked towards the waiting-room the Dove roared down the runway and was airborne.

I put her suit case in the boot and her night-bag and parcels in the back of the car.

'I wonder how I'll like Pela?' she said as we drove off from the airfield.

'You won't recognize it.'

She shifted in her seat to get comfortable.

'So many changes.'

At the main road I turned towards Niko.

Hilda looked back. 'You're going the wrong way.'

I kept the car going.

'You must sign Charles Rushton's book,' I said. 'It won't be there much longer.'

'What do you mean?'

'Oh, I don't know. I've got an idea we'll be thrown out of these houses.'

'You're morbid.'

'Maybe, all the same we're an anachronism.'

We drove through Niko station to the Residency. The flag was flying and Charles was at home.

'Nip in quietly and sign the book,' I said, 'I don't want to see him. He makes me depressed.'

She stepped into the kiosk at the side of the drive. 'There's been nobody there for three weeks,' she said when she came out.

'The old order changeth,' I said fatuously.

I turned the car and we drove back through the station past neat houses with hedges of croton or clipped casuarinas, and painted name boards stuck in the ground outside.

'Is Pela like that?' Hilda asked as we joined the main road.

'Sort of,' I said. 'The mud houses have gone and now there are three types of bungalow according to salary grades and a big house for me in four acres of land.

'It sounds marvellous,' she said.

We headed eastward along the new tarmac road.

'And there's electricity and piped water.'

She put a lighted cigarette in my mouth.

'It all helps,' she said.

'Thank the ministers, and for this road, too.' I pulled up to allow a lorry to pass. 'And wait until you've seen the schools and hospitals.'

We left the tamarind and locust bean trees of Niko and went smoothly along the new road through the orchard scrub. Early storms had freshened the countryside but the days were still hot, and with rain not far off it was oppressive and humid.

A herd of humped cattle moved slowly across the road ahead of us.

'Why have they been able to do all these things?' Hilda asked as we waited.

'Why have who been able to do all what things?'

The herdsman waved a long stick and laughed.

'The ministers.'

I shrugged my shoulders.

'I suppose we'd set the stage for rapid development, or maybe they're not so sensitive about the taxpayers' money.' I lit a cigarette and shouted at the herdsman. 'But there's more to it than that. They're alive and vital and eager; there's no stopping them.'

'What does the Mudela think of the changes?'

'Harama?'

'Yes.'

The herdsman waved his stick as the last of the cattle crossed.

'Harama's an old man,' I said, 'he's too old for changes.'

'Do you see much of him?'

'Every Tuesday, and he returns the call on Thursdays. He thinks he can carry on as his father did. He can't see that Pela's the concern of ministers. The politicians say that I encourage him.'

'Do you?'

'Are you serious?' I said, 'where do you think that would get him, or me, for that matter?'

'I don't know.'

'I do,' I said.

I savoured the news from home—the operation for appendicitis, music lessons, increased school fees, good reports about the younger boy.

The road dipped and cut through a bamboo thicket on each side of a culvert. It was too soon in the season for water but cool air rose from the moist ground. In the shade of the bamboos a large drill lay on its side and its blue and red features made a splash of colour on the tarmac. Flies had gathered and very soon vultures would find the body and tear it apart. Half an hour later we drove into Pela. White-turbaned crowds thronged the road through the town and trumpets sounded and there was a rhythm of drums. I saw Harama's gaudy umbrella above the heads of the crowds; he was on his way back from the Mosque.

Lepers on the roadside were demanding alms and girls pushed through the crowds with head-loads of cassava, hawking their goods in monotonous sing-song. A rearing horse mounted by someone of consequence made a commotion and I was compelled to pull up. While I waited a youth brought a blind man to the window. He held out a tin basin.

'King of the world,' he declaimed. 'Owner of untold treasure; Allah give you victories over your enemies and hide your secrets.' He put his hand to his stomach. 'I am hungry.'

'Go,' I said, 'for the sake of Allah give me the space you occupy.'

'Very well, oh Lion,' he said without offence. 'May Allah give you long life.'

I got the car moving again.

'Why did you swear at that blind man?' Hilda said. I was pre-occupied and did not hear her properly.

'What did you say?'

'Why did you swear at that blind man?' she repeated.

'He's a scoundrel; he's boss of the blind men and gets a cut of everything they beg.'

We drove slowly on along the narrow street. A procession of drummers held us up at the town gate and then we passed through to the road for the government station beyond. We drove alongside the polo ground past the new office buildings and had reached the Education Officer's house about fifty yards from the Residency. We got on to the circular road at the tennis courts. Hilda interrupted my thoughts.

'I'd never have believed you if you had told me twenty years ago that I should see that in Pela.'

A girl with blonde hair drawn neatly back in a bun stood listening attentively to a black woman gripping a perambulator. A three-year-old girl pulled on her dress and an older girl stared at us.

'That's the D.C.'s wife with the two children—Ilse Roebuck, she's a German—and the other woman is Mrs Demeta, the doctor's wife.'

'Mrs Roebuck'll soon have three children,' said Hilda, and then she exclaimed, 'Oh how lovely, how perfectly lovely.'

The *ponciana regia* at the beginning of the drive was in full bloom, a gorgeous medley of yellow and scarlet.

'The cassias and the tulip tree at the back are good this year, too.'

Ali came out to meet us. He had put on his best uniform.

'Welcome, madam,' he cried, 'welcome.'

Then cook appeared wearing his apron and grinning with delight.

'Welcome, madam; are the children well?'

'All well, cook,' she said. 'How's your wife and children?'

'My wife has just delivered another female child.'

Vusa the gardener rushed across the lawn shouting idiotically.

'Welcome, madam, welcome.'

'Go in,' I told her. 'You'll have the horse-boys and all the women here in a moment.'

I got the baggage out of the back of the car and gave it to Ali and followed her into the cool shade of the hall.

There were no social diversions at Pela. Women refused to leave children at night for dinner parties or bridge. On library nights we went to the club but there were no dances there now. Contractors' men who were building the bridge over the Libia came in working clothes and stayed drinking until midnight. At the beginning of September we gave a party to government staff. Out of the twenty-seven who came nineteen drank Coca Cola or squash and seventeen were non-smokers. There were only ten Europeans.

When they had gone Hilda looked at the clock. 'A quarter past ten, in the old days the party would have hardly begun.'

'It costs less,' I said.

She shook up the cushions 'Everyone's so earnest and correct and I don't know what to say to them.'

Ali was clearing the ash trays.

'Bring whisky and soda,' I said.

Hilda poured out a tot and passed me the decanter.

'Well, I don't have to wash up,' she said, 'I mustn't forget that.'

'Africa, the white woman's paradise,' I said.

'You wouldn't have thought so to hear some of them talking.'

In October egrets flew in over the station, the sign that the rains were over. The harvest began to ripen and we were infested by

earwigs and flies For a few weeks the air was fresh and sweet
At night the stars were bright, the moon rose with dazzling brilliancy and we sat overlong outside before dinner. Hilda left in
November. Because of *harmattan* haze there could be no flagstop at Niko and I drove her to Huta for the internal service to
Belemba.

CHAPTER XXIX

I was away five days. I could have got back in two but I stayed three days with Shellard, the P.C. at Huta. It was just after four o'clock when I put away the car and walked into the house. Ali met me saying that Roebuck had asked me to telephone at once. There was no reply from his house; when I rang the office McIntyre replied.

McIntyre, a broad young man from Dunedin with a pugnacious face, was hard working and competent.

'Where's Roebuck,' I said.

'He's gone off with Mena to Shomu. There's been hell to play there—anti-tax demonstrations.'

I had an uneasy feeling that I had failed in my duty, an irrational feeling of guilt which I always had when anything happened when I was out of the Province.

'When did this happen?'

'This morning. Roebuck couldn't wait. He told me to give you the gen.'

'Come up at once,' I said.

District Council committees assessed and collected the tax in their areas. The minimum rate was twenty-one shillings but the committees were supposed to levy on income. Assessment methods were crude and the committees were content to get as much as they could without causing an outcry. A Central Council precept put up the tax and it had been raised again by a government levy of ten shillings towards the costs of new services.

Roebuck, Bemana and Tai had been round the districts to check the assessments and had reported that they were fair.

McIntyre's car tyres crackled on the gravel. His shrunken stockings and faded shorts exposed his muscular legs.

'Mrs Wood get away O.K?' he asked as he came in.

240

His casual manner was slightly offensive.

'Yes, thank you,' I said. 'Sit down. What's happened?'

He stretched back and grinned.

'They've set fire to the district office and burned furniture, typewriter, records and all—and broken open the safe. That's the last I heard.' He grinned again. 'God knows what's happened since. Roebuck and Mena left about twelve o'clock.'

I felt old and tired. The thought of violence appalled me. I got up and offered McIntyre a cigarette.

'No thank you,' he said.

'What about a drink?'

He shook his head.

I remained standing.

'What started it?'

'It's the government levy. They refuse to pay it.'

He kept his eyes fixed on me as I stared at him.

'They don't want schools, hospitals and the rest of it, then?'

He leaned back in the chair.

'No, sir!' he said easily. 'They can do without all that if it's going to cost them ten bob.'

I felt anxious but no longer dejected. Action of some sort was better than the idleness. There was still work to be done.

'That's all?' I said.

'Not all—they don't like the methods of the assessment committee.' He pursed his lips. 'They say they are tyrannical scoundrels oppressing the poor.'

'There's a NUDA council at Shomu?'

He nodded. 'They are all NUDA councils in that part.'

I walked up and down the room. I saw Hilda's sewing glasses on the side table. It seemed a long time since she had sat there. Without interrupting my main train of thought I decided to pack the glasses and post them at once.

'The whole thing's political then?'

I was disconcerted by the amused manner with which he watched me. He spoke with a trace of a New Zealand accent.

'What isn't in this place?'

I glanced at him as I walked to and fro.

'Very little,' I said, 'and of course it gets hot at midday—just the weather for riots.'

McIntyre was someone I could talk to, but I was really thinking out loud when I paused and stood facing him.

'This thing could spread.'

His change of expression affected me more than what he said. 'I'll say it could.'

'All right, Mac, tell the postmaster to keep the line open tonight. I may want to telephone Belemba.'

There was a chill in the air but women traders sat patiently behind stands on the roadside and though the light was failing, tailors, leather workers and smiths were still working outside their houses. Along the labyrinthine alleys leading away from the road smoke rose from hundreds of closely-packed compounds and there was the acrid stench of burning horse dung. Boys on bicycles weaved their way among the sheep and goats; wandering children turned and stared and then continued to play. I drove by the dyepits and the new co-operative shop. The haze gave the failing sunlight a grey metallic effect. Girl hawkers raised their voices but not with the hopeful cries of midday. People moved slower as though wearied by the work of the day. A donkey brayed somewhere. Sounds blended into the subdued murmur of normal evening activity. Then there was a sudden outburst of drumming, an unmistakable festive uproar. It was an unusual time for a wedding or funeral. I drove on towards Harama's compound. It was from there that the drumming came. I left my car outside and walked in. Six drummers, four men and two youths, were beating out furious rhythm. Coins lay in the dust at their feet but the drummers, gibbering with concentration, kept up their performance. Women and girls postured and twisted to the rhythm of the drums, more women joined them and a jostling crowd pressed forward all round. Household servants, lolling against the buttresses of the main entrance, laughed and chattered among themselves. I spoke twice before one of them broke away and led me along the passage to the inner chamber. It was dark and a minute later he returned with a lamp. Then Harama bustled in with the short tottering steps of an old man trying to hurry. His head was covered with a soft hat and he wore a matching gown of white calico. He was panting when he sat down.

I replied to his greeting, then I said, 'I'm surprised by the drumming and dancing, Harama, you must have had news of this trouble at Shomu.'

He made an expansive gesture and smiled. 'They're happy out there.'

His animation disturbed me.

'What makes them so happy?'

He put his hands flat on the table and leaned forward.

'I want my people to be happy. It is good that they should be happy. You must not be surprised.'

His mouth twitched and he dribbled. I said nothing and he added—it seemed to me rather inconsequentially—'how are you, my friend?'

'I'm worried about this trouble at Shomu,' I said.

Thick mud walls and the warren of passages could not muffle the drumming outside.

Harama was evasive, peering at me as though he were not sure he had heard me aright.

'What is that now, about tax, I think?'

'You know what I mean, Harama. I mean the riots and damage to property. A mob has burned down the district offices.' I pushed my face towards him. 'This is very serious, my friend.'

He no longer smiled. He had retired into himself and was withdrawn from me.

'You know what I mean,' I repeated.

He stirred and spoke slowly in a weak voice.

'It's the new local government, my people don't like it. Our old way was better.'

Pity welled up in me but I shook my head.

'We're not going into all that again,' I said, but I did not think he heard me for he continued 'and the tax is too much. My people can't pay it.'

'That's not true, Harama.'

His lips moved, but no sound came.

'What do you say, Harama?' I said.

'I've always been a friend of white men,' he mumbled. He held out his left hand. 'Why don't you help me?'

'And I'm your friend. That's why I've come. I'm here to help you.'

243

My nerves could not stand the noise of the drumming much longer.

Harama shook his head slowly. I was conscious of a feeling of crisis.

I touched his arm. 'Harama,' I said, 'if these riots spread immense trouble will come to your people.'

He lay over the table and his back heaved as he silently wept into his hands.

I put my hand on his back. 'Listen to me,' I said. 'One person can stop this trouble and only one person.'

He raised his head. Curiosity steadied him and he was more composed.

'Who?' he said, 'who is that?'

I pointed at him.

'You,' I said. 'You are the only person who can stop this trouble. And you must.'

He cowered at the suggestion.

'Oh, no,' he said, 'I can do nothing.'

I brought my hand down on the chenille covering.

'Harama, you must go round the Province and tell the people— they are your people—to pay their tax at once. Believe me this will be the best thing you have ever done. All the world will see your people obey you. You can do more than these councils.'

He gaped and was about to speak when Buramo came in. Buramo greeted me correctly but without any expression and then turned to Harama.

'It's evening prayer time, Master,' he said.

Harama struggled up. Buramo gave him his arm and drew out the chair.

Harama nodded and smiled at me. 'It's evening prayer time. You must excuse me, my friend.'

I moved round the table to detain him. 'I beg you, for the sake of Allah, to do what I say.'

He smiled and nodded again.

'It's evening prayer time. Thank you for coming.'

I left the house and walked round the fringe of the crowd in the compound. The sun had gone down and it was colder. Shea-butter dips and small fires burned on the roadside.

It was just after ten o'clock when the Land Rover pulled up. Roebuck's greying hair had begun to recede. Bushy eyebrows overhanging lively brown eyes met at the bridge of his nose and matched his moustache. An alert manner and his well formed features gave him a conventional military appearance. He was not over forty but looked older.

'Well, James?' I said when Ali had brought in drinks.

Roebuck drew on his pipe.

'Mena and I left at noon for Shomu with twenty-eight men. The office buildings were still smouldering but the rioters were gone. We were told that some of them had gone by lorries to join a meeting that afternoon at Lampedi. We were stopped by road blocks, the first eight miles out of Shomu and the second twelve miles on. We were held up again about two miles this side of Lampedi. There were trees across the road and they had moved out stones and built up a barrier. When the men got out of the truck crowds came from both sides of the road about fifty yards ahead. Some of them were carrying muzzle loaders, the rest were armed with clubs and sticks.'

I looked at Mena; he nodded and Roebuck continued.

'It's mainly burned bush there—easy to dodge about in, but still quite good cover. While the men were clearing the road the crowd came closer and started throwing stones. Two or three fired but we were well out of range.'

Mena opened a note-book. 'They fired three times,' he said.

Roebuck paused, looked at Mena and went on again. 'In open country our men couldn't do much with heavy boots and equipment. I agreed with Mena that unless they came closer it would be better to concentrate on clearing the road and push on to Lampedi.'

I touched the bell. Roebuck poured out a second drink but Mena waved Ali away.

Roebuck continued: 'We ran into a crowd of three thousand at Lampedi. They gave way for us with a lot of jeering and shouting and we pulled up in the centre of the town on the north side of the market where the lorries park. For half an hour they milled about shouting and waving sticks. At half past three four men came forward. They said they had nothing against me or the police but they refused to pay the levy and alleged that the assessment committee was corrupt and was victimizing NIC tax payers. I told them I would take a deputation back to Pela and I was sure that you would investigate their complaints. They said they would consult their people. We waited an hour then Mena and I walked through the town. Most of the crowd had gone but when we came back we found a couple of hundred had collected near the council offices. We moved the Land Rover and the truck towards them. I went forward with a megaphone and told them to disperse or we should use force. They became noisy and I could hear shouts of "Let's rush them." "Let's burn down the offices." The noise was deafening and even with the megaphone I could not make myself heard.'

Roebuck turned to Mena. 'I asked Hophni to disperse the mob and restore order.'

'Yes?' I said.

Mena breathed hard. 'We sent over tear-gas but they rushed to the other side away from it. They were waving sticks and moved in on us again. I drove them back with a baton charge. We made five arrests. They came back again. A man with a club was in front inciting the mob. I was afraid for the safety of my men and I got on the bonnet of the Land Rover and drew my revolver. I held one round over my head. I put the round in the breach and fired.' 'I hit him in the knee.' Mena breathed hard. 'In the meantime some of the mob were smashing windows in the council office and pushing in burning corn stalks. I put in another round and fired again. They ran off, one of them was holding his shoulder. The crowd fell back but began to form up again. We made two more baton charges. Order was then restored but smoke was coming out of the district office. We put out the fire. I treated the injured man and brought him back in the truck with the prisoners.'

Mena folded his arms and waited for what I had to say.

'Have you had any hints of trouble on this scale?'

Mena compressed his lips.

'No, sir, I have not, normal grumbling about tax and harmless party bickering, that's all.' He shook his head. 'The whole thing's a mystery.' He again shook his head. 'I'd like to know what's behind it.'

I turned to Roebuck.

'You think these disorders were organized and that there may be more?'

'I should say most certainly.' He put down his pipe. 'Big crowds don't appear out of thin air—somebody must bring them together. I think we must expect more trouble. I didn't feel we settled anything at Lampedi.'

An owl hooted close to the house. A car passed along the road at the end of the drive.

'What reinforcements do you want?' I asked Mena.

He looked at Roebuck. Roebuck knocked out his pipe.

'It's not so much reinforcements for the local detachment,' he said, 'they should be kept for normal police duties. We really need a mobile force of about two hundred for patrol duty up and down the road from here to Marovo—that's if we're right in our appreciation of the position.'

Mena nodded. 'I agree—a sort of fire brigade to stop the thing spreading, while you can find out what's behind it.'

A nightwatchman down in the trading section sounded twelve on a rail metal.

'Herbert Gregg's acting Inspector General. I'll try and get through to him now.'

I walked out to the drive and stood while they got into the Land Rover.

'How's Ilse?' I asked Roebuck.

'She's fine,' he said, 'getting tired of waiting, of course.'

'When's "D" Day?'

'Just over a month, we reckon.'

The driver pressed the starter.

'I hope all goes well.'

The vehicle moved slowly away.

'She'll be all right,' Roebuck called back, 'we've got great confidence in Demeta.'

Gregg was in bed. He listened to what I told him without interrupting.

'We'll fly two hundred men to Niko by freighter tomorrow and I'll get Huta to arrange transport and radio trucks to meet them.'

'Can I have George Crawshay?' I said.

'He's on leave.'

'Who'll it be then?'

'Holworthy, I expect,' he said.

'Who's he?' I asked, but the line went dead and I told the operator to go.

CHAPTER XXX

The Land Rover pulled up in the *porte-cochère*. Most people knew that the space was reserved for my car. I went out to the hall as Holworthy came in. I felt a stab of doubt when I saw his luxuriant moustache. Long waving hair was brushed into tufts at the sides of his head and big bushy eyebrows met over his prominent nose. He had an amused manner as he looked at me with large brown eyes and gave a fatuous salute with a quivering hand.

'Greggo sends his chins,' he said.

'Come in,' I said.

He sat down and thrust out his legs. He wore suede ankle-shaped shoes, crocheted string stockings and extravagantly-cut Ghurka-style shorts.

'I hope you don't mind the wagon under the porch?'

'What will you have to drink?' I said.

'Mothers' ruin, old boy, if I may.'

Ali glared at him when he came in with the drinks.

Holworthy took a cigarette from the box.

'That boy gave me an old-fashioned look.'

'He's never seen anything like you before.'

He laughed. 'What a lot the poor fellow's missed.'

'Are the others coming?' I said.

He put down his glass with a tap. I rang for Ali and told him to leave the gin.

'Pardy and Mena?' he said. 'They've gone over to that school where the men are quartered.'

He reached for the gin. He took his second drink slower.

'Tell me, old boy,' he said, 'when do you think we'll get away?'

I thought for a moment.

'I hope within three or four weeks,' I said.

'Goody,' he said. 'I'm glad it's not longer than that.'

'This is a pretty big operation, you know.'

'Yes, yes, but the Council of Ministers' Reception is on the fourteenth of next month.' He spoke with a humorous drawl. 'Not a single pale face concerned in arrangements—can you beat it—all in the hands of our sun-tanned brothers. There's every promise of the biggest balls up of all time. I wouldn't miss it for worlds, no sir!'

'What's Pardy like?'

He tilted his head.

'So so, just so so. He's an ex London bobby. Good with a drunk in a lane, I daresay, but not a lot on top.'

'Mena's a good man,' I said.

Holworthy gave me a quizzical smile.

'Mena?' he said doubtfully. 'He's come up the long way. Probably sound on routine but dicey in a jam, I imagine.'

He shook bitters into his glass, poured out more gin and stared round the room with critical interest.

'You do yourself pretty proud in these Residencies,' he said with an envious inflexion. 'It must have been a piece of cake in the old days, the squire in the big house and all that.'

He started humming.

'Tell me, old boy,' he said, 'what are you going to do when our chums put the skids under us and give us the push?'

'You mean after Independence?'

'Yep.'

'If there's a job for me I may hang on for a couple of years. What are you going to do?'

'Me? If they press money on me to go, I'll be off like a bat out of hell.'

He started humming again.

'Have you had much experience with crowds?' I said.

He looked startled.

'Me? God, yes,' he said. 'In India . . .'

Ali came in.

'One white man and Mr Mena outside,' he announced.

'Well, don't keep them waiting,' I said.

Pardy was over six feet with thick short-cropped fair hair and an expression of surprise on his square sun-burned face. His short-sleeved shirt exposed freckled muscular forearms. He looked shy and spoke with a countryman's burr.

Mena had sandals on his bare feet and was wearing his uniform shorts and a coloured shirt of a thick woven material.

He stood at attention when I greeted him.

Ali brought in the drinks tray. He poured out squash for Mena, added water and ice and asked him to taste it.

He turned to Pardy and said, 'Good evening, sir.' He carefully avoided an excess of froth as he poured out a bottle of beer.

I began to feel happier. I saw Roebuck's Wolseley through the window. McIntyre was in front with him; Bemana and Tai sat at the back.

When I introduced Roebuck to Holworthy I said: 'You've not met Colonel Roebuck?'

Roebuck's face hardened. 'Please, sir,' he protested.

Holworthy blinked and his jaw fell open.

'Are you Jimmy Roebuck?' he said with excitement.

Roebuck spoke frigidly. 'Yes,' he said.

Holworthy was not deterred by his manner.

'I've been wanting to meet you. My brother-in-law knew you in Cairo.'

McIntyre grinned and winked at me. The rest of the room stood awkwardly excluded by Holworthy's banalities.

'Sammy Bolt—he was in the Gunners.'

Roebuck looked puzzled and shook his head.

'Never heard of him,' he said.

I moved a card table into the middle of the room.

'Let's get started,' I said, 'have you got the map, James?'

Roebuck unrolled a linen-backed map of the Province.

'The road due westward from Pela runs through four district headquarters,' I said. 'That's where the trouble lies. You've had no reports from the rest of the Province, Mena?'

Mena stood at attention. 'No, sir,' he said. He pointed to three district areas to the east and two to the north and one to the south of Pela.

'Everything's normal here. The people are paying their tax without any trouble.'

'And the rest of the Province?' I asked.

He stood at attention again but strain was beginning to affect him and he seemed tired.

'Bad, sir,' he said. 'Very bad. They've burned the houses of the Shomu assessment committee. The Lampedi District Council offices have been burned and they have looted the houses of councillors. The chairman and clerk of Gizo District Council and some councillors from Marovo District came in today demanding protection. Gangs from Lampedi and Shomu have been there, and there are strong rumours of trouble.'

'Unless we do something soon, there may be trouble all the way through?'

'Indubitably, sir,' he said.

Holworthy laughed. Roebuck looked up and frowned.

'There's not a shadow of doubt about it,' he said.

We made our headquarters at Logie Lodge, five miles down a side road ten miles west of Lampedi, four hundred feet up on the flattened peak of a hill. It was not an ordinary resthouse. It was fifty years since Alistair Logie, Provincial Commissioner, trekked from Pela with a party of police to bring peace to the area which had long been troubled by raids and internecine fighting. He stopped the bloodshed and punished the leaders, then he called their followers together and told them to build him a house on the top of the hill, a house which would be seen for many miles around as a perpetual reminder of the fate which befalls those who make war on their neighbours. For nearly a year the warriors had shuffled and sweated carrying heavy loads of bright red mud up the hill while others, kneading and battering, shaped it into four-foot thick walls. Then they collected reeds and cornstalks and laid a steep gabled thatch over poles and hard wood beams.

Those days were gone, but the house remained with its large airy rooms, its whitewashed walls, its baronial-like dining-room and spacious hall. It was the nearest approach to a perquisite of office for the provincial commissioners who came after him, a comfortable centre from which to tour the western part of the province or a retreat for a week-end or a holiday. Visitors from all over the territory asked permission to stay there and enrolled themselves as 'Friends of Logie Lodge'. Much had been done with the money they gave—rows of pewter pots hung from a dining-room dresser, there was a wooden settle in the hall, hide-covered chairs, ordered from England, stood round an open hearth. Glass, cutlery, china and pots and pans accumulated, and there were good beds in most of the rooms. An overhead tank was fed from a ram and piped water had been put in. Visitors brought presents. Big game trophies ranged round the walls and a pair of elephant tusks stood one on each side of the hearth. There were framed watercolours of the view from the house, and someone had given a set of pen and ink sketches: 'The long and short of it', 'If you know a better hole', 'Tommy gets the bird', 'Why did I leave home'. There were twelve of them. No one knew the people and the drawings were patchy with mould. Shelves over-flowed with paper-back books. Copies of *Punch*, *Blackwoods* and *Country Life* were piled high on a side table. In the Visitors' Book in the hall were the names of the people who had stayed there—the smudge of a dog's paw 'Micky his mark', 'Tom and Rosemary Clarke, a most heavenly honeymoon', four different Governors and their retinues, shooting parties, and page after page of names, facetious comments, apologies for broken glass, effusive thanks and much more. My own name was there in Daubney's Christmas party twenty-seven years ago when Geoffrey Palthrop fell down the steps and knocked himself out.

A feeling of decay pervaded the place. Everything cost more and people could not afford to be as generous as they had been. The rugs were threadbare and the curtains were ragged.

Tolu, the steward, brought me complaints about the refrigerator, there were not enough sherry glasses, someone had gone off with a towel, new lamps were wanted. Tolu was too old to keep the place clean and dust lay over the furniture and the brass was no longer polished.

I came out to the terrace when I heard the car. The light was failing and there was *harmattan* chill in the air. It was the third day Roebuck and Holworthy had been out on the road between Gizo and Marovo. I had not seen them since breakfast.

Investigations had started at Lampedi and Shomu, witnesses' statements were being taken and already thirty-seven men were in custody. Roebuck had posted Tai to Shomu and Bemana to Lampedi to get the councils working again. Mena and Pardy were standing by with the police at the foot of the hill.

Holworthy got out first.

'Well?' I said.

He was in a bad temper.

'Everything ticketty-boo as usual,' he said.

'See or hear anything?'

'Not a sausage. I don't know what we're here for.'

'It's because you're here that nothing's happening.'

He looked disbelieving and turned away.

'Could be, but I doubt it. You had a flash in the pan and the thing's fizzled out.'

He unbuckled his Sam Browne as he went into the house.

Roebuck took a haversack and vacuum flask from the shelf under the dash-board. He moved stiffly as he got out.

'Holworthy thinks we're wasting his time,' I said.

He shrugged his shoulders, shivered slightly and stared at the hazy obscurity of the landscape below.

'He wants to get back to Belemba, that's the trouble, he misses the fleshpots.' He shrugged his shoulders again and raised his left hand in a gesture. 'Let's hope he's right. We don't want trouble.'

'You saw nothing at Gizo or Marovo?'

'Absolutely normal as far as I could see and no reports from the plain-clothes men.'

We talked for five minutes and then went into the house. A minute later there was a gun shot and we went outside again to see what had happened.

Holworthy was on the terrace with a gun and his orderly was holding a guinea fowl.

'I don't allow shooting here,' I said. 'Please don't do it again.'

Holworthy ejected the cartridge case and reloaded.

'No?' he said.

If I were not careful our mutual dislike would be forced into the open.

'There's never been any shooting at Logie Lodge,' I said patiently. 'We like to see the guinea fowl and francolins coming up to the house in the evening. We put down corn for them and they are practically tame.'

He broke open the gun again and picked up the cartridges.

'Well, for crying out loud, fancy that!'

He began to move off and then, as though he had thought of something, he turned back and faced me.

'I'm just about browned-off with doing nothing. There's

plenty for me to do in Belemba. I've been brought up here on an alarmist report.'

An attraction of Logie Lodge was the open hearth. In the *harmattan* season when the nights became chilly Tolu laid a log fire and with the smell of wood smoke and in the mellow lamp light it was pleasant to sit in a circle for drinks before dinner. Pardy and Mena had come up for the night, Holworthy was now genial and talk flowed easily. We decided the full force should remain three more days and if there were no incidents Pardy should remain after that with fifty men to make arrests on the information we were getting about the Shomu and Lampedi disturbances. We had a third drink and then a fourth.

Ali spoke to me when we got up for dinner. 'There's a man outside wants to see the D.C.'

'Mr Roebuck, you mean?' I said.

He scowled, 'He says it's urgent—there are two men with him. He looks like a policeman.'

Roebuck said, 'I'll see what it's about.'

We sat down and the boys brought us soup in earthenware pots.

Roebuck appeared in the verandah archway.

'Do you mind coming? Holworthy ought to come too.'

Three men waited in semi-darkness near the flower pots in the hall at the main entrance. One in sandals cut from an old motor tyre wore a shirt hanging outside a cloth round his waist. He was holding a note-book. With him there was a middle-aged man in native dress, tall and of good presence, but who now looked anxious. The third—a young man in his twenties wearing shorts and a white shirt—stood in the background. The man with the note-book was the most self-possessed of the three. He came to attention when we walked out to the hall.

'Corporal Faga of the Special Branch,' he reported. He nodded at the older man. 'Mr Pitelo, Chairman of the Gizo District Assessment Committee.' He looked half over his shoulder. 'And Mr Ofala, the Clerk to the Council. We have information that people are gathering to move on Gizo tomorrow to demonstrate against tax assessments. A large crowd is expected.'

The chairman edged forward. His explosive manner of speaking belied his dignified appearance.

'The council are willing to meet these people and if necessary amend the assessments. We'll hear anything they've got to say to us. We only want to do the right thing.'

He kept repeating himself, and I finally said, 'All right, we understand. Is there any chance of talking to them?'

He sighed and spoke to the clerk.

'The trouble is they won't listen. We must have police protection until they come to their senses.'

Holworthy said, 'Corporal, are you quite sure of your facts. You are not passing on rumour?'

The corporal stood at attention.

'My information is reliable. There will be trouble at Gizo tomorrow.'

'I'll join the party,' I said when we sat down again.

Holworthy, who was on my left, looked concerned.

'I don't think we ought to play it that way,' he said knowledgeably and then paused and looked at me. 'You would prefer me to be frank?'

I felt uneasiness at his confident assurance.

'Of course,' I said.

'Frankly, I believe you would be in the way.' He held up a hand. 'Don't get me wrong. It'll be up to Jimmy.' Roebuck looked up but said nothing. 'If he asks me to restore order, it becomes a police operation and the ball's in my court.' He wagged a forefinger. 'As I see it we should keep you behind the scenes for the present.' He grimaced and made a deprecative gesture. 'If things get too hot for us,' he laughed and gestured again, 'they might, you know, then you come in and appreciate the situation and decide the next step.' He looked across the table at Roebuck. 'Are you with me, Jimmy?'

Roebuck said 'Yes' without expression and went on eating. Holworthy smiled at me.

'We mustn't commit our heaviest gun too soon.' He seemed to be humouring me. 'We'll keep you informed by sitreps over the air.'

I regarded him in silence for a moment.

'What are your proposals then?'

He leaned back and looked round the table.

'I'll escort Jimmy to Gizo tomorrow. Mena will bring a hundred men. Pardy, you'll remain with your lot in reserve.'

Roebuck agreed and we left it like that.

We sat drinking coffee and talking but at half past ten I got up. 'We may have a heavy day tomorrow, I think we all ought to turn in.'

Holworthy protested. 'The night's a pup. Boy,' he shouted, 'bring brandy.'

'I don't want brandy,' I told him. Roebuck also refused. Mena and Pardy went off to give their men orders.

Just before bedtime Holworthy, Roebuck and I went outside. Ali was waiting with a letter when we came in.

'Who brought this?' I asked.

'Liftana, office messenger,' he said, 'he's waiting for an answer.'

I wondered why McIntyre should be writing to me.

'When did the messenger come?'

Ali adapted his manner to what he supposed was the state of my affairs.

'Now,' he said gravely, 'just three minutes ago.'

'This is Demeta's handwriting. It's for you, James,' I said handing the letter to Roebuck.

I watched while he opened the envelope. He compressed his lips as he read. He suddenly peered at the close writing and looked shocked. His hand trembled as he re-read the letter.

'Bad news, James?' I said.

He pushed the letter into his pocket.

'It's about Ilse. There've been complications. Demeta says she is bleeding.'

'She's not due yet?'

'No, not for another three weeks.' He took out the letter and read it again. 'He says she's got *placenta praeva*. He's talking about a Caesarean section. It's urgent, he says, if we want to save the child. He wants permission to operate.' Roebuck looked in despair. 'What shall I do?'

'Go back to Pela at once, of course. Don't bother to pack anything.'

He sighed. 'Do you mind?'

'My dear fellow!'

'I'll get back as soon as I can.'

I put my hand on his shoulder.

'No you won't, you'll stay at Pela until Ilse is O.K.'

'I'd better get off then.' He called for his boy. 'I'm sorry this had to happen now.'

'Forget it. Knock up McIntyre when you've seen Demeta. Tell him to come out at once.'

We walked with him to his car. 'Give my love to Ilse.'

Holworthy said nothing until the car rolled down the hill.

'This is a bloody nuisance. Just when something's about to happen, Roebuck has to go. The old timers are right, families get in the way of the job out here.'

'McIntyre will go with you tomorrow,' I told him.

We went back to the house.

'McIntyre, yes,' he said thoughtfully. 'I must say I prefer Jimmy Roebuck—we speak the same language. Still, it can't be helped.'

'What about a little tiddley before we hit the hay?' he said.

'I'm going to bed,' I said.

Holworthy, McIntyre and Mena left with the police after breakfast. It was too soon to make a report to the Civil Secretary, but I wrote a private letter to Gregg. I had a salad and a slice of pineapple for lunch. After that I went out on the terrace. Balsams, petunias and zinnias, regularly watered, flowered in earthenware pots. Oleanders, frangipane and the hibiscus bushes would bloom after the first rains. Streaks of earth showed the presence of white ants in the bougainvillea trellis put up in Daubney's time. It would not last much longer.

The haze cleared by mid-morning and a brassy sun filled the sky. The orchard scrub shimmering in the heat spread out below, a medley of brown, russet and yellow with black patches where the dry grass had been fired, a few knobbly trees and here and there a cluster of huts. Languor hung over the scene. The heat and the glare were too much to encourage much movement. I walked round the house to the back. The corporal in charge of the radio van and one of his men were stretched out on mats in the shade of a mango. The third had soaped himself and was sluicing his bare body at the stand pipe near the boys' houses. I told him to stop wasting water. The corporal stood up and reported no signals from Gizo. He stretched out again as I returned to the house.

I undressed, pulled on pyjama trousers, took a book, and lay on my bed. I wondered if I had been right in agreeing with Holworthy to keep out of their way, and I wondered what I should do if the situation was too much for them. I worried about Roebuck and tried to picture what I should do if Ilse died. I was drowsy but my restless mind kept me from sleeping.

The sound of a car rose from the back of the house and then grew fainter as it moved out on the spiralling road up the hill, then got louder again as it came round and took the last slope. I put on slippers and went on the verandah. Lizards scurried away on the coconut matting. The females were dun-coloured and four or five inches long. The males were much bigger and had long tails and bright yellow heads. After the shade of my room the heat outside assaulted me like the heat of a furnace. My shadow was a pool round my feet.

There was a gear-change as the Land Rover made the final ascent. I expected to see Pardy but I saw it was Holworthy. He opened the door before the vehicle stopped and nearly fell as he got out.

'The situation is completely out of hand,' he cried before I could greet him.

There were damp patches down to his waist on each side of his shirt. His mouth hung open and there was a wild look in his eyes.

'All my tear gas is finished. The crowds keep coming back at us. Half my men are injured. We can't hold out. They'll over-run us. They're absolutely mad. They're burning houses and stoning us. There must be ten thousand of them. I tell . . .'

'Take it easy,' I said. 'Where's Mena and McIntyre?'

He flung out his hands in an impatient gesture.

'Oh they're still there. I was cut off from them and got away.'

The shadow of a circling hawk moved over the ground and a few yards behind Holworthy a black whydah bird with a fantastically long tail flapped its wings without making pro-gress.

I gaped at him.

'You left them to come back here?'

He was calmer now and a shiftiness came into his manner.

'Yes, it was more important that I got back here to report to you personally.'

We stood in the sun. Holworthy took off his cap and wiped his brow. The driver was watching us.

'You had a radio van. You could have signalled. There's a reserve unit standing by here.'

'Signal,' he cried. He shook his head. 'There was no time.'

I let it pass and he met my eyes uneasily.

'You've got rifle men. If there was danger of the police being over-run you would have been entitled to fire.'

He pushed his face at me.

'Yes, and carry the can at the inquiry. It's all right for you to say that sitting here on your backside.'

'Shut up,' I said.

He looked ugly. His voice was hoarse.

'Am I to get reinforcements? I can't restore order with the men at my disposal.'

I could not understand him.

'Reinforcements?' I said. 'I don't understand.'

'Yes, reinforcements, that's what I said.' He blinked at me. I said nothing.

'Well, what do you say?'

'Where the hell can I get reinforcements,' I said wearily. I turned away and spoke to the driver.

'Tell Mr Pardy to come.'

'Just a minute,' Holworthy raised his voice. 'What do you think you're doing?'

The driver looked first at Holworthy and then at me.

'Go on,' I told him. 'Tell Mr Pardy to come at once.'

Tyres threw back gravel as the driver started the vehicle. He turned and headed down hill.

Holworthy's mouth fell open and he narrowed his eyes.

'I hope you know what you are doing. You realize you're giving orders to my men?'

'Yes, that's all right,' I said. 'Will you excuse me, I must put on some clothes.'

Holworthy followed me into the house. He put out his hand as I turned to my room.

'Just a minute,' he said. I stopped. 'Well?' I said. He scowled. 'Perhaps you'll tell me precisely what you are proposing to do.'

I was beginning to feel sorry for him.

'I'm going to signal Mena I'm joining him with Pardy and bringing fifty men. You stay here with the remaining fifty we'll hold in reserve for the time being.'

'You're going to Gizo?'

'Yes, that's the idea.'

'You must be mad. You've no idea of the danger.'

'No?' I said.

'And what's more,' he went on, 'you've no right to assume tactical control of the police. That's my job.'

I looked hard at him.

'I think you've got fever. Take some aspirin and paludrine and lie down.'

'I shall protest you know.' Holworthy's voice broke as he tried to assert himself. 'You'll be held responsible for any casualties.'

I put my hand on his shoulder.

'Do what I say, Holworthy,' I said, 'there's a good fellow. You've got a temperature. You're unfit for duty.'

He passed a hand over his face, looked at me for a moment and then frowned.

'Now you mention it, I have got a headache. Maybe I ought to lie down.'

'Have a hot drink and sweat it out. You'll be better in the morning.'

I put on plimsolls and shorts and pulled on a shirt and the Land Rover was back. Pardy was waiting outside. His placidity was refreshing after Holworthy's behaviour.

'Mr Holworthy's sick,' I said. 'I want you to come with me to Gizo with fifty men. Mena and McIntyre may be in trouble.'

'Very good, sir,' he said.

'I'll drive,' I told Holworthy's driver.

He got out and I took the wheel. Pardy's long thighs pushed his knees up to the dash-board.

The road to the west is a minor road, untarred and dusty in the dry season, but it forms the single main trade artery for the dense population in that part of the Province. Peasant farmers living miles north and south of it bring their produce along bush tracks by head load and donkeys—foodstuffs, palm kernels, ground nuts and cotton—and sell at the road-side markets where middlemen buy it and send it by lorry to Pela.

We met no one until we passed through Gata, a hamlet fifteen miles from the Lodge on the bank of a dry stream. A gang of men came out of the shade of a large banyan. A half-grown youth threw a stone and then shouted, 'You'll be killed if you go to Gizo.' Seven miles further west on the outskirts of Gizo we saw smoke.

CHAPTER XXXI

Straw thatched mud houses spread out in a shallow bowl across the cattle route from the East. The road from Lampedi enters through the old part of the town where the local inhabitants live, farmers, craftsmen and small traders. Half a mile on near the big cattle market there is a floating population of strangers, long-haired Arabs from Timbuktu, veiled Tuaregs and their slaves, Arabs from Darfur and pagans from Matiri with star-shaped throwing knives. Nomadic herdsmen mingle with thick-lipped coast negroes and Southern Mundama dealers.

A crowd of more than a thousand barred our way into the town. They were screaming and shouting and setting fire to houses and corn stores. A tremendous shout went up when they saw us. Pardy and I got out and went up to a man who was pointing at houses and urging his followers to set fire to them.

I touched his shoulder. 'What's wrong?' I asked.

He collected himself for a moment and looked at me and then beyond at the police truck.

'Keep out,' he said. 'This is nothing to do with you. We don't want to fight the police. We're fighting NUDA and the council.'

A crowd gathered. 'Go back,' they shouted, 'you'll be killed if you try to stop us.'

I attempted to parley, but no one listened.

'We'll have to use force,' Pardy said.

I went after the man I had spoken to first.

'I warn you,' I said, 'if you don't stop people may get hurt.'

He pushed forward crowding me and I caught the stench of stale sweat. He spat and then looked me up and down.

'You and the police are like a cooked corncob, ready for eating. Go back where you came from.'

He pointed at houses with the Bull symbol stuck on the door and two men went forward with blazing corn stalks to fire the thatch. While I had been talking rioters had moved behind us carrying fire to the police trucks and throwing bottles and stones at the men. Pardy ordered a baton charge. The crowd dispersed down the main road and along alleys and lanes leading off. We drove on another hundred yards but the mob re-formed and again advanced on us.

Pardy shouted through a megaphone, 'I shall fire if you don't disperse.' He held up his revolver and twice repeated the warning.

A man with a blazing torch headed a gang with muzzle loaders and clubs.

'Fire,' he screamed, 'go on, fire, you only use blanks.'

When they were twenty yards off but still coming on they threw bottles and stones at us. There were bangs from the muzzle loaders. Two policemen fell and then Pardy fired. The mob wavered but started to come forward again. Pardy fired a second time and ordered a baton charge to arrest ring leaders. From then on we moved at walking pace through the jeering crowds thronging the roadway. A Volkswagen bus lay in a storm water gully with its wheels in the air. Blackened shells of mud huts smouldered from blazing thatch which had fallen inside. Smoke rose from the remains of the council offices. A sustained uproar came from somewhere ahead. The volume of sound rose as we drove along the widening road past the infant welfare centre and the animal health office towards the cattle market. The whole area was filled by a crowd like a vast audience centred on Mena's police trucks. I ordered them to give way but I was immediately surrounded by an angry mob and a man with a club kept pushing forward defying me to move him.

The haze softened the rays of late afternoon sun and it became cooler. A light breeze from the north-east had spread the tear gas through the crowd. It was either that or the baton charges which started the crowd moving away. Debris, sandals, scraps of ragged clothing, stones, broken bottles and sticks littered the deserted market. A police sergeant stood watching prisoners climb up the back of the truck.

'We'd just about had it,' McIntyre said.

His shirt was spattered with blood. There was a gaping wound on the bone below his right eye.

'I don't like the look of that eye,' I said.

He winced when he touched the wound.

'It's nothing,' he said.

I looked again at the eye.

'You ought to see Demeta. The eye may be damaged.' I peered closer. 'There's no sense in taking chances with your sight.'

He pushed out his chin and looked obstinate.

'Lay off, please sir,' he said. I'm all right. Where's Holworthy?'

I had forgotten Holworthy.

'He's at the Lodge. There seems to be something wrong with him.'

McIntyre snorted and used a coarse expression.

'I'll say there's something wrong with him.'

The police formed lines near the truck. Mena broke away from consultation with Pardy.

'We're keeping fifty men here,' he said, 'the injured men can go back with Pardy.' He looked uncertain. 'I don't know whether Mr Holworthy will have orders, but I'd like a truck to come back with the men's rations.'

'You'll get your rations,' I said.

I called to McIntyre, 'You must come back.'

He glared at me.

'No,' he said, 'I'm staying here.'

'You can't stay here. You need a night's rest and a couple of days off.'

'Please, sir, don't fuss.' McIntyre spoke impatiently. 'I'll kip down here with Hophni in the school.'

He looked at Mena. 'O.K. Hoph?'

Mena nodded. 'Certainly Mac, that'll be fine.'

McIntyre turned to me again. 'I'll be all right. The driver will bring my kit when he comes back with the rations.'

I missed McIntyre and Mena. Pardy was busy with daily routine and I only saw him at meals and he went to bed straight after dinner. Holworthy's growing familiarity was hard to combat. Two days after the Gizo disturbances he put on red kid mules and a dressing gown and suggested a drink. Ali had just lighted the lamps and the mellow light and blazing logs encouraged the

265

intimacy I wished to avoid. We had been talking about Mena but for a moment conversation had lapsed.

'I suppose he did well in the circumstances.' Holworthy's manner was tolerant. 'Quite a spot for an officer of his experience to find himself in.'

I grunted and Holworthy tapped cigarette ash in the hearth. It was perhaps a minute before he spoke again.

'What do you think?' he asked.

'About Mena?'

'About the way he handled the Gizo situation?'

What Holworthy wanted was hesitation and then possibly a little faint praise. We would then agree that Mena might have done better but for an African officer of limited experience he had done as well as could be expected. This would have found its way into the official report.

'I think his handling of the situation was masterly,' I said.

Holworthy laughed and again tapped off ash.

'Oh come,' he said good-humouredly, 'just between these four walls, are you quite happy about the shooting?' His face was composed and smiling. 'You don't think he was trigger happy?'

I could not control my contempt but the lamp was behind me and he could not see my face in the shadow.

'I don't understand you,' I said.

He looked faintly amused.

'You know what I mean. Was the shooting really necessary?'

I spoke with great emphasis.

'What is remarkable is that there was so little shooting.'

'Maybe, maybe.' He spoke as though conceding a point. 'Still, I can't help feeling things might have been different if I had been there.'

'But,' I said, 'surely that is the whole point, you should have been there.'

I was afraid that I had been too outspoken but he smiled.

'Yes, of course, but these things happen, first Jimmy's missus and then I get the grand daddy of all goes of malaria.'

I heard Pardy's Land Rover outside. He touched the horn as he was getting out; the door slammed and he came in.

He greeted Holworthy. 'Glad to see you up, sir. I hope you're feeling O.K.'

I observed a change in Holworthy's manner. He now seemed lethargic and tired.

'Thank you very much,' he said. 'I am better but I'll have to go easy.'

Pardy remained standing.

'It doesn't do to rush things,' he said and then added, 'they say it takes a week to pick up after fever.'

'Sit down, Pardy,' I said, but he continued to stand.

'Hophni's just come through on the radio. He says there's going to be a demonstration at Marovo.'

'Marovo, when?' I said.

'The day after tomorrow.'

Holworthy put down his glass and stood with his back to the fire. He re-tied his dressing gown cord and glared at Pardy.

'How the hell does Mena know? I thought the whole bloody affair was over.'

Pardy faltered; he seemed surprised by Holworthy's petulance.

'We get information from Special Branch men in the villages.'

Holworthy picked up his glass.

'Yes, but is it reliable? I wouldn't put it past some of them to cook up reports. They all want promotion.'

He sat down again and stared at the fire.

'Thank you, Pardy,' I said. 'I'll see Mena tomorrow. I'd like to get up there before the crowds start to collect.'

Holworthy turned and looked at me.

'You're not going there?' He sounded incredulous. 'Surely you should send McIntyre.'

'You think so?' I said.

He snorted. 'You know best but that's the way I'd play it.'

'Will you come?' I said.

'How can I?' He made a gesture of helplessness. 'I'll be in touch on the radio.' He sighed and stared again at the fire. 'It would be better if you stayed too. It's not right that you should get mixed up in these brawls.' He picked up the poker and sparks rose up the chimney as he stirred up the logs. 'Still, I suppose you know what you're about. If you must go, Pardy will go with you.'

I had thought Pardy might come with me but I said, 'I think it would be better if Mena came'.

Holworthy nodded significantly.

'Perhaps you're right,' he said and then spoke to Pardy.

'Tell Mena from me to take a hundred men and deploy them before the crowds collect. A show of force may stop them getting excited.'

'I prefer not to have the men in the town when I meet the crowd,' I said.

Holworthy scowled.

'I don't get it. What is it you want?'

'The men should stand by at Yara a mile south of the town. We'll take a plain clothes man with a bike in the Land Rover. He'll tip off the police if we want them.'

Holworthy spoke with studied unconcern.

'It's a matter of opinion which is the best course. I won't press my view.'

Marovo means meeting place, it is where the fabulous warrior Limotu, coming southward, met his bride Palolu and decided to settle. It stands on pleasantly wooded high land with shea and locust bean trees in an area where there is still an abundance of game. The town has two landmarks. A high rock stands to the north with a massive flat face white streaked like lime marking. The people call it Limotu. To the south there is the rocky hill Palolu. The boulders round the base where hyenas hide by day are called her children. The resthouse stands fifty feet below overlooking the town.

Marovo depends for its prosperity on trade in foodstuffs. Farmers in the surrounding hamlets send in yams, beans, maize and guinea corn for sale in the market. But the town is also well known for its potters and brass workers whose handiwork is seen in markets far to the south and often finds its way to Belemba.

Mena joined me at Gizo and we drove up to Marovo the night before the demonstration was expected. A hundred police were to follow at dawn and stand by at Yara.

The district council chairman, Moses Oframa, a man with an egg-shaped bald head and a lined and cadaverous face, had been Chief Clerk in the Lands Office in Belemba, and when he retired came back to Marovo. He was a sensible man who desired to serve his people. I cared less for Jallo the deputy Chairman who came with Oframa to the resthouse. He was undersized and slightly deformed and always seemed bad tempered and quarrelsome.

Three members of the tax assessment committee and Tatata, the council clerk, came with them.

'We don't want any palaver here,' Oframa said earnestly. He wore a well-cut English suit and a gold watch chain. He was well over sixty but he was alert in a precise and didactic manner. 'We want to stand well in the eyes of the world as responsible people capable of running our affairs. If tax payers have grievances we are always prepared to deal with them constitutionally.'

Oframa spoke with renewed assurance when the others murmured agreement.

'Nobody has put forward complaints to me.' He held out his hands in an appealing attitude. 'I am willing at any hour of the day or night to hear them. I know people don't like paying more tax, who does? but I have said repeatedly, if we are to have more amenities they must be paid for. I think people were beginning to understand this and moreover my council are not responsible for the Central Council precept or for the government levy.'

Jallo kept shifting in his chair waiting for Oframa to finish.

'The whole thing's political,' he said. 'NIC have hired hooligans to make trouble. There's a gang of them moving from district to district inciting people.'

'The NIC secretary told me he knows nothing about it,' I said.

Oframa slowly shook his head. Jallo snorted, then muttered to his companions.

'Do you believe him?' he said. 'Do you expect him to admit it?'

'I suppose not,' I said.

Jallo's gaze shifted to Mena.

'I hope we shall have police protection for our property. We don't want a repetition of Lampedi and Gizo.'

Mena smiled tolerantly.

'We'll do our best,' he said. 'We always do.'

Jallo was not satisfied. He wagged a finger at Mena.

'I hope your realize the gravity of the danger,' he said.

'Mr Jallo,' I interposed, 'we shall have a hundred men standing by at Yara. They can be in the town within ten minutes of the first sign of trouble.'

Jallo raised his voice and turned to the others for support.

'You ought to have more men and you ought to have them in the town waiting.'

I ignored the outburst and spoke to Oframa.

'I'll sit with you and the council tomorrow,' I said. 'We'll talk to the people when they come.'

'Very good,' Oframa said. 'Benches and a table will be put out in front of the native court in the square.'

'You're mad,' Jallo said. 'These people won't listen to reason.'

'We'll try,' Oframa said, 'we'll try.' He bowed to me. 'We must leave now and we'll meet in the morning.'

'Good night, Mr Oframa,' I said.

I heard raised voices as the party followed Oframa down the path to the town.

On a clear day there was a good view from the resthouse, but now the scene was obscured by *harmattan* haze. As night fell it turned cool and Mena and I sat in our camp chairs by a fire until bed time.

Just before midnight I was roused by prowling hyenas. They wandered off and I was on the point of sleep again when I heard a new sound. It was a faint bugle call from far away in the bush. It was followed by drumming and horn blowing.

A table, two chairs and rows of benches were set out in front of the native court building. Oframa, Jallo and eight other councillors were waiting when Mena and I arrived. A plain clothes man reported that a crowd of four thousand were moving towards the town.

Oframa and the councillors were uneasy and looked to me to do something.

'Who's their leader?' I asked.

Oframa conferred with the councillors.

'We believe their leader is Alama Kalada, headman of Buto,' he said.

'Try and get him to come on ahead of the crowd,' I suggested to Mena.

A trader named Aruda who acted as NIC branch secretary was said to know him. When Mena came back he said Aruda had agreed to tell Kalada I wanted to see him.

By nine o'clock the town square was ringed with Marovo people. An hour later the sun broke through the haze and it was as hot as midday. Half an hour later there was a commotion as a party of men pushed through the onlookers.

Kalada was a tall man with fine cut features. He was an impressive figure in white gown as he strode across the square looking neither to the right nor the left. Seven men straggled behind him and stood a few paces off when he reached the table. His manner was enigmatic and almost sad when he acknowledged my greeting.

'Mr Kalada,' I said, 'I believe there is a very large crowd outside the town. There are no difficulties which cannot be resolved by discussion.'

He raised his eyebrows and looked at me with a suggestion of a smile.

'I agree,' he said, 'but a good deal of heat has been generated. The people are in an ugly mood and are not easy to placate.' He looked at the councillors. 'These NUDA council people have been arrogant and dictatorial. . . .'

Oframa jumped up and banged the table.

'That's a lie,' he shouted. 'We've always been ready to hear complaints.'

I laid a hand on him.

'All right, Mr Oframa,' I said. 'Let me do the talking.'

Kalada's expression was unchanged. He ignored Oframa and waited for me with courteous attention.

'I don't want the whole mob here,' I said. 'Let me meet their representatives and hear what they have to say.'

Kalada remained silently staring at the people fringing the square and then with a scarcely perceptible glance at Oframa he said, 'It'll take some time to arrange.'

'I'll wait,' I said.

He bowed, turned and strode across the square ahead of the men who had come with him.

I sent to the resthouse for a flask of tea and more cigarettes. Mena's man reported the crowd was restive and that Kalada could hardly restrain them. Oframa said it was insulting to be kept waiting so long.

Kalada returned at three o'clock with a delegation of about

two hundred. Benches were brought out from the court and the school. Kalada stood close to the table and the rest of the party sat on the benches behind him.

'You speak on behalf of all these people?' I said to him.

'I do,' he said.

'Very well, I will hear what you say.'

Kalada consulted a note-book.

'Tax has been increased too much. The assessment committee has shown favour to NUDA members. The council are spending too much in the town and neglecting the villages. There is hardship because of the government levy for schools, hospitals and roads.'

Kalada paused to look at his note-book. There were more people in the town centre.

Mena nudged me. 'The mob is moving in,' he said.

'Continue, Mr Kalada,' I said.

'The court is corrupt and illegal demands are made by council employees.'

'Those are serious charges,' I said, 'you will have to be precise.'

'I will give details,' he said.

'Lastly,' he turned to the people behind him, 'this new form of local government is repugnant to us.'

The delegates shouted agreement and repeated their shout when he added, 'our old methods were better. Harama is our chief and we obey only him.'

I spoke in an aside to Mena.

'You'd better send your man off.'

I promised Kalada I would report what he had said to the Civil Secretary and investigate specific complaints. Oframa agreed to review tax assessment and I said I would consult the Minister about reform in the court.

Kalada took a long time in explaining to the delegates what I had said.

I stared round me. Vultures ousted from the square by the crowds perched on roof tops and in the baobabs behind the court house. I could see a ripple of movement in the growing crowd fifty yards up the road. I had left my dark glasses at the resthouse and the hot glare of the westering sun on the red mud houses had given me a headache.

Kalada was still talking to the delegates.

Mena whispered. 'They're priming muzzle loaders at the back of the crowd. I don't think Kalada can control them.'

'Where are the police?' I said. 'It's time they were here.'

He nodded. 'I'll meet them and bring them in by a side road to split up the crowd.'

Mena went to the back of the court house to his Land Rover. Kalada returned to the table.

'We'll give Mr Oframa a list of the people who're over-assessed.'

'Yes, all right,' I said.

'And we'll get answers about the other things from you.'

'Yes, certainly. Come and see me at Pela sometime.'

'Thank you,' he said.

'You'll take the crowd away now?'

'Yes, we'll go now,' he said but he remained standing at the table. 'I can definitely tell everyone that tax assessments will be reviewed?'

'Certainly,' I said. 'Isn't that so, Mr Oframa?'

'We've agreed to all that,' Oframa said.

Kalada beckoned to the men on the benches to rejoin the crowd. And then Jallo raised his voice. It seemed to me he spoke with provocative truculence. He shook a fist at Kalada.

'That doesn't mean taxes will be reduced,' he said. 'Some may be increased. It's only a review if you know what that means.'

Oframa tried to silence him, but he was too late. The angry shouts of the delegates were taken up by the mob behind and rippled up the tightly-packed road beyond. Above the tumult of voices someone set up an ululation like a rallying call. A stone was thrown, more stones followed and the crowd surged forward.

'Go back, go back,' shouted Kalada, but there was now no hope of restraining them.

Oframa, Jallo and the other seven councillors ran to houses behind us at the far end of the square. For a moment I stood alone then someone gripped me from behind. I could see the movement of muscles under the brown skin of his arms. Somebody else took my thighs from in front. More men came and I was lifted and half carried to a house on the side of the square. I

273

struggled to get out but five men, Kalada among them, barred the doorway to keep me inside. I saw the mob round the council offices battering in windows and doors with benches. Men rushed past the doorway with blazing cornstalks setting fire to thatch.

I was affronted by the indignity of my position. 'Let me out at once,' I demanded.

Kalada and another man pushed me back.

'This is nothing to do with you,' he said. 'If you stay here you'll be safe.'

I struggled to get out but they pushed me sprawling back into the room and then shut the door. It was a single room hut with rough door frame set in the mud. Some light came from a space above the door and from a slit in the wall. The thatch was smoke-blackened inside from fires during the rains. Yams piled against the wall and there was a heap of guinea corn heads, some cassava, a few calabash bowls and a food pestle and mortar. I picked up the hard wood pestle and battered the door until the timbers broke away from the hinges. I pushed aside the broken wood and went out. Distraught men rushed about in every direction shouting and screaming. For a fleeting infinitesimal measure of time I knew I had received a violent blow on my head.

I was in bed at the Residency. The mosquito net was tossed up but I had not heard Ali come in and there was no tea tray on the side table. There was someone sitting in a wicker chair by the bed reading one of my books. The situation was beyond me, my head ached and my thoughts were confused. The man was wearing a white coat. I made an effort and identified him as the senior male nurse from the hospital.

'You are Mr Pagana,' I said.

He took my temperature and felt my pulse, keeping his eyes on his watch and moving his lips. He took out the thermometer, inspected it carefully and then shook down the mercury. He made notes with a ball-point pen.

'How long have I been here?' I asked.

'Excuse me, sir,' he said, 'I must telephone Dr Demeta.'

When I moved I felt pain in my right thigh and in my back and side. There was a dressing above the elbow of my left arm. My forehead was grazed and I seemed to have a swollen eye.

Roebuck came with Demeta. Their solicitous manner disturbed me.

'Hello, James,' I said, 'how's Ilse?'

Roebuck spoke in a soothing tone.

'She left Niko last Saturday. Miss Comben the Senior Sister at Huta will be in the same aircraft and has promised to help with the children.'

'And how about the new baby?'

'She's fine, we're delighted we've got another girl.'

There seemed nothing more to say about that.

'When can I get up?' I asked Demeta.

'How do you feel?'

'Hungry.'

'I'm not surprised, you've been unconscious for two days. I want you to keep quiet. I don't think your skull's damaged but you've had bad concussion.

Mena came just before tea time. He asked me if I knew who hit me.

'No, Hophni,' I said, 'I don't. What happened after?'

'It was dark when we picked you up. The rioters had trampled over you.'

I felt my swollen eye.

'It's a good thing they didn't wear boots,' I said.

Mena touched his left arm above the elbow. 'You've got a burn here. Blazing thatch fell on you.'

'Who brought me here?'

'I did. Dr Demeta told me I ought to have left you at Marovo. You might have had a fractured skull.'

'I'm glad you didn't,' I said.

Demeta kept me in bed for two weeks and forbade any work, but I read and wrote letters. The *Courier* and the *Graphic* came up by air in weekly bundles to Huta. They had changed in the last year. They were now full of flash-light photographs of grinning Europeans and Africans clutching glasses at receptions and cocktail parties, and talk about Independence celebrations. There were long reports of an action about a disputed title of land required for an airport extension, the usual police court news, and sports reports. Dufu had left NUDA and joined NIC. In a statement in the *Courier* he spoke of an 'agonizing re-appraisal of the his political beliefs'. At the bottom of an inside column of *Graphic* I read 'Seven people were killed and forty-three injured at tax demonstrations at Marovo in Pela Province. The police report that all is now quiet.'

CHAPTER XXXII

The demonstrations had been unexpected, but the speed at which conditions returned to normal was no less remarkable. Tax was quickly paid and the councils were meeting again. Everyone wanted to forget the affair but there was the aftermath. Most of the men charged with offences were released on bail but they would be brought up for trial at a special magistrates' session. And a letter signed by the Civil Secretary informed me that the Governor had appointed Mr Justice F. S. Peake and Mr J. Y. A. Calder, Q.C., as special commissioners, 'to inquire into the causes of civil disturbances in certain districts of Pela Province'. I had expected something of the sort. It was the additional terms of reference which surprised me, 'and to determine how far Harama the Mudela of Pela had discharged the duty laid upon him by Section 4 of the Chiefs Ordinance of maintaining order and good government and interposing for the prevention of crime'.

Peake made a list of requests and I gave him all he wanted. Roebuck went to live with McIntyre and the D.C.'s house was prepared for Peake and Calder. It had never been settled whether a Puisne Judge took precedence over a Provincial Commissioner in his own province. For me the issue was an anachronism but I fancied Peake might still think it important. I called on him first and he called next day when I was out. He sent me a formal letter. 'Not only must the inquiry be impartial,' he wrote, 'but must also manifestly appear to be so. For that reason,' he went on, 'the commissioners will meet you only on public occasions.' He made me feel I was somehow on trial. I had no wish to see him, but I was sorry I could not entertain John.

They spent the first week at Pela, a week in each of the four districts, and five days again at Pela before they left for Niko to fly back to Belemba.

They took my evidence last. I knew what Roebuck, McIntyre

and Mena had said and could add nothing. We agreed that the disturbances were a symptom of maladjustment to change, a distrust of the new councils based on ignorance and resentment of insolence to Harama. Hysteria had been whipped by a few ill-disposed persons by focusing attention on tax increase. I offered the opinion that the system of local government was sound and that tax assessments were reasonable. I said I knew of no grounds for fearing a repetition of disorder.

Peake was tired and querulous. He had put on weight since I had seen him at Belemba and had become a fat little man with a fleshy clean-shaven face and grey wispy hair. He wore glasses with bifocal lenses and held up his face to see properly when he took notes. His manner was pompous but his questions were fair.

I had finished my evidence.

'I've got some notes here,' he said. 'There was something I wanted to ask you.'

He shuffled through papers and began to mutter. John Calder pointed and he said, 'Ah yes', and looked back at me.

'Do you agree that when an administrative officer requests the help of the police to disperse a riotous assembly it is entirely at the discretion of the senior police officer what tactics he employs?'

'Certainly,' I said.

He made a note and looked up again.

'It is suggested there were occasions when you assumed tactical direction of the police.'

'What occasions were those, sir?'

He frowned. 'During the disorder at Gizo and later at Marovo.'

'In the absence of Mr Holworthy, who was unfit for duty, Mr Mena was in full control of police dispositions on both those occasions.'

Peake pursed his lips and peered at his notes.

'It is suggested that the riots at Marovo and the subsequent loss of life and damage to property would have been averted if police in strength had been deployed in the town when there was reason to expect a riotous assembly.'

'Suggested by whom, sir?'

Peake flushed and deliberately put down his pen. He placed both hands flat on the desk and leaned forward.

'Mr Wood,' he said, 'would you kindly refrain from questions and confine yourself to the observations put to you.'

John Calder said something and Peake glared at him. There was an exchange of whispers and then Peake looked more composed.

'Mr Wood,' he resumed, 'my colleague is of the opinion that it would not be improper to disclose the source of the suggestions. I am not sure that I agree with him, but I do not propose to pursue the point.' He looked at his notes. 'The suggestions were made by Mr Ferdinand Jallo, deputy chairman of Marovo District Council, and Mr Cedric Holworthy, Superintendent of Police.'

'I am of the opinion,' I said, 'that Mr Mena took a well calculated risk in holding back police at Marovo. There was every hope that if a crowd assembled they could be persuaded to disperse without a display of force.'

'Events show that these hopes were ill-founded?'

'Yes,' I said.

'It is suggested that you exerted undue pressure on Mr Mena and that he was not exercising independent judgment.' Peake took off his glasses and stroked his face. 'If this is so you are now attempting to justify your own judgment.'

'Does Mr Mena say that I exerted pressure on him?'

Peake ignored my question. 'Well?' he said.

I made an effort to control myself.

'I believe the police action was competently directed, reasonable in the circumstances and based on a sound appreciation of the situation as it then appeared. The felling of trees across the road could not have been foreseen.'

Peake glared at me.

'I take it you maintain that you did not exert pressure on Mr Mena?'

'I did not. In any event Mr Mena is an experienced and competent police officer who would not be influenced against his own judgment.'

Peake thrust out his lower lip and tapped the desk.

'You've still not said whether or not you believe in the light of developments it would have been better if police had been deployed in Marovo before the rioters moved into the town.'

'That is a hypothetical question. I can't offer an opinion on what might have happened if the police had taken any of the other courses open to them. My opinion, for what it is worth, is that there might have been more violence if the rioters had found police waiting for them.'

Peake yawned and turned to Calder.

'Have you anything?'

Calder shook his head.

It was a quarter to two and one of those humid days which come at the end of the dry season. A canvas punkah swung over the bench but in the body of the court there was no movement of air and sweat ran down my body.

Peake and Calder conferred in undertones. I had got a headache and was tired of standing.

'Do you still require my presence?' I asked.

They both looked up. Peake glared as though he resented my interruption.

'You will be told when you may stand down,' he said.

'Very well,' I said.

'I'd like you to address yourself to a new matter.'

'As you wish.'

'What action did Harama the Mudela of Pela take towards the maintenance of peace and good order during the period of the disturbances?'

I had not expected the question.

'I don't know,' I said.

Peake put down his pen again and leaned over the desk.

'Are you not Provincial Commissioner in charge of this Province?'

'I am,' I said.

'Yet you tell me you don't know what the paramount chief of the Province did in the course of these disturbances?' He sounded shocked by my ignorance. 'I take it these disturbances were sufficiently unusual to demand your special attention?'

'Chiefs exert their influence in directions not always evident to Europeans. The traditional organization is complex. It is often impossible to say what a chief is doing or not doing.'

Peake looked sceptical. He slipped a tablet into his mouth and made an aside to Calder.

'Well, we do know, do we not, that these mysterious methods

of working did not prevent grave public disorder in four districts of this Province?'

'It might have been more widespread.'

'Maybe it need not have happened at all.'

Peake wrote up his notes and then again asked Calder if he had any questions.

Calder's voice sounded melodious after Peake's testiness.

'Mr Wood,' he said quietly, 'did you at any time discuss the disturbances with the Mudela?'

The punkah creaked as it swung over the bench. Peake was writing when I replied.

'I did,' I said.

They both fixed their eyes on me. Peake's mouth fell open.

'You did?' he said with a rising inflexion.

'Yes, sir, it was my duty to do so.'

'And what course did the discussion take?'

'I suggested to him that he was the only person who could stop the spread of disorder.'

Peake leaned over the desk and breathed hard.

'This is most important,' he said, 'most important. Please recall as precisely as you can what he said in reply.'

'He said he could do nothing.'

'Could do nothing or would do nothing? There is a distinction.'

'Could do nothing.'

'Did he in fact try?'

'I've dealt with that particular point.'

'Ah yes, the mysterious activities, the labyrinthine channels, we don't know about.'

His manner was unpleasant. He raised a finger and pointed at me.

'Let me put it this way. After you made your suggestion did you have any reason to suppose he acted on it? Let us forget all about the invisible filaments of chieftancy power. Did he visit the disaffected districts, did he attempt conciliation, did he call any meetings to discuss outstanding differences? Did he, in fact, do anything at all to your knowledge?'

'No.'

'No,' Peake repeated with an air of finality. His pen scratched as he wrote. He blotted his notes.

'I've no more questions. Mr Calder?'

John Calder smiled at me. 'Perhaps you would like to add something for the record?'

'Thank you,' I said. 'I should like to place on record my sincere belief that whatever Harama did or did not do, he had what he conceived to be the best interests of his people at heart.'

Peake barely listened. He was collecting his papers.

'Very well, that will be noted,' he said. He unstrapped his brief case. 'The inquiry is closed.'

It was three o'clock and I was dispirited when I went out into the hot sun. I wondered uneasily what injury I had done to Harama.

The dry season was over and high winds heralded the onset of rains. The lights failed at the house and I supposed a branch had fallen across the line somewhere. I sat in darkness until Ali brought in a Tilley lamp. As I picked up my book I heard a car in the drive. I walked out under the *porte-cochère* to see who was there. McIntyre's station wagon pulled up.

'I'm not disturbing you, I hope?' he said.

'Come in Mac,' I said.

There was a livid scar under his right eye and four pairs of stitch marks. Demeta had been anxious about the injury but McIntyre had treated it lightly. I had persuaded him to see the specialist in Belemba and he had flown down in the aircraft with Peake and Calder.

'How's your eye?' I asked.

He snorted. 'I must have plastic surgery when I get home.'

'Is the sight improving?'

He frowned. 'It's better. I can see light and dark now and I have started driving again. They tell me there's no permanent injury.'

I had heard differently, but I said nothing.

'That's good,' I said, 'have a drink?'

'I won't thanks, I've just had supper.'

His manner was awkward and I wondered what he had come for. I exhausted my small talk and left him to say what he wanted. He slowly lighted a pipe.

'I had a crowd up from the Central Office earlier this evening,' he said.

It was not the sort of thing McIntyre would come up to tell me. He was constantly having Africans to his house and meeting them in the town.

'It's good of you to hold these regular sessions,' I said. 'I must say I'm too lazy.'

He looked embarrassed. 'It's more our job than yours to make the effort, and anyway I enjoy it.'

Conversation flagged again.

'What do you talk about?' I said.

He shrugged his shoulders.

'Oh, anything, the new constitution, Independence, parliamentary procedure, England, Nigeria, Russia, the Congo, the United Nations. They ask a lot of questions.'

I pumped the lamp and turned the pricker.

'I thought the Information people put out a lot about those things.'

For the first time he brightened.

'These boys are keen. They don't believe everything they read. They like to argue.'

There seemed nothing more to say about that. He was unresponsive to other subjects.

'Are you sure you won't have a drink?' I said.

'Quite sure,' he said.

We sat on a few minutes longer. He put down his pipe and spoke hesitantly, almost diffidently.

'I suppose you've known Harama a long time?'

'Yes, on and off for about twenty-seven years. I've been posted out of the Province some of that time, but I've always kept in touch with him.'

'What was he like in the old days?'

'First-class horseman, a good shot, quite illiterate, of course, but very straight. He used to ride miles settling disputes. He liked to have me around and I often went with him.'

McIntyre folded his arms and regarded me in thoughtful silence. When he spoke there was almost an envious note in his voice.

'They must have been good days,' he said.

Conversation petered out again.

'Why did you ask about Harama?' I said.

'I'm interested,' he said.

There was another silence. I felt he was making demands on me.

'Come clean, Mac, what's all this about?'

'Buramo came with the crowd this evening.'

'Oh,' I said, 'I didn't know he was one of your group.'

'It's the first time he's been. He stayed on after the others left.'

'Oh yes,' I said.

The lights came on again and Ali came in for the lamp.

McIntyre was looking straight at me. Apart from the scar his eye looked quite normal. He spoke hoarsely with the trace of accent which came into his voice when he was agitated.

'Do you want the real gen about the riots?'

'The riots! Oh dear me no, Mac, we don't want to go over that again. Let's forget it.'

He made a sweeping gesture as if to brush irrelevancies aside.

'I don't mean the stuff Peake and Calder wrote down.'

I was not sure I wanted to hear any more.

'What precisely do you mean?' I asked.

'Harama organized the demonstrations. He told the people not to pay taxes and to smash up the council offices.'

I wished he had not told me.

'Harama wouldn't have done that,' I protested, but I knew McIntyre was sure of his facts. 'He's too old, he couldn't organize anything.'

'I'm sorry, sir, but that's just what he did. I got the whole story from Buramo. Hooligans joined in the disturbances. Harama never expected them to go as far as they did.'

'Buramo told you this?'

'Yes, he had to tell someone. He was bottled up with worry. He was present at the meetings in Harama's house when the thing was fixed up.'

McIntyre shrugged. 'You might say he is implicated.'

'Now he feels he's done his duty?'

McIntyre nodded. 'That's about it.'

I smiled at him.

'And now you feel you've done your duty too?'

He picked up his pipe again. He spoke with a wry smile.

'What are you going to do about it, sir?'

'Nothing,' I said.

'No, I didn't suppose you would. Still, I thought I ought to tell you.'

I walked out with him to his car.

'Thanks for letting me know, Mac,' I said, 'you've done exactly what you should. Good night.'

'Good night, sir,' he said. 'I'm sorry I've tossed this thing at you.'

'Not to worry,' I said, 'just keep it under your hat.'

I went back in the house and picked up my book but I held it unopened. I knew I was not really surprised by what I had heard. I was glad it was McIntyre who had got hold of the news. If it had been Roebuck he would have wanted the inquiry re-opened and fresh statements taken. There would have been charges against Harama.

CHAPTER XXXIII

The strong manilla envelope was addressed by name to me. It had been franked in the Civil Secretary's office. A second envelope, sealed and marked Top Secret, was enclosed. It contained a stencilled typescript of the commissioners' report. With the Governor away Mathews was in charge and Peter Metcalfe was acting Civil Secretary. He wrote privately to say the report would be considered by Mathews and the Council of Ministers on the following Thursday.

'With Independence in the offing and so much going on no one's very interested in Pela,' he wrote, 'but I thought you would like to know the form. The commissioners' findings will be noted, Harama may get a rocket. It depends how the Ministers feel. Mathews will, of course, do what they tell him.' There was a friendly message from Margaret and an invitation to stay with them when I passed through Belemba.

The wire staples broke away and the pages came loose when I pressed down the report on my desk. The first part contained a description of the disturbances at Shomu, Lampedi, Gizo and Marovo. Then followed an analysis of the police action and the conclusion: 'We are satisfied that the police only employed force by the use of fire-arms and otherwise when peaceful persuasion had failed to disperse riotous assemblies. We are of the opinion that the degree of force used was the minimum reasonably necessary to prevent felonious crime and for police protection. We find that the police officers discharged their duty in an exemplary manner and in particular wish to draw attention to the conduct of Mr C. E. G. Holworthy, Superintendent of Police, who although seriously indisposed and in spite of the force at his disposal being greatly out-numbered by rioters, frequently displayed outstanding resolution and skill but for which the disturbances might have reached far greater proportions.'

I turned to the next part—'The Cause of the Disturbances'. They wrote about the introduction of the new system of local government and the methods of tax assessment, and concluded, 'We cannot assign the outbreaks of violence to any one simple cause. The disorders had the appearance of spontaneity; they were not the outcome of long premonition; no single person formed a rallying point for a disaffected peasantry. For a brief period contagious mass hysteria took possession of a normally law-abiding community and drove them to excesses which they now regret and deplore. We have asked ourselves what could have induced such people to act in this way. We do not believe it was the level of taxation. People of substantially similar resources in other parts of the Province have paid tax at similar rates without the slightest demur. We see in the riots a local manifestation of maladjustment to change. Those placed in authority by the process of popular election and those subject to this authority were not intimately identified. On the one hand there were councils with progressive and ambitious notions asserting an intellectual superiority over a peasantry with no real understanding of the function and status of the new councils and who in large numbers had abstained from voting at the council elections. The friction engendered by the juxtaposition of these incompatible elements sparked off. . . .'

There was more in Peake's prosy style but no clear explanation for the disturbances. They wrote with greater conviction in Part III where they dealt with Harama. They summed up in the last paragraph 'The inauguration of the new statutory local government with the devolution of a large measure of authority from the centre to a number of District Councils giving them autonomy over a wide range of local affairs, renders the position of the paramount chief anomalous to a great extent. He retains certain traditional functions as far as they do not conflict with statutory provisions and he is *ex officio* president of the Central Council. But in day to day administration he has virtually no executive function. Nevertheless, a chief if he so chose could, by virtue of his exalted position, contribute in many ways to the social, political and economic advancement of his people. We believe that active support of the new form of local government would do much to ensure its success. There is much which must be left to choice by a traditional chief of what he thinks fit and proper for him to do. But he also has certain duties of which he cannot divest himself. Section seven of the Chiefs' Ordinance imposes on a paramount chief the duty "To maintain good order and government and to interpose for the prevention of crime in the area over which he exercises traditional authority". There may well be occasions when it is beyond the power of a chief to discharge this duty effectively but this does not relieve him of the duty of attempting to do so. Indeed, until he has made this attempt it would be wrong of him to assume incapacity. Evidence is not wanting to prove that Harama, Mudela of Pela, not only failed to maintain good order and government and interpose for the prevention of crime in the area of his traditional authority, but that he also made no attempt to do so during the disturbances in Pela Province. We are particularly persuaded of this by the evidence of Mr J. G. Wood, Provincial Commissioner, that he specifically reminded Harama of his duty in this respect and that Harama, while being fully aware of the gravity of developments, made no effort whatsoever to dissuade his people from the course of violence on which they embarked. We should be falling short of our duty if we failed to record our opinion that Harama, Mudela of Pela, was guilty of gross dereliction of duty. . . .'

I heard nothing for ten days then I received a second Top Secret letter from Peter Metcalfe. This time it was formal and short. There were two blue documents enclosed with it.

'*I, Stephen Alridge Mathews, Knight Commander of the Most Distinguished Order of St Michael and St George, Officer of the Most Excellent Order of the British Empire, for the time being discharging the duties of Governor and Commander in Chief of the Protectorate of Mundama, in exercise of powers conferred upon me by Section II of the Chiefs' Ordinance, after due inquiry, hereby order in the interests of good order and government in the Province of Pela that Tubo Harama shall from this day cease to enjoy the rights and privileges appertaining to the Mudela of Pela and shall forthwith cease to be known by that title.*'

It was signed, dated and sealed. I was ordered to return the original to the Civil Secretary with an affidavit that I had served the copy on Harama. My heart stopped beating and I let the paper fall. I had expected Harama to be rebuked and I had wondered how I should do it. I had not expected this. I was overwhelmed by the wrongness of the thing. I told myself I would have no part in the humiliation of the old man. I would rather resign.

A gust of cool wind sent papers flying off my desk. There was a smell of rain. My orderly came in and bolted the windows. As he picked up the papers I lay forward with my head on my arms.

'Are you all right, master?' he said.

I looked up at him. He was standing at the corner of my desk holding the papers.

'Put down the papers,' I said. 'I'm all right.'

He still waited.

'Shall I tell Ali to come?' he said.

'No, it's all right,' I said, 'you can go.'

When he had gone I rang the exchange and gave the D.C.'s number.

'I want to see you, James,' I said.

He sounded harassed.

'Could you make it half an hour? I've got an office full of people.'

'No,' I said, 'please come at once.'

The wind dropped. There was a rumble of thunder and the rain fell straight down. In a few minutes a torrent of water gushed from the roof gutter. The warm humidity of the room was oppressive. I reopened the windows and stared at the blurred scene outside. The pathos and tragedy of Harama affected me like a grievous bereavement.

Tyres swished on wet gravel. Roebuck brought his car to the side of the house as near as he could to my office. He pushed out a golf umbrella and made a dash for the door.

'What a day!' he exclaimed. He stood the umbrella in the corner near the door. His manner changed when he faced me. 'What's wrong?' he said.

'Sit down, James,' I said, 'look at this.'

His face set in serious lines as he read.

'Well?' I said.

He read the paper again and looked blank when he held it out to me.

'Well?' I repeated.

He shook his head. 'This is a bad show.'

'It's monstrous!' I said.

I stared at him with incoherent anxiety. He took a cigarette and I pushed the matches towards him.

'When will you serve it?' he said.

'Serve it! You don't think I'm going to serve it. I'll send the thing back and resign. You'll have to take over.'

He was neither sanguine nor hesitant. He spoke quietly.

'You can't do that, sir. You've got your orders.'

'No,' I said. 'I'll see them in hell first.'

Roebuck folded his arms and his manner changed.

'You won't like what I am going to say,' he said.

'Say what you like.'

He stared across the table at me.

'I know there's a personal bond between you and Harama. That's why I'm sorry this thing has happened, but maybe because of this personal bond you've shut your eyes to a lot. Harama's only getting what he's asked for. He's made no effort to come to terms with changes. He's quite out of touch. In fact, to put it bluntly, he's been a definite obstacle to progress.'

'Yes, James,' I said, 'go on.'

'It doesn't matter who the man is, you can't have a single person delaying reforms.' He paused. 'May I be frank with you?'

'Always be frank, James,' I said wearily. 'Always do your duty without fear or favour. That's what we are paid for. We're a disciplined service.'

He flushed for a moment and then compressed his lips. We were on the verge of a quarrel.

'It's in the best interests of this Province that Harama should go and I've known it for a long time.'

He had quickly regained his composure and regarded me with steady unwavering eyes.

'Maybe you think I ought to go too,' I said.

Rain splashed in from outside. Roebuck got up and closed the windows. He went on in a gentler tone.

'I know how you feel about this.'

He would have said more but I gave him no chance.

'You can't even begin to understand how I feel,' I said. 'This old man means more to me than anyone in this country. I don't care what he's done, you've got to take him all in one piece. I couldn't live with the memory. . . .' I made a gesture. 'You had better get back to your office. You must have work to do.'

I pushed back my chair and went to the window. Roebuck took his umbrella and paused in the doorway.

'Promise me one thing,' he said. 'You'll sleep on this before you make a decision.'

I did not turn round but I shrugged acquiescence.

'All right, James, I'll promise you that.'

I thought of Harama for the rest of the day and at night the thought persisted and robbed me of sleep. I heard cocks crowing answering each other all over the station before I dozed off. I woke late with a feeling of impending disaster and my thoughts turned at once to Harama.

Rain had now fallen for twenty-four hours and it was still raining as I drove to the town. Life must go on, I thought, the rain would give a good start to early planting. I had read my instructions before leaving and rehearsed the translation of the document. Water quickly drained through the sandy earth but where the road fell at the trading section the stores stood like islands in a sheet of water. My feelings were numbed. I had a pad with me to make a note of anything Harama said. I drove through the gateway. I wondered if I were dramatizing the task which had been forced upon me, and whether I was being sentimental. In the immense changes taking place Harama would be forgotten within a few years of his death. I was one of many British officials, a name filed somewhere just as long as I drew a pension. The drains were torrents carrying away debris of the dry season and the town was desolate. The men were away on the land making the most of the rains. Craftsmen were working indoors out of sight. Bedraggled sheep crossed the road. I turned in at Harama's compound. There was no drummer at the entrance to announce me. I heard a child crying in one of the huts and a woman's voice raised in anger. An old man, too old for work, stared without any expression from an open doorway. I told myself I would be completely impersonal. I should serve the paper without a word of sympathy or regret. I refused to think of the upheaval which would follow. I should have warned Mena of the risks of disorder. But there was no turning back. If I did not do it now I knew I should never do it. I stepped into the entrance to get out of the rain and a youth came out of a side room, the son of Harama's old age who sometimes carried the state umbrella.

'Is Harama in?' I said.

He looked blank. 'I don't know,' he said. 'I've not seen him today.'

He was overawed and wanted to go.

'Wait,' I said. 'Tell Buramo to come.'

I again rehearsed the translation I had made of the paper.

Buramo muttered a reply to my greeting as if I were unwelcome. There was something in his manner which disturbed me. He had a worried expression and I wondered for a moment whether he had got news of Harama's deposition.

'I've come to see Harama,' I said.

Buramo stared at me, lips parted, motionless and silent. His strange behaviour increased my uneasiness.

'Can't you speak?' I said.

'Come this way,' he said.

He turned off the main passage and took me into a part of the house I had not seen before. We passed two ante rooms each with a man sitting on the floor outside. He stopped at the third.

'In there,' he said.

It was a small bare room like a cell. The only light came from a slit high up on an outside wall. A triangular-shaped charm made from sewn leather and two small gourds were fixed over the entrance and an ovoid object of baked mud with porcupine quills embedded in it hung from the ceiling. Harama lay on his back on a grass mat on the floor. His out-turned feet made two little peaks in the blanket. White stubble sprouted from his shaven head. His eyes were closed. He was breathing stertorously through his open mouth, and a long yellow tooth stuck out over his lower lip.

'How long has he been like this?' I asked.

Buramo seemed bemused and I repeated the question.

'Since seven o'clock this morning. He fell down and we brought him in here.'

The old-fashioned telephone was fixed to the wall at the main entrance to the house. I waited there and stared at the rain.

Demeta wore a raincoat of plastic material and a topi with

a waterproof covering. I lead the way to the room. He looked at Harama with professional concern, bent down and raised an eyelid then he drew back the blanket and felt his pulse. He straightened up again.

'He ought to be in hospital,' he said.

Buramo spoke for the first time.

'Harama would not like that. If Allah ordains, he will recover.'

We ignored the interruption.

'Can you do anything for him?' I said.

Demeta shrugged his shoulders and looked at Harama again.

'He's had a stroke before and he's well over seventy. Still, you can't say and we can at least give him nursing.'

I went out with Demeta.

'I'll look in again this evening,' he said. He buttoned his raincoat and put on his topi. Ducks waddled across the compound. 'They like this weather,' he said. He gave me a nod. 'I'll telephone you about half past five.' He ran through the rain to his car.

The image of the old man stayed with me for the rest of the day. Demeta telephoned that a room was being prepared and an ambulance would be sent for Harama in the morning. The rain stopped at six o'clock and I went to the club. Two contractors' men were arguing with the steward about change. I told him to pay whatever they asked. I walked round the station, about a mile by the circular road, and I was tired but still restless when I got back. I tried to read after dinner, but a swarm of flying ants infested the house shedding their wings and it became impossible to sit near a light. I dropped my book and walked on the verandah. The rain had brought out frogs and an ear-splitting chorus rose from the compound. The croaking stopped and dance music came across the station from the engineer's radio set. When Ali left I told him to leave the door open; I was too restless to sleep. I walked down the drive to the road. After the rain the air was fresh and sweet and the stars were very bright and there was a new moon. Mosquitoes buzzed around my face. I stood on the road undecided whether to go on or return and then out of the deep silence of the night there was an uproar of drumming. It grew in volume and was taken up from all parts of the town. It was followed by bursts of fire from muzzle loaders. The barbaric tumult reached a crescendo and continued with undiminishing volume. A Chief was dead. I too mourned. I mourned the passing of someone eager, healthy and young. My eyes were wet. I swallowed and then made no attempt to hold back. Tears rolled down my face as I walked back to the house.